P9-DCB-881

"YOU HAVE COME TO SEE THE HORSES," STRONG WOLF SAID.

Suddenly alone with him, his night-black eyes stirring her insides so pleasurably, Hannah went to him and framed his face between her trembling hands.

Hardly able to believe that she could be so bold, so reckless, she guided his lips to hers.

When his arms pulled her against his lean, hard body, Hannah's head swam with the ecstasy of the moment.

Strong Wolf whispered against her lips. "You want to see the horses now?" His hands stroked her back, the heat of his touch reaching through the thin fabric of her cotton blouse.

"Later," Hannah whispered back, her voice unfamilar to her in its huskiness.

Strong Wolf whisked her fully up into his arms and held her close as their eyes met in unspoken passion. He kicked the door shut, then kissed her feverishly as he carried her toward his bed.

Other *Leisure* and *Love Spell* books by Cassie Edwards:

TOUCH THE WILD WIND
ROSES AFTER RAIN
WHEN PASSION CALLS
EDEN'S PROMISE
ISLAND RAPTURE
SECRETS OF MY HEART

The *Savage* Series:

SAVAGE QUEST
SAVAGE TEMPEST
SAVAGE BELOVED
SAVAGE ARROW
SAVAGE VISION
SAVAGE COURAGE
SAVAGE HOPE
SAVAGE TRUST
SAVAGE HERO
SAVAGE DESTINY
SAVAGE LOVE
SAVAGE MOON
SAVAGE HONOR
SAVAGE THUNDER
SAVAGE DEVOTION
SAVAGE GRACE
SAVAGE FIRES
SAVAGE JOY
SAVAGE WONDER
SAVAGE HEAT

SAVAGE DANCE
SAVAGE TEARS
SAVAGE LONGINGS
SAVAGE DREAM
SAVAGE BLISS
SAVAGE WHISPERS
SAVAGE SHADOWS
SAVAGE SPLENDOR
SAVAGE EDEN
SAVAGE SURRENDER
SAVAGE PASSIONS
SAVAGE SECRETS
SAVAGE PRIDE
SAVAGE SPIRIT
SAVAGE EMBERS
SAVAGE ILLUSION
SAVAGE SUNRISE
SAVAGE MISTS
SAVAGE PROMISE
SAVAGE PERSUASION

CASSIE EDWARDS

Savage RAGE

LEISURE BOOKS NEW YORK CITY

A LEISURE BOOK®

June 2007

Published by

Dorchester Publishing Co., Inc.
200 Madison Avenue
New York, NY 10016

If you purchased this book without a cover you should be aware that this book is stolen property. It was reported as "unsold and destroyed" to the publisher and neither the author nor the publisher has received any payment for this "stripped book."

Copyright © 1995 by Cassie Edwards

All rights reserved. No part of this book may be reproduced or transmitted in any form or by any electronic or mechanical means, including photocopying, recording or by any information storage and retrieval system, without the written permission of the publisher, except where permitted by law.

ISBN-10: 0-8439-5884-7
ISBN-13: 978-0-8439-5884-3

The name "Leisure Books" and the stylized "L" with design are trademarks of Dorchester Publishing Co., Inc.

Printed in the United States of America.

Visit us on the web at www.dorchesterpub.com.

I

Nymph-like, she is fleet and strong.
—WILLIAM WORDSWORTH

Saint Louis, Missouri—1853

The small room was dark and airless. There were no mirrors. There was no dressing table. The sparse furnishing consisted of only a bed with a lumpy mattress, a bedside table on which sat a kerosene lamp, and a hard-backed chair. The only window was at the very top of the room, near the ceiling, purposely giving no one access to it.

Feeling like a caged panther, Hannah Kody paced the room nervously, the long skirt of her black dress tangling around her legs as she made her swift turns.

She stopped and looked up at the window. Outside white puffs of clouds floated across a brilliant blue sky. The sun was straight overhead. It was noon. Soon someone would come and break the silence that was near to driving her mad.

"Isolation," Hannah breathed out in a low, agitated whisper. "I've been put in isolation!"

She ran her fingers through her flowing waist-length golden hair. Never would she part with her hair! She would not allow anyone to chop it off, almost to her scalp. She was in a convent in Saint Louis, Missouri, not of *her* choosing. So she was certainly not going to part with her hair only because it was the rule of the convent to do so. It was required of all young women who entered the teachings of becoming a nun.

"Hah!" she whispered, and began pacing again. "Just let them try. Even if I have to stay in isolation until hell freezes over, I won't part with my hair."

Hannah had been called a tomboy all of her life and hadn't minded it. But she didn't want to have short hair like a boy! She had always treasured her long, flowing golden hair. As she saw it, it was the only thing beautiful about her.

She knew that she was tall and lanky. There was nothing she could do about that.

But she could certainly make sure nothing happened to her only asset—her hair!

"Mother, Father," she agonized in a whisper. "Why did you do force this sort of life on me? I don't want to be a nun!"

Of course she knew their reason, and had fought them every inch of the way. But, due to her father's bullheaded determination to change her into a lady, she had lost the battle. He had said that if her very own parents couldn't tame her tomboyish ways, surely the sisters at the convent could!

Hannah had been there only a short time, but it had seemed an eternity. And as far as she was concerned, nothing about her had changed, except for making her even more rebellious than before.

"I'll show them," Hannah whispered. She plopped down on the chair in an unladylike manner, her legs widespread, the skirt hiked up past her knees. "I'll make them want to send me away. They will grow tired of battling me as I stubbornly fight for my rights."

She gazed up at the window again and daydreamed that she was riding on a horse in a wide-open meadow, the ground dotted with a beautiful tapestry of wildflowers.

Her hair was blowing in the wind.

The horse was galloping hard, its mane flying.

If she closed her eyes even now, she could smell the horseflesh. She could feel the wind and sun against her face. She could capture that wonderful feeling of freedom!

The sound of a key being placed in the lock of the door drew Hannah back to the present. She eased up out of the chair and backed against the wall in the deeper shadows. Although she suspected that someone was bringing her dinner, she never knew for sure whom to expect to walk through the door. Every nun in the convent had tried to scold her into obedience. But all had turned away, sighing, or whispering beneath their breaths some small prayers for her salvation and forgiveness.

Hannah could scarcely feel the beat of her heart as she watched the doorknob turn. Although hungry for food *and* company, and hoping that food was just outside the door, she did not look all that forward to eating. She had not only been placed in isolation, she had been given small portions of food, and nothing tasty.

Nor had she had a cup of tea or coffee since she had been in isolation. She had been on a ration of water.

When the door slowly opened and Hannah could smell a familiar perfume, that which her mother wore, her eyes widened. She gasped softly when her mother and father entered the room. She became numb, for

surely they had been told about her being so uncoop-
erative, and had come to shame her into obedience.

"Hannah," her mother said, moving in a dignified
glide across the room in her lace-trimmed, pale blue
velveteen dress, her arms outstretched toward Hannah. "My sweet darling. How could they treat you this
way? Never would I have expected this or I would
have fought much more aggressively your father's decision to place you here."

Hannah welcomed her mother's soft hug. Ah, but
she was such a short, petite woman, someone Hannah
would have loved molding herself after. But she had
inherited her father's tall height, his *lankiness*.

She returned her mother's embrace, relishing the
familiar aroma of her mother's French perfume, yet
watching her father over her mother's shoulder as he
stood just inside the room, somber.

He was dressed in an expensive dark suit, a dia-
mond stickpin glittering in the folds of his ascot at his
throat. His long legs were stiff as he slowly rocked
back and forth on his heels while staring back at Hannah with his piercingly dark eyes, those which she had
most definitely not inherited. Hers were green, as
green as spring grass, like her mother's.

She could smell the cigar scent of her father, yet
even that could not hide the overpowering smell of
medicine that clung to him and his clothes, which he
acquired from his daily medical practice. He was a
well-known surgeon. He had wanted Hannah to follow
in his footsteps.

She had refused. She wanted no part of attending
medical school. And she most certainly didn't want to
be imprisoned by hospital walls, reeking of medicine
herself, day in and out.

For so long it had been Hannah's dream to train

show horses. Until her parents had interfered, she had been working with a trainer, learning his skills.

Unlike her older sister, who was a senior in college, and her brother, who now owned a ranch—thanks to their rich father, who had backed both their ambitions—Hannah had vowed never to accept her father's "charity" by him giving her a start in a career, especially one not of her own choosing.

She wanted to pay her own way—earn her keep.

She didn't want to be beholden to anyone, especially not her overbearing father, *the* Howard Kody, whose name was known throughout the midwest for his skills at doctoring.

"Hannah," her father said, his voice deep and gravelly. "Grace and I have come to take you from the convent."

Hannah was taken aback by what he said. She eyed him speculatively as her mother moved to her side.

"Father, what did you say?" she gulped disbelievingly. Could it be true? she wondered anxiously. Could he actually care enough for her feelings that he would end this charade that he had forced on her? Did he truly care for her so much that he would put her feelings before his?

"I said we've come to take you from the convent," Howard said, then had no time to say anything else. Hannah rushed across the room and flung herself into his arms. It had been a long time since she had been given any reason to hug him. She had not known until now how much she had missed his powerful arms around her, his breath stirring her hair as he leaned his cheek into it.

They embraced for a moment longer, then Howard gripped Hannah by her shoulders and held her at arm's length.

"Thank you, Father," Hannah said, tears streaming

from her eyes, now realizing he cared so much for her. She even felt somewhat guilty for having disappointed him.

"Grace, get Hannah's things together," Howard said, nodding toward his wife of thirty years. "Then we'll go and try and clear things up with Sister Kathryn. We've got to make her understand why this had to be done. When she hears that our son is going blind, and that this is the only reason we are taking Hannah from the convent, she will understand."

"Yes, she'll understand that a sister's place is with a brother at times like this," Grace said, going to take a satchel from beneath the bed. "Hannah is needed there, to see after his best interests, especially since *we* can't stay with him. And Chuck most certainly will not leave his ranch to live with *us*."

Hannah paled. She looked in jerks from her father to her mother, then back at her father, her eyes wavering. She had been wrong to think that her father had had a change of heart for *her* sake. He was taking her from the convent for someone else. Not for her, or *her* feelings!

She wrenched herself free of her father's grip. She glared at him and wiped the tears from her eyes as she squared her shoulders.

Yet she couldn't find the words to tell him how he had just let her down again, as he had so often in her life.

Then his words about her brother sank in. Blind? Her brother was going blind?

"How bad *is* Chuck?" Hannah blurted out, now feeling guilty for having thought of herself, when all concerns should be centered on her brother.

"His eyesight is quickly failing him," Howard said solemnly. "Damn it all to hell, anyway. He has followed his dreams to the Kansas Territory, established a ranch, and now *this*."

"Will he go totally blind?" Hannah said, her heart aching over her dear brother's misfortune.

"Seems so," Howard said, then turned to Grace when she brought Hannah's satchel to him.

"Father, Mother said something about me looking after Chuck's best interests," Hannah said, swallowing hard. "What does that mean? That I am going there? To live with him?"

"Yes, Hannah." Howard nodded. "You will be his eyes."

"His . . . eyes . . ." she said more to herself than to her parents. She weighed this in her mind. She wanted to find the good in how her life would change again.

Yes, she was jubilant to leave the convent. And in Kansas she would be able to ride horses in the open range. She would be as free as the wind, to do as she pleased; the outdoors had always beckoned to her, as if it were her lover.

But she could not allow herself to be jubilant over her quickly changing future, and that in her brother's misfortune came a beacon of light for *her*. She was deeply saddened over her brother's worsening condition.

"Do you mind traveling to Kansas, dear, to help your brother in his time of need?" Grace asked, placing a gentle hand to Hannah's cheek. "You and Chuck have always been close. It will delight him to have you with him."

"Of course I don't mind," Hannah said.

Then she stepped away from her mother and turned glittering, mutinous eyes to her father. "But I wish just once that I could be allowed to make my own decision about something," she blurted out. "I *am* eighteen, you know."

"And so you are," her father said, sighing. "And so you are."

She inhaled a quivering breath, then left the room with her parents.

After bidding a good-bye to Sister Kathryn, Hannah left the convent with a wild, thumping heartbeat. She could hardly wait to board the riverboat that would take her to the Kansas Territory. She would be with her brother again. And without her parents or the sisters there to dictate her every move, she would finally know the true meaning of the word *freedom*.

For the first time ever, her life would be hers, to do with as *she* pleased!

2

From her little head to her little feet
She was swayed in her suppleness to and fro
By each gust of passion; a sapling pine,
That grows on the edge of a Kansas bluff!
—FRANK DESPREZ

Two Weeks Later, Kansas Territory

"And how do you like living with your big brother?"
Chuck Kody asked as he squinted through his thick
eyeglasses, trying to see Hannah across the large oak
dining table. "It's quite different from living 'midst the
hustle and bustle of Saint Louis, isn't it, sis?"

Since she was no longer under the scrutiny of her
parents, or the sisters at the convent, Hannah was feeling at peace with herself for the first time in weeks.
Except for her concern over her brother's failing eyesight, she would feel that finally all was well in her
world.

She shoved her empty breakfast plate aside, saddened that he couldn't see well enough now to see
her give him a warm smile.

"I love it," she said, rising from her chair. She went
to Chuck and stood behind him, then draped her arms
around his neck and lay a cheek on his head. "I'm
glad to be here with *you*."

He reached up and patted one of her hands. "It's not the same, though, is it?" he said thickly.

She leaned around him and kissed his cheek. "No, it isn't," she said, her voice drawn. "I wish I could wave a magic wand and tell your eyes to be like they were years ago when we went horseback riding every morning before breakfast. Now *that* was living, big brother. I don't think I've ever felt as alive as then."

"Damn my eyes," Chuck said in a low growl. "I can hardly see an inch ahead of me now, much less ride a horse."

Hannah stepped away from him as he inched his chair back and rose slowly to his feet. She flinched when he stumbled over the leg of the chair, causing it to fall over with a loud crack against the polished oak floor.

"Hell," Chuck said, bending and searching for the chair with his hand.

"I'll get it for you," Hannah said, tears filling her eyes to see his helplessness.

"No," Chuck said. He reached a hand out to stop her. "Please don't patronize me, Hannah. I'm not that helpless. Not yet, anyhow. It's just a damn chair. Anyone can knock over a damn, stupid chair."

Covering her mouth with her hands, Hannah stood back and watched him grope around for the chair.

Once he found it, she could see how his hands trembled as he locked his fingers around the back of the chair. She wanted to rush in and get it upright again for him, so that he would not have to feel the helplessness that he was surely experiencing.

She sighed heavily as the chair was finally in place at the table.

She then watched as her brother searched around for his cane, then sighed again when he found it.

As he inched himself along, feeling his way across

the room with his cane, Hannah walked beside him. She didn't dare place a hand to his elbow and help him. Although she was there for that very purpose, she had discovered upon first arriving at the ranch that it had not been *his* decision at all to have her there, to see to his every need. It had been her father's. He had taken it upon himself to interfere in his son's and daughter's lives again.

She knew, deep down, that her brother was thankful she was there, no matter the circumstances. And she certainly had not minded her father manipulating her life this time, either. It had gained her freedom from the convent.

How wonderful it was to be out here in the wide-open spaces where she could look for miles and miles and see the vastness of the land. Just seeing it made her feel free, sometimes even wild, as though she were one with the land and the animals.

While horseback riding, she had even taken advantage of her newfound freedom to go and take a look at the Potawatomis Indian village not far from her brother's ranch. In fact, their land adjoined Chuck's. It was hard to tell where their land stopped and Chuck's started. Only a small portion of his ranch, used for pasturing cows, was bordered with a fence.

Thus far, Hannah had not come face-to-face with any Potawatomis people. The thought intrigued her, especially since they were her neighbors.

"You go on, now, Hannah, and take your morning ride," Chuck said as they entered the parlor.

"If I didn't know better, I'd think you were trying to get rid of me," Hannah joked back.

"Never," Chuck said, stopping to turn to her. He searched with his hand until he found her face. He ran his fingers over her features. "Sweet Hannah. You don't know how good it *is* to have you here. Please forgive me if I get grouchy sometimes. I'm finding it damn hard to adjust to my affliction. Please always remember, though, that having you here helps lighten the burden."

"I hope so," she murmured. "I only wish to do what is best for you."

Her gaze moved over him. He was a tall, handsome man. Although he could buy any expensive suit he wished, he usually wore fringed buckskins. He had told her that he wore the buckskins because they were more comfortable. She knew that the true reason was because they were easier to get into, with no buttons to maneuver into buttonholes.

His collar-length hair was the same color as hers, as golden as Kansas wheat. And his eyes, although having failed him, were still a sparkling green.

He was very muscular, even though he was no longer able to get out and do much physical labor. But she had seen him exercise, knowing himself the importance of keeping his muscles alive and active.

"I'll let you know when I need your help," Chuck said, settling down in a chair before a slow-burning fire in the massive stone fireplace. "Now, you'd best get on your way before the heat of the day makes it too uncomfortable for you to ride. These cooler mornings, when even a fire feels good to my bones, are the best time for riding. Remember that you aren't here to be my maid. I have enough help to care for the house and to see to the cooking."

"Yes, and most seem dependable," Hannah said, thinking that there was one man who seemed less than trustworthy.

Tiny Sharp, her brother's foreman.

There was something about the man that bothered Hannah. It wasn't altogether the way he looked at her. It was not a look of a man who was interested in

a woman, and she understood. With her tall height
and lankiness, she saw herself less than desirable for
any man.

No, it was something else. He was shifty-eyed. He
seemed to always be looking at her with a silent
loathing!

She gazed around at the luxurious room. This alone
could place envy in the heart of any man. Perhaps
the foreman resented her brother for being this rich.
Perhaps he resented her for being there, to see after
her brother's interests.

Expensive, gilt-edged paintings hung from the walls.
The furniture was plush and comfortable, the coverings made of rich maroon velvet, matching the
drapes at the two windows that were made of the
same fabric.

Crystal vases caught the glitter of the rays of the
morning sunshine pouring through the windows, taking on the look of sparkling diamonds. A grandfather
clock made of beautiful mahogany ticked away against
one wall. A foot-pedal organ sat against the wall opposite it.

"Go on, Hannah," Chuck said, nodding toward her.
"I'm going to rest, then play the organ for a while."

"I won't be gone—" she began, then stopped when
the sound of someone arriving on a horse drew her
attention to the window.

"See who that is, sis," Chuck said, stiffening. "Tiny
shouldn't be back yet. He and some of the cowhands
were supposed to be out checking the far pasture. I've
lost a cow or two these past weeks."

"Perhaps the Indians stole them?" Hannah said,
walking toward the window.

"No. I don't think so." Chuck said, rising from the
chair. He stood with his back to the fire and leaned
his full weight on his cane. "As long as deer, buffalo,

and other wild animals roam this land, that's what the
Potawatomis will eat. Naw, they wouldn't bother my
cows. Anyhow, thus far, Strong Wolf and I see eye to
eye on most things. I don't think he'd want to chance
having me as his enemy by stealing my cattle."

Hannah stepped up to the window and peered outside. "Is Strong Wolf a young warrior?" Hannah said,
her gaze locked on the handsome Indian who had just
reined in beside the hitching rail just outside of
Chuck's house. She knew horses well from her love
of them and recognized that the Indian's was a lovely
bunched-muscled chestnut stallion.

"Yes, I'd say Strong Wolf is perhaps thirty," Chuck
said, slowly making his way across the room.

"Then, I think he's just arrived at your doorstep,"
Hannah said, unable to take her eyes off the warrior.
She had seen many Indians while living in Saint Louis.

She had even talked with some on the waterfront
when they had come to trade. Because of this she had
learned not to fear them.

Looking at this Potawatomis Indian made her knees
feel strangely weak. Perhaps it was because he wore
only a brief breechcloth that was only soft squares of
buckskin, hanging from the waist in front and back by
a belt. This attire somewhat unnerved her, for it did
not leave much of his anatomy to her imagination.
That shamefully excited her more than she wished to
admit, even to her*self*.

Strong Wolf had a fine-boned frame, a long, trim
torso, and muscular thighs. He was powerfully built
and sat tall in the saddle, with intense dark eyes. He
had a firm, but almost sensuous mouth. The lean line
of his jaw showed strength. He had a strong, determined face with hard cheekbones and flat planes. He
carried his head high on a pair of well-knit shoulders.

And his waist-length black hair was parted in the middle, a red band holding it in place.

"Come with me outside on the porch, Hannah," Chuck said, breaking her concentration. "Let's see if it *is* Strong Wolf. If so, I wonder why? He rarely makes it a habit of coming to call. I usually go to him when something needs to be talked over."

"How, Chuck?" Hannah said, turning to wait for him. "If you can't ride . . ."

"I'm not totally helpless, sis," Chuck said, interrupting her. He frowned at her. "Whenever I have the need to leave my ranch, I travel by way of horse and buggy. Tiny, my foreman, usually accompanies me. Perhaps now *you* can if the need arises for me to go and speak with the Potawatomis leader."

"Is he their chief?" Hannah asked softly.

"No, his grandfather is still chief," Chuck said, squinting as he tried to see his feet while taking guarded steps across the room. "About a year ago, Strong Wolf led a portion of his Potawatomis people from Wisconsin to establish a village nearby. He told me that he will return one day to lead the rest of his people here. He came without them only because he wanted to be sure he could find land suitable to their needs. He found it here, on land that lies adjacent to my property."

"His grandfather is chief?" Hannah said, still watching from the window, the handsome Potawatomis leader having not yet caught her gawking at him like some starstruck schoolgirl. "Does that mean that Strong Wolf will one day be chief?"

"Yes, after his grandfather passes on to the other side," Chuck said, nodding. "Also, Strong Wolf told me that he was born with the name Sharp Nose until he had a vision. His name was changed then, so that

he would enter the chieftainship with the name
Strong Wolf."

"I see," Hannah said, then remembering what her
brother had said about her accompanying him to the
Potawatomis village made her heart leap with
excitement.

"I do hope that I can go with you to the Indian
village," she murmured.

Knowing that she would soon be eye to eye with
the handsome Indian, Hannah's pulse raced. She went
to the foyer with her brother, then the door. Her fingers trembled as she placed her hand on the doorknob
and turned it.

She held the door open for her brother and watched
his steps as he went out to stand on the porch, then
followed him and stood beside him. Up close, she was
taken even more by the Potawatomis warrior. He was
so noble in appearance, so wonderful to look at.

When Strong Wolf's eyes met hers, Hannah grew
strangely warm at the pit of her stomach. Her cheeks
turned hot with a blush, for never had a man affected
her in such a way.

She could even see something different in his eyes
as he gazed at her. It was the way she would expect a
man to look at her if he found her pleasant to his eyes.

"What brings you here this morning, Strong Wolf?"
Chuck asked, squinting as he tried to make out Strong
Wolf's features amid the shadows that his eyes saw
now, instead of actual things.

Strong Wolf gazed at Hannah a moment longer before responding to Chuck's question. From afar these
past few days he had watched her riding horseback.
He had at once been taken by her free spirit.

And not only that. To him she was intriguingly
beautiful, with her long, flowing golden hair, her well-

rounded breasts, and her small waist and glowing cheeks.

Unlike any woman he had ever seen before, she was tall and slender like a reed, with a sublime, long neck. He was not disappointed when he saw her eyes were as green as the grass, vibrant, and filled with mystery, yet innocence. Her pale skin looked as smooth as a pebble or a carved stone.

Today she wore a pretty dress, fully gathered, with little puffed sleeves trimmed with lace that draped to the elbows.

Hannah was aware of how Strong Wolf was studying her, causing her to blush and look away. Could he possibly see something in her that he liked? she wondered to herself. Thinking that perhaps he did made her insides glow with strange feelings she had never experienced before.

Oh, Lord, had destiny brought her here to meet this man? she wondered. Had her father been led into the decision of sending her here because of some hidden force urging him to?

Her heart was beating within her chest like the claps of wild thunder as she imagined being alone with this Potawatomis warrior, asking him his true reason for staring at her in such a way.

Surely she was being foolish; he studied her because she was a white woman. Perhaps he saw her as . . .

When he looked suddenly away from her and began talking in a cold tone to her brother, Hannah lost her train of thought and listened to his accusations about a dam having been built that was interfering with the lives of his people.

"I know of no such dam," Chuck said, stunned by the change in Strong Wolf's behavior toward him. He had thought they had gained some respect between them, some camaraderie.

But surely he had been wrong. Friends trusted one another. They gave each other the chance to delve into the truths of that which troubled one another.

"You own this ranch, yet you do not know what is happening on its soil?" Strong Wolf said, dismounting his horse. His eyes occasionally moved to the woman, then forced them away again. He had come to get answers from this man. Not get caught up in feelings for a woman.

"Yes, I do own the ranch and the pastureland that surrounds it," Chuck said stiffly. "And I would be the first to admit that just perhaps I don't know everything that goes on, as I should. I have a foreman. He is in charge of much that happens."

"This foreman. He is called Tiny?" Strong Wolf said, folding his arms across his chest as his jaw tightened at the remembrance of watching the tiny little white man roaming around too close to land that was, by treaty, the Potawatomis.

"Yes, my foreman is a small man," Chuck said, nodding.

"Then you must order this man to remove the dam that he built across water that I secured for my people when I touched the goose quill to treaty papers with white leaders," Strong Wolf said flatly. "My people are a home-loving group. They never seek fame in war. As you know, I will soon guide more of my people to this land of sunshine and blowing grasses. I seek peace in all things. But if I must fight for my rights in this new land, I *will*."

Strong Wolf stepped closer to the porch. "You must prove to me that you are no liar, that when you say you know nothing about a dam, you know *nothing*," he said thickly, his face twisting. "I do not ever wish to believe that you are a wily, treacherous, and deceitful man who has been led into bad roads of life."

As Strong Wolf occasionally looked at Hannah, she was given the opportunity to see into his beautiful midnight black eyes. They seemed to look into her very soul.

Thus far she had just stood there and listened, not saying anything in the defense of her brother, for this Indian's confidence as he talked so openly and fearlessly to her brother greatly impressed her.

But being strong-willed and hardheaded, Hannah could no longer keep her silence. "I've heard enough," she said, stepping between Chuck and Strong Wolf. "No one is going to talk to my brother like that. Not even *you*, Strong Wolf. My brother is an honest, God-fearing man. You should be ashamed of yourself for thinking otherwise!"

She was aware of her brother giving off a gasp behind her. Her knees weakened as she stared at Strong Wolf, whose eyes were wide with obvious shock of seeing a lady interfering in business between two men.

Suddenly Hannah was no longer as confident when his eyes narrowed into hers. Fear grabbed her at the pit of her stomach. Yet she stood her ground and lifted her chin, defying him with a set stare, willing her eyes not to waver.

"And who is this woman?" Strong Wolf suddenly blurted out. He took one step sideways so that he was again face-to-face with Chuck. He had never before seen such a forward woman. He was not so repelled and angered by it as he was impressed.

"This is my sister Hannah," Chuck said, still in a partial state of shock over Hannah speaking up in such a way. Yet shouldn't he have expected it? She had always been outspoken. And he never held that against her. She had always been able to fight her own battles in life.

Except for when their father had placed her in the

convent. He had worried about that stifling her spirit. He knew now that had not happened.

"Hannah?" Strong Wolf said, turning slow eyes her way again.

She smiled sheepishly at him, then turned quickly away and watched Tiny as he approached on horseback toward them.

"Who is that, Hannah?" Chuck asked, squinting his eyes, trying to see.

"Tiny," Hannah said, glowering at the tiny man.

"Just the man I need to see," Chuck said.

Tiny dismounted and stepped around Strong Wolf, their eyes locked in silent battle. He went on the porch and stood beside Chuck.

"Chuck, what's he doin' here?" Tiny grumbled, nervously fingering a rust-colored mustache. Freckles were thick on this thin, weather-beaten face. His widebrimmed Stetson hat was sweat-stained. His chaps were briar-scratched.

"Tiny, Strong Wolf says he found a dam built across a stream that belongs to him," Chuck said, his voice guarded. "You did it, didn't you, Tiny? No one else would."

"I had help, if that's what you mean," the tiny, redheaded man said, sneering as he gazed at Strong Wolf.

"You know you're wrong, don't you, Tiny?" Chuck said, his voice sounding tired.

"I had to," Tiny argued. "It's necessary for the operation of the gristmill that has recently been built at the ranch."

"Tiny, destroy the dam," Chuck said, heaving a deep sigh. "We can find other ways to run the gristmill."

"But, Chuck, this is the *only* way," Tiny argued.

"Tiny, we don't want no trouble with the Potawatomis, now, do we?" Chuck said impatiently.

"You'd think they'd understand," Tiny grumbled.

"The dam you built has interfered in my people's lives," Strong Wolf said, not allowing this man to sway the rancher against the decision that he had already made. "When the hunt for game is slow, then fish in the stream is good for my people's cook fires. The dam *must* be destroyed. And that is my last word. It is *final*."

Chuck turned to Tiny, his jaw tight. "Remove the dam, damn it," he growled out. "Remove it immediately."

Strong Wolf breathed in a slow, quivering breath. He was glad that this confrontation was settled with the landowner, yet he did see a troubled path ahead with the tiny man. He could see the rage in the depths of his gray eyes as Tiny continued to glare at him. Strong Wolf could see how he clasped and unclasped his hands into tight fists at his sides.

Yes, this was a man who would not accept defeat all that easily. But Strong Wolf was a much better man than he, and would never let the man best him.

Confident that the dam would be removed and that he had been wrong to test the waters of friendship with this landowner, who until now had offered him friendship, Strong Wolf gazed intensely at Chuck.

"Friends still?" he said, squaring his shoulders.

"Yes, friends still," Chuck said, nervously clearing his throat.

Strong Wolf turned slow eyes to Hannah. "Friends?" he said, his eyes locking with hers.

Hannah's whole insides melted when she met his direct, intense gaze. Her knees weakened as she reached a hand out toward him. "Yes, friends," she murmured, her heart leaping when he placed his powerful hand in hers and shook it.

Tiny emitted a disgusted groan from the depths of

his throat, then stalked away. Day by day his hate for the Potawatomis was growing inside him. And today was the last straw! His schemes, thus far, to discourage these Indians from staying in this area had not been severe enough. The Indians' farmland was thriving. Their people were well and happy. Yes, he must turn to more severe measures to change this.

All that Tiny had schemed to own—all of Chuck's land and possessions—was threatened, not only because of the stubborn Indian, but now also because Chuck's sister was there to care for him. He had wasted too much time waiting for Chuck to become completely blind so he could swindle Chuck out of all that he owned—a ranch and hundreds of acres of farm and grazing land. He had never suspected that Chuck would have a relative come to live with him, to help him with his affliction, especially not an interfering sister.

As Tiny saw it, Chuck's sister was an obstacle to his plans, and the Potawatomis had land that he wanted for his own ranch. He was now not only Chuck's foreman, but also his bookkeeper, and if he had calculated right in placing the wrong entries in Chuck's ledgers, Chuck's land would soon be Tiny's.

And he must act soon, before Hannah was shown the ledgers.

Tiny sneered, then laughed to himself when he thought of how asinine Chuck had been to trust Tiny to care for the journals. Chuck no longer had the ability to even add up figures to see if they balanced.

"I'll be the richest man in all of Kansas Territory, Tiny gloated to himself as he swung himself into his saddle. He grabbed up his reins and took one last look at Strong Wolf, then wheeled his horse around and rode away.

"Come again soon, Strong Wolf," Chuck said as

Strong Wolf released Hannah's hand. "We shall have council here for a change, instead of at your village. I feel I should do something to make up for this inconvenience caused you today."

"You have done enough by ordering the removal of the dam," Strong Wolf said, his eyes still on Hannah. What he saw today in the woman was something he wished to ignore, yet his heart told him that was impossible. There was too much about her that was different from most women. His intrigue of her touched him to the very core of his being.

"Tiny was just looking out for my best interests," Chuck said, sighing. "But I do have my doubts about him sometimes."

"It is not my place to discourage you about those who work for you; yet I cannot help but say that if I were you, I would be wary of that man," Strong Wolf said, then turned and went to his horse. "I have my duties to see to. I must leave."

He gazed at Hannah again. "We shall meet again, I am certain," he said. He nodded to Chuck, then rode off in an easy lope on his beautiful chestnut stallion.

Hannah's heart beat soundly as she watched Strong Wolf ride away. He sat so tall and so masterfully in his saddle. His shoulders were so squared and muscled. And she loved the way his dark, waist-length hair fluttered in the wind.

"Sis?"

Chuck's voice broke through Hannah's reverie. Red-faced, she turned to him. "Yes?" she murmured.

"What do you think?"

"About what?"

"About Strong Wolf."

"In which way, Chuck?"

"Hannah, am I wrong, or did I feel strong feelings being exchanged between the two of you?"

Hannah gulped hard. She sucked in a wild breath. "You noticed this?" she murmured. "You can't even see all that well, yet detected something evolving between me and Strong Wolf?"

"Besides my eyes, my other senses have been enhanced, and, yes, Hannah, I felt something happening between you and my Potawatomis friend."

"And if you are right?" Hannah murmured. "How would you feel?"

Hannah became unnerved by Chuck's sudden silence.

3

Was that thunder?
I grasped the cord of my swift mustang,
Without a word.

—FRANK DESPREZ

Hawk, a Sioux and the son of Star Flower and Buffalo
Cloud, was traveling alone on horseback, his destination Kansas. His village was not far from the village
of Strong Wolf's people in Wisconsin. He was thinking
back to what his mother had said to him before he
had left for this long journey. She had told him that
it was now time to follow the scent of skunk that had
been left along the trail made by Strong Wolf and
his friend Proud Heart, who were now settled in the
Kansas Territory.

The fathers of Strong Wolf and Proud Heart were
responsible for the death of Hawk's uncle, his mother's brother. Hawk never knew his uncle Slow Running, but his mother had told him often how much
she had loved him.

And she had stood beside her brother when he had
gone against the Chippewa, the Sioux people's natural
enemy. And since his death at the hands of Chief
White Wolf and his companion Sharp Nose all those

years ago, she had lived with resentment, with revenge on her mind.

She had ordered her son to do the avenging. She had told him that she had waited long enough for this to happen. She had told Hawk to go now to the Potawatomis's newly established village. There he was to avenge his uncle's death by killing the sons of those two warriors who were responsible for her brother's death!

From the beginning, when his mother had first approached him to do this for her, Hawk had told her that he could not kill those whom he himself did not see as enemies.

He had finally agreed to do what she had asked of him after his mother had repeatedly reminded him that he owed her so much. Because of her having trouble giving birth to him, she couldn't have any more children.

Even *he* held himself to blame for his mother's barren womb. And how could he not? She had never let him forget that he was the reason she could never have any more children.

Yes, he owed her anything she asked of him.

Also, he had agreed never to tell his father, Buffalo Cloud, what he and his mother had conspired to do. His father, the peace-loving man that he was, would never approve.

As he rode onward, Hawk's thoughts centered on Proud Heart's sister, Doe Eyes. He hadn't told her, either, what he must do for the sake of his mother. He had been forced to leave Doe Eyes behind, his one and only love, although both hearts would be broken by such a silent farewell. Because of tensions between families, theirs had been a forbidden love, one that only they had secretly shared.

When wild thunder rolled across the hills in the distance, Hawk sank his moccasin heels into the flanks of his white mustang. He was anxious to get this done and over with. His mother had told him not to return home again until the deed was done. He *must* hurry and return home alive and well, for he would be chief after his father.

"How am I to kill people I do not even hate?" Hawk despaired to himself, having not even known the man whose death he was avenging. Like his father, Hawk was a peace-loving man.

"And she expects them both to die," he whispered to himself. "How . . . can . . . I?"

He lifted his eyes to the sky. "Doe Eyes, if you could just be here, to comfort my bleeding, troubled heart!" he cried to the heavens.

4

She seemed to hear my silent voice!
—JOHN CLARE

Doe Eyes, a beautiful Chippewa maiden, and the daughter of White Wolf and Dawnmarie, had learned of Hawk's journey to the Kansas Territory. Against her parents' wishes and ignoring their protests, she had found warriors to accompany her to the Kansas Territory in search of Hawk.

Riding on a gentle mare, she was on Hawk's trail even now. No one seemed to know why Hawk had just suddenly left Wisconsin. She only suspected why, and had planned to try and get to him before he did something he would regret for the rest of his life. Her parents believed that he was seeking his own destiny away from a demanding, unreasonable mother.

She believed he was following the orders of this cruel, heartless mother. And she shivered inside to even think of what this might be.

Though troubled, Doe Eyes looked beautiful, serene, and confident as she rode her horse through tall, blowing grass. She wore a belted dress of animal skins left open on both sides to make her ride on the horse more comfortable. She wore a necklace of deer and panther teeth.

Her skin had a smooth copper sheen, her facial features were perfect. A single braid hung down her back.

As evening drew nigh, the sky in the west was red. Suddenly Doe Eyes heard a faint rumble of wild thunder in the faraway hills.

"Hawk, where are you?" she cried to the heavens.

5

Did you ever see a woman,
  for whom your soul you'd give?
If so, 'twas she, for there never
  was another so half fair.
          —H. ANTOINE D'ARCY

With a panther's tread, Strong Wolf moved noiselessly through the thick grass and placed the last stick of dynamite amid the rocks and rubble that still lay in place across the stream.

"The paleface lied," Strong Wolf said as he stood back with his friend Proud Heart and gazed at the dam that had not been removed. It was noon, the next day after the visit to Chuck Kody's ranch.

"The rancher must have waited until I was gone, then told his foreman *not* to destroy the dam," Strong Wolf growled out between clenched teeth. "How could I trust so easily?"

Since sunup today Strong Wolf and Proud Heart had waited and watched for the white men to come and tear down the dam, as promised, since it had not been torn down already.

When they realized that the dam was not going to be removed, they had gone to a shack that sat far back from the rancher's lodge, where they had seen Tiny store many sticks of dynamite. They had stolen several sticks of the dynamite and had returned determinedly to the dam.

"Do we have enough of the white man's power sticks in place?" Proud Heart asked, himself studying the dam. "Perhaps we should have removed the dam with our hatchets. There would be less danger involved, and noise."

"We do not have the time to waste hacking away at limbs and debris with our hatchets," Strong Wolf said flatly. "And, yes, we have enough dynamite sticks in place."

"But the noise that dynamite makes is as powerful as the sticks are effective," Proud Heart said. "It will draw the white men from the ranch."

"Let them come," Strong Wolf said, his eyes filled with an angry fire. "We have done what should have been done already." He gave Proud Heart a smug smile. "And will we not be gone when the white men get here? We will leave this place as soon as we see that the dynamite has done its business."

He placed a hand on Proud Heart's shoulder. "My friend, it is my plan to make things right for our people in all ways," he said thickly. "What we do today assures our people water and fish without them having to travel so far to the river to get what is required for survival. And we gave the white men a chance to take back what they had placed on our own land. The man whose land lies adjacent with ours is deceitful. He only pretended to give the orders for his foreman to destroy the dam. But it will soon be done. That is all that matters."

He dropped his hand to his side. "And, my friend," Strong Wolf said, walking toward his horse, "let us finish what we have started. The sooner we have this chore behind us, the sooner you can return to your wife Singing Wind."

"You should have a wife to go home to also," Proud Heart said, walking beside Strong Wolf, but not to mount his horse. It was *his* duty to set the dynamite off, while Strong Wolf saw that no one was near who might get harmed by the blast.

"In time, Proud Heart," Strong Wolf said, swinging himself into his saddle.

Proud Heart gazed up at him and cocked an eyebrow. "There seems to be something in the way you said that, that teases me into wanting to know if you may have met a woman," he said. "Have you met a woman who tugs at the strings of your heart?"

"My friend, I would not urge you to travel this far from your own people, the Chippewa, whom you left behind in Wisconsin, to be with me as I searched for land for *my* people, the Potawatomis, only to keep secrets from you," Strong Wolf said, grabbing up his reins. "I was not certain myself until yesterday that I had something to share with you. I did not tell you yet what transpired yesterday between myself and a woman because we have been occupied by other things besides idle chatter."

"Than you *have* found a woman?" Proud Heart asked, eyes wide.

"There *is* a woman, and I have not had to travel far to look upon her loveliness," Strong Wolf said.

"Then *who*?" Proud Heart prodded. "Where did you see her?"

"Her skin is fair, her hair is golden, her eyes are the color of grass," Strong Wolf said, his insides afire at the mere thought of Hannah.

"You ... are ... in love with a white woman?" Proud Heart stammered out.

"Yes, and do not act as though you are appalled at my choice," Strong Wolf said. "Is your mother not, in part, also white?"

"Yes, that is so," Proud Heart said, nodding. "My mother is part white and part Kickapoo. But she claims the Kickapoo side of her heritage much stronger than her white. As you know, she plans to travel to Mexico to search for her Kickapoo people. She promised her mother long ago, before her mother passed on to the other side, that she would find her people before *she* grew too old to travel. That proves my mother's dedication to the Indian side of her heritage, does it not? This woman who tugs at your heartstrings. Is she able to boast of being part Indian?"

"I have not yet been given the opportunity to question her about anything that I wish to know," Strong Wolf said. "But I know without asking that, yes, she is all white by blood kin. Never have I seen anyone as fair as she."

"Who, Strong Wolf?" Proud Heart said, leaning closer to Strong Wolf. "Tell me her name. Do I know her myself?"

"Yes, you know *of* her," Strong Wolf said, his eyes dancing into Proud Heart's. "You have watched her as I have watched her ever since she arrived on the great white boat on the river a few sunrises ago."

"The woman who now lives at the white man's ranch?" Proud Heart said, now recalling Strong Wolf having watched the woman from afar when they had seen her horseback riding with the skills and bravery of a man.

"She is the one," Strong Wolf said, nodding.

"But is she not kin to the man who deceived us today?" Proud Heart persisted.

"Yes, she is his sister," Strong Wolf said. "But that will not matter to me. I want her, not her brother. And I will have her."

Strong Wolf wheeled his horse around. "Now, let us finish here what we have started so that perhaps I may see her again today," he said thickly. "She so pleasures my eyes."

"She *is* different in appearance than most women," Proud Heart said, stepping back from Strong Wolf's steed. "She is tall. She is free-spirited, a woman who rides a horse like a man and who seems to know her mind as *well* as any man."

"And that is what intrigues me about her," Strong Wolf said, smiling down at his friend. "Now, prepare to set off the dynamite."

He gave Proud Heart a steady stare. "Make sure I am far enough away," he said somberly. "And also make sure you are safely hidden before the dynamite explodes."

Proud Heart nodded, then turned and walked back toward the dam.

Strong Wolf watched his friend for a moment longer, then rode off in a soft lope, his eyes ever searching for anyone who might happen by on horseback.

As he looked, he went back over in his mind that which he and Proud Heart had just been discussing.

The woman!

In his mind's eye he saw her now, as though it were yesterday, and how there seemed to have been some magical force reaching between them, making them aware of their feelings for each other.

Until now he had never thought about falling in love this quickly, this intensely.

His head seemingly in the clouds, he rode onward, unable to think past Hannah's lovely smile, her beautiful hair, and how statuesque she was!

And he had seemed to have won a vote of approval from his best friend, for, except for those brief moments when Proud Heart had questioned him about

Hannah's skin color, Proud Heart had not discouraged his interest in the white woman.

That made Strong Wolf smile, for Proud Heart was to him like a twin. All things good and bad they shared together. Their long affection had made them kin—brothers!

6

At first I viewed the lovely maid,
In silent, soft surprise.
　　　　　　　—ROBERT DODSLEY

Dressed in a long riding skirt, a calico blouse, well-fitting boots, and wearing three-quarter length butter soft gloves, Hannah rode in a soft trot on a fine pinto horse. Silver earrings dangled from her pierced ears, and her long, luxuriant hair was held back from her face with small combs.

She rested a hand on the knife sheathed at her waist as she rode onward. Hannah felt dispirited, for she had been unable to sleep all night. She couldn't get Strong Wolf off her mind, or the dam. She had told her brother that she was going horseback riding this morning, while hiding the truth from him that she was actually going to see for herself if Tiny had followed her brother's orders and destroyed the dam.

She also hoped that she might see Strong Wolf again. He had awakened feelings inside her that she had never known were there. She hoped to be with him again, to test these feelings, these wondrous sensations that warmed her through and through.

And what was absolutely perfect, was that her brother and the Indian were friends. That would make her relationship with him, should he feel the same about her, less forbidden. She recalled how women were mocked and ridiculed back in Saint Louis when they had married an Indian brave.

Well, this wasn't Saint Louis, she thought stubbornly to herself. This was Kansas, where she was free to do as she *pleased*!

Smiling, confident of her feelings and with whom she wished to share them, Hannah rode onward.

It was summer on the plains. Fields of golden sunflowers faced eastward. Colonies of plants wandered across the hillsides.

When she reached the river, she rode slowly beside it and watched for the stream that forked away from it, where Tiny had placed the dam. The river was carried along on a weak current green with algae. Sometimes rocks and sometimes rich green moss fringed the riverbank. But for the most part, cottonwoods and sycamores held back the banks and probed the sky with their canopies.

Farther away, the oaks, hickory, and maple trees claimed the higher ground. In their shade grew the inner forest of pawpaws, buckeyes, and occasionally crab apple trees.

Most of the sunny places were dominated by walls of horseweeds. Some were left with a permanent lean in their growth, a reminder of the spring's higher water.

Finally she came to the stream that she was looking for. Slowly she rode beside it, her eyes searching for the dam, hoping she did not find it. If Tiny hadn't removed it, that would be a blatant show of disobedience of her brother's orders, which could cause her brother undue stress.

"I do so hope it's gone," she whispered to herself as she edged her horse around a cluster of white birch trees. "Not only for my brother, but also for Strong Wolf. I would hate to think that he might blame my brother if Tiny . . . ?"

She got distracted for a moment by two groundhogs that were playing and chasing one another. She followed them into the trees and rode within the thick foliage beside the stream, where she could only now barely see the water.

Suddenly the groundhogs darted into small holes in the ground. Hannah shrugged and turned her horse back in the direction of the water, just in time to see the dam through a break in the trees a short distance away.

Anger filled her heart in hot splashes. "The damn nitwit," she whispered to herself. "Tiny *didn't* do as Chuck told him. *Damn him.*"

Then when she came out of the cover of the trees and she was on the banks of the stream again, something else grabbed her attention. What she saw caused her heart to skip several beats and a cold sweat of fear to cover her.

She could hear the pounding of her blood in her ears as her eyes looked in jerks at the many sticks of dynamite that she saw positioned in various places in the dam. Then a cry of panic filled her throat when she saw the wick that crawled along the ground like a snake to a thick stand of rock and brush.

Proud Heart suddenly rose from behind his protective hiding place. He waved frantically at her. "The fuse has been lit!" he shouted. "I cannot stop it! Leave! Ride away quickly!"

Strong Wolf had rode up one side of the stream and down the other, his eyes watching.

When he heard Proud Heart shouting, his heart leapt with alarm.

Someone was dangerously near the dam.

And it was time for the dynamite to explode!

Who was near the dam?

Was it the rancher's men?

If so, should he even warn them?

Wouldn't it be a welcome loss if they died?

But not wanting to think such things, even if he did despise the small white man, he nudged his horse's flanks with the heels of his moccasins and raced along the banks of the creek to warn them.

When he saw Hannah ahead, seemingly disoriented from fear, his insides grew weak with panic. He had not even thought about the possibilities of her coming this far from the ranch, alone.

But she had!

And if he did not reach her in time, if she didn't regain her senses and ride away, she ... could ... be killed!

He knew the chances were great that even he could be killed if he tried to save Hannah, but nothing would keep him from trying!

He drove himself onward in desperation, fear having quickened his heartbeat. His flesh crawled at the thought of what might happen to Hannah *and* himself, if he wasn't quick enough.

When he reached her, he swept an arm out for her and grabbed her from her horse.

Just as he slid her onto his lap and rode away in a fast gallop only a short distance, the explosion erupted behind them. Debris flew everywhere. Hannah's horse reared and rode away. Strong Wolf held his own horse steady.

A dislodged rock flew through the air and hit Hannah in the forehead. Knocked unconscious, she grew limp in Strong Wolf's arms.

Strong Wolf rode quickly into the thickness of the trees. When he felt that he was safely away from danger, he drew tight rein and slid from his horse, Hannah in his arms.

Strong Wolf carried Hannah to an overhang of rock and lay her on a bed of moss beneath it. He knelt over her, inspected her wound, and discovered only a small contusion rising on her forehead, the skin not even broken.

As he cradled her head on his lap, and had her so close that he could smell the sweet fragrance of her skin and hair, he was suddenly overwhelmed with fears that had been forgotten while he had only watched her from afar.

But now with her so close, with her unaware that he was able to hold her and study her, the fears that has plagued him always in his past, haunted him again.

While watching this woman these past days, knowing that destiny had drawn her here for him to love, how could he have forgotten his secret past?

The secret was so dark, how could he ever think that this woman could be told?

Surely no woman would understand!

Because of his ugly secret, Strong Wolf had centered his life around his people. He had made his people the main focus of his life.

Not women!

Even now he knew that he should turn his eyes from this woman and never think of her again!

With this particular woman, it should be even easier to fight off feelings of needing her, for in a sense, she was his enemy. Her very own brother had lied to him! Had betrayed him!

Weary of allowing himself to remember why he shouldn't love this woman, or any woman *ever,* and knowing that the blast would bring the rancher's foreman, Strong Wolf lifted Hannah into his arms and carried her toward his horse. Before he placed her in the saddle, Proud Heart rode up.

"Are you well, my brother?" Proud Heart asked anxiously. "Were you injured?"

Then Proud Heart's eyes moved to the woman.

"I am not injured, only she is," Strong Wolf said, placing her on his horse, swinging himself in the saddle behind her. "But it is only a flesh wound. She will soon awaken."

"*Then* what, my brother?" Proud Heart asked warily. "What will you do with her then? Take her with us? Or return her to her lying brother?"

"I am not certain just yet what I should do with her," Strong Wolf said, his insides torn with needs and wants. "Go on to the village without me. The deed is done here. The dam is no more."

"You could have been killed because of that woman," Proud Heart mumbled out as he gazed with contempt at Hannah.

"But my lungs still draw breath into them, do they not?" Strong Wolf said, glowering at Proud Heart. "My brother, do not allow this woman to come between us. I shall do what I must. It is truly no concern of yours."

"Anything or anyone who enters your life is my concern because my friendship to you is forever," Proud Heart said, then turned and rode away.

Strong Wolf watched Proud Heart until he could see him no more, then rode in the opposite direction.

Hannah slowly awakened. She was first aware of the horse's movements, then opened her eyes and saw that she was not in control of the horse. She was on someone else's steed, being held there by someone's muscled arm.

She turned with a start as she gazed with wide and questioning eyes at Strong Wolf.

Strong Wolf's eyes locked with hers, then he drew tight rein and stopped his horse.

"What happened?" Hannah asked, reaching a hand to her throbbing brow. She didn't remember how she had gotten on Strong Wolf's horse with him. The last few minutes seemed altogether blocked from her memory.

"Strong Wolf, why am I with *you*?" she asked, stunned by so many things. Why was she there? How had she gotten injured? Why was Strong Wolf so . . . so . . . strangely quiet and withdrawn?

When he helped her from the horse, still he said nothing.

Hannah tried to steady herself, to stand alone, but her knees buckled beneath her.

She was surprised when Strong Wolf offered no help and allowed her to fall to the ground. When she gazed up at him, she froze inside, for he no longer seemed friendly. Instead she felt that by the way he was glaring at her so contemptuously, it was as though she were his ardent enemy!

"Strong Wolf?" she said, reaching a trembling hand toward him. "Please . . . ?"

But . . . still . . . he ignored her!

7

Her hair that lay along her back
Was yellow like ripe corn.
——DANTE GABRIEL ROSSETTI

As Strong Wolf continued to glare at her, Hannah
slowly pushed herself up from the ground.

After she was back on her feet she started to back
away from him, their eyes still locked in silent battle.

When he reached out and grabbed her by a wrist,
stopping her, Hannah gasped and paled. "Please tell
me what's wrong," she said, her voice tremulous.
"Why are you treating me like this?"

In small flashes her memory was returning. She recalled why she had left the ranch; to see if the dam
had been destroyed. She recalled now having seen the
dynamite planted in strategic places in the dam, and
then . . .

"Your brother deceived me," Strong Wolf finally
said, interrupting Hannah's train of thought; her re-
membrances of what had brought her to this moment
in life.

"My brother deceived you?" Hannah said, her eyebrows forking. "How?"

She reached her free hand to her brow, where she

felt a slight swelling of the skin. It was just now beginning to throb.

The blast!

She now recalled the blast!

Shortly afterward, it was as though a black veil had been drawn over her eyes when she had been knocked into unconsciousness.

"Your brother played the role of a friend and then the role of one who speaks with two tongues," Strong Wolf said, confusing Hannah even worse by how he explained his feelings.

Then it came to her.

The dam!

Strong Wolf surely thought that Chuck had gone back on his word and had allowed the dam to stay in place across the stream, after all.

"If you are speaking of the dam, you are wrong to accuse my brother of being responsible for it having not been removed," Hannah said, pleading at him with her eyes. "It's apparent to me that his foreman blatantly ignored his orders."

She flinched when he tightened his grip on her wrist, paining her.

"And why should I believe you?" he grumbled. "You can lie as easily as your brother. Do you not share the same blood in your veins? You could share the same ease at lying!"

"My brother and I are both honest people," Hannah said, firming her chin. "Neither of us make a habit of lying, especially about something like this. It was obvious to me yesterday when you and Chuck were together that he deeply admires and respects you. I could tell that you felt the same about him. He would do nothing to jeopardize the friendship. I am sure that you wouldn't, either."

She paused, then said—"You *wouldn't,* would you?" she breathed guardedly across her lips.

"I have often been forced to place friendships behind me," Strong Wolf said, then released her wrist. "Always my people's welfare comes before anyone else's."

Hannah rubbed her wrists. She gazed at him questionably, not knowing if she had gained ground with him, or if he still wished not to believe her or Chuck.

She then looked from side to side and asked, "Where's my horse?"

"The blast of dynamite frightened it away," Strong Wolf said, torn with what to believe. He wished to think that this woman whose very nearness made his heart do strange flip-flops could be trusted.

Yet he could not allow a woman to be the cause of his defenses weakening. Many Potawatomis people were responsible for him keeping his sense of logic. They had to remain the main focus in his life. He could not allow himself to trust too easily, even when it was a woman he wished to be free to love.

"Using dynamite was an irresponsible thing to do," Hannah suddenly snapped, placing her fists on her hips. "Not only could I have been killed, but also *you.*" She moved her fingers to the lump on her brow. "I'm lucky this bump is all I have to show for your ... your ... negligence."

"I warned your brother about the dam," Strong Wolf said stiffly. "He did not listen. I chose the quickest way possible to rid the land of it."

"I still say that was the wrong way to handle the situation," Hannah said, then glared at him. "And I told you that my brother isn't responsible for the dam not having been removed. Why can't you believe me? Tiny was supposed to remove it. He *didn't.*"

"If what you say is true, then your brother must

find a way to make sure that what he commands done from now on, is *done*," Strong Wolf said.

"Then you believe me?" Hannah asked, her eyes wavering into his.

"Perhaps a little," Strong Wolf said, folding his arms across his chest.

"Either you do, or you *don't*," Hannah said, frustrated.

He said nothing back to her.

"Well, *I* know one thing for certain," Hannah said, turning to walk away. "I'm going to find my horse. I'm going home. I'm tired of bantering with you. I don't know how else I can convince you that my brother is innocent of that which you accuse him."

Strong Wolf watched her walk away for a moment, then something came to him so quickly: a plan that he felt was necessary. He did not have the time to think it through before he went and grabbed her by a wrist again, stopping her.

Their eyes met in silent combat, and he was reminded of so long ago, when it *was* the practice of the Potawatomis to take captives. Despite the momentary terror of such abduction, victims—especially women—were generally welcomed as new members of the community to which they were taken, sometimes hundreds of miles away.

Most captives accepted their new roles, replacing the tribe members who had been lost to disease, nature, or battle.

But this was now, and this was a *white* woman. This was a *spirited*, stubborn white woman. *She* would not accept such fate as easily.

"You are not going anywhere until I am ready to allow it," he said thickly, their eyes in silent combat again as she stared in disbelief at him.

"Are you saying that I ... am ... a captive?" Hannah said, paling.

"If I must hold you as ransom, to get assurances from your brother that are true, yes, for now you are my captive," Strong Wolf said, disbelieving that he had actually said that.

Never before had he done this.

But never before had he felt the need to. He was afraid that if he did nothing to make the rancher realize the true importance of keeping the water running free, then another dam would appear across the stream before there was another sunrise.

Hannah stared up at him for a moment, seeing in him so much that made her insides melt. Even though he was treating her wrong today, she could still feel something special flow between them.

It was in his eyes that his words betrayed his heart!

He wanted her. She could tell it. She could feel it.

And, oh, she so badly wanted him. It would be heaven to be held by him. His muscled arms could make her feel so protected, so loved!

But at this moment, they were enemies. And she would fight for her freedom!

Wrenching her wrist free, Hannah turned and ran. "My father imprisoned me at the convent!" she shouted over her shoulder. "No one will imprison me ever again!"

Strong Wolf was again in awe of Hannah's spirit, of her will to fight for her rights! He admired this in her, and he wanted her even more than before. She would be a challenge for any man. And he had always enjoyed challenges of all kinds!

He ran after her.

When he caught up with her, he swung an arm around her waist and wrestled her to the ground until she lay flat on her back. Straddling her, holding her

wrists to the ground over her head, he watched her
breasts heaving beneath the thin fabric of her cotton
dress, then looked into her eyes that were filled with
the fire of defiance.

"You are even more beautiful when you are angry,"
he said, then crushed her lips beneath his as he gave
her a frenzied, passion-filled kiss.

His loins flamed.

Her head spun.

Both were startled by the intensity of their feelings
for one another.

Her heart pounding, dizzied by the rapturous, heady
sensations whirling within her, Hannah wrenched her
lips free.

"Please don't," she whispered, her eyes pleading
with his. "I ..."

Before she could say any more, Strong Wolf was on
his feet. His one hand still on one of her wrists, he
yanked her up from the ground.

His jaw tight, Strong Wolf forced Hannah to walk
toward his horse. When they reached his steed, he
placed his hands at her waist and lifted her into the
saddle. He then swung himself into the saddle behind
her and held her in place as he locked an arm firmly
around her waist.

"You can't do this!" Hannah cried, trying to pull
his arm away from her waist as he urged his horse
into a fast gallop. "Let ... me ... go!"

Strong Wolf ignored her as best he could, all the
while still feeling the taste of her on his lips and seeing
the heaving of her well-rounded breasts.

If he continued this plan of taking her captive, she
might end up hating him forever. He could not force
her to love him. Those things had to come naturally,
from true feelings.

As she had returned his kiss, he knew that she had

not *yet* grown to hate him. There had been feelings in the kiss. Passion had been exchanged between them. He did not want it to be short-lived, yet he would look the fool now if he released her.

And he would *not* let himself look less a man to her, ever!

Yes, he had started something that he would have to finish, no matter the end result. He had lived without her until now. So could he the rest of his life, if forced to.

"Strong Wolf, I *must* be set free," Hannah cried as she looked over her shoulder at him. "My brother is almost blind. I have come to the Kansas Territory for the sole purpose of being his *eyes,* to look after him and help him with his decisions. Don't you see? I can't leave him at the mercy of men like Tiny Sharp! He disobeyed my brother! I must return to the ranch and tell my brother! Who knows what Tiny will do next? I must be there to make sure he doesn't do anything else that can cause harm to my brother!"

Strong Wolf heard the true pleading in Hannah's voice, and listened hard to what she said, yet could not alter his plans.

"If you will set me free now, before this goes any further, I won't tell anyone about your plan to abduct me," Hannah cried. "I promise, Strong Wolf. I won't tell anyone. Not even my brother. I just want to return home so that I can tell him that Tiny disobeyed him!"

The more she spoke, the more she pleaded with him, Hannah's words reached inside Strong Wolf's heart. He knew that she spoke the truth about her brother, having been saddened himself when he had noticed how Chuck's eyesight was responsible for him being awkward and unsure of his movements.

He knew that it *was* possible that Tiny Sharp *had*

taken advantage of Hannah's brother. Strong Wolf so badly wanted to trust Chuck, *and* believe the woman.

Deciding to trust and believe, Strong Wolf released Hannah. He had just been given another reason to admire, to fall in love with, this woman. Her loyalty to her brother touched him deeply. Strong Wolf knew now that she was someone he could not deny himself of loving, as he had all other women he had ever known before her.

He wheeled his horse to a sudden stop.

Hannah gazed in wonder at Strong Wolf. She scarcely breathed as she waited for him to speak, to explain why he had stopped. Her pulse raced as his eyes met and held with hers. She could not stop this crazy, rapturous spinning within her when he looked at her in such a way, so penetrating, as though he was looking into her very soul!

"You are free to go," Strong Wolf said, his own heart pounding at the way her eyes talked to him. "I will take you home. Hopefully your horse will find its way back to your brother's ranch on its own."

"Oh, thank you," Hannah said softly, having to hold herself back when she so badly wanted to fling herself into his arms and hug him. "And I understand your feelings toward such men as Tiny. You have surely been faced with many of the same type of men throughout your life."

She knew that there had been many injustices performed against the red man. She had just never been in the position of having seen it face-to-face before.

"But, please don't put my brother in the same category as such men as Tiny," she blurted out. "He is kind, gentle, and most times way too generous."

She gulped hard. "I'm even afraid that he won't fire Tiny," she said, a bitter edge recognizable in her voice.

"He'll see some good about keeping him on, even after I tell him the ugly truth about him."

"Being your brother's eyes, perhaps you can make him see the wrong in allying himself with the tiny white man," Strong Wolf said.

He held her closer as he rode off. He fought off the need that was rising within his heart, to kiss her again, to hold her.

So aware of his hard, lean body so close to hers, snuggled against her backside, Hannah became breathless. Her heart pounding fiercely, her face became hot with a blush as his arm grazed against her breasts. She could almost feel the heat of his flesh through the thin fabric of her white calico blouse.

They rode awhile, then Hannah's breath caught with surprise when Strong Wolf suddenly wheeled his horse to the side and rode in another direction. Fearing that he had changed his mind, and that he had decided to take her captive after all, she pulled at his arm, but he held her too tightly. She had no choice but to see what he had planned for her now. She had to wonder at what point he had changed his mind?

And, *why*?

With a wariness that she had never felt before with *any*one, Hannah watched all around her as Strong Wolf continued taking her farther and farther away from her brother's ranch. Her brain was a mass of confusion as Strong Wolf rode through a forest of thick, tangled greenery, where things were heavy with shade. Ages of decayed leaves scented the air with their earthy smell as the quiet life of the forest kept its secrets.

Suddenly Strong Wolf wheeled his horse to a stop. He helped Hannah to the ground, and then slid from the saddle and tethered his reins to a low-hanging limb.

Hannah didn't attempt to escape from him. She had no idea where she was. She did know that she was many miles from civilization. She was at his mercy. She had no choice but to follow beside him as he gripped her by the arm and led her down a narrow path beneath the trees.

Suddenly before her was a misty smoke hanging over a body of water, surrounded by an impassable sinking mire. Through the smoky mist she could see a cave that had been sealed up with great boulders of rock.

She was glad when Strong Wolf stopped, even though this place of mystery somewhat terrified her.

When he turned to her, she took a step away from him.

Unable to hold back his feelings any longer for this woman, Strong Wolf reached for Hannah and snaked his arms around her waist.

His heart racing, he yanked her against him and kissed her. He held her tightly within his embrace as he could feel her shoving against his chest, in an attempt to get free.

Then he loosened his grip when he felt her grow limp in his arms and willingly return his kiss with wild abandon. He wove his fingers through her hair and held her closer. He gyrated his body into hers, overwhelmed by the raging heat that was building within him, stunned by how she responded as she clung and melted against him.

Stunned by her feelings, so carried away by his kiss that she had momentarily forgotten that she was still his captive, Hannah wrenched herself free and ran away from him, up the tangled path.

"Hannah, do not be afraid," Strong Wolf cried after her. "I meant you no harm. Stop. I will willingly return you to your brother's ranch."

His words, the sincerity in which he said them to her, and the promise of ecstasy that she had found while within his arms, that which she had never found while with any other man, made Hannah stop and turn slowly around to face him.

When he stepped up to her and took her hands within his, she found herself helpless beneath his passion-filled, midnight eyes.

"I want to know everything about you," Strong Wolf said thickly. "I want to be with you so that I can know what makes me feel this bonding with you. You have affected me differently than any other woman. *You* are different. It is this difference that has led me into behavior that is quite unlike me, a powerful leader, who will one day be chief of my people."

"You say that I am different in your eyes than other women," Hannah said, hoping that she was right to trust him. "How am I different from other women you have known? I find it hard to understand why you would even want to be with me. I am tall and lanky. I even find myself ugly when I look into the mirror."

She paused, then her eyes wavered into his. "Do you pretend an attraction to me only to get closer to my brother?" she said, her voice breaking. "Is it to seal a bond between yourself and my brother so that you would be assured of no longer having cause to feel a strain between one another?"

Strong Wolf placed his hands to her waist and held her at arm's length as his eyes devoured her. "Your mirror lies when you gaze into it," he said huskily. "I have never seen anyone as lovely. And, no, I do not lie to you about my feelings. This is no game. This is not done purposely to gain tighter friendships and trust between myself and your brother. Those things I achieve on my own, in my own time. And I had achieved a closeness with your brother until the incident with the dam. But now I know that I was wrong to doubt him. I see Tiny as my problem. Not your brother.''

He drew her closer. "You and I could have so much together," he said thickly. "So much is already there to build upon. What are the depths of your feelings for me?"

Hannah's heart swam in a rapturous sweetness to have him speak to her in such a way, to know that he could look past her shortcomings and love her. It did not seem real. It was like a fantasy, that which she had read about many times in novels.

He brushed her lips with a kiss, then held her close. "Speak to me, my woman, of your feelings," Strong Wolf whispered.

Hannah sucked in a wild breath of rapture and closed her eyes. Her knees were weak. The excitement of the moment was so intense, her throat was dry.

But in her mind's eye she was seeing her brother back at the ranch, almost helpless against Tiny Sharp. She was wrong not to hurry back to him, to warn him.

Although she could spend forever like this, in this man's arms, she knew that there were more important issues now than giving in to her feelings that stole her senses away.

"How do I feel?" Hannah murmured, easing from his arms. "I dare not say just yet. Please give me time to think about us, about *everything*. For now, I must return home quickly to my brother. I know he heard the blast made from the dynamite. He has to know that Tiny disobeyed his orders. I need to be there to help stand up against that small creature, who in his mind, thinks he is a giant among men."

Strong Wolf chuckled. "That is an amusing comparison," he said, taking her hand. "Come. I will take you to your brother's ranch."

He led her back up the tangled path, toward his horse.

Before they got there, he stopped and held her hands. "I will look forward to our next time together," he said. "Perhaps then you will be free to talk with me, to share with me."

"I promise that I will," Hannah said, then went on with him to his horse.

The ride was not long until the ranch house came into sight.

Strong Wolf reined in his horse.

"I will not take you the rest of the way," he said thickly. "I have you close enough so that you will not have far to walk. Until you speak with your brother and clear up what has happened today, I will stay my distance."

Hannah nodded. She slipped from the saddle and gazed up at him again.

She became breathless when he reached down, swept an arm around her waist again, and drew her back onto his lap and kissed her. He then released her again and placed her on the ground.

Dazzled by the kiss, Hannah was speechless as she gazed up at him. Their eyes locked for a moment, then he rode away.

Hannah sucked in a quavering breath. She was numb by the experience with Strong Wolf. Sweetly, deliciously numb.

8

Oh, what a plague is love!
How shall I bear it?
She will inconstant prove,
I greatly fear it!
—ANONYMOUS, 19TH CENTURY

Breathlessly Hannah walked toward her brother's
house, admiring it. It was a large, one-story log ranch
house, surrounded with elms, oaks, and maple trees.

Far back from the house stood a bunkhouse and
other outbuildings. A great gate surrounded the
house, giving the entrance to the grounds.

Hannah paused long enough to look over her shoulder a last time, to see if Strong Wolf was still watching
her. Now so close to her brother's house, surely Strong
Wolf could see that she was safe enough to go on
alone, without him watching her.

She sighed with relief when she discovered that he
had rode away. She had worried about him lingering
too long. Under the circumstances of what had happened, she didn't want him to be anywhere near this
place when she laid down the law about Tiny.

Tiny had to go!

She walked determinedly toward the house, but before she reached the front steps, several cowhands and
her brother came out on the porch.

"Where the hell have you been?" Chuck asked, squinting hard in an attempt to see her. "I've been beside myself with worry, Hannah. And, Hannah, I didn't hear you arrive home on a horse. Where is it? What happened? You're a skilled rider. No horse would get the best of you, unless . . . unless."

"Chuck, I'm all right," Hannah said, interrupting him. "Please don't be so upset. I can explain everything."

She glared at the armed men, pistols heavy at their hips, then looked at Chuck again. "What are these men doing here so well equipped with firearms? What were you going to do, Chuck?" she said, her voice wary. "Send a posse out looking for me?"

"Hannah, what was I to think?" Chuck said, nervously raking the fingers of one hand through his hair. He leaned on his cane with the other hand. "You've been gone for hours."

Quite aware of the eyes of the men on her every move, Hannah went up the steps. She could feel their eyes roving over her, and not because she was something pleasant to look at. She knew that she was disarrayed. Her hair was windblown. Her skirt was filthy from having been on the ground more than once on this turbulent day. Her blouse was ripped, and she knew that her face must be dirty. And not only that. She had a lump on her forehead the size of a goose egg.

"Chuck, you can send the men away," she said, giving her brother a hug. "I'm home. I'm safe." She leaned into his embrace when his free arm snaked around her waist.

She relished the warmth of her brother's show of devoted love for a moment, then stepped away from him to glower at the men.

Chuck nodded at the men. "As you can see, my

sister is all right," he said thickly. "You can leave. But
I would appreciate it if a couple of you would go
searching for her horse. If it's out there somewhere,
disoriented, it could be bait for wolves or that pesky
panther that's been wandering much too close to my
property."

A sudden panic, a warning, leapt into Hannah's
heart. If the men went out now to look for her horse,
they might come across Strong Wolf before he had
the chance to get farther from her brother's property.
She had no idea what Tiny had told her brother about
what had happened.

One thing for certain, no one could have missed
hearing the loud blast made by the dynamite. Her
brother had to know already that someone *had* destroyed the dam. He might think it was Tiny, or he
might know that it wasn't. If he didn't understand the
situation, he might think that Strong Wolf was guilty
of some wrongdoing.

And he wasn't. The property on which he had used
the dynamite was *his*. And even though he had abducted her, he had set her free.

"Why, there it *is*," one of the cowhands said, gesturing toward the lovely pinto horse as it came into sight
in a slow trot.

Hannah couldn't believe her eyes when she saw the
horse headed toward the corral, just in time to keep
the men from looking for it.

"Before my eyes got this bad, I personally trained
that pinto to return home, but I thought it had forgotten," Chuck said. He smiled. "Now I have both my
sister and my favorite horse back home."

The men tipped their hats to Chuck and Hannah,
then sauntered from the porch and went back to their
usual chores.

Chuck reached his free hand out for Hannah.

"Come, sis," he said, sighing heavily. "Let's go inside. Does a cup of coffee sound good to you?"

"A bath is more to my liking," Hannah said, taking his hand, squeezing it affectionately.

They went inside to the parlor.

But before Chuck could tell the servant to get two cups of coffee, he stopped with a start. "Lord," he gasped out, paling.

Hannah's eyebrows forked. "What's the matter?" she asked softly. "Chuck, you look as though you've seen a ghost."

"It's Strong Wolf," Chuck said in a rush of words.

Hannah paled. "What *about* Strong Wolf?" she asked warily.

"Sis, you have to know how worried I was when you didn't return home," Chuck said, his voice drawn. "Damn it all to hell. Not only have I been upset this entire afternoon over Tiny having not removed the dam, forcing Strong Wolf to destroy it with dynamite, I have been beside myself with worry about *you*."

"So you *do* know that Tiny didn't remove the dam," Hannah said, trying to keep calm since her brother was too suddenly concerned over Strong Wolf.

"You know that Strong Wolf dynamited the dam," Hannah said guardedly. "Is that what you are upset over? What's wrong, Chuck? Tell me."

Chuck lowered his eyes. "Since you were gone so long I . . . I . . . thought that perhaps Strong Wolf had abducted you as revenge for the dam not having been destroyed," he said.

Hannah paled. "You . . . thought . . . that . . . he abducted me?" she said, recalling in her mind's eye that very abduction, and later when Strong Wolf said that she was free to go.

"What else was I to think?" Chuck said, lifting his eyes, squinting toward Hannah.

"Chuck, what did you do when you thought that I was abducted?" Hannah asked, her heart pounding.

"Chuck, what . . . did . . . you do?" Hannah persisted when he still did not answer her.

When he still failed to respond to her questions, she clasped his shoulders with her trembling fingers. "Chuck, for God's sake, tell me," she said, her voice rising in pitch as alarm arose within her. "What . . . about . . . Strong Wolf?"

"I sent several of my cowhands to the nearby fort to ask for their help in finding you," Chuck said, his tone worried. "Of course, I told them to tell those in charge at the fort about Strong Wolf's threats, and that . . . he . . . dynamited the dam."

He waved a frustrated hand in the air. "Damn it, Hannah, he stole dynamite from my storage shack," he said, his voice tight. "Why the hell did Tiny have to ignore my orders about the dam? None of this would be happening."

"So you are saying that right now, at this very moment, a posse might be out there looking for me?" Hannah rushed out. "They might even be on their way to Strong Wolf's village to arrest him?"

"My cowhands haven't been gone for long," Chuck said softly. "I waited until I couldn't wait any longer. Maybe they haven't reached the fort yet."

"I'm absolutely stunned by what you have done," Hannah said, trying not to shriek at her already distraught brother.

But because of her brother's fears and insecurities, Strong Wolf was in danger.

"How could you?" she said, her voice breaking. "Don't you know that Strong Wolf wants nothing but friendship from you? This damn man you have hired as a foreman is a ruthless son of a bitch. Chuck, you've got to fire him."

She looked toward the bunkhouse, then over at Chuck. "You have fired him, haven't you?" she asked warily.

"No," Chuck said, his jaw tight. "And I'm not about to. He knows my business front and back. I couldn't do without him, sis. Not yet, anyhow."

"I just can't believe this is you letting someone like him get the best of you," Hannah said, her eyes wavering as she gazed at her brother.

Then another thought came to her that made her feel ill at her stomach. "Where *is* Tiny?" she asked. "If he's not here, please don't tell me that he's among those men who were sent to the fort."

"Yes, I . . ." Chuck said.

But Hannah didn't wait to hear any more of his explanations. She ran from the porch toward the corral, where the pinto had just been taken. She was glad that the saddle was still in place. She shouted at the cowhand to leave it on the horse.

Ignoring her brother's shouts to stop, Hannah rode away, urging the pinto in a hard gallop. If at all possible, she had to get to the fort in time to ward off a conflict between Strong Wolf and the military.

But if she was too late, and Strong Wolf had already been incarcerated, she would plead his case and tell those in charge at the fort that he was innocent of all crimes accused. Yes, he stole the dynamite, but only to do what Tiny had neglected to do. But she was going to side with Strong Wolf for having used her brother's dynamite to destroy the dam.

And no one but herself and Strong Wolf knew of his intention of abducting her. That, for certain, could not be held against him! No one but herself and Strong Wolf would have to even ever know about it!

But one thing that she couldn't understand was the fact that her brother had excused Tiny's blatant refusal to obey his orders. She might have a struggle on her hands to get rid of the conniving little man.

"But I will find a way," Hannah whispered to herself.

She wasn't going to allow this man to get any more of a foothold on her brother's life than he already had. She would find a way to discredit him.

She only hoped that she would be in time. This man might have more tricks up his sleeves.

But for now, she only wanted to concentrate on Strong Wolf and *his* welfare. He and his people had suffered enough at the hands of white men!

She sorely regretted that one of those white men was ... her ... beloved brother.

9

The cold fear that follows and finds you,
The silence that bludgeons you dumb.
—ROBERT SERVICE

Holding his hat at his side, Tiny Sharp stood before Colonel Patrick Deshong's desk at Fort Leavenworth. Chuck's other cowhands were standing at the back of the room, listening, as Tiny tried to explain the day's events that centered around Strong Wolf being accused of not only stealing dynamite and using it on a dam, but also of having possibly abducted Hannah.

While drumming his fingers on the top of his oak desk, the colonel glared up at Tiny with angry, impatient brown eyes. "Chief Strong Wolf uses reason before he acts," he said. "He's a man of peace. He would not do anything foolish that could threaten the safety and well-being of his people."

He laughed throatily. "Abduct a woman?" he said. "That isn't like him. You go and tell Chuck that his sister is probably enjoying her outing on horseback. Tell him that if she doesn't return by sunset, though, to come and tell me. I'll put together a search party for her. But until then, tell Chuck not to jump the gun. He's worrying too much."

"That lady could even now be in the clutches of the Potawatomis," Tiny said, placing his palms on the colonel's desk, to allow him to lean closer. "If anything happens to her, you'll be responsible."

"Get your filthy hands off my desk," Colonel Deshong said, leaning closer to Tiny. "And don't come in here mouthing off to me about who's responsible for what."

Tiny eased his hands off the desk and straightened his back. "And are we to also ignore the damn fact that Strong Wolf stole the dynamite and threatened the countryside by settin' it off? A damn Injun don't know nothin' 'bout dynamite. If he'd miscalculated, not only the dam would be blown up, but half the human race in these parts."

"You don't give the chief credit for much, now do you?" Colonel Deshong said, pouring tobacco into the bowl of a pipe from a small pouch.

"Why should I?" Tiny said, plopping his hat back on his head. "But I see I'm wastin' my time here. You don't give a damn 'bout anythin' much except yourself and the comforts of your soldiers here at the fort."

He swung a frustrated hand in the air. "Let the damn redskins take over everything," he shouted. "See if I care."

As Tiny and the men stamped from the colonel's cabin, they could hear him laughing behind them. Tiny turned with doubled fists as the colonel followed them outside, puffing on his pipe.

Colonel Deshong slipped the pipe from between his lips. "Tiny, do you want to know what I really think about what you told me today?" he said, his eyes dancing with amusement.

"Don't think I do," Tiny said, turning again to stamp away.

"I think you made it all up in an attempt to get Strong Wolf in trouble," Colonel Deshong shouted, not one to give up that easily when he had not yet said his piece. "Be sure the next time you come to the fort, it's not with tall tales that take up my precious time."

Tiny swung himself into his saddle. He grabbed up his reins as he waited for the rest of the men to mount their steeds. He glowered at the colonel, then wheeled his horse around and rode off in a hard gallop through the tall gate of the palisade walls that encircled the fort.

"He'll be sorry!" Tiny said as he looked over at Clem, his best buddy and partner in mischief. "No one gets away with talking to me that way."

"There ain't much we can do about it," Clem said. He reached a hand and scratched at the stubble of whiskers on his chin. "The colonel is pretty much in charge in these parts."

"Well, he may be in charge, but I don't take to being ignored, *and* being accused of saying things that ain't true," Tiny shouted, raising a fist in the air.

"Again I say, Tiny, there ain't much we can do about it," Clem said, sinking his heels into the flanks of his horse to catch up with Tiny again, when Tiny raced on ahead of him.

"What am I to tell Chuck?" Tiny said as Clem sidled his horse closer to Tiny's. "He was genuinely worried about his sister. What if she *has* been abducted? Chuck'll have my hide for not convincing the colonel to go and search for her at the Injun village."

"Perhaps we should go on to the village ourselves and take a look," Clem said, again itching his whiskered chin, a habit when he was nervous.

"Naw, I don't want to risk that," Tiny said, his eyes squinting as he tried to make decisions that would work in his favor. "There ain't much love between me and that Injun leader. He'd as soon shoot me as look at me."

He laughed into the wind. "Especially over that dam," he said.

"You're lucky Chuck didn't have your hide over that," Clem said, now resting his one hand on the butt of his holstered pistol. "You should've removed the dam. Chuck was adamant about that, Tiny."

"Well, I was just as adamant about keepin' it where we built it," Tiny spat out angrily.

"But you knew that Strong Wolf wouldn't stand for that dam bein' there," Clem argued back.

"I had to take a chance of him bein' too much of a coward to remove it," Tiny said. "He's known for his peaceful ways, ain't he? Well, who's to say he might have been too afraid of stirrin' up trouble by removin' the dam. It was a chance worth takin'."

"Yeah, and it could've cost you your job," Clem said, laughing sarcastically.

Tiny glowered over at him. "I'm too valuable to Chuck for him to fire me," he said thickly. "He may have brought his sister to Kansas, but damn it all to hell, Clem, I'm the 'eyes' he truly needs. I'm the one who knows how to take care of the journal entries. His sister doesn't. I keep our men in line. His sister doesn't. And I know the land, every inch of it. His sister doesn't."

"Yeah, I see what you mean," Clem said, then strained his neck when he saw someone approaching them in the distance.

He nodded at Tiny. "Ain't that a Potawatomis brave headin' our way?" he said, pointing.

"Yeah, I believe so," Tiny said, a slow smile tugging at his lips. "And would you look at the meat and pelts on the travois he's draggin' behind his horse? I'd say his hunt went quite well today, wouldn't you?"

"Much better'n ours," Clem growled out, chuckling.

Tiny looked over his shoulder at the other cowhands. "Want to have some fun?" he shouted, yanking his rifle from the gun boot at the side of his horse.

Everyone shouted and nodded. They hollered and whooped as they waved their rifles in the air.

"You aren't going to kill him, are you?" Clem said, hesitating at taking his own firearm in hand.

"Naw, but when we get through with him, he'll wish he *was* dead," Tiny said, laughing throatily. He looked over his shoulder again. "Come on, men. Follow my lead. It's been awhile since we've had such an opportunity as this. The damn Injun should've known better than to go hunting by himself. He's at the mercy of *Tiny Sharp*."

"What *are* you going to do, Tiny?" Clem asked, still hesitant about joining the others.

"Are you with us, or ain't you?" Tiny said, giving Clem a threatening scowl.

"I'm with you all the way," Clem said, seeing that he had no choice.

"What's got into you today, Clem?" Tiny asked as they thundered onward toward the Indian who had taken notice of them and had turned his horse and travois around, in an attempt to get away.

But the weight of the travois stopped a hasty enough retreat. It was heavy with butchered meat and pelts that had been taken from the animals that the brave had killed today.

"It just seems like we get closer and closer to bein' found out by Chuck," Clem said, finally lifting his rifle from his gun boot. "We take chances every time we do something that ain't proper. Take the dam for example. Damn it, Tiny, we should've destroyed it and gone on about our business. All I'm interested in is my paycheck. Nothin' more."

"You can't tell me that your heart ain't pumpin' a hundred miles an hour at the thought of havin' fun at this here Injun's expense, now, can you?" Tiny said, laughing into the wind when Clem smiled over at him.

"I thought not," Tiny said, then leaned lower over his horse as he rode in a faster gallop toward the Indian.

When he felt that he was close enough, he straightened his back, raised the rifle into the air, and fired off a warning shot to the Indian.

Tiny laughed boisterously when the Indian stopped and leapt from his saddle and began running away from the advancing men on foot.

"You'd better stop or I'll blow your damn head off!" Tiny shouted at him.

The Indian stopped with a start, turned slowly around, then stood with a stubbornly lifted chin and glared at Tiny as he halted his horse only a few feet away.

"Why do you stop me?" the Potawatomis brave asked, holding his hands away from his sides, so that the men could see that he wasn't going for his sheathed knife at his right side.

Tiny looked over his shoulder. "Bring his horse and travois of meat over here!" he shouted at his men. "We've some meat inspectin' to do."

Tiny was aglow inside at this opportunity to get back at Strong Wolf by being able to take his anger out on one of his braves. It had not taken long for Tiny to decide that if the soldiers refused to make Strong Wolf pay for having stolen his dynamite and for having blown up the dam, then it was up to Tiny to do what he could.

And to hell with Hannah, he thought to himself, where*ever* she was. It served her right if she was lost. The stubborn bitch. Tiny saw her as just a mite too big for her breeches. The way she rode horses, she was unlike any lady he had ever seen. And she had a mouth on her that could scald a cat!

"What are we to do now?" Clem said, wrenching Tiny from his deep thoughts.

Tiny slid from his saddle as the Indian horse and travois were brought closer. He patted the horse, ran his hand over the animal's withers, then went back and knelt down beside the travois.

He studied the meat and pelts. For just one man, this Indian had been lucky at hunting. Tiny imagined that this meat was for the brave's family. The pelts were either for trading, or to be used for the comfort of the brave's family during the upcoming wretched months of winter.

He pushed himself back up from the ground. With his rifle clasped tightly, he went to the brave who was dressed in only a breechclout and moccasins. He turned and gazed at his men.

"We have us a thief in our midst!" he shouted. "This Injun is guilty as sin of stealin'."

"Bird in Ground is no thief," Bird in Ground said, his dark eyes wide with surprise over having been wrongly accused.

Tiny turned slow eyes to the brave. "Bird ... in ... Ground ... ?" he said, then mocked the Indian by saying his name over and over again.

Then Tiny sobered and leaned into the Indian's face. "I've heard of strange names before, but this one takes the cake," he said, chuckling.

Tiny turned his rifle around and jabbed the Indian's stomach with the butt end. "You thief," he hissed out. "Don't you know those were my hogs you killed today?"

He was amused by the expression on the Indian's face at the mention of hogs. Tiny didn't own a hog, or cattle. The time would come, though, when he would own everything that was now Chuck Kody's.

But only if he played his cards right. *And* if he could figure out what to do about Hannah. He hoped that she *was* lost today. He hoped that panthers, wolves, or wild hogs would get her and rid his life of at least this one complication.

"Hogs?" Bird in Ground said, trying to bear the pain that the rifle had inflicted on his gut. "I hunt and kill deer today. I kill raccoons. I kill muskrats. Not hogs." He gestured toward the travois. "Do you not see the pelts? Hogs have no pelts."

"You are not only a thief, but also a skilled liar!" Tiny said, slapping the Indian across his face with the back of his hand.

"Clem, get the Injun's rifle from his horse," Tiny said, watching a trickle of blood flow from the Indian's nose.

Clem did as he was told.

"Clem, shoot the rifle into the air," Tiny said, now watching blood trickle across the Indian's lips and into his mouth. Yet the Indian stood stoic and stiff, looking straight ahead.

Clem fired off the rifle, frightening Bird in Ground's horse away, the travois stumbling along after it, rocking precariously from side to side.

"No!" Bird in Ground cried. He broke into a run, to go after his horse. But he did not get far. Tiny ran after him and tackled him.

As Tiny held Bird in Ground down, he looked up at his men. "After I stand up away from him, don't allow this son of a bitch to get to his feet," he said, his eyes flashing. "You know what must be done to keep him there."

Tiny rose away from Bird in Ground. The cowhands circled around the brave. Some hit him with the butts of their rifles. Some kicked him. Others hit him with their fists. They did not stop until he lost consciousness.

When they stepped away from him, Tiny's lips quavered into a smug smile at the sight of the blood all over the Indian's body. "That'll teach Strong Wolf to mess with me," he said, giving one last kick to Bird in Ground's side.

Bird in Ground groaned. His eyes slowly fluttered open. He gazed over at Tiny as Tiny knelt down beside him.

"Can you hear me when I talk?" Tiny asked, watching Bird in Ground slowly, painfully, nod.

"Good. Bird in Ground, I know you have a wife and child," Tiny said, smiling smugly. "I've seen you with your family."

Panic leapt into Bird in Ground's eyes. He struggled to get up, but went limp again from the pain and broken ribs.

"Now, listen closely to what I am going to tell you," Tiny warned. "If you value your family's life, you will tell no one who did this to you today. If you do, your whole family will die. If not by my hand, by someone else's, for I have a lot of friends, Bird in Ground. All you need to remember is not to tell who did this to you. Do you understand? Nod if you do."

He smiled smugly when Bird in Ground slowly nodded, then looked away from Tiny.

"I think we're finished here," Tiny said, rushing to his feet. "Let's get out of here before someone happens along. I'm not quite ready yet for a noose around my neck."

Leaving the brave lying at the edge of the road, bleeding and half-unconscious, the men rode away in a hard gallop.

Tiny sat smugly in his saddle, his eyes dancing. He let out a loud whoop and holler as he waved his hat in the air.

10

Graceful and useful all she does,
Blessing and blest where'er she goes.
—WILLIAM COWPER

Hannah felt many eyes on her as she entered the wide gate at Fort Leavenworth. She drew a tight rein on her pinto before Colonel Deshong's cabin, not at all surprised when several soldiers surrounded her.

"Who are you?" one of them asked as he grabbed her reins. "What do you want?"

"I've come to see Colonel Deshong," Hannah said, looking guardedly from man to man, wondering if they actually saw her as a threat.

"*I'm* Colonel Deshong," Patrick said as he stepped from his cabin in his full uniform. His coat shone with brass buttons, the shoulders gold with cord and tassels. "What can I do for you?"

Hannah turned her eyes quickly to the man, finding him dignified in appearance. His complexion ruddy, he was stout, with neatly groomed reddish blond hair that hung to his shirt collar.

"I've come to speak in behalf of Strong Wolf," she said. "I want to prove that he did not kidnap me. My brother was wrong to send his cowhands here with false accusations. Strong Wolf is innocent of the crimes he is accused of."

She swallowed hard when she caught a look of surprise in the colonel's eyes, and then tightened inside when his brow knitted into a frown.

"First, my day is interrupted by Tiny Sharp, who seemed hell-bent in having Strong Wolf incarcerated," Colonel Deshong said, twining his fingers around the handle of the saber that hung at his right side. "And now I have a woman coming to speak in the Indian's behalf."

"And what is wrong with that, sir?" Hannah said, boldly lifting her chin.

"Nothing, nothing," Colonel Deshong said, a slow smile tugging at his lips. He nodded toward one of his soldiers. "Help her down from her saddle."

"Sir, I am quite capable of mounting and dismounting my horse by myself, thank you," Hannah said, grabbing her reins from the man who held them. "And, sir, I didn't come to pay you a social call. I just need to know your plans for Strong Wolf. Have you, or have you not, sent a battalion of men to arrest him?"

"No, and I don't intend to," Colonel Deshong said, clasping his hands together behind him. "You see, ma'am, I would trust Strong Wolf's word before I would trust Tiny Sharp's."

Hannah sighed with relief. "Thank goodness," she said, her shoulders relaxing.

"Come on inside and have a cup of tea with me," Colonel Deshong encouraged. "I know your brother well. I admire the man. I would like to become more acquainted with his sister."

"Thank you for the invitation," Hannah said, her tone having softened since she saw Colonel Deshong as no threat to Strong Wolf. "But I'm sure I've distressed my brother terribly by having taken off so quickly on horseback to come and speak in behalf of

Strong Wolf. I must hurry back and apologize to him, and set his mind at ease that I am all right."

"I have to know, ma'am, how you know Strong Wolf?" Colonel Deshong asked, forking an eyebrow.

Again Hannah stiffened. She looked guardedly around her, feeling the men's eyes on her, awaiting her answer.

"I . . ." she began, but was reprieved for the moment when a commotion behind her drew all of the attention away from her.

She looked over her shoulder and paled when she discovered Chuck entering the courtyard. A cowhand was driving his horse and buggy too recklessly through the crowd of gawking soldiers.

"Chuck," she said in a loud gasp.

"Hannah, damn it, you've got to quit doing these reckless things," Chuck scolded as he squinted up at her through his thick eyeglasses. He waved his cane at her. "Get in here with me. You can take the reins. Adam will take the pinto home for you."

Colonel Deshong stepped down from the porch and went to Chuck. He placed a gentle hand on his arm. "And besides being angry at your sister, how are you doing, Chuck?" he asked, his voice filled with concern. "Your eyes. Have they worsened?"

"I wish I could say no to that question, but the truth is, Patrick, I can scarcely see one inch ahead of me," Chuck mumbled as Hannah climbed into the buggy beside him and took the reins.

"You've got quite a spirited sister there," Colonel Deshong said, chuckling. He smiled over at Hannah. "I don't believe I got your name, ma'am."

"Hannah," she said, returning the smile. "Please call me Hannah."

"It's nice to make your acquaintance, Hannah," Colonel Deshong said, reaching over to take Hannah's free hand. He squeezed it affectionately, then dropped his hand back to his side. "Chuck, you've got to tell your sister the dangers of riding alone. Not all Indians are as peace-loving as Strong Wolf and his people. And most certainly she can't trust all white men. It's dangerous as hell for her to be taking off on her own like she did today."

"Yes, I know," Chuck said. "What about Strong Wolf? Have you sent men to arrest him?"

"Do you think your sister would be sitting there all calm and collected if I had?" Colonel Deshong said, laughing softly.

"And so Strong Wolf isn't going to be arrested?" Chuck said.

"Naw," Colonel Deshong said, again clasping his hands behind him. "And let me tell you something about your foreman, Chuck. He came here with a pack of lies about the Potawatomis leader."

"Lies?" Chuck said, forking an eyebrow. "What lies?"

"He said something about Strong Wolf blowing up a dam, and about Strong Wolf having abducted your sister," Colonel Deshong said, his voice filled with sarcasm. "You'd best tell him to watch his mouth or it's going to get him in trouble."

"Patrick, I sent him here," Chuck said thickly. "I was scared to death that something had happened to Hannah, because she didn't arrive home when I expected her to. I ... I ... should have known better than to think that Strong Wolf would have anything to do with her disappearance."

"By God, Tiny wasn't lying after all?" Colonel Deshong said, eyes widening.

"Not this time, Patrick," Chuck said, nodding. "Nope. Not this time. And I feel lousy as hell for

having shown that I don't altogether trust Strong
Wolf."

"Chuck, I'm going to tell you what I told Tiny,"
Colonel Deshong uttered. "I told him that *if* you *did*
send him to me about your sister's possible abduction,
that you should not jump to conclusions so quickly. I
absolutely knew that Strong Wolf wouldn't abduct a
woman, especially not your sister. You and Strong
Wolf have a history of being friends. How could you
accuse him of such a thing?"

"Well, now, Patrick, that is a good question," Chuck
said, scratching his brow. "One I thought I had an
answer to."

"And that is?"

"Strong Wolf threatened me, that's what."

"He threatened you?"

"About the dam that was built across the stream
close to my ranch."

"Then, Tiny didn't lie about that, either?"

"No. Afraid not. You see, Strong Wolf *did* blow up
the dam, and with dynamite he stole from my very
own shed."

"But this dam—" Colonel Deshong crossed his
arms. "It's against what is set down in law, Chuck,
when treaties were signed with the Potawatomis. No
streams, creeks, or rivers can be dammed up. You
know that as well as I. I'm surprised that you author-
ized Tiny to do that."

"I didn't, Patrick," Chuck said, his shoulders suddenly slouching.

"Then, I'd say you'd better get you a new foreman,
or set the law down on the one that works for you,"
Colonel Deshong said, placing his fists on his hips.

"Yeah, I see that some changes must be made,"
Chuck said, nodding.

He reached over and patted Hannah on the knee. "Honey, take me home," he said, his voice weary.

Hannah lifted the reins. "Good day, sir," she said, smiling at the colonel as an ally, for it was obvious that he despised Tiny as much as she did.

Yet there seemed something else about the man that made her uneasy. It was the way he stared at her, as though he was trying to read her thoughts. And she had to believe that it was because of her obvious devotion to Strong Wolf. She knew to expect more questions from the colonel later.

"Come sometime when you can have that cup of tea with me, Hannah," Colonel Deshong said.

She nodded, then slowly turned the buggy around.

"And, Chuck, you come, too," Colonel Deshong said, giving them a half salute. "We've much to get caught up on."

"I don't get out much, anymore," Chuck shouted back at him as Hannah rode off toward the wide gate. "But I'll think about it. I'll come if Hannah will."

Adam followed on the pinto.

"I guess Tiny should be back home by now," Chuck said, sighing. "I wish I hadn't mistrusted Strong Wolf all that quickly. We've had such a special friendship."

"He probably won't even ever know about what you did," Hannah said, giving him a soft look. "And, Chuck, I'm so sorry that I gave you cause to worry. I know that I shouldn't have taken off like that. I'm here to make your life easier, not to make more of a hardship on you. Will you forgive me?"

"There's nothing to forgive you for," Chuck said somberly. "It's me. I've got to relax more. I've got to quit being suspicious of everything everyone does. But when you didn't come home when I expected you to and the dam had been blown to bits by Strong Wolf,

I couldn't help but think that just maybe he kidnapped
you to spite me for having not removed the dam."

Hannah swallowed hard and looked away from him.
She knew that he didn't see well enough to see her
face, to see that she was uneasy every time he mentioned Strong Wolf possibly having abducted her. He
had. But only she and Strong Wolf would ever know.
She wasn't about to tell anyone. Most certainly Strong
Wolf wouldn't.

He frowned over at her. "And, Hannah, I want you
to listen to me, and pay attention to what I say,"
Chuck said, his voice drawn and angry. "Patrick was
right in telling me to warn you about the dangers in
riding alone, especially for so long a time. You are
too foolhardy. Too daring. I forbid you to go horseback riding again. I'll send Adam with you. And don't
you argue, Hannah. After what happened today, my
mind's made up."

"Chuck, I can't do as you say," she blurted, aware
of him emitting a gasp of horror. "I just want you to
be patient with me, to try and understand that I need
to be alone. I need to go horseback riding. I need to
feel free."

Knowing that he had no choice but to sit back and
allow Hannah to do as she wished, he sighed, then
squinted over at Hannah. "All right, sis," he said somberly. "I do understand. If you will recall, I used to
feel the same as you."

Hannah wrenched her eyes from him. She was so
sad for him, yet her thoughts drifted now to Strong
Wolf.

She was so glad that Colonel Deshong had trusted
Strong Wolf. And because of his trust, Strong Wolf
was free.

Smiles, that with motion of their own,
Do spread and sink and rise,
Oh! Might I kiss the mountain rains
That sparkle on her cheek.
— WILLIAM WORDSWORTH

Strong Wolf rode beneath a shadow of trees toward his village, glad that he had chosen not to abduct Hannah, after all. Now they might have a future together ... *if* he would allow himself to love a woman.

Always when he thought that he might, his past came to him in flashes. The ugly secret that he carried around with him, to haunt his every waking hour, might still keep him from this woman whose very presence caused his senses to swim with passion.

"I must have her," he whispered, then drew a sudden tight rein when he spied something up ahead beside the road that sank dread into his very soul.

He was stunned at the sight for a moment longer, then sank his heels into the flanks of his horse and rode onward in a hard gallop.

When he drew tight rein again, he hurriedly slid from his saddle and knelt on one knee beside the silent, bloody form of a Potawatomis brave from his village.

"Bird in Ground," Strong Wolf whispered, lifting

the brave's face from the ground. He leaned low over
his brave, and placed his cheek against his mouth, glad
to feel the hot breath of Bird in Ground on his flesh.

"He is alive, but ah, just look at him!" he cried
aloud, causing birds to stir in the trees overhead and
fly away.

"Bird in Ground," he said, trying to arouse him.
"You must awaken and tell me who did this to you."

Bird in Ground did not stir.

Strong Wolf looked around for the brave's horse.
He saw no steed, but caught the shine from the barrel
of the brave's rifle as it lay just partially exposed from
a thick bed of grass about a foot away.

Then his eyes jerked around when he heard many
horses approaching in the distance. Through the dust
he saw soldiers on horseback riding his way. Were
they headed for his village to arrest him for having
stolen the dynamite and for having destroyed the
dam?

Wanting to protect his brave from any more harm,
and wanting to get to his village quickly, Strong Wolf
lifted Bird in Ground into his arms and carried him
to his horse.

After getting the brave positioned in his saddle,
Strong Wolf mounted the horse behind him and held
Bird in Ground in place as he twined a muscled arm
around the injured brave's waist. He started to ride
away but stopped when the soldiers made a sudden
turn in a different direction away from his village.

Strong Wolf breathed more easily when he realized
that they were not after him, after all.

Wanting to get Bird in Ground to the village for
medical treatment, Strong Wolf did not take the time
to search for his horse. He rode away, with Bird in
Ground still unconscious in his arms, wondering who
did this.

And when he found the guilty party, he vowed to make him pay in blood. When he got through with him, he would leave him way more bloodied than Bird in Ground!

Strong Wolf spied the log cabins of his village a short distance away, among the birches. He nudged his horse's sides with his knees and rode onward.

There was much wailing and crying when Strong Wolf entered his village with Bird in Ground. Strong Wolf drew tight rein before Bird in Ground's lodge, where his wife and children waited for him, desperation and fear etched on their faces.

"Who did this?" Proud Heart said as he ran up to Strong Wolf to help him take Bird in Ground from the saddle.

"He cannot speak now," Strong Wolf grumbled as he gently handed Bird in Ground to Proud Heart.

Strong Wolf then dismounted and went with Proud Heart and Bird in Ground's family into the lodge. "But when we find the one who is responsible for this fiendish act against one of our own, pity him!"

"My husband," Sweet Wind cried as she knelt beside Bird in Ground.

Strong Wolf took a basin of water and a cloth to Sweet Wind. He knelt down on the other side of the bed as she began washing the blood from his body. Proud Heart comforted the children beside the lodge fire.

"Awaken, my brother," Strong Wolf said. "You must tell me who did this to you. A search party will be formed. We will find the one responsible. He will pay for the crime!"

Bird in Ground's eyes slowly opened, his lashes stuck together with dried blood. He gazed up at Strong Wolf, then looked slowly over at his wife.

"My husband, you are home, safe with your wife

and children," Sweet Wind murmured, gently stroking a cloth across his bloody and battered chest. "I am so sorry for you. Who could do this to you?"

"I ... made ... good hunt today," Bird in Ground said, reaching a trembling hand to his wife's cheek. "Plenty meat. Plenty hides."

He looked at Strong Wolf again. "Did ... you ... find my horse and travois?" he stammered out, each word paining him.

"No, they are gone, but we will send braves to search for you," Strong Wolf said. He took one of Bird in Ground's hands. He gently clutched it. "My brother, tell us who did this. Time is wasting. We must go and find the guilty party before he gets too far."

Bird in Ground closed his eyes. He recalled the threat about his family, that if he told who did this, they would die!

"I know ... not ... of their names," he said, hating the lie as much as he hated the men he lied for!

"There was more than one?" Strong Wolf said, his eyebrows raising.

"Yes, that I can tell you," Bird in Ground said, moaning when pains shot through his abdomen.

"Describe them," Strong Wolf said.

Bird in Ground turned his eyes away and said no more.

Disappointment grabbed at Strong Wolf's heart, for he knew that this brave knew at least how to describe his assailants, but had been warned into silence.

"Bird in Ground, I will say no more now, but when you are well again and can see the logic of pointing out who did this to you, I will question you again," Strong Wolf said, rising to his feet.

Bird in Ground looked in panic up at Strong Wolf. "Do not ask, for I will not tell," he said, then again looked away in shame.

Strong Wolf stiffened. He looked over at Proud Heart, whose own jaw was tight with disappointment. Then he left the lodge. He was almost certain who was responsible. But he couldn't take action without having absolute proof!

Streaked with purple, opaque shadows, the world was red in late sunlight as Strong Wolf entered his lodge. He sat down before his fire thinking about the bitter disappointments he had been forced to face in his lifetime.

But most of all, he feared loving the white woman, for if she turned her back on him once she knew the secret of his past, he was not sure if he could endure the disappointment.

"Should I even chance it?" he whispered.

12

And soon her swimming eyes confessed
The wishes of her soul.
                    —ROBERT DODSLEY

The sun was low in the sky, rising slowly, splashing
the heavens with a beautiful pinkish tint as Hannah
rode the pinto beneath a heavy umbrella of trees. She
had scarcely slept all night. As soon as daybreak broke
along the horizon, she had quickly dressed in a riding
skirt and blouse and had left the house while her
brother was still asleep.

She was filled with many tumultuous feelings, most
of which now centered on Strong Wolf. His kiss had
sparked something within her that she could not shake.
Every time she thought about being in his arms, she
felt warmly weak inside. Her heart would thud suddenly at the mere thought of his name.

Even now, her breath quickened when she realized
where her morning travels had taken her. She was
being drawn to the mystery cave; to the misty, smoky
haze. Had she been drawn there for a purpose? she
wondered to herself. If so, what? Why?

With a wildly beating heart, Hannah dismounted
and tethered her horse's reins to a low limb of a tree.
Breathless, she moved down the footpath.

Anxiously she recalled the other time that she had

been here with Strong Wolf. It had been easy to drift into his arms, to allow the kiss.

Yet she was not sure of Strong Wolf's intentions toward her. Although he had denied it, what if he *did* only want to use her, in order to have a closer alliance with her brother? Their lands connected. Could Strong Wolf want more than just the land that he had been given by treaty?

And *she* had to be careful of this wild freedom she had found in the Kansas Territory. She shouldn't allow herself to go too far with her feelings toward a man she scarcely knew; with a man she perhaps couldn't even trust!

Her heart fluttering the closer she walked into the thick, misty smoke, she became alert to every sound, of the warm summer morning. The air was of a crisp freshness and a sweet breeze swept down over the pine-covered hills.

She came through a thick clump of young trees and thought she heard a noise. She held her breath to listen, her right hand resting on a long knife sheathed in her belt.

She listened to the call of birds in the distance and the hum of bees, but heard nothing more, only those sounds made by Mother Nature.

Hannah's footsteps faltered again when she heard a noise that sounded like padded footsteps. She sucked in a wild breath of fear when a twig snapped behind her.

She turned with a start and gasped in surprise when she found Strong Wolf there, gazing intensely at her through the smoky haze.

Hannah returned his gaze openly, fearlessly, lovingly, her heart melting into his as he moved toward her.

She quickly noticed that today he wore his usual

beaded moccasins, but instead of a breechclout, his attire was brown deerskin leggings with long, soft fringes on either side, and a deerskin shirt with bright-colored beads sewn tightly on it. His hair was long and loose, held in place by a red bandanna tied about his brow.

"You have come to see the smoking of unknown fires, or was your purpose to come here today, to see if I would answer the silent beckoning of your heart and come here also?" Strong Wolf suddenly said.

He reached a hand out and brushed some tendrils of Hannah's hair back from her face.

"I'm not certain why I am here," she murmured, an unleashed passion for him consuming her through and through.

"It was the same restlessness, the same pull, that has drawn us both here, to unlock the secrets of our hearts," Strong Wolf said. His fingers gently slid down the contours of her face, stopping to cup her chin within the palm of his hand.

Slowly he urged her lips toward his. "In my restless dreams I saw us here, together," he said huskily. "Was it a dream that also beckoned you?"

"No, I didn't even sleep well enough last night *to* dream," she said in a whisper. Her heart beat so hard from his lips being so close, she felt light-headed.

"And what did you think about when you were awake?" he said, his lips brushing against hers as he whispered. "Did you think about Strong Wolf? Did you think about this?"

He swept his arms around her and crushed his lips to hers, his hard, strong arms pressing her against him so that their bodies strained together hungrily. The heat of his passion was pulsing and pressed tightly inside his breeches, paining and dizzying him.

Afraid of the passion that was so overwhelming her,

afraid to move this quickly into something that she might regret later, Hannah shoved against Strong Wolf's chest until she managed to get free.

Her chest heaving, she turned her back to him. "We mustn't," she murmured. She placed her trembling hands to her cheeks and felt their heat against her palms.

Understanding a woman who might be reckless in some ways, more careful in others, Strong Wolf did not press the issue. He sucked in a breath and waited for his heartbeat to slow down, then reached a gentle hand to Hannah's wrist and turned her to face him.

"I feel much for you," he said thickly. His gaze took in her flawless features, the soft glimmer of her hair. The whites of her eyes were almost luminously clear. "You feel much for me. And one day soon we *will* go farther than kissing. But not today. I see that you are not ready."

Hannah's eyes blinked nervously as she gazed up at him. She was stunned by this man's understanding; of his patience.

She felt guilty now for having suspected him of wanting her for more than the sake of wanting. He had sincere feelings for her that matched those she felt for him.

"Thank you," she murmured, shyly lowering her eyes. "Any other man would . . ."

"I am not just any other man," Strong Wolf said thickly.

"Yes, I know," Hannah said, lifting her eyes to his.

She trembled inwardly when she saw how his eyes were glazed and drugged with desire. She was keenly aware of the slope of his hard jaw and his finely chiseled face; that his lips still were only a feather's touch from hers.

Suddenly she flung herself into his arms. "Hold

me," she murmured. "Just please hold me. I love how it feels to be held by you."

"Tell me how it feels," Strong Wolf said, burying his nose in the depths of her fragranced hair.

"I ... feel ... needed," Hannah said, closing her eyes to the ecstasy as his lips brushed against her ear, his breath hot against it.

"I do need you," Strong Wolf said, his thumb lightly caressing her flushed cheek. "As you also need me."

"Yes, yes," she whispered, not fighting it when he placed a finger beneath her chin, his mouth seizing hers again in a fiery kiss.

She twined her arms around his neck and returned the kiss as his hands were now on her throat, framing her face.

Never had she imagined that a man's kiss could be tender and overwhelming at the same time. Never had she imagined that being with a man could be so bliss-fully sweet. Her want for him was erasing all doubts, all caution. If he touched her where she painfully ached, she would now allow him to do with her what-ever he wished.

The secret place between her thighs was throbbing and burning with sensations that were new to her. She had scarcely ever been aware of that part of her anat-omy until now.

She felt an urgency; a fire that had become ignited. She felt consumed by the heat of desire!

Strong Wolf could feel her responding much too eagerly to him, and knew that she still was not ready. Although every nerve ending in his body cried out to take her on that road of paradise with him now, he knew to wait until later, when he *knew* that afterward she would not regret having allowed it.

He wanted her to be ready, to participate with him with an open heart. Regrets could kill passion before it even began. He wanted no regrets from this woman. Only a total commitment!

His pulse racing, the heat in his loins almost unbearable, Strong Wolf crept from Hannah's arms. He placed a gentle hand to her cheek as she gazed up at him questionably.

"Later, my woman," he said huskily. "When it is right for us to come together in the way we both hunger for, only then shall we fully explore our feelings for one another."

"Yes, later," Hannah murmured, stunned again that he had not taken advantage of the moment. She knew now that it was right for her to love this man.

She took Strong Wolf's hand as he reached it out for her.

"I will take you home," he said, his eyes smiling into hers.

"I don't need an escort," she said, that independent side of her surfacing again.

"I shall, anyhow," he said. He could not allow a woman to set down all of the rules.

"Yes, please do," Hannah said, suddenly realizing that when he wished to be dominant, he would be. And something inside her wanted to allow it.

"It is best to be more careful on your outings," Strong Wolf said as they walked back up the path. "One of my braves was beaten unmercifully by an unknown assailant yesterday. Who is to say the same men would not stop at doing the same to a woman?"

He paused. "Or worse," he added, his voice drawn. "Being forced sexually is worse than being physically beaten by guns, fists, and kicked by feet."

Going cold inside at the thought of being taken by force by a stranger, Hannah looked quickly up at Strong Wolf.

"Your brave, did . . . he . . . die?"

"No, but he will not hunt for his family for many sunrises," he said solemnly. "He would not be able to ride or shoot."

"How horrible," Hannah gasped. "Did he tell you who did it?"

"He had been threatened into silence," Strong Wolf said flatly.

"I wonder if . . ."

"Yes," he said, interrupting her. "If you are thinking that Tiny Sharp might be responsible, yes, I suspect he might be. But there is no proof. Without proof, my hands are tied. I do not wish to stir up trouble between my people and the pony soldiers by acting only on suspicions."

"But if Tiny . . ."

He interrupted her again. "He will pay for his sins, one way or the other," he said, his voice thick with venom.

They grew quiet when they reached the tethered horses, surprising Hannah that Strong Wolf's was grazing contentedly beside hers. She gave Strong Wolf a questioning stare.

"Yes, I arrived after you," he said, smiling amusedly. "I was drawn *to* you, and to the smoking of unknown fires."

He helped her on her horse, then mounted his own. They rode off, side by side, in a slow lope.

"You have referred to the smoky haze back at the small pond as the smoking of unknown fires," she said, glancing over at him. "What causes the smoke? Who sealed up the cave?"

"No one knows where the smoke comes from or how or why the cave was sealed up with boulders," Strong Wolf said, resting a hand on the butt end of the rifle sheathed at the right side of his horse. "It is a place of mystery. Perhaps in time, the mystery will be unfolded to us."

They rode onward, talking and becoming more acquainted.

Then, to Hannah's surprise, she was riding past Strong Wolf's village. Although most lodges were log cabins, there was also a scattering of bark-covered wigwams, surely housing those who would not let go of their past so easily.

The log cabins were single-family dwellings, constructed of vertical poles plastered over with mud, and covered by roofs of bark and thatch. Hobs were left in the gables of the houses to provide an escape for smoke.

"The one side door on our lodges opens to a room with an earthen floor," Strong Wolf said, when he noticed Hannah studying them. "There is a fireplace, and comfortable furnishings. Clustered together, we have fifty permanent lodges."

"It is quite impressive," Hannah said softly. "But I am surprised to be here. I was so involved in talking with you I had not noticed that we had strayed this far from the road." She paused and gazed questionably at Strong Wolf. "Did you lead me here purposely?"

"Yes, I wished for you to see how peaceful it is at my village as my people move around doing their usual chores," he said. "I wish for you to become more and more acquainted with my way of life, for one day I hope that it will also be yours."

Hannah's lips parted in a low gasp, and her cheeks flamed with color.

He planned for her to marry him.

And why should she be so shocked? she wondered to herself. Everything he had done while with her had pointed to the fact that he cared for her this much.

And she cared deeply for him.

But marriage? Could she truly leave her way of life
and marry an Indian? Did she care this much for him,
that she could enter another world so different from
her own?

And then again there was her brother. Chuck de-
pended on her. How could she let him down by leaving him? It was apparent that he was no longer able
to function alone.

"You have grown quiet," Strong Wolf said, his eyes
wavering into hers. "Does the thought of marriage to
a Potawatomis warrior who will one day be chief leave
a bitter taste in your mouth?"

Alarmed by how he had taken her silence, Hannah
sucked in a wild breath. "No," she quickly said. "How
could you even think that?"

"A woman's silence can sometimes speak more than
a woman's words," Strong Wolf said.

"Please only pay attention to my words," Hannah
said, reaching over to touch his arm. "Sweet man, you
know how I feel about you. But as I said before, I
need time. There is so much in my life right now that
troubles me. My brother. I so fear for my brother."

"If he would send his foreman away, much in his
world would be better," Strong Wolf said, covering
her hand with his. He lifted her hand to his lips and
kissed it, then released it so that she could grip her
reins more securely again.

"I know," Hannah said softly. "But sometimes he
is even more stubborn than his sister."

"You are stubborn?" Strong Wolf said, his eyes
dancing into hers. "I will enjoy learning all of your
traits."

He then looked away from her and gestured toward
his village with a wide sweep of his hand. "Can you
see, my woman, the village I am so proud of having
established?"

"Yes, and I see it as quite industrious," she said as she watched women at work in large fields of corn.

His eyes followed hers. "You see the women?" he said. "They are magical in their growing of corn. There is always much corn bread, corn stew, and corn-meal. The women are sowing beans and squash today around the hills where the corn is already growing."

"I never realized the garden area was so large," Hannah said, turning to look at Strong Wolf. "Yet I see small gardens next to each home. What is planted there?"

"With plows and hoes furnished by your government, my people grow not only corn, beans, and squash in the fields, but also peas, potatoes, pumpkins, and melons in the smaller gardens next to their homes," he said. "But corn is our principal field crop."

"And who cares for your personal garden?" Hannah asked, her eyes wide.

"Since I have no wife, nor a sister, my people loan me women to care for my crops," Strong Wolf said, smiling when he could almost read her mind, thinking that should she marry him, she would have to labor hard from day to night.

"Do you mean to say that the men never help in the gardens?" Hannah dared to ask.

"Men hunt, women grow," Strong Wolf said matter-of-factly, now knowing for sure that she asked the question because she was thinking of her future with him. "You see, my woman, the hunt is a labor meant only for men. A man knows where to hunt, when, and what. But that does not always mean that they will find meat on the day they choose to hunt. A woman always knows that her chore will not walk away and hide from her, as animals are wont to do."

Hannah laughed softly. "I see," she murmured.

"Yes, when they are available for the hunter, away

from their hiding haunts, the Potawatomis sees the
deer, buffalo, and bear as especially prized. But also
he hunts for turkey, pigeons, squirrels, rabbits, and ah,
so much more that the forest houses."

He paused as he looked through the cover of the
trees, toward the stream that snaked across the land
close to his village. "And the stream is bountiful with
fish," he said. "Sturgeon is our major fish catch."

"And then you have a variety of nuts, berries, and
herbs in the forest," Hannah interjected. "Also plums,
persimmons, grapes, mulberries."

"You see how easy it is to learn ways of the Potawatomis?" Strong Wolf said, laughing softly at how she
had joined in the conversation about food and game.
"We Potawatomis, when nature is good to us, have
enough from the forest in ways of berries and nuts,
to feed our family from June to August."

Hannah watched young braves standing near the
fields. "What are the boys there for?" she said, pointing to them.

"They are there to drive away birds and animals
while the women do their planting," Strong Wolf
explained.

Several acres of uncultivated land that stretched
away from the village at the right side was covered
with blue grass, which made excellent pasture for
horses. As they left the village behind and rode past
the grazing horses, Hannah admired them.

"I have always wanted to own many horses," she
blurted out. "It was my dream as a child to train
horses." She looked over at Strong Wolf, her eyes
wavering. "My father never understood. He wouldn't
allow me to have my dream."

"You come to my village any time and choose your
favorite horse, and it is yours," Strong Wolf said.
"You can now, if you wish."

"Truly?" she said, her eyes widening. Then she sighed. "Thank you for offering, Strong Wolf. But it's best that I don't. I truly must hurry home. I must see about my brother. He's surely been up from bed for hours and is worrying his head off about where I am. We mustn't give him cause again to think that I was taken hostage."

"Again?" Strong Wolf said, forking an eyebrow.

She told him about what had happened yesterday.

She could tell that he hadn't taken to the story too well, especially the part where her brother had actually gone as far as having sent Tiny and his men to the fort to report that she was missing, with suspicions that Strong Wolf was responsible.

"But, Strong Wolf, how can you be angry at my brother for thinking you abducted me," Hannah murmured. "You *did,* if only for a short while."

They exchanged smiles, then rode onward until they reached the outskirts of her brother's ranch.

"I will now leave you, but not because I wish to," Strong Wolf said, reaching over to place a hand behind her neck. He drew her lips to his and gave her a lingering kiss, then grabbed his reins and wheeled his horse around.

He gazed at her for a moment longer, then rode away.

He was filled with wonder about this woman. Surely she was his destiny. He had to find a way to conquer the ghosts of his past. That was the only way he could ever feel free to love her.

And he must have her.

His life now would be incomplete without her!

Hannah watched him ride away, filled with sweet memories of today that would linger within her heart forever.

She loved him.

Her heart skipped a beat when she saw her brother on the porch of the ranch house, slowly pacing back and forth.

Again she had let him down by worrying him.

But this was a small sort of letdown compared to what it would be if she chose to leave him, to marry Strong Wolf!

"Chuck!" she shouted. "I'm home! I'm home!"

When he turned toward her voice, stumbled, and almost fell from the porch, a part of her died inside.

How could she ever turn her back on his need?

How?

13

You kissed me! My soul in a bliss so divine
Reeled and swooned like a drunkard,
When foolish with wine.
                    —JOSEPHINE SLOCUM HUNT

Hannah stood beside the organ as Chuck played another song. He knew the keyboard well, and he had
memorized the songs.

"It's so beautiful, Chuck," Hannah said, leaning
over to give him a kiss on his cheek.

"My music, my ability to play the organ, is something that can never be taken from me because of my
damned eyesight," Chuck said, his fingers moving up
and down the keyboard as he played a waltz.

He then rested his hands on his lap as he turned to
Hannah. "I know that you're anxious to take your
morning ride," he said, squinting through his thick-
lensed glasses. "Go on, Hannah. But promise me that
you won't go far."

She knelt down beside the bench and peered up at
him. "Chuck, do you remember me telling you about
the horses that I saw at Strong Wolf's village?" she
said, taking his hands, squeezing them affectionately.

"Yes, you saw them while on your outing yesterday," he said, nodding.

"Chuck, I'd love to go and see them again today,"

she said, searching his face. When she saw his jaw tighten, she knew what to expect next.

"I don't want you going that far, sis," he said solemnly. "You were gone too long yesterday."

"I was gone that long yesterday because I went somewhere else besides Strong Wolf's village," she said. "I'm intrigued by the mystery cave and the place of smoking waters. I went there first, then went to Strong Wolf's village."

Chuck paled. He eased his hands from Hannah's. "How did you know about the cave? About the smoking waters?" he said thickly. "That's not something you would just happen upon."

Feeling trapped, Hannah went silent. She hadn't told Chuck about her abduction, which was how she had discovered the cave and smoking waters. So how could she explain?

"Chuck, I'm in love," she blurted out, seeing the shock register on his face as he jerked his head back as though having been slapped.

"You . . . are . . . what?" he gasped disbelievingly.

"I'm in love," she repeated. "With Strong Wolf. He took me to the mystery cave and the smoking waters. He showed them to me."

She was not about to tell her brother that she had received her first kiss from Strong Wolf while there. That sort of secret must stay between only herself and Strong Wolf.

"He . . . took . . . you there?" Chuck said. He paused, then reached a hand to Hannah's face and ran his fingers slowly over her features. "Sis, I wish you would stay home today. Don't go to the Potawatomis village. Don't see Strong Wolf anymore. Haven't I got enough complications in my life? Must I have to worry about this?"

"There's nothing to worry about," Hannah said,

taking his hand. "Chuck, I'm a big girl now. I can take care of myself." She paused, then went on. "And I have never felt anything for a man until now."

"Hannah, surely it's only an infatuation," Chuck said, easing his hand away. "He's an Indian. He's going to be a powerful chief. Surely that is what attracts you to him."

"There is much more about him than him just being an Indian that makes me feel good inside," Hannah said, sighing. "And, Chuck, he *loves* me. Truly loves me. Please be happy for me. For *us*."

"How can I be happy?" Chuck complained. "Hannah, you are so inexperienced in these things. You even shied away from too many social functions in Saint Louis. Most girls, when they enter that age of discovering boys, did everything they could to attract one for herself."

"I was never truly shy, Chuck," Hannah defended. "I . . . I . . . just wasn't interested. That's all."

"That strengthens what I said a few moments ago," Chuck said, his voice shallow. "You are . . . inexperienced, Hannah."

"I'm going to marry Strong Wolf," Hannah blurted out before she even had the time to think. Her face heated up with a blush as she watched her brother's reaction.

When he only stared at her and said nothing, she was relieved, but worried about her brother's feelings. If she married Strong Wolf, that meant she would leave Chuck to fend for himself!

Chuck said nothing else about it. He knew not to. He knew that once his sister had made her mind up about something, no one could change it. He saw now why his father had placed her in the convent. He had hoped to tame her wild heart.

"Maybe that's what you need," he suddenly blurted.

"What?" Hannah said, forking an eyebrow.

"A husband," Chuck growled out. "Maybe a husband could handle you better than father, or I *ever* could."

"Chuck, I thought you, of all people, understood me. How could you even want me to be as you call it—handled?"

"I'm sorry, sis," Chuck said, heaving a sigh. "I used the wrong word." He gestured toward the door with a flick of a hand. "Go on, now. But be careful."

"I will have the rifle with me at all times," Hannah said. She went to Chuck and kissed him. "And you know how skilled I am with firearms. Father taught me well enough."

"Yes, and he has regretted ever since that he turned you into a tomboy," Chuck said, turning to place his fingers on the organ keyboard again.

"I'm not a tomboy, Chuck," Hannah said. "I'm a woman!"

But she knew that he didn't hear her. He was playing the organ, the music purposely much louder.

Hannah watched her brother playing the organ for a moment longer, then turned around and stamped from the house.

She was glad to be out on the open range. She couldn't forget her brother's expression when she had told him that she was in love with Strong Wolf, and that she might even marry him. His look reminded her of all of the white people who looked to Indians as untamed savages, and that in the white world, it was forbidden for a white woman to marry a redskin!

"Well, I will show them all," she whispered to herself. "There is no law on this earth that will keep me from loving Strong Wolf!"

She flicked her reins and sent her horse into a hard gallop in the direction of Strong Wolf's village. But she kept an occasional look over her shoulder for the likes of Tiny Sharp. Her brother still had not fired him.

And as long as he was in the area, she couldn't let her guard down. She trusted him no more than she trusted a snake!

14

Would you but come,
While lies were yet moist with your breath;
While your arms clasped me round,
In that blissful embrace,
While your eyes melt in mine,
Could e'en death e'er efface.
                    —JOSEPHINE SLOCUM HUNT

Strong Wolf sat as motionless as a ghost beside his fireplace. The bowl of his pipe rested on a knee as he thought over a request that had just been made of him.

First he looked at Colonel Patrick Deshong, and then Claude Odum, the Indian agent for the area. They were there to have council with Strong Wolf.

Colonel Deshong had voiced first their reason for being there.

Claude Odum, a close friend and ally with Strong Wolf, had voiced his opinion on the matter.

Both men saw the importance of a road being built on land that lay just adjacent to Strong Wolf's, on the far side away from where his land hugged up against Chuck's.

Still thinking, Strong Wolf coiled the fingers of his right hand around the long, tender stem of the pipe and placed the tip to his mouth. The glow of the fire crept through the pipe's smoke, making the room take on an eeriness, the silence a strained one as Claude and Patrick breathed shallowly in their anxious waiting.

Strong Wolf's thoughts went to Bird in Ground and

how he had been unmercifully attacked and beaten by interlopers on Potawatomis land. Bird in Ground still refused to point an accusing finger at whoever was responsible.

This made Strong Wolf think that just perhaps it *might* benefit him and his people to have a road on Potawatomis land, on which white men would travel. Too often the white people used his land, anyhow, to get to the river. This often brought them too close to the village. His people needed their privacy.

"If I agree to a road, can I say where it will be built?" Strong Wolf suddenly said as he again rested the bowl of his pipe on his right knee.

"Most assuredly," Patrick said, his eyes lighting up to know that Strong Wolf was seriously considering giving them permission.

"Then I will say now that it will be placed far enough from my village to ensure not only my people's privacy, but also their safety from whites," Strong Wolf said, laying his pipe aside. It had already been passed to Patrick and Claude, strengthening their bond of friendship with Strong Wolf and his Potawatomis people.

"Yes, I assure you that it will not interfere at all in your hunt, or your daily lives," Patrick said, nodding.

"Then, it is agreed upon," Claude said. "The council was good today, Strong Wolf."

"It has been too long since you came and shared more than council with me and my people," Strong Wolf said, smiling over at Claude. "You have not shared a meal with the Potawatomis for many sunrises now."

He looked over at Patrick, then shifted his gaze back to Claude. "Will you both share food with me today?" he asked.

He nodded toward the fireplace, over which hung a

piece of savory meat roasting on a spit. Coffee was
simmering in a pot in the coals at the edge of the fire.
"Does it not tempt you?"

"Yes, quite," Patrick said, chuckling.

"*I* have the time," Claude said. "How about you,
Patrick?"

"My duties await me," Patrick said, then laughed
softly. "But don't they always?" He nodded. "Yes. I
could stand a bit of food before I return to the fort.
Thanks for offering, Strong Wolf."

They laughed and joked, enjoying one another's
company as they ate the roasted venison and unleav-
ened bread, and drank the Potawatomis's brand of
dark, strong coffee.

"It has been refreshing being here today, away from
the troubles that always await me at the fort," Patrick
said, setting his empty wooden platter aside. He
chuckled low. "There is always something to add another gray hair to my head."

"Should I be as lucky as you to have such a head
of hair, I'd welcome a gray one or two every day,"
Claude said, chuckling as he ran his hand across his
bald head. "Damn it, I'm only thirty, and I've already
lost my hair."

The sound of a horse arriving just outside Strong
Wolf's cabin drew their conversation to a close. Strong
Wolf went to the door and opened it. His eyes widened and his heart did a strange sort of somersault
when he saw Hannah dismounting her pinto. He
smiled a silent welcome to her.

She returned the smile.

"Good morning," she said, her insides swimming
with rapture when he reached out and grabbed one
of her hands.

"You have come to my lodge," Strong Wolf said
thickly. "That is good." He held her hand for a mo-

ment longer, relishing the feel of her flesh against his, then released it.

"Is this a bad time?" Hannah asked, looking over her shoulder at the two young braves holding the reins of two horses that stood as though waiting for someone just outside Strong Wolf's lodge. She looked into his eyes again. "Do you have company?"

"Company?" Strong Wolf said, arching an eyebrow, unfamiliar with that word being used in such a way.

Understanding his confusion, Hannah worded her question differently. "Is someone here already?" she murmured. "If so, I can come back later."

"Yes, there are people here," he said, glancing over his shoulder at Claude and Patrick, whose eyes were intensely watching what was transpiring at the door. He stepped aside and smiled at Hannah. "Come inside. You can join our council."

Hannah paled. "You are having council?" she asked, her voice guarded. "I'm sorry. I have chosen a wrong time to come and ask to see your horses. I can come later."

"Horses?" Strong Wolf said. "Ah, yes. I offered to show them to you. You are to choose the one you wish to have as your own."

"I haven't come to take a horse," Hannah quickly corrected, wincing when she saw an instant hurt in his eyes.

"Perhaps later, but not today," she quickly interjected.

"Please do come inside," Strong Wolf urged. "I do not believe that Colonel Deshong and Claude Odum will mind if you join our council."

Hannah tensed with the mention of Colonel Deshong. When she had gone to the fort to defend Strong Wolf, this man had been too inquisitive about her relationship with Strong Wolf.

Now he would be even more curious.

Yet she had no choice now but to step inside and face the man again. She knew that when Strong Wolf stepped aside, the men inside the lodge had been given full view of her. They had also heard him invite her in to join their council.

She had to wonder what sort of council; what had drawn Colonel Deshong here? Had he changed his mind? Was he going to arrest Strong Wolf after all?

Strong Wolf placed a gentle arm around her waist as he led her into the lodge. She smiled wanly at the colonel, then looked over at the other man. Dressed in buckskin, he was tall, extremely thin, and bald. His dark eyes were friendly as he held out a hand of friendship for Hannah.

"I'm Claude Odum," Claude said, offering his name before Strong Wolf got around to making introductions. "I'm the Indian agent for this area. And you are?"

"Hannah," Hannah murmured, taking his hand, gently shaking it. "Hannah Kody. My brother Chuck owns a ranch not far from here."

"Why, yes, I know Chuck," Claude said, his smile fading. "I've recently heard about his eyesight failing him. I'm sorry."

"Yes, it's quite hard on my brother," Hannah said, swallowing hard.

"And what brings you here today, Hannah?" Claude asked, dropping his hand to his side.

"Horses," Hannah said, feeling awkward as she turned slow eyes to the colonel, knowing that he was watching her, curious.

"Horses?" Claude said, forking an eyebrow.

She looked quickly back at him, glad not to face the colonel's questions yet. "Yes, Strong Wolf offered to show them to me. You see, as a child it was my ambition to train show horses. I ... somehow ... got sidetracked."

"And how did that happen?"

"My father. He had different plans for me."

"Those were?"

"He is a physician. He wanted me to follow in his footsteps and work in the same field as he."

"A woman physician?" Colonel Deshong suddenly said, sending Hannah's gaze his way. "Now, that might prove interesting."

Hannah's spine stiffened. "Had I aspired myself to be a physician, I would have been as good as any man in that field," she quickly defended.

"Out here, so far from civilization, a woman doesn't need to aspire to anything, does she?" Colonel Deshong said, giving Hannah a slow smile.

Hannah felt trapped. She gave Strong Wolf a harried, pleading look.

He responded quickly, having noticed her uneasiness.

"Hannah is a woman of good heart," Strong Wolf said thickly. "She is caring for her brother in his time of need."

"I see," Patrick said.

"I truly must be on my way," Claude said, reaching down on the floor for his coonskin hat. He plopped it on his head, then reached out and again took Hannah's hand. "Hannah, it has been delightful. I hope I will have the pleasure of seeing you again."

"Thank you, sir," Hannah said, smiling up at him, his height surely at least six foot five inches. "It has also been my pleasure. I look forward to seeing you again."

She placed her hands behind her back and clasped them together so that she would not have to offer a handshake to the colonel as he also got up to leave.

It was obvious that he had purposely unnerved her. She had to wonder why. While at the fort, she had found some qualities about him that she had admired.

But today? She saw too much in him that she didn't trust, or like.

"Hannah, you take care of yourself while riding alone," Colonel Deshong said, his eyes momentarily locking with hers. Then he placed a hand on Strong Wolf's shoulder. "It's been good to talk and dine with you, Strong Wolf. And thank you for your permission to build the road. I'm now in your debt, you know."

Strong Wolf nodded, then walked Patrick and Claude to the door. "Come and have council anytime," he said, watching them mount their horses.

After they were gone, he turned and gazed at Hannah. "You have come to see horses," he said thickly. "Do you wish to see them now? Or later?"

So suddenly alone with Strong Wolf, his black eyes stirring her insides so pleasurably, Hannah went to him and framed his face between her trembling hands.

Hardly able to believe that she could be as bold, as reckless, she guided his lips to hers.

When his arms swept around her waist and yanked her against his lean, hard body, Hannah's head swam with the ecstasy of the moment.

Strong Wolf whispered against her lips. "You want to see the horses now?" he whispered, his hands stroking her back, the heat of his hands reaching through the thin fabric of her cotton blouse. "Or later?"

"Later," Hannah whispered back, her voice unfamiliar to her in its huskiness.

Strong Wolf whisked her fully up into his arms and held her close as their eyes met in an unspoken passion. He kicked the door shut, then kissed her feverishly as he carried her toward his bed.

Hannah twined her arms around his neck, fearful,

yet anxious, for what would soon transpire between them. She could not, she *would* not, fight the want, the need, any longer.

She now realized that she had not come today to see Strong Wolf's horses.

She had come to share much, much more than that with him; her very soul!

15

The love that is purest and sweetest
Has a kiss of desire on the lips.
—JOHN O'REILLY

Undressed and already in bed, Hannah lay nestled beneath a luxurious rabbit fur blanket that had been woven from long strips of cottontail pelts. As she watched Strong Wolf undress, she became breathless remembering a moment ago how his fingers had so gently disrobed her. She had felt awkward when he had gazed at her body as he had tossed each garment aside. She had always thought that she was too thin and gangly ever to please a man.

But after she was fully undressed today, and Strong Wolf moved his fingers over her flesh for the first time, she had felt as though she were floating; the experience was so pleasant.

She had learned quickly how wonderful it was to share such moments with the man she loved. She had gradually relaxed and had allowed herself to enjoy how it felt to be touched and caressed.

Now she was waiting to be able to touch and caress Strong Wolf's body. Although not practiced at such things, she knew her love for him as well as her instincts would guide her.

When his manhood sprang into view as he slipped

his buckskin breeches down his muscled legs, Hannah sucked in a wild breath of wonder.

He was so huge there.

So long.

So *thick*.

So well proportioned!

Surely he knew well the art of pleasuring.

But she feared the pain that might come with being with him sexually for the first time, especially now that she saw how he would so magnificently fill her.

Shame came to her in splashes, to realize where her mind had taken her. It was hard to believe that she had even initiated what was transpiring. She was aching beneath the soft tendrils of down at the juncture of her thighs. When Strong Wolf had only briefly caressed her there, she had felt as though she might explode with feelings!

Her heart pounded as Strong Wolf stood so beautifully nude before her, his one hand gently moving on his manhood as he came and knelt over her on the bed.

With his free hand he unfolded the rabbit blanket from around her, revealing her full, silken nudity to him.

"My woman, place your hands on me as I take mine away," Strong Wolf said huskily, gasping with pleasure as Hannah reached up and gently placed her eager, trembling fingers around him, feeling the heat of his flesh against hers.

"Now stroke me," he encouraged, his eyes two points of fire as he gazed down at her.

As though hypnotized beneath his passion-filled eyes, Hannah moved her fingers on him. When he closed his eyes and gasped and moaned with pleasure, she was aware of how this even enhanced her own

rapture. She was swirling in a storm of passion that
shook her innermost senses.

"Enough," Strong Wolf said, reaching for her hand,
gently laying it at her side.

He moved his fingers on himself again for a moment, then placed those fingers to her lips, just beneath her nose. "Smell and taste me."

Smiling seductively up at him, feeling devilishly feminine, Hannah flicked her tongue out and licked his
forefinger.

When he placed his finger into her mouth, she
sucked on it, closing her eyes in rapture as he placed
the heat of his manhood where she throbbed between
her thighs.

He did not try to enter her.

He just moved himself in circles on her womanhood,
causing her to become crazed with needful pleasure.

He took his finger away from her mouth, then
sealed her lips with a frenzied kiss as his hands molded
her breasts within them. She drew a ragged breath
when he kneaded her breasts, having never felt anything as delicious.

Strong Wolf felt the heat rising inside his loins as
he rolled her breasts against the palms of his hands.
As her nipples hardened against his flesh, he circled
his thumbs around each of them, then softly pinched
them.

Hannah moaned when Strong Wolf's mouth went
to a breast and moved over a nipple, his teeth gently
nipping. She whimpered tiny cries when his hands
moved down her body and he stroked her where the
heat of his manhood still lay in waiting. Hannah
opened her legs more to the pleasure.

Her head tossed from side to side as his fingers
caressed more earnestly against that piece of her flesh
that she had been unaware of until today. The more

he caressed her, the more her insides grew mushy with pleasure.

Then suddenly she felt his hand leave her. Quickly he plunged his heat into her pulsing cleft. The pain of his entrance was excruciating. Hannah cried out, her wide eyes gazed into his as he watched her reaction to this first time of having been entered by a man.

"Relax," he whispered, brushing a comforting kiss across her lips. "Take a deep breath. Close your eyes. Let the joy take the place of the pain."

Breathing hard, not wanting to be disappointed, the pain having drawn her into realities that troubled her, Hannah nodded and closed her eyes. She was thinking about how shameful and whorish she was behaving.

Hadn't Chuck told her that she was inexperienced with men?

Was this what he meant?

That she was so inexperienced that she would go too easily to bed with the man she loved?

Tears splashed from her eyes as she tried to make some sense of what she was doing here, in such loose behavior.

Yet as she lay there thinking, feeling remorse, things slowly began to change back to something wonderful.

As Strong Wolf kissed her so sweetly, his hands holding her close while his thrusts came slowly and gently inside her, she felt the same old thrill that she had felt when only gazing upon Strong Wolf.

"Is it better now?" Strong Wolf whispered into her ear as he gently brushed her hair back from her face. He flicked his tongue into her ear, causing Hannah to shiver sensually.

"Yes, so much," she whispered back, her voice quivered in her building excitement.

He showered her face with soft kisses as he placed

a hand to one of her thighs and urged her leg around his waist, and then her other one.

Her soft thighs opened wide now, Strong Wolf moved even more deeply inside her, her moist inner flesh clasping him in a warm, clinging embrace.

Her hips moved and rocked.

She pressed her pelvis against him.

Strong Wolf kissed Hannah long and deep, his tongue flicking between her lips. His pleasure was mounting. He moaned throatily as he kissed her more hungrily, his hands beneath her, lifting her closer.

He could feel the excitement rising.

His thrusts came to her in a wild, dizzying rhythm.

He gripped her shoulders and as he made one last, deep plunge, her body spasmed against his in her own climax.

Then their bodies became still. Strong Wolf held her tightly against him. His tongue parted her lips. Her tongue flicked out and touched his.

His hand moved downward, following the curve of her hips, her buttocks, and then around to touch that very core of her heat.

He was still inside her, pulsing.

He withdrew, stroked himself until life came to him again, then he filled her again and began his rhythmic strokes as he kissed her passionately.

They found their pleasure a second time, then Strong Wolf rolled away from Hannah, breathing hard, his heart lost to her forever.

Nestled into his bed of sweet-scented grass, Strong Wolf pillowed Hannah's head against his chest as she lay on her side beside him.

"You are so quiet," Strong wolf said, placing a finger beneath her chin, directing her eyes into his. "Do you wish not to be here? I know that you enjoyed our lovemaking, so it is not that you wish to run away from. What is it? Why do you not smile?"

Hannah gazed up at him, then smiled. "I am so amazed at what we have found together," she murmured. "I am with you with such ease in this way. I find it hard to believe that I am, and that I have enjoyed it so much. I love you so much. Surely that is why it came so easy for me today." She laughed softly. "I came to see your horses, not to initiate lovemaking with you."

"In your heart, you know that we should have made love even before today," Strong Wolf said, again stroking the tender flesh of her womanhood. "Even now, as I touch you, do you wish ever to leave me?"

"No," Hannah choked out, the pleasure spreading inside her again. She held her head back and sighed.

He leaned over and kissed the hollow of her throat, then covered a breast with his lips and flicked his tongue around the nipple.

"Surely we can't do it again, so soon," Hannah managed to say in a choked sort of whisper.

He turned her so that her back was to him. He drew her up close behind him as one hand reached around and cupped a breast, while the other hand caressed her where she was alive again with need of him.

"We will make love a different way," Strong Wolf whispered huskily against her ear, bringing her slowly to her knees in front of him.

Hannah felt the heat of his manhood probing from behind at the heart of her desire. She leaned her hips back and slowly lifted a leg, then sighed with pleasure when she felt him enter her again with his wild, rhythmic thrusts.

As he thrust inside her, his fingers stroking her swollen nub, she closed her eyes and allowed herself to be carried away again on clouds of rapture.

Strong Wolf closed his eyes. He took his time, savoring each moment that he was inside her, her flesh so warm against his, so tight, so wet. He could feel his manhood being sucked farther inside her as Hannah squeezed with pleasure.

"Lord," she cried, feeling the sweet rapture of their togetherness again. "How can it be? It is so wonderful, Strong Wolf. Pleasure me! Pleasure me! I can't get enough!"

He leaned over far enough to kiss her as she turned her head to one side to receive his lips against hers.

They kissed wildly.

They floated.

The soared.

They again found the bliss of sharing.

Afterward, when they were dressed and sitting beside the fire, they shared a meal that a Potawatomis woman had brought to them at his bidding. They feasted on a meal of cooked turnips and milkweed buds.

Hannah marveled over him having coffee to serve her.

When their meal was finished, Strong Wolf added dry willow twigs to the fire. The fire was already fueled by brambles, huge logs, and small ears of green corn.

Soon bright flames shot up and filled the room with a pleasant golden glow, the smoke lifting up through the chimney and wafting into the early afternoon air.

"I enjoyed the milkweed buds," Hannah said, then took a sip of coffee as she crossed her legs at her ankles, the rabbit fur robe spread beneath her on the floor soft and comforting. "I never imagined they could be eaten, much less be so tasty."

Dressed in his full buckskins, his long black hair drawn back from his eyes with a leather band, Strong Wolf scooted closer to Hannah. He took her half-emptied cup from her and set it aside, then snuggled her closer as they stared into the fire.

"In the spring, the Potawatomis women are eager for greens," he softly explained. "The early sprouting green plants are added to the soup kettle. They use fiddleheads, marsh marigold leaves, fresh milkweed shoots, and sprouts of bracken fern in their cooking. Also roots of lilies, jack-in-the-pulpit, cow parsnips, and American lotus."

"I never knew there could be so many that could be eaten," Hannah said, gazing up at him.

"Often the plants we eat are not only for the pleasure of eating, but also eaten to heal," he said, then realized that Hannah tensed when her pinto whinnied outside.

"I must really go," she said, searching his face with her eyes, adoring him.

"Stay," he said thickly, placing a gentle hand to her cheek as she withdrew away from him.

"I can't," she murmured. "My brother. You know that he needs me."

"I need you," Strong Wolf said, then shook his head, as though to clarify what he had just said. "But I will not be selfish. I understand your brother's needs."

He placed his hands to her upper arms and drew her close so that their lips were only a breath away. "But I understand my need of you, and I am not certain how long I can go now without having you again," he said huskily, his eyes dark with passion. "You must find a way to be with me. And not only for an afternoon. For *always*."

He twined his fingers through her hair and yanked her lips against his. He gave her a fiery kiss, his free hand reaching inside her half-buttoned blouse to stroke a breast.

Breathless, shaken by the intensity of their feelings

for one another, Hannah wrenched herself free. "I
don't know how I can work things out," she murmured. "If at *all*."

She rose to her feet and went to the door.

He followed her, took her by the wrists, and swung
her around to face him again. "You must find a way,"
he said, his eyes imploring her.

She sighed, then she flung herself into his arms.
"Please understand," she cried. "Please don't put such
a demand on me. I so love my brother. I feel sorry
for him. He is struggling for his very own survival!
We, you and I, at least have each other."

He tilted her chin with a finger. "That is not
enough," he said thickly. "We ... must ... be
together!"

"I must go," she softly cried. "Although the maids
are there to care for my brother's needs in some respects, he needs me for others. It is late afternoon. I
should have left long ago."

"The horses?" he questioned. "You didn't choose
a horse."

"As I said earlier, Strong Wolf, I didn't come to
choose a horse, only to look," Hannah said, then
slowly smiled up at him. "And I'm not sure yet if I
came even for that reason. It seems not."

"Never regret what we have done here today,"
Strong Wolf said, troubled by his fears of ever loving
a woman, or taking a wife.

Would she find out?

Would she understand?

Was there a need for her to *know,* he wondered.
Only one woman knew, and she had only been ten
winters of age.

But even then she had turned her head away with
disgust when she had discovered the truth about him!

Would ... Hannah ... do the same? he despaired.

He believed that Hannah's love for him was strong enough never to turn away from him.

And was not her heart big toward her brother's affliction? Surely if she ever witnessed that which abhorred so many, she would not be repulsed.

They stepped outside together. A young brave had brought fresh hay for Hannah's horse. She thanked him as he looked up at her with wide, admiring eyes.

Then she gazed at the sky. Purple flecks of night were already appearing along the horizon.

"I will see you safely home," Strong Wolf said. "Little Sky, go for my horse."

The young boy nodded anxiously and left to do as he was told.

Hannah looked around her at the activity in the village. A large fire was being built in the center. Children were gathering around the fire, laughing and talking, as the pungent wisps of the smoke curled up toward the darkening sky. She watched as some of the children fed the fire more green ears of corn.

"The children seem so content," Hannah said, smiling up at Strong Wolf.

"They should be," he said, taking the reins of his horse as Little Sky brought his steed to him. "The children are always glad when the sun hangs low in the west. Soon will be the time when old legends are told around the fire."

"Oh, how I wish I could stay and hear them myself," Hannah said, then shivered inside when she realized just how late it was, and how long she had been gone. She trusted that her brother would not be as worried this time.

Strong Wolf helped her into his saddle. "I see a time when you will be here to hear all of the tales told by the elders, as well as the gossip of the women during the day," he said, then went to his own horse

and swung himself into his saddle. "When we are married, Hannah. When we are married."

The thought sent a thrill through her heart, yet
again there was that torn feeling.

How could she marry him?

How could she ever leave her brother?

She rode away with Strong Wolf, smiling at the children who ran along beside her pinto, laughing and
reaching up for her. She was envisioning another child
that might one day be smiling at her from the crowd
of other children.

Hers and Strong Wolf's!

How wonderful that would be, she allowed herself
to think.

Then the moon appeared as they left the village.
She *had* stayed too long.

16

Beloved, I, amid the darkness greeted
By a doubtful spirit-voice,
In that doubt's pain.
—ELIZABETH BARRETT BROWNING

Hawk had finally arrived at his destination. He had
watched the Potawatomis village from a butte all afternoon, and he had not yet seen Strong Wolf or
Proud Heart.

Then suddenly he rose up on his knees and placed
a hand over his eyes. Squinting he saw two figures on
horseback ride from the village. He knew Strong Wolf
well enough to recognize him from this distance. He
was riding with a lady away from the village.

And not just any lady.

She ... was ... white!

While waiting and watching today, feeling some
bonding with the people that he watched, Hawk had
felt a great shame over having come this far for only
one purpose. How could he do harm to two warriors
with whom he had shared some of his youth?

He had visited their village.

He had played games with them.

He had challenged Strong Wolf and Proud Heart
often in arm wrestling.

They had shared equally the victories!

They had shared in these things until his mother

had ordered him against it when they had reached eighteen winters.

Since then, Strong Wolf and Proud Heart had seen him as someone who might be an enemy, since he could no longer speak with them or join games with them.

It was rumored, even, that Strong Wolf and Proud Heart had been told that Hawk would one day kill them for his mother!

He had not denied the rumor face-to-face with them, for to do so would be to go against his mother while speaking with them!

And now his mother *did* want Hawk to kill them. Men that he had for so long admired and wished to be friends with again?

He had decided today to observe Proud Heart and Strong Wolf for several days, then decide what he must do, the promise to his mother lying heavily on his heart and mind.

For now, he wished to see where Strong Wolf was going with the lady. He would hurry from the butte, and then stay his distance so that he would not be noticed.

It was strange to be there now, with Strong Wolf so close, and not be able to greet him as a friend greets a friend. He was playing the role of an ardent enemy, and Strong Wolf wasn't even aware of it.

It didn't seem fair.

Hawk was remembering back to the time when everyone thought that Strong Wolf and Doe Eyes would be married once they grew up to be of marrying age.

Only they had seemed to know why that had never happened. It had never been explained to anyone.

He did know, though, that there had been a strain between Strong Wolf and Doe Eyes since both were around ten winters of age. Something had happened then to change their feelings for one another. After the unknown incident, Strong Wolf and Doe Eyes had avoided each other like they were worst enemies.

Hawk's loins ached over missing Doe Eyes, feeling that he had thrown away his future only to please his mother!

As each day passed, he saw the foolishness of the promise he had made to his mother, a mother who most saw as wicked!

17

When we have run our passion's heat,
Love hither makes his best retreat.
                            —ANDREW MARVELL

Hannah breathed in the morning air as she rode toward Strong Wolf's village. To prove her devotion to her brother, she had stayed home for several days, and assisted him in every way possible.

Her brother had even begun instructing her about the ledgers, which she found boring.

Hannah had also stayed home these past few days to get her thoughts straight on how she felt about Strong Wolf. Yes, she loved him. She adored him.

But to have made love? To have given herself to him so easily?

She knew that she should feel ashamed, but no matter how long or hard she had thought about it, no shame had entered her heart.

Her love for Strong Wolf was pure. It was *right*. Loving and making love with him was a part of her newfound freedom that she had fought so hard to achieve. And she would not deprive herself of it!

She ran a hand over the rough material of the denim breeches that she had chosen to wear today for her outing. They were Chuck's pants that he had worn years ago when he was much thinner. Luckily he had not thrown them out. The pants well defined the curve of her hips and thighs. In fact, they fit her a mite *too* snug. But the length had been perfect, for she and her brother were of the same height.

She had also chosen a red plaid flannel shirt from her brother's closet, and a wide-brimmed Stetson hat. When she had walked into the dining room for breakfast, and had leaned over to kiss her brother, he was able to see just enough with his failing eyesight, that she was all spruced up like a man.

Chuck had surprised her by agreeing with her outfit. He said that dressing like a man might make things less dangerous for her while she took her daily ride on her horse. She would be less a target for men who might have been without a woman for too long. Settlers were moving into the area daily. Some were men whose wives had died while on the long journey. Others were bachelors.

He had gone as far as to encourage her to wear a gun and holsters.

Smiling, she patted the pistol at her right hip, then slid her hand down to rest on the butt end of the rifle where it lay snuggled within its walls of leather, sheathed at the pinto's right side.

Flicking the reins, she rode onward. She held her face up to the warm sun. The breeze was refreshingly cool. The sky was a turquoise blue.

And then Hannah became aware of the sound of a horse coming up from behind. She looked over her shoulder and tensed when she quickly recognized Colonel Deshong, flanked on each side by soldiers. She had to believe that he was also headed for Strong Wolf's village, for she was almost there.

Begrudgingly, not wanting to be bothered with the colonel again, Hannah wheeled her pinto around and stopped. When the colonel and his two soldiers reined in beside her, she smiled smugly. She said nothing as the colonel's gaze swept over her, then gave her a wondering stare.

Hannah removed her hat and ran her fingers through her long golden hair. "I can tell you aren't used to seeing a woman wearing breeches," she said, laughing softly.

"No, can't say that I am," Patrick said, a slow smile tugging at his lips. Again his eyes roamed over her. "Are you on your way to Strong Wolf's village?"

Hannah's eyes narrowed warily. "Yes, and you?"

"Yes," Patrick said, squirming uneasily in his saddle.

"You were there only a few days ago," Hannah said, their eyes locking. "Do you make it a habit to visit this often, Colonel?"

He smiled again. "Do *you*?" he said ruefully, his eyes dancing.

Hannah's jaw tightened. "I've come to see Strong Wolf's horses," she murmured.

"I believe that was your excuse the other time I saw you there," Patrick said, still staring at her in an amused manner.

"Excuse?" Hannah gasped, relieved when suddenly Strong Wolf appeared on horseback as he came around a bend in the road, riding toward them.

She broke away from the colonel and rode to meet Strong Wolf, drawing tight rein as he drew rein beside her.

At first Strong Wolf stared at her, obviously stunned by her attire. Slowly his eyes moved over her.

Then he gazed into her eyes, touching her with them as though they were a caress. "I was on my way to see *you*," Strong Wolf said thickly. "Too many days have passed since we were together."

"I . . ." Hannah said, interrupted when Colonel Deshong and his military escorts came and drew rein beside them.

"Patrick?" Strong Wolf said, forking an eyebrow. "I did not receive word that you were coming for council."

"I sent none," Patrick said, his expression solemn.

Strong Wolf gazed from Patrick to Hannah, then back at Patrick. "Come," he said, gesturing with a hand toward his village. "We will go and have council. Patrick, I am curious to see what has brought you to my village again so soon. Usually many sunrises pass before you wish to have another council with Strong Wolf."

"Yes, but I had a need much sooner than that this time, Strong Wolf," Colonel Deshong said, his uneasiness revealed in how he fidgeted with the horse's reins.

"Then, come," Strong Wolf said, nodding. "We shall have our council."

He turned his dark eyes back to Hannah. "Come also," he said. "You will once again be a part of my council." His eyes again swept over her attire, obviously puzzled by it.

Then they rode off together.

When they arrived at his village, all but the two military escorts entered Strong Wolf's lodge. They became comfortable in chairs before the fireplace where a fire burned. Hannah watched the ritual with the long-stemmed pipe as it was passed from Strong Wolf to Colonel Deshong, and back again to Strong Wolf, who then set it aside on the hearth.

"Now, tell me what has brought you once again to my lodge where you are always welcome for council," Strong Wolf said to Patrick, folding his arms across his chest.

Ignoring Hannah's presence, Patrick rested his hands on his knees, the knuckles whitening as he clasped them there. "I am embarrassed to have to admit to you that we are low on supplies at the fort," he said, his voice weary. "There is a cholera epidemic upriver. The riverboats are no longer getting through with supplies. They aren't allowed to, fearing the spread of the dreaded disease."

"Cholera?" Hannah gasped. She stared over at the colonel. "Is Saint Louis plagued with the disease?"

"No, it's the smaller towns downriver from Saint Louis," Patrick said.

"Thank God," Hannah said softly.

"We'd best hope the disease doesn't reach as far as Saint Louis," Patrick said solemnly. "The result could be catastrophic."

Hannah shook off a chill that encompassed her at the thought of her family being in possible danger. She hugged herself, then tried to relax and listen as the colonel explained to Strong Wolf why he was there.

"Strong Wolf, my men are in dire need of meat," Colonel Deshong said. "The men under my command were trained to be soldiers. That is where their skills lay. Not in hunting. Do you think your warriors might go on the hunt and bring us some deer at the fort? I ... we ... would be forever grateful."

There were a few moments of strained silence. This request seemed to be an unusual one, for Strong Wolf's eyes had lit up with surprise as the colonel had spoken it. Strong Wolf rose from the chair and stared a moment longer into the fire.

Then he turned and gazed at the colonel as Patrick rose slowly from his chair. Strong Wolf placed a hand on the colonel's shoulder. "My friend, many deer will lie at your doorstep this very day, before the moon chases the sun from the sky."

Heaving a great sigh, Colonel Deshong smiled

broadly. "You are a true friend," he said. "I will repay you, somehow, for your help."

"Payment comes in continued friendships and freedom of councils between two friends," Strong Wolf said, then walked the colonel to the door and opened it. "You will have deer meat on your table soon."

"Thank you," Patrick said, giving Strong Wolf an affectionate hug.

Colonel Deshong then left the lodge and rode away with his companions.

Strong Wolf went back to Hannah and took her hands in his as she rose from the chair. "And you will come on the hunt with me and my warriors?" he asked, surprising Hannah.

"I'd love to," Hannah said. "But is it all right? Are women allowed on the hunt?"

"You are allowed because I am the voice of my people," Strong Wolf said thickly. "Also, this hunt today is not for my people's cooking pot. It is for the white man's. So I see no taboo in having you join the hunt."

"Strong Wolf, I'm amazed at your generosity toward the colonel," Hannah said as they stepped outside together. "First you gave permission for a road to pass through your property. Now you have agreed to send your warriors out on a hunt for meat for the soldiers."

"What one gives, comes back twofold," Strong Wolf said, chuckling.

Then he turned her to face him. He placed his hands at her waist, his eyes raking over her, again looking at how she was dressed.

"A woman in man's clothes?" he said, his lips tugging into an amused smile. He gazed into her eyes. "How is it that you wear such clothes?"

"A whim of mine, I guess," Hannah said, softly shrugging as she smiled devilishly at him.

"Whim?" Strong Wolf questioned, forking an eyebrow. "What is this thing called 'whim'?"

"A notion, a sudden desire," Hannah said, finding his innocence in these sorts of things so refreshing. "Like it was a whim on your part to allow me on the hunt."

They both laughed, then she stood back and watched as Strong Wolf gathered enough of his warriors to make a successful hunt, Proud Heart among them.

Then Hannah was in awe when Strong Wolf came to her and placed protective leggings over her denim breeches, made by tying a piece of animal skin around them.

"These are worn to protect against prickly bushes in the forest," he said as he and his men placed the same protective coverings around their legs.

As a young brave went for Strong Wolf's and Hannah's horses, Strong Wolf went inside his lodge and grabbed up his bow and quiver of arrows.

When they left the village on horseback, Hannah was honored to be with Strong Wolf, and glad that none of his warriors appeared to resent her presence. Proud Heart was riding on Strong Wolf's right side, she the left.

She sidled her horse closer to Strong Wolf's. "Thank you for letting me come," she said softly. "Will you also allow me to kill a deer, myself? I am skilled with firearms. As a child, my father taught me well the art of shooting."

"We shall see first how many deer offer themselves to us today," Strong Wolf said. "You see, my woman, we are like our brothers the wolves. We hunt the deer, but we do not kill them all. But we do take what we are allowed to take, because if there are too many deer left alive to fend for themselves, they will starve. We only thin out the deer population with our hunt, so that the Deer People will be stronger and their children's children will survive to support our own future children."

"You speak of things with such depth and knowledge," Hannah said, in awe of how he saw things and the rules by which he lived. "I would have never thought about what is best for the deer population. And I doubt that many white people do. They should learn from *you*, Strong Wolf, your people, the true knowledge of the hunt."

"A deer is not just an animal," Strong Wolf further explained. "All things have a living spirit within. Everything, even animals, have guardian spirits of their own."

"You have to be so much more aware of things for the welfare of your people," Hannah said, thinking about how easy things were for the white people. "I so admire you and your people."

"It has been this way since the beginning of time for the red man," Strong Wolf said. "And when the white man came and took the forest animals in such numbers, it became even harder for my people."

She became aware that even while he had been talking, his eyes were on the ground, as were his warriors'. "Are you tracking a deer?" she asked, trying to see what they saw among the dried, rotted leaves on the forest floor.

"Yes," Strong Wolf said, without looking her way. "Our quarry is a buck with several antlers and much meat on it. He will be the first kill for my friend, the colonel. Hopefully the buck will lead us to more like him."

Hannah followed alongside Strong Wolf as the trail

led to a high ridge. And then they swung to the east, away from the wind, so that the wind would not carry their scent toward the deer.

They made a wide half circle, then came out above where the buck was feasting on the leaves of a tree below them.

"We will dismount here," Strong Wolf said, nodding over at Hannah, then nodding at Proud Heart and his warriors as they each dismounted. "And now is the time for us to clear our minds. Do not think of the deer as we approach it. A deer hears a hunter's thoughts if his thoughts are *on* the deer."

Hannah's heart thumped wildly within her chest as she yanked her rifle from its gun boot. She watched Strong Wolf and his braves clasp onto their bows, then followed beside Strong Wolf as they moved stealthily through the thick stand of birch trees.

She occasionally gave Proud Heart a nervous glance as he would say something softly to Strong Wolf. She was too proud to ask what was being said. When Strong Heart wanted her to be included, he would include her despite Proud Heart's interference.

Strong Wolf held out an arm, stopping everyone. "We will wait for the deer to come up the trail again," he whispered to Hannah, the others seeming to know without being told. "He is just down bow range. He is alert to all sounds. We must now wait in silence."

Hannah nodded. She gripped the rifle tightly, her eyes watching the narrow trail that led up from the ravine where the deer was taking its time eating.

Strong Wolf said a quiet prayer to himself, asking the deer to forgive him, then drew an arrow from his quiver. He notched the arrow on his bow and drew the string back as he heard the deer's feet shuffling along the trail.

Strong Wolf held his breath as he waited and watched.

Hannah's eyes were wide. She had also heard the deer approaching. She could even now hear the deer breathing!

When the deer came close enough, Strong Wolf let out his breath and loosed his arrow.

Proud Heart loosed his, the others standing back and only observing. Their time would come when the next deer was spotted.

The two arrows dove straight into the middle of the deer's side, just above its front leg.

Hannah's fingers felt frozen to the gun. She couldn't pull the trigger. She was in awe of how quickly the arrows had sank into the deer's body. She watched the deer take one leap, then tumble to the ground.

Hannah ran beside Strong Wolf as he went and knelt down beside the deer. The buck heaved a heavy sigh, then shuddered and died.

Having never before been this close to a buck such as this, Hannah was in awe of its size. She reached out and touched the antlers, then pulled back her hand when Proud Heart hoisted the deer over his shoulder and carried it to his horse.

After the deer was secured on the horse's back behind the saddle, they repeated the search and kill until six deer were downed.

"That should be enough meat for the white men's table," Strong Wolf said as he secured the last kill on the back of his own horse. "Let us now deliver what we have promised."

The journey back to the fort was silent and full of reverence. The hunt was a time of solemnness. Respect to the dead had to be paid.

The wide gates of the fort were open when they

arrived. They rode on inside and drew tight rein before the colonel's cabin.

Shirtless, Patrick came outside. A cigar hung from the corner of his mouth. His eyes danced when he saw the deer. "And so you did it," he said, giving Strong Wolf a quick smile. "You actually did it."

"Did I not say that I would?" Strong Wolf said, dismounting. He loosened the ropes around the deer that lay across his horse's back.

"You did in one afternoon what would take my men a month to do," Patrick said, chuckling. He watched Strong Wolf lay the deer at his feet, then stepped around the deer and clasped his hands on Strong Wolf's shoulders. "Thank you, my friend. Thank you."

Strong Wolf nodded.

Patrick lowered his hand to his side and stepped back as the other deer were placed on the porch.

Patrick then gazed at Hannah. A small smile tugged at his lips. "And so you also joined the hunt?" he asked.

"I watched," Hannah said, stiffening.

Strong Wolf and his men mounted their steeds. The colonel gave Strong Wolf a salute, then Hannah wheeled her horse around and rode beside Strong Wolf from the fort.

When they rode a short distance, Hannah wheeled her horse to a stop. Strong Wolf stopped beside her, motioning for his men to go on without him.

"I must get back home," Hannah said, reaching a gentle hand to Strong Wolf's face.

"We took much time hunting when, if not, we could have been together in the privacy of my lodge," Strong Wolf said, taking her hand and kissing its palm.

"There will be another time," Hannah said, feeling

the sweet stirrings of need at the pit of her stomach. "But for now, I must put my brother's needs first."

"Go," Strong Wolf said. "But soon we shall be together again, alone."

"Yes, soon," Hannah said.

Her insides stirred sensually when he reached over and placed a hand behind her neck, and then leaned and kissed her.

When he moved away from her, Hannah's insides were trembling. When he rode off, she watched him for a moment, then looked in the direction of her brother's ranch.

She looked at Strong Wolf again.

Suddenly she rode after him.

When he heard her approaching, he looked over his shoulder and gave her a knowing smile. He wheeled his horse around and waited for her.

18

Words from my eyes did start—
They spoke as chords do from the string.
                              —JOHN CLARE

Tiny and several cowhands under his supervision sat
on horseback on a butte watching a young Potawatomis brave fight off bees as he climbed a tree to get
at the bee's hive of honey.

Tiny chuckled, finding it amusing as first one bee
stung the young brave, and then another.

"He's a persistent son of a bitch, ain't he?" Tiny
said, glancing over at Clem, who sat on a horse beside
him. "We'll just wait for the young savage to do the
dirty job of gettin' the honey. Then we'll take it from
him and bring it back to the bunkhouse."

He could already taste the honey. When the cook
served biscuits the next morning, they would have the
pleasure of spreading honey on the thick gobs of
butter!

"I ain't never seen anythin' like it," Clem said as
he idly scratched his whiskered chin. "Honey ain't
worth all of those stings."

They were surprised when the boy jumped to the
ground, went to his pony, and got an ax.

"Well, I'll be damned," Tiny said, leaning forward
to take a closer look. "He's goin' to cut down the
whole damn tree to get at the honey."

"He'd better be prepared to run, that's all's I can
say," one of the other men said, chuckling. "When
that hive falls to the ground with the tree, bees are
goin' to scatter everywhere."

"I think we'd better go on our way ourselves," Clem said, spitting over his left shoulder. "I don't want no bees to come after me. Honey ain't worth it."

"Aw, you're just a yellow-bellied coward," Tiny complained. He gestured with his hand. "Go on home like a dog with its tail tucked between its legs. Who cares? But don't you go askin' for honey for your biscuits tomorrow."

Clem's eyes wavered, then he set his jaw firmly and stayed in place.

The boy labored hard for the next half hour or so. Then suddenly the tree started leaning first one way, and then the other. There was a creaking sound as it swayed.

Then the young brave stepped quickly away as the tree fell to the ground. Bees flew everywhere from having been disturbed, but Wind on Wings was not disheartened. He stepped among the bees and fell to his knees where the honeycomb lay temptingly on the ground.

Frustrated, the bees returned to the hive, buzzing frantically around it as Wind on Wings ran to his pony and placed the honeycomb inside his parfleche bag and sealed it.

Smiling triumphantly and ignoring the bees that had followed him to his pony, Wind on Wings swung himself into his saddle and rode off.

But he didn't get far. Tiny and his men soon blocked his path, giving Wind on Wings more of a fright than the dozens of bees ever could. His eyes wide, he reined in his pony and stared from man to man.

"Little savage, what'cha got there?" Tiny asked, inching his horse closer to Wind on Wings's pony.

Wind on Wings straightened his shoulders, to show that he was not afraid. "Let me pass," he said, now realizing that he should not have gone so far from his village alone.

His father had warned him. His father had reminded him of what had happened to Bird in Ground. Wind on Wings had ignored the warning. Bird in Ground was always getting into some sort of trouble. Wind on Wings scarcely ever did.

Now he had taken one chance too many, leaving his own hunting grounds to follow the bees. Like a bear who was tempted by honey, so was Wind on Wings. Nothing tasted as wonderful!

But he was on land that belonged to the white rancher. He was trespassing, and knew that he might have to pay dearly for his carelessness.

"Tsk, tsk," Tiny said, mockingly shaking his head back and forth. "Seems you cut down a tree that belongs to my boss. And why? For that honey you have in that bag on your horse." Tiny reached a hand to the boy's wrist and squeezed it tightly. "Give me that honey, you stupid brat."

"Yes, the bear tree belongs to white man, but the honey is *mine*," Wind on Wings said, lifting his chin defiantly. "I fought for it. I won it!"

"Like hell it's yours," Tiny said, sneering into the young boy's face. "Give it up, or else."

"It is mine!" Wind on Wings said, crying out in pain when Tiny twisted his wrist backward.

Tiny nodded at Clem. "Get the damn honey," he ordered.

Clem didn't budge from his saddle. "Boss man wouldn't like what you're doin'," he stuttered out. "Tiny, we managed to not get caught after beating up that brave the other day. We're takin' too much of a chance by accostin' a second brave. I say let the kid have his honey and we go on our way. We're supposed to be trackin' down a stray cow. Not humiliate a young brave."

Tiny released the boy's wrist and slid out of his saddle. He went to Clem, grabbed him by the collar, and yanked him to the ground. He doubled a fist and hit him. "Now, do as I say, or you're fired!" he shouted.

"I *quit*," Clem moaned, rubbing his sore jaw. He scrambled to his feet. "You son of a bitch, I hope Chuck figures you out soon, or his whole ranch will suffer for it. I wouldn't blame the Potawatomis if they came and burned down his entire place!"

"Get outta here," Tiny said, pointing to the road. "And if you breathe so much as one word to Chuck, I'll hunt you down until I find you. I'll thrust a knife in your ribs. Do you hear me? Not one word to Chuck."

"All I want is to get as far away from you as I can," Clem said, grabbing his hat. Plopping his hat on his head, he glared at Tiny for a moment, then swung himself into his saddle. "You tiny son of a bitch, I hope you get caught and are thrown in jail. Hangin' ain't good enough for the likes of you. I hope you rot in *hell*."

He rode off.

Tiny stared after him, then turned to the other men. "Do I have some help here, or do I have to fire the whole lot of you?" he shouted.

The men dismounted and surrounded the child's pony. Tiny reached for the boy's wrist, yanked him from his pony, and shoved him to the ground. One foot on his chest, he nodded to the parfleche bag. "Carl, get the damn honey," he said to one of the cowhands. "Jess! Baldie! Come here and help me with the kid."

Tiny placed his fists on his hips as he glared down

at Wind on Wings. "You had no right to cut down that tree," he snarled. "You have no right to the honey."

"Is . . . honey . . . this important to you?" Wind on Wings stammered, wincing when Tiny ground the heel of his boot deeper into his abdomen. "Take it. I will go home. I will tell no one what you did today."

"You'll not rat on me, huh?" Tiny said, laughing sarcastically. He looked from Jess to Baldie. "Let's show him what we do with kids that rat on people so's he'll think twice before doin' it."

Tiny offered the first kick to the boy's side. Jess and Baldie followed with their kicks.

Then Tiny knelt down over the boy and doubled up a fist. He hit him until he lay unconscious on the ground.

"I think we went a mite too far this time," Baldie said as he took a shaky step away from the child. "Tiny, he looks dead to me."

"Naw, only knocked out," Tiny said, shrugging. "Let's get the honey and get outta here. Serves the savage right for trespassin' and destroyin' property."

Tiny grabbed the parfleche bag from the boy's pony. After securing it to his own horse, he took one last look at the boy, then rode off with his men, laughing boisterously.

Wind on Wings groaned as he tried to open his eyes to see. But they were swollen closed. Struggling up from the ground painfully, he reached blindly for his pony. When he could not find him, he gave a soft whistle.

The pony came to him and nudged him gently in the side. Even this hurt Wind on Wings, even though his pony had done this countless times before to prove his loyalty to the young brave.

Wind on Wings moaned as he pulled himself up into his saddle. Then he reached for the reins and nudged his pony in the side with his bare knees. "Shadow, take me home," he said in a strained whisper.

The pony turned in the direction of his village. Bleeding, bruised, and bee-stung, Wind on Wings swayed back and forth in the saddle, his head hung. He had to stay alert until he reached his home so that he could be safe again.

19

Breath & bloom, shade & shine—wonder,
wealth, and-how far above them—
Truth, that's brighter than gem,
Trust, that's purer than pearl.
                              —ROBERT BROWNING

Hannah rode beside Strong Wolf into the outskirts of
his village. She had decided that she would stay for a
short while, then return home.

She had begged Chuck not to worry about her if
she was gone longer than he wished. He understood
now that she loved Strong Wolf and that she was torn
between needs—between two men and their needs
for *her*.

Feeling eyes on her, Hannah looked over at Strong
Wolf and caught him watching her. "Why are you
looking at me like that?" she asked, laughing softly.

"Do you see my lodge up ahead?" Strong Wolf said,
gesturing with a hand toward it.

Hannah looked away from him and gazed at his
lodge as they slowly approached it on their horses,
then looked over at Strong Wolf again. "Yes, I see
it," she murmured. "We will soon be there."

"We will soon be together there," Strong Wolf said,
his eyes dancing into hers. "My woman, the lodge is
boring now when you are not a part of it."

Hannah smiled shyly and looked toward his lodge

again, an eyebrow lifting in wonder when she found a woman now standing at Strong Wolf's door, watching their approach.

Strong Wolf caught sight of the woman also. "Lotus Blossom?" he said, taken aback by how she stood there now, tears streaming from her eyes. He slapped his reins, nudged his horse in the flanks with his heels, and hurried to his lodge.

Hannah came up behind him, dismounted, and went to his side as he placed gentle hands on the beautiful Potawatomis woman's shoulders.

"What has happened?" Strong Wolf asked as Lotus Blossom gazed up at him with tears.

"It is my son Wind on Wings," Lotus Blossom said.

Her husband came suddenly up behind Strong Wolf, then stepped around him and stood at his wife's side.

"Our son arrived home bloody and bruised, and only half-conscious," Black Bear muttered. He doubled his hand into a tight fist and lowered it to his side. "It is *again* the work of white men." His eyes filled with angry fire as he glared at Strong Wolf. "This must be stopped!"

"A name," Strong Wolf said, his spine stiffening. "Did Wind on Wings give you a name of who did this to him?"

"He knows *no* white man's name," Black Bear said venomously. "I have taught him to stay far from them. Until today, he listened to the warning of his father."

"*Where* did this happen?" Strong Wolf urged.

"He said nothing about who or where," Black Bear said, folding his arms angrily across his chest. "It is the same as with Bird in Ground. He has been frightened into silence."

"How can we know who to go after if your son does not speak out and tell the name of the guilty party?" Strong Wolf said, frustrated.

"All my son said, to possibly help in our search for those responsible, is that they stole his parfleche bag from him," Black Bear said.

"Why would white men want his parfleche bag?" Strong Wolf said. "They can get them by trade cheap at the trading post. Why would they beat your son only to get a parfleche bag?"

"Because it was filled with honey that Wind on Wings took from a bear tree," Black Bear uttered.

"Oh, now I see why this was done," Strong Wolf said, slowly shaking his head back and forth. "It was not so much a need of a parfleche bag, *or* honey. It was to have an excuse to batter one of our children."

"Find a man with a parfleche of honey, and you will find the man who led the attack on my son," Black Bear said, then placed a comforting arm around his wife's waist and led her back to their lodge where their son awaited their gentle care.

Hannah placed a hand on Strong Wolf's arm, drawing his attention. "Do you think Tiny did this?" she asked, seeing how even the name made Strong Wolf's jaw tighten.

"He and countless others who look to the red man as savages could have done this," he said. "It is hard for me to see how they can label the red man savages when they who do this today are the true savages!"

Strong Wolf's warriors surrounded him, some on foot and some still on their horses. He handed out the instructions on how to search for the ones responsible for having done this today. He explained about the parfleche bag of honey!

Strong Wolf went to his horse and grabbed the reins. Hannah followed. "Please let me go with you," she asked, her eyes pleading up at him. "Perhaps I can help in some small way. If Tiny is found with the parfleche bag, I would like to be there in behalf of my brother. I would love to have the opportunity of taking the man to Fort Leavenworth. It would delight me to see him locked behind bars."

"If we find the men responsible for the child's beating, they will not be taken immediately to the fort," Strong Wolf said heatedly. "My people will first have an opportunity to get vengeance in their own way, for I truly believe that when we find these men who did the dirty deed today, we will also find the men who attacked Bird in Ground."

Hannah gazed at him for a moment longer, wondering what sort of vengeance would be used against the white men, then hurried to her horse and mounted it, thinking that whatever the men got, they deserved. She now knew that she took her life in her own hands every time she rode alone in the Kansas Territory. Anyone who could be this vicious against children, surely would have no qualms against attacking a lady, and raping her.

She shuddered at the thought, then rode out of the village with Strong Wolf and his warriors. She knew to watch for a freshly cut tree. From there they would follow the tracks, which hopefully would lead them to the ones responsible for the young brave's attack.

Strong Wolf attempted to follow the tracks of Wind on Wings. He became disgruntled and disappointed in the young brave, for the tracks led away from Potawatomis land. That would mean that his attack had occurred on Chuck Kody's property.

Strong Wolf had not stressed enough to the young braves *not* to venture away from the land of their people. If they did, they only tempted ridicule! Even senseless beatings, for to so many white men an Indian was something nonhuman!

"Aren't we now on my brother's property?" Han-

nah suddenly asked as she sidled her horse closer to
Strong Wolf's.

"Yes. And the young brave's tracks led this far.
They go farther still on your brother's land."

"Then, that means that perhaps it *was* Tiny," Hannah inferred.

"The only way of proving it was, is to find the parfleche bag of honey on his horse," Strong Wolf said,
glancing over at her. "And, I am sure, whoever stole
the honey made sure not to carry it on his steed for
long, knowing that if he was caught, he would pay for
what he did to the young brave."

Strong Wolf drew a tight rein and turned to his
men. "Our search stops here!" he shouted. "The same
as Wind on Wings, we are trespassers. We must return
to land that is ours."

Hannah looked ahead and saw a tree that lay across
the ground. Bees were still buzzing around the fallen
hive. She could see some traces of honey dripping
from it.

"There is the tree," she said, then turned to Strong
Wolf. "It must be the tree that Wind on Wings told
us about. See the bees buzzing around the hive?"

Strong Wolf's eyes narrowed as he stared at the
tree, then at the hovering of bees. Then he gazed at
Hannah. "Still we must retreat off land that belongs
to your brother," he said thickly. "I will not give your
brother's cowhands an excuse to accuse the Potawatomis of going back on treaties that were signed in
good faith. This is your brother's land. One of our
young braves crossed upon it. He destroyed your
brother's property when he cut down the tree. He
meant to steal the honey he so eagerly sought. It is
only best now to return to my people." He reached a
hand to Hannah's cheek. "It is best that you go on
to yours."

"No, I wish to stay with you," Hannah said, her eyes wavering. "Strong Wolf, I feel responsible for what happened to that boy today."

"And why would you?" Strong Wolf said, lowering his hand away.

"Because it was on my brother's land that the young brave was so badly injured," Hannah said, lowering her eyes.

"Had Wind on Wings obeyed his elders, he would have not been in the wrong place at the wrong time," Strong Wolf said. "The blame falls solely on the one who went against orders."

"Still I wish to stay with you," Hannah said, her eyes pleading into his. "The sun is still high in the sky. I have time."

"If you wish, come," Strong Wolf said, then wheeled his horse around and rode off, Proud Heart at his side, the warriors dutifully following.

Hannah rode quickly to Strong Wolf's other side.

The ride back to his village was steeped in solemn silence. Hannah's thoughts were on Tiny, and how she would again try to urge her brother to fire him. Surely her brother couldn't condone what Tiny did today, and she was almost certain that it was he who had caused the bruises and cuts on the young brave.

"You are quiet," Strong Wolf said as he gazed over at Hannah.

"I'm thinking about the cruelties of life," Hannah said somberly. "There is so much I don't know, and perhaps never will."

"Yes, it is the same for me, and I am looked to as one who knows much about life, because I am my people's leader who will one day be a proud *chief*," Strong Wolf said, his eyes weary. "But one must learn to live a day at a time and let things work out as they will, hopefully well enough to survive until the *next* day." He paused. He nodded. "Yes, it is hard, this thing called survival."

His heart skipped a beat when he saw movement up ahead, and then discovered who was suddenly there, awkwardly in the path because he had not moved quickly enough to get hidden.

"Hawk?" Strong Wolf stammered out, drawing a sudden tight rein. His horse came to a halt. Strong Wolf stared at the man he knew from his other homeland in Wisconsin. Hawk! Chief Buffalo Cloud and Star Flower's son Hawk, with his hawklike features that emphasized his wide, dark eyes.

Hawk's heart sank to know that he had been discovered. He had followed Strong Wolf and then had circled around. He had thought that he was far ahead of Strong Wolf, when in truth, he came out right in his path!

Knowing that he had no choice, Hawk rode up to Strong Wolf. "And so we meet again," he said.

"And so we do, but what are you doing here, except to spy on me and my people, and also Proud Heart who you have been urged to believe is your enemy!" Strong Wolf growled. He nodded to his warriors. "Seize him! You see him as I do, as our enemy! His mother threatened long ago to avenge her brother Slow Running's death!"

Proud Heart rode up beside Hawk and leaned into his face as Hawk's hands were tied behind him. "And so your mother sent you to do the dirty work?" he hissed. "She sees that my death, and Strong Wolf's, is even more important than my powerful chieftain father's? Than Strong Wolf's powerful chieftainship? Well, she was wrong to send you to do the dirty work."

Strong Wolf peered into Hawk's eyes. "How long have you been here spying on us?" he asked angrily.

"How long have you been hidden like a frightened snake coiled in the grass close to my village?"

"Strong Wolf, I ..." Hawk began, but he was stopped when Proud Heart gave a yank on his horse's reins and led him away from Strong Wolf toward their village.

Strong Wolf sighed and his shoulders grew limp as he gazed hopelessly to the ground. "If not one thing, it is another," he mumbled. "Why can't there be love and peace among men? Why?"

"Who *was* that?" Hannah finally had the chance to ask. "Was he here to kill you and Proud Heart?"

"I am not sure what his true plans were, Hannah," Strong Wolf said as he softly nudged the flanks of his horse to urge it into a soft lope. Hannah kept up beside him. "Hannah, Hawk has never been one to cause problems. The fact that he is here, I am sure at the orders of his mother, surprises me. *And* I am certain that he would not be here unless ordered to come. His place is with his people, as mine is to be with mine."

"He is not Potawatomis, then? Nor Chippewa?" Hannah said, trying to follow Strong Wolf's logic.

"No, he is Sioux," Strong Wolf said softly. "His mother, Star Flower, is wicked to the core. She has tried to make her son as wicked."

"What about his father?" Hannah prodded. "How does he feel about all of this?"

"Chief Buffalo Cloud is a fair, kind man," Strong Wolf said solemnly. "He married Star Flower because she is a temptress in her loveliness. After their marriage, I am sure he discovered her true self."

"But why didn't he leave her?" Hannah said softly.

"Because her beauty outweighs her evil in the eyes of her husband," Strong Wolf said, recalling the exquisite features of Star Flower.

They rode on until they reached the village. Hannah

dismounted and stood back and watched, stunned when Hawk was placed on a stake in the center of the village after not being able to deny why he was there, on Potawatomis land.

"This is not something I wished to do," Hawk pleaded as his buckskin shirt was ripped from his chest. "It was my mother! How could I refuse her? Because of me she has a barren womb!"

"That is why you came to avenge your uncle's death?" Strong Wolf said incredulously. "Because your mother made you feel guilty over her not being able to bear her husband any more children?"

Hawk hung his head in shame.

"Remove him from the stake!" a woman's voice rang out at the far edge of the village as three horses came into sight, a woman on one of them. "Remove him *now*. He does not deserve to be treated this way, Strong Wolf!"

Strong Wolf's heart leapt into his throat when he recognized the voice. He turned on a heel and stared at the woman of his past, the very woman who so long ago had reduced him to less than a young brave in her eyes!

"Doe Eyes?" he gasped.

Proud Heart took an unsteady step backward. "Sister?" he said in a low gasp, his eyes filled with wonder. "Sister Doe Eyes?"

Hannah paled at Strong Wolf's reaction to the woman entering the village. She stared at the woman and saw her loveliness.

And Hannah was instantly jealous!

20

My heart aches, and a drowsy numbness pains
My senses, as though of hemlock I had drunk.
                                              —JOHN KEATS

Doe Eyes ran to Hawk when nothing was done to release him. As she gazed up at him, she desperately sobbed his name and clutched at his hands. "Why did you leave without me?" she cried. "You did not even say a good-bye. Is your love less for me than mine is for you?" She glanced over at Strong Wolf, then Proud Heart, then pleaded up at Hawk with her dark eyes. "Tell them, Hawk. Tell them that you are here only because your mother forced this upon you."

"They already know, but they do not listen," Hawk said, his voice breaking. "I was wrong, Doe Eyes, to leave in such a way. I should have never listened to my mother. Our future, yours and mine, is what suffers from her misguided, evil ways."

"That proves, Hawk, that she has no feelings except for herself," Doe Eyes said, her voice rising in pitch. "Think of yourself, Hawk. Not your mother. Tell Strong Wolf and Proud Heart that you are sorry, that you meant them no harm."

"It . . . is . . . too late," Hawk said, his eyes locking with Strong Wolf's. His eyes shifted slowly to Proud Heart.

Having never seen, or known of Doe Eyes's affection for Hawk, Strong Wolf was rendered speech-less. Their love for one another had been kept from everyone. And as he listened to them, he could not help but think that what they said was all a ploy, to hide the truth that they had worked together on this plot against him and Proud Heart.

Strong Wolf had learned long ago never to trust Doe Eyes. She had so coldly turned him away after she had learned of his secret past.

No one since had made him feel as small, as useless. Doe Eyes was a woman without a heart, and he sus-pected that she would do anything to reduce him to a pitiful nothing again in everyone's eyes!

Hannah was too stunned to move as she watched this woman with Hawk, someone who had surely meant something to Strong Wolf in his past. Since Hannah had known Strong Wolf, no one had ever rendered him speechless as he seemed to be now in the presence of this woman! It was as though he was in a spell!

Hannah wanted to shake him, to bring him back to his normal self, yet still she felt helpless in what she was witnessing today. She just stood there, an ob-server, an outsider, feeling useless, and wishing she had gone on to her brother's house. She regretted having to see Strong Wolf placed in this position.

Doe Eyes ran up to Strong Wolf. "Please, Strong Wolf, please release Hawk," she cried, her hands in tight fists at her sides. Tears streamed from her eyes. "Please believe me when I *know* that Hawk's mother is the reason he is here spying on you and Proud Heart. He was forced to come to the Kansas Territory."

When Strong Wolf refused to respond, she went to Proud Heart and flung herself into his arms. "Brother, please help me," she begged. "Help me to make Strong Wolf see reason."

Proud Heart eased her from his arms and glared down at her. "Sister, did I ever know you?" he said. "And what of our parents? Surely they do not approve of you being here!"

"I knew you would not understand," she said, then ran back to Strong Wolf and grabbed him by an arm.

He recoiled and yanked his arm away.

"Hawk would never harm you nor my brother!" Doe Eyes said, dropping her hands to her sides. "If so, would he have not done it already? He has been here long enough to do you both harm, then return to Wisconsin."

Strong Wolf gazed down at her, his eyes narrowed with hate. "You have no right to be here," he said venomously. He gestured toward Hawk. "*He* has no right to be here, no matter the reason. He is a man. He is a warrior. He could have stood up to his mother and told her that a man does not obey a mother!"

"You know his mother," Doe Eyes cried. "She is strong-willed. She has a way about her! A son is rendered helpless before her, even if he *is* a powerful warrior who will one day be chief of his people!"

"He who follows the skirts of his mother is ... not ... a man!" Strong Wolf emphasized between clenched teeth.

"Does it truly matter?" Doe Eyes sobbed. "Free him. He will leave you, untouched."

"He would leave me untouched?" Strong Wolf said, then laughed fitfully. "You, who have no feelings, come into my village and try to pretend that you do? Pity Hawk if he has fallen into your trap. That means he has become ruled by *two* women, not one."

"Strong Wolf, I know that you have had bad feelings for me for many moons now," Doe Eyes said, wiping tears from her cheeks. "I beg you not to take your feelings for me out on Hawk."

She lowered her eyes, then looked slowly up at him again. "I'm sorry for having treated you so badly when you professed your love for me those many years ago. I'm sorry for having hurt you like I did with my rejection, and in the way that I did it, so thoughtless, so cruel. Please don't take it out on Hawk! I can't help but love him!"

Hannah stifled a gasp, yet knew that she shouldn't be surprised. Strong Wolf's reaction to this beautiful Indian maiden's presence was curious.

A part of Hannah was jealous over knowing that Strong Wolf had loved another woman.

Another part of her knew that it didn't matter that he had, for he loved *her* now.

"What I do with Hawk, and how I choose to do it, has nothing whatsoever to do with you," Strong Wolf said, glaring down at Doe Eyes. "You were dead to me many years ago. You do not exist in my heart, mind, *or* my world. I look at you now and see nothing. When you talk, I hear only the wind!"

Doe Eyes followed Strong Wolf's eyes as he turned to the white woman. She knew now that his heart was filled with another woman, and her skin was white. She watched Strong Wolf with much interest, and then the lady.

As Strong Wolf gazed at Hannah, he could see the wonder in her eyes. He now knew that he might be forced to tell her the full truth about the relationship between himself and Doe Eyes, and finally explain about the dark secret that had caused Doe Eyes not to love him.

But now, for the present, he had Hawk to deal with!

He went to Hawk and glared at him. "You say you are innocent?" he said, folding his arms across his powerful chest. "That you would not have killed me and Proud Heart had you not been caught in the act of spying?"

"Had I planned to truly do it, it would have been done!" Hawk cried. "The opportunity was there. I was so close to you both, sometimes I could have reached out and touched you!"

"I should have smelled your snake breath," Strong Wolf snarled.

"Free me, Strong Wolf," Hawk said, squaring his shoulders. "I will return to my people. I will never cross your path again."

"Return to your people and be ridiculed by your mother because you did not do as she ordered?" Strong Wolf said, laughing. "I think not."

"I have learned much by being away from her willful ways," Hawk said. "I have learned that if I am ever to be a leader of my people, I must learn to be more like my father, whose strength and prowess gain the admiration of your people. When I return and stand up to my mother, then my people will be able to look up to me as a man worthy of my father's title of chief."

"Even if I set you free, so that you could return, unharmed, to your people, you will never have the same respect and admiration as your father, Chief Buffalo Cloud." Strong Wolf laughed sarcastically.

"Give me the chance to," Hawk said, his eyes wide as he gazed over at Strong Wolf.

"You beg like someone who still hangs to a mother's skirt tail," Strong Wolf said, again laughing at Hawk.

"To live, I will do whatever I must," Hawk said, firming his jaw.

"If you were a true man, one who would be a great leader, you would die like a man!" Strong Wolf said, then grabbed his knife from the sheath at his right side and sliced the ropes at Hawk's wrists and ankles, freeing him.

"Thank you, thank you," Doe Eyes cried, running to clutch onto Strong Wolf's arm.

He glared down at her and wrenched his arm free. "Wench, thank not this man who hates the very sight of you," he said. "If it were you on the stake, I would laugh and walk away from you."

Doe Eyes gulped hard, inched back away from him, then went and flung herself into Hawk's arms. "Let us leave this horrible place," she cried.

"He goes nowhere," Strong Wolf said, slipping his knife back into its sheath. "I do not release him out of kindness. He now has to prove his innocence to me, or never walk, alive, from this village of the Potawatomis!"

Doe Eyes turned burning eyes to Strong Wolf. "You will not allow either of us to leave this place alive," she said, glowering at Strong Wolf. "For so long you have resented me. Now you have the chance to silence me forever!"

"Again all I hear is the wind when you speak," Strong Wolf said, placing his hands on Doe Eyes's upper arms. He bodily set her aside to get to Hawk, then glared into Hawk's eyes. "The test today is a simple one, but the sort long used by my people when someone has gone against them."

Hawk said nothing.

Does Eyes ran to Proud Heart. "Again I implore you to help me, my brother," she cried. "Help *Hawk*. For my sake, brother? Please?"

"Doe Eyes, when you chose to travel the road of life with Hawk, you knew then what the end would be for you where family was concerned," he said. "I hardly know you now as a sister."

"And all because I love Hawk?" she uttered.

"That, and also long ago my feelings for you changed when you put ridicule on the shoulders of my best friend Strong Wolf," Proud Heart said, his voice breaking. "I knew not what caused the ridicule, but I did know that it caused pain in my best friend's heart. That pain then became my own, your *brother's*."

Doe Eyes stepped away from her brother, then went and clung to Hawk's arm.

Touched by Proud Heart's words, his loyalty as a friend, Strong Wolf stared at him for a moment, and exchanged smiles with him when Proud Heart turned his eyes to him.

Then Strong Wolf nodded to a warrior. "Bring a mustang to me that has not yet been tamed for riding," he said solemnly.

The warrior nodded.

He returned soon with a feisty black mustang that yanked its head back and forth against the rope that was tied around its neck. Its dark eyes were filled with spirit. Its body was powerfully muscled, the mane sleek and shining beneath the rays of the afternoon sun.

"Hawk, you will ride this pony," Strong Wolf said, taking the rope from the warrior and giving it to Hawk. "If you can break it by taking the devil out of it, then your innocence will be proved and you can leave before the moon replaces the sun in the sky."

Hannah was surprised that such a small challenge as this would be enough to free Hawk!

"Follow me," Strong Wolf said as he glared at Hawk.

Hawk held onto the rope, occasionally eyeing the frisky mustang, as he followed Strong Wolf to the outskirts of the village, where there was room for him to go through the process of taking the wildness out of the mustang.

Marking the path of the public trial, the Potawatomis people stood in two parallel lines, their faces solemn.

Hannah stood beside Strong Wolf, her heart pounding with excitement as she watched Hawk trying to mount the steed. She had ridden many spirited horses in her lifetime. She had enjoyed the challenge of taming them, then training them to become something wonderful, gentle, and loved.

Like an arrow sprung from a strong bow, the horse, with extended nostrils, plunged forward. With all of his might, Hawk drew the strong reins in.

The horse halted with wooden legs.

Hawk was thrown forward by force, but he did not fall off.

The maddened creature pitched with flying heels. The line of men and women swayed outward.

Then they moved forward again, safe from the kicking, snorting thing as Hawk managed to hold it at bay.

The mustang was fierce with its large black eyes bulging out of their sockets. With humped back and nose to the ground, it leapt into the air again.

He did this over and over again, but still Hawk did not fall from the steed, or let up on fighting for his freedom.

Doe Eyes watched, afraid for her loved one. Should he lose, *she* would lose, and he was all that she wanted out of life.

"Do not fail," she whispered.

Then she raised a fist into the air. "Fight for your life, Hawk!" she screamed. "Choose life and *me*."

Hawk fought hard to stay on the mustang as it went

in mad, crazed circles, its mane shaking back and forth
as if it were insane.

Then suddenly the steed came to a shimmering stop.
Wet with sweat and shaking with exhaustion, it stood
with its head hung.

Heaving hard, sweat pouring from his brow, Hawk
slid from the horse. He went around and faced the
mustang, their eyes locking. He reached a hand toward it, smiling broadly when the horse nuzzled the
palm of his hand as though he were a friend for life.

Loud shouts came from the men and women. The
wild mustang was conquered!

Strong Wolf went to Hawk in two long strides.

Hawk turned and faced him.

Strong Wolf placed his hands on Hawk's bare shoulders. "You have proven yourself," he said. "You can
go. And the horse is *yours*."

"Strong Wolf, please believe me when I say that I
have never wanted to be your enemy," Hawk said. "I
want a family! Not enemies! I have never hated you.
It is my mother's hate that has come between us. I
want you as a friend."

"This friendship you speak of, it is not won as easily
as a horse is tamed," Strong Wolf said, dropping his
hands to his sides. "But I do not enjoy having enemies. If you wish, you do not have to leave just yet.
Stay awhile with my people."

"Yes, I wish to stay," Hawk said humbly. "It will
be hard to explain to my mother how I have turned
my back on her wishes."

"When the time comes to face her, it will be the
same as you having just tamed the mustang," Strong
Wolf said. "You will also tame your mother."

Strong Wolf gazed over at Doe Eyes, then looked
somberly at Hawk. "Hawk, never give Doe Eyes cause

to turn away from you, for she does this easily, the
cool-hearted woman that she is."

Hawk's eyes widened. He said nothing as Doe Eyes
came and stood beside him, her hand clasping his, but
the warning caused him to gaze at Doe Eyes in wonder, again wishing that he knew what had transpired
between Strong Wolf and Doe Eyes those many years
ago. To make Strong Wolf this bitter, Doe Eyes must
have done something very questionable.

He cast the wonder from his mind. He loved her.
She loved him. He trusted her love, as she trusted his.

"And how long will you stay?" Strong Wolf asked,
avoiding Doe Eyes's steady stare.

"Until you return to your people, then I shall also
return to mine," Hawk said. "That is, if you will allow
me to stay this long among you and your people."

"I no longer see you as my enemy," Strong Wolf
said. "So stay as long as you wish."

Proud Heart stepped forth. He gave Doe Eyes a
quick, uneasy stare, then placed a firm hand on
Hawk's sweaty shoulder. "If Strong Wolf sees you as
a friend, then so shall I," he said, stiffening when he
heard his sister emit a low, grateful sob.

"Hawk, make camp down by the stream," Strong
Wolf said, nodding toward it. "Tomorrow you can
build a lodge that will house you and Doe Eyes until
our return north."

"You are both kind and forgiving," Hawk said, suddenly hugging Strong Wolf, and then Proud Heart. "If
not for my mother, we could have been such friends
as adults."

"We are adults now, and we shall share adult friendship," Strong Wolf said.

Then Hawk stepped back from Strong Wolf and
Proud Heart, smiled awkwardly at those who stared
at him from the circle of people, then took the horse's

reins, Doe Eyes's hand, and walked away toward the stream.

Hannah watched, absolutely in awe of this man she loved, and how generous he was to everyone. He had even made a friend out of an enemy!

Your eyes smile peace.
The pasture gleams and glooms
'Neath billowing skies that scatter amass.
　　　　　　—DANTE GABRIEL ROSSETTI

Hannah went with Strong Wolf to his lodge, Doe
Eyes's words staying with her like glue. Strong Wolf's
warning to Hawk about Doe Eyes made her realize
even more that Strong Wolf's past had not been
pleasant.

"Let us sit by the fire," Strong Wolf said. He gently
took Hannah by an elbow and led her down onto the
rabbit-fur blanket that was spread out on the floor
before the hearth. "Food has been brought and left
for us. Truly you are hungry, Hannah."

"Yes, quite," Hannah said, studying him as he la-
dled moose meat stew from a black pot that hung over
the fire on a tripod into two wooden bowls. She could
tell that he was still disturbed by what had happened
today. She felt that surely Doe Eyes had affected him
the worst. Her mere presence had made him nervous.

Hannah was filled with such wonder about what this
woman had done to Strong Wolf in the past, to make
him so unnerved with her in the present. Had he loved
her this much?

Suddenly she knew what she must do. Marry
Strong Wolf.

"The stew is good," Strong Wolf said, watching Hannah as she slowly sipped stew from her spoon. He could tell that she was deep in thought.

And he knew about whom.

Doe Eyes.

Doe Eyes had placed many things in many people's hearts and minds today. He hoped that doubt was not inside Hannah's heart now; doubt of him and his true love for her.

"I was but a child of ten when I foolishly loved her," Strong Wolf blurted, drawing Hannah's eyes quickly to him. He angrily broke off a piece of fried bread between a thumb and forefinger. "I have since then despised her."

Hannah lay her dish aside and moved on her knees before Strong Wolf. She took his platter and set it aside, and also the piece of bread that he had not yet eaten.

"My love," she said, framing his face between her hands. "I care not about Doe Eyes, or what she was or was not to you in your past. This is now. We, you and I, are in love. And if you think me not too bold, I wish to marry you."

Strong Wolf's lips parted in a soft, surprised gasp. He gazed at her at length, then swept her up in his arms as he rose to his feet. "Bold?" he said, laughing drunkenly. "Do I think you are too bold? Never. What you said came from the heart. I will answer you from my heart. Yes I want you. Yes I want you to be my wife!"

Inside he was warm with happiness. He fought off the shadow of doubt of taking a wife. His past! The secret that he had protected since he was ten winters of age! If he married Hannah, surely one day she would discover the secret when he least wanted her to. It could happen at any moment. Even while they were making love!

Yet he would chance anything to have a future with her.

He gathered her close and kissed her. Then he carried her to his bed and lay her across it. He knelt over her and kissed her again. His one hand kneaded her breast through the fabric of her shirt. His other hand stroked her at the juncture of her thighs, although her breeches were an impediment to him truly touching her there.

"I know the answer!" Hannah said, quickly drawing her lips from his. She sat up on the bed, her heart pounding like wild thunder at the thought that just came to her. It was a possible solution to her concern over her brother.

"What answer?" Strong Wolf said, brushing soft kisses across her brow.

"My sister!" Hannah said, placing a hand to his cheek as he stared into her eyes. "My sister's schooling is almost complete. Perhaps she will consider making a life for herself in the Kansas Territory and at the same time live with Chuck at his ranch and see after his welfare."

She kissed Strong Wolf, then gazed excitedly into his eyes again. "I shall send a wire to my parents tomorrow about our upcoming marriage," she said, her eyes bright. "I shall also send a wire to Clara. Oh, pray, darling. that she will agree to come and take my place at our brother's ranch."

"And if she doesn't?" Strong Wolf said, taking her hands, drawing her against his hard body.

"Then I shall find someone dependable to stay with him," Hannah said determinedly. "I love you. I wish to be with you. Yet I also want to make sure my brother's welfare is taken care of."

"And I am sure that you will," Strong Wolf said, again holding her close. He nestled his nose into her hair. "My woman is able to achieve anything she wishes to achieve."

"Do you truly think I was too bold by asking you to marry me?" Hannah asked, leaning away from him, their eyes locking. "It is not the proper thing to do, you know."

A terrible explosion in the distance rocked the planked floor beneath the bed, causing the bed to tremor precariously.

"Now what?" Hannah said, rushing from the bed with Strong Wolf. Hand in hand, they went outside and stared into the heavens as billows of black smoke spiraled into the sky not that far from the village.

"What could that be?" Hannah said, shielding her eyes with a hand as she watched the smoke continue to waft into the air.

"It must be investigated," Strong Wolf said. He shouted at several warriors who had been brought from their lodge by the same explosion.

Proud Heart came to Strong Wolf.

"Proud Heart, gather together many warriors," Strong Wolf said, already half running toward the corral. "Come. Follow me."

Hannah went with Strong Wolf. She swung herself into the saddle as Strong Wolf mounted his steed. They waited for the warriors to ready their horses, mount them, and then they all rode away in the direction of the smoke and stench of fire.

When they reached their destination, they discovered a bridge on fire that had not been built all that long ago just off Indian property, burning timbers tumbling down into the stream.

"Who could have done this?" Hannah said, watching the flames eating away at the rest of the bridge. "Why?"

The sound of horsemen coming up on them made

Strong Wolf and Hannah turn at the same time, just in time to see Tiny ride up, his cowhands quickly surrounding them.

"We gotcha," Tiny said, his eyes dancing as he clutched to a rifle. "We caught you in the act!"

Hannah sighed heavily. "Tiny, what on earth are you talking about?" she said, edging her horse closer to his.

"Just you stay right there," Tiny warned, aiming his rifle at Hannah. "You're in on this as sure as I'm sittin' here."

"And you are full of sour wind!" Hannah barked back. "If anyone is to blame, it is *you*. You did it to cast blame on Strong Wolf. You just hoped he'd come to see what had caused the explosion. You son of a bitch, you set off the dynamite and hid until Strong Wolf and his warriors came to investigate."

"And so aren't you full of it," Tiny snarled back. "Just shut up, Hannah. You've no room to talk. You're just as guilty as Strong Wolf, because you are *with* him." He chuckled. "Just wait until Chuck sees you behind bars with the savages. He'll split a gut, that's for sure."

"You're a sick, miserable man," Hannah said, her teeth clenched.

"*You* should've minded your own business and stayed at the ranch with your brother," Tiny spat out. "What happened today is an obvious Potawatomis plot to disrupt the white community. This time Colonel Deshong will hear me out, when I cast blame Strong Wolf's way."

Another man on horseback came into view. Claude Odum soon drew a tight rein beside Strong Wolf. "And what were you saying?" he said, directing his question at Tiny.

"Strong Wolf blew up the bridge, that's what," Tiny said, nodding toward Strong Wolf.

"Tiny, now, why would Strong Wolf blow up a bridge close to land where a road he has only recently approved of is being built?" Claude said sarcastically. "It isn't logical, now, is it? Don't you think you'd best change your story as to who did the dynamiting today?"

Tiny went tight-mouthed on him.

Claude leaned closer to Tiny. "This looks more like a double cross to me," he accused. "Something that you might do to make it look like Strong Wolf was responsible."

Hannah edged her horse closer to Tiny's. "And Strong Wolf has my alibi, to prove that he wasn't anywhere near the bridge," she said, boldly lifting her chin. "He was with me back at his village. We were in his lodge when the explosion rocked the earth."

Tiny glowered from Claude, to Hannah, then to Strong Wolf.

Boiling mad, Hannah watched Tiny ride away. "He's gone too far this time," she murmured, then turned to Strong Wolf. He had been much too quiet while she had debated things with Tiny. "Strong Wolf, did I say something wrong?"

Strong Wolf's lips tugged into a smile. "You said everything right, my woman," he said, reaching over to kiss her.

Claude Odum chuckled beneath his breath, drawing Strong Wolf and Hannah apart.

"Now, will someone tell me what's going on here?" Claude said as he gazed from Hannah to Strong Wolf. "I heard the explosion. I came as soon as I could. Who *did* set off the dynamite?"

"Are you thinking that perhaps Strong Wolf had a

hand in this, after all?" Strong Wolf said, his smile fading.

"Naw," Claude said, relaxing his shoulders.

"Then let's forget about it. It's Colonel Deshong's problem," Hannah said. She smiled over at Strong Wolf. "I believe I have a trip to make to Fort Leavenworth. Will you accompany me there tomorrow, Strong Wolf, so that I can send the wire to my parents and my sister?"

"A wire?" Claude said, forking an eyebrow. "What's this about a wire?"

"Hannah and I are going to be married soon," Strong Wolf said, lifting his chin proudly.

"And I am sending a wire to my family to let them know," Hannah said, smiling over at Strong Wolf. She was glad to see that he seemed more relaxed, perhaps able to place the traumas of today behind him, in the hope of their future together.

"Congratulations," Claude said. "And if you don't mind, I'd like to accompany you to the fort tomorrow in case Tiny might have tried to stir up trouble over today's explosion."

"That would be fine," Hannah said.

She turned and gazed at Strong Wolf, who again seemed quiet and filled with thought. She wondered if he was thinking about another time, another place, another woman?

Yet, she reminded herself, he had loved Doe Eyes when he was ten.

Still there seemed too much between them that made Hannah uneasy. She knew now that she would only be truly sure of Strong Wolf after they had spoken wedding vows.

She hoped that could be soon, then again, there were always unseen problems to delay the best of plans, especially here in the Kansas Territory!

22

O, keep a place apart,
Without your heart,
For little dreams to go!
—LOUISE DRISCOLL

The next day at Fort Leavenworth, Claude Odum stood back with Hannah as Strong Wolf talked with Colonel Deshong. Hannah's purpose for having come to the fort had been sidetracked the minute Patrick had seen Strong Wolf enter the door. The bridge. There were many questions about the bridge.

"And, Patrick, do you suspicion that I, Strong Wolf, had anything to do with the bridge being destroyed?" Strong Wolf asked, stiffening his shoulders.

Strong Wolf's corded muscles showed through the material of the fringed buckskin shirt, they were so taut in his building anger with the colonel. His word! Did not his word mean anything?

"Don't get your nose out of joint, Strong Wolf," Patrick said, rising from his chair. "I have to ask questions. That's what I'm getting paid for."

As everyone mutely watched, Patrick went to his liquor cabinet and poured himself a shot of whiskey.

He gave a look over his shoulder at Strong Wolf, then thought twice about asking him if he wished to have a drink. He knew that Strong Wolf didn't approve of "firewater."

Nor did Claude Odum, who showed his displeasure.

Patrick tipped the glass to his lips and drank the whiskey in one fast gulp, then slammed the glass back down inside the liquor cabinet.

He sauntered back to his desk and eased down in the chair, then gazed over at Strong Wolf again. "Now, what were we saying?" he said, easing the awkwardness of the morning by pretending their discussion was unimportant.

Feeling insulted by the behavior of Patrick today, Strong Wolf leaned over and placed his hands flat on the desk, so that he was closer to his face. "I ask you again," he said, his voice edged with anger. "Do you suspicion that Strong Wolf and his warriors are responsible for blowing up the bridge?"

"Strong Wolf, if I had, I would have sent my soldiers to your village to arrest you," he protested. "Now, I hope that sets things straight between us so that we can go on to something else." He cast Hannah a forced smile. "Like what Hannah is doing here this morning?"

Hannah started to take a step forward.

Claude gently grabbed her wrist and eased her back to his side, realizing that Strong Wolf wasn't finished with the colonel yet.

Hannah looked questioningly over at Claude. He slowly shook his head back and forth, and she soon understood.

"I am glad that you trust me," Strong Wolf said, drawing the colonel's eyes back to him. "We both, in good faith, have touched the goose quill to treaty papers."

Strong Wolf straightened his back and folded his arms across his chest. "But I must admit, Patrick, that I, a man with copper skin, do not always understand the white man's law," he said solemnly. "It is too often like walking in the dark. Whites complain that redskins are intruders upon their rights. Yet we, the so-called intruders, are the first true Americans. How smooth the language of the whites when they can make right look like wrong, and wrong like right." Strong Wolf stated.

"Strong Wolf, in my case I must listen, always, to both sides when a crime is committed," Patrick said, heaving a sigh.

"Have I not shown in many ways my friendship toward you?" Strong Wolf demanded. "Is that not enough? Enough to believe Strong Wolf over evil white men? Strong Wolf has always been the white man's friend. I have always spoke well of those who are good at heart. I feel that you, a great war chief, would not hurt my people. You know that *my* objective is not *war*. Had it been, I would have attacked and killed the war chief and his soldiers long ago!"

"Don't threaten me," Colonel Deshong said, his eyes squinting angrily. "And as far as friendships go, when someone says they have proof of even a friend's guilt, I have to investigate."

"I am a *true* friend," Strong Wolf said tightly. "And to strengthen my friendship with you, the war chief for this territory, I offer to go again for more meat for you and your men." He offered to do this, knowing that with men like Tiny around, he needed this strengthening of camaraderie with the colonel.

Colonel Deshong's eyebrows forked. "As a matter of fact, we *do* need more meat," he said, smiling up at Strong Wolf. "You *are* a true friend for offering to bring more for our tables."

"You will soon have it," Strong Wolf said, then looked more somberly down at Patrick. "And do not forget that favor when evil men might again wrongly accuse me of crimes I have not committed."

"And now that that is behind us, what has brought this lovely lady to the fort with you, Strong Wolf?" Patrick said, rising form his chair. He went to Hannah. "You surely did not come just to listen to the two of us have a heated discussion."

"No, not quite," Hannah said, laughing awkwardly. She lifted her chin, causing her long golden hair to tumble down her back, her dress more feminine than usual. And today she was not riding a horse. She had come in a buggy. "I have come to ask you to do a special favor for me."

"Why, certainly," Patrick said, clasping his hands behind him as he rocked slowly back and forth. "Just ask and it is yours."

"Would you please send a wire to my parents and my sister in Saint Louis?" Hannah said, sending a beaming smile over at Strong Wolf, who stood with his eyes on her.

He had placed his anger behind him and now waited for her to announce their upcoming marriage.

"Why, I would be happy to," Patrick said, unclasping his hands. He reached a gentle hand to Hannah's arm. He led her to the desk and handed her a pen. "Just write down what you wish to be sent, and I shall do you the honors."

Hannah took the pen, smiled over at Strong Wolf, then dipped the pen in the inkwell. She wrote out the message that her parents would soon be reading, and then one for her sister.

She knew to expect an explosion from her father and pitied her mother having to be the one to calm him. He would have to understand that Hannah was no longer his concern; she was a woman with her own mind.

And as for Clara? She knew that Clara would be happy for her. But would Clara be willing to give up

her ambitions of teaching? She was just about to grad-
uate from college.

Hannah only hoped that Clara would care enough
for Hannah's future with her husband to come and
help her establish it. Her hand trembled as she wrote
that note to her sister. It was the most important of
the two!

She signed her name to the notes and handed them
to the colonel. "I believe I have covered everything
in my notes to my parents and my sister," she said,
smiling to herself at his reaction when he read them,
then stared up at her.

"Yes, sir, I am going to marry Strong Wolf," Hannah said, linking her arm through Strong Wolf's. "As
soon as my parents can accept the marriage and will
arrive here to share the happy event with me."

"We would like for you to be there also," Strong
Wolf said, addressing Patrick.

"It would be my pleasure," Patrick said, nodding.

Hannah turned soft eyes to Claude. "And you,
Claude," she said, smiling at him. "Would you
please?"

"Why, most certainly," Claude said, smiling widely
over at her, and then Strong Wolf. "I would have been
hurt to the core had you not included me."

Hannah turned to Strong Wolf and hugged him,
then watched as Patrick sent the wires.

When it was done, she sighed. "And now to await
the responses," she said, giving Strong Wolf a nervous glance.

Strong Wolf placed an arm around her waist. "We
will go now."

Claude went to Strong Wolf and placed a hand of
friendship on his shoulder. "Congratulations," he said,
his eyes warm. "Just let me know when to be there
for the wedding. I wouldn't miss it for the world." He

stepped away from Strong Wolf and gave Hannah a gentle hug. "I wish you all the happiness in the world."

"Thank you," she said, returning the hug.

Patrick went to Strong Wolf and shook his hand. "I envy you," he said, giving Hannah a glance. "My wife passed away a few years ago. I've never considered marrying again. But should someone like Hannah come along and give me a second glance, I think I'd jump at the opportunity of having such a woman to grow old with."

"Why, thank you," Hannah said, surprised. She even welcomed the colonel's arms around her as he gave her a pleasant hug.

She then walked to the door with Strong Wolf, for the moment feeling content.

"I've much to discuss with Patrick," Claude said, as they stepped outside onto the porch. "And if a wire comes in from your parents, I'll personally bring it to you, Hannah."

"I hope that will be soon," Hannah said, stepping up into her buggy.

Strong Wolf swung himself into his saddle and rode beside her buggy through the wide gate of the fort, then rode in silence until the fort was far behind them.

Then he reached down and grabbed Hannah's reins. "Do not return home just yet," he said, his eyes imploring her. "Too many things have gotten in the way of our being together. Let us hide ourselves in the woods today so that we can be alone. No one will find us to interrupt our moments together."

"I had planned to spend the rest of the day with Chuck," Hannah said, her heart thumping at the thought of doing otherwise. "I feel as though I have neglected him, Strong Wolf. Soon I will have to tell him our plans. I don't want to have any regrets."

"I need you," Strong Wolf pleaded. "For a little while, Hannah? Then you can return to your duties to your brother."

Understanding his needs, which matched her own, Hannah nodded. "Yes, darling," she murmured. "For a little while. I want nothing more than to be with you."

He leaned down and kissed her, then led the way through the forest until they came to a slow, meandering stream, over which hung a thick foliage of oak and elm trees. The shade was cool. The breeze was gentle. Everywhere overhead birds sang and flew from branch to branch. Squirrels scampered beneath the trees, gathering long lost acorns from last autumn.

"It is absolutely perfect," Hannah said, gazing around her. Wild roses climbed the trees, in pinks and reds, their fragrance sweet and spicy.

Strong Wolf removed a blanket from his buckskin bag that lay across his saddle. He took the blanket and spread it on the ground close to the stream.

He reached out a hand for Hannah. She went to him and sat down beside him. For a while they watched the minnows at play in the water.

Then Strong Wolf turned Hannah toward him and drew her into his arms. His lips came to hers in a frenzy of kisses, his hands quickly unbuttoning her dress.

As he lowered the dress down to her waist and her breasts were revealed to him, he moaned as his hands swept around them, their softness, their firmness, sending a burning passion through him like a whip crack.

Hannah abandoned herself to the wondrous feelings that swam through her as his hands kneaded her breasts, his lips drugging her. She reached up beneath his shirt and ran her fingers over the smoothness of his skin, over his muscled chest, then gently pinched his nipples until they became hard against the palms of her hands.

Needing more than this, wanting everything today, Strong Wolf eased away from Hannah and yanked his shirt off. He stood up over her as he slipped his breeches down, the urgency he felt for her springing into sight.

"Remove your clothes," he said as he kicked his breeches away, then stepped out of his moccasins.

Hannah moved to her knees and slipped her dress over her head and tossed it aside, then as he watched her, she lay down on her back and slid her undergarments slowly and seductively down her legs.

Swallowing hard, passion overwhelming him, Strong Wolf knelt down beside her and grabbed her undergarments and yanked it away from her. He removed her shoes and stockings, then straddled her and probed with his throbbing hardness between her thighs, where she opened herself to him.

Her blood quickened, and she closed her eyes in ecstasy when he entered her in one quick thrust, filling her magnificently.

She shuddered with desire and tossed her head back and forth, moaning throatily as he moved within her.

Strong Wolf wove his fingers through the soft glimmer of her hair and brought her lips to his, his free hand moving over her silken body, touching and caressing her secret places.

Her whole body quivered as the slow thrusting of his pelvis brought her ecstasy. She swept her arms around his neck. Her soft, full thighs opened more widely to him as she placed her legs around his waist.

She clung and rocked with him, sighing against his lips as he reverently breathed her name while kissing her.

His hard body against hers, the way they were locked together, so sensually, made a flood of emotions overtake Hannah. How could she have lived before him? She had not known that such paradise existed on this earth. Her breath quickened with pleasure as his lips brushed her throat, and he sank his mouth over a breast, his tongue flicking the nipple.

"I adore you," she whispered, her face hot with her building passion. "I love you. I shall always love you."

Strong Wolf gazed into her eyes and swept damp locks of her hair back from her face. "You are mine forever," he whispered.

He once again claimed her lips with his in a heated kiss, his tongue thrusting between her lips, touching hers, the fires of his passion burning, spreading, heating up his insides like an inferno.

"More," Hannah whispered, hardly recognizing her voice in its huskiness, or herself, in her brazenness. Her voice quivered emotionally with excitement. "Don't stop. Love me. Fill me more deeply. I need you! Please, Strong Wolf. More!"

Responding to her need, the very air charged with their building pleasure, Strong Wolf plunged himself more deeply into her pulsing cleft, feeling the clasping of her moist inner flesh. He gripped her shoulders. His mouth brushed her cheeks, her ears, then lightly and tenderly kissed her eyelids.

"My woman," he whispered into her ear. He felt his temperature rising, her spasmodic gasps proving that she was nearing her own sought-for release.

He pressed his cheek against one of her breasts and fell back into a wild, dizzying rhythm inside her, his

breath filling the morning air with its gasps of
pleasure.

"Now!" Hannah cried, feeling the familiar sensations that came moments before finding total ecstasy
within the arms of her beloved. "I feel it. Oh, Strong
Wolf, *now*!"

She clung to him as she became overwhelmed with
pleasure, the spasms of his body proving to her that
they had reached the ultimate of pleasure together.

Afterward they lay together, clinging, breathing
more easily. Hannah was suddenly aware again of the
birds in the trees overhead, of the soft spiraling of the
sun as it laced its way through a break in the trees,
and of a distant voice of frogs vibrating from the thickets that grew down into the stream.

"I really must go," Hannah said, easing gently from
Strong Wolf's embrace. "I promised Chuck that I
would study the journals again today. I ... I ... just
can't seem to understand their entries."

Strong Wolf grabbed her by the wrist and brought
her down beside him again, but only to give her one
last kiss. He kissed her, then rose with her from the
blanket and dressed.

"One day soon you will not have to think of journals," Strong Wolf said, sliding his fringed, buckskin
breeches up his muscled legs. "You will be my wife.
It will be good to know that when I come to my lodge,
you will be there."

"Always," Hannah said, going to him, running her
fingers over his chest. She leaned down and flicked
her tongue over one of his nipples, smiling when she
heard him suck in a wild breath of pleasure.

"My woman, do you wish to return to your brother
today?" Strong Wolf said, taking her gently by her
shoulders, leading her away from him.

"Yes, I *must*," Hannah said, eyes innocently wide.

"Then, do not torment this man who will soon be your husband by sending his heart into another spinning," he said, laughing softly. He bent over, grabbed his shirt, and quickly had it over his head.

"One day soon I shall torment you all I wish," Hannah mocked as she finished dressing. "For I will be with you both day and night. I shall torment you mercilessly with my kisses and caresses."

She ran her fingers through her hair in an effort to remove the tangles, then gasped with pleasure when he drew her against the hard frame of his body to kiss her again.

She gyrated her body against his, wanting more, regretting having to leave him. "I need you," she whispered, her one hand feeling his own need through the fabric of his breeches. "Should we, perhaps, wait awhile longer?"

"No, it's best not," Strong Wolf said. He eased her away from him. "You go your way. I will go mine. Soon our paths will not have to cross, but come together as one. We will only say good-bye for short intervals when I am gone to tend to the duties of my people."

Sighing, Hannah watched him shake the blanket out, then fold it and return it to his parfleche bag. She walked then to her buggy and climbed onto the seat.

Taking up the slack reins, she gazed over at Strong Wolf as he swung himself into his saddle.

"We don't dare kiss good-bye," Hannah said, knowing that to even touch him again would most certainly alter her plans for the day.

"No, we dare not kiss again," Strong Wolf said, smiling at her. "Nor even touch. Good-bye for now, Hannah. We will be together again soon."

"Yes, soon," Hannah whispered as he wheeled his horse around and rode away from her.

Now familiar with the land, Hannah knew her way back to her brother's ranch. She had only a short way to go, already at his pastureland.

She gazed in the distance at her brother's ranch house, admiring it. Then she looked at the outbuildings and gazed at the bunkhouse. She could see several men mulling about there, and thought of Tiny.

"The weasel," she murmured. "But how on earth am I ever to get my brother to fire him? Even this last incident probably didn't convince him that he is up to no good. What *is* his hold on my brother?"

Her brother had explained away Tiny's latest attempts at discrediting Strong Wolf, by saying that Tiny was hardly different from a large majority of white people who didn't like Indians.

Yet she felt as though she had achieved something by her latest talk with her brother. As she had talked against Tiny, the very man who made the daily entries in her brother's journals, she had watched Chuck take out a magnifying glass to study the figures on the pages.

She could tell by his reaction, that although mainly seeing shadows and light as he had looked at the figures, he had seen something that had caused him to glance up at her, his face pale with discovery.

He *had* seen something questionable in the entries!

Yet again he had scoffed about it, saying that Tiny wouldn't have the nerve to try and alter the figures.

Not knowing anything about bookkeeping, Hannah felt helpless, yet at least she knew that her brother's suspicions had been aroused.

And if Clara would agree to come and see to Chuck's best interests, *she* would know whether or not

Tiny was scheming to swindle her brother, for she was a skilled mathematician.

"Clara, you've got to come," she whispered, then rode on toward the house, frowning at Tiny as she passed by him.

His sly smile sent goose bumps up and down her flesh.

23

Thou must be true thyself,
If thou the truth wouldn't teach.
                    —HORATIUS BONAR

The next day, Strong Wolf and several warriors were
on the hunt for the colonel's meat. Three deer were
tied to the backs of horses, with plans to kill at least
one more before heading back to the fort with the
friendship offerings.

As Strong Wolf rode onward, a blue heron flew out
from the brush, its wide wings flapping in a slow beat.

Looking down at the ground, Strong Wolf saw the
whiteness of thistle seeds, that which the Maker had
placed on the earth as a cushion for those who traveled often in the forest.

He saw jewelweed, balm against the sting of nettle
and poison ivy. He also saw the three-leaved rasp-
berry, the fox grape, and the leaves of ginger.

Yes, he thought to himself, it was a good place for
his people, a land of loveliness. He was proud to have
led them there, although he was constantly faced with
challenges with the white man.

The hunt was needed today to again guarantee solid
friendships with those at the fort.

He was willing to do this as long as they, in turn,
displayed their ways of friendship toward the
Potawatomis!

The sun was warm on Strong Wolf's bare chest. His breechclout fluttered in the breeze as he spied another deer in the path a short distance away.

He drew a tight rein, his horse stopping at the command.

He yanked his bow off his shoulder, slipped an arrow from the quiver and notched it to the bowstring, then took steady aim. He whispered his prayer to the deer.

He looked quickly elsewhere when a sudden spattering of gunfire rang through the dense forest, the sparks of the blast catching Strong Wolf's eyes just as he saw movement.

Proud Heart rode up to his side. "White hunters!" he cried.

Soon they realized that the white men were more than that. While one of the white men went and stood over the downed deer, the others came out of hiding on horseback from all sides and surrounded the Potawatomis braves, their rifles aimed at them.

Lowering his bow to his side, the arrow still notched, Strong Wolf looked slowly from man to man, recognizing none of them.

"And so what have we *here*?" one of the whiskered men said, laughing in a strange sort of snort. "A pack of savages."

"Who are you, and what are you doing on land of the Potawatomis?" Strong Wolf asked, his voice guarded.

"Oh?" one of them said, forking a thick eyebrow. "I don't see no signs anywhere sayin' this is Injun land." He gazed over at the man beside him. "Frank? Do you see any sign sayin' this land belongs to anyone in particular? Wouldn't you say anyone can hunt here that wants to?"

Frank edged his horse closer to Strong Wolf's.

"Yeah, even Injuns are fair game on the hunt, wouldn't you say?" he said, chuckling.

Suddenly Strong Wolf's bow was grabbed away from him and tossed to the ground, his arrow falling limply away from the string.

White Beaver, one of Strong Wolf's most valiant braves, was knocked from his horse with the butt end of a rifle.

Strong Wolf watched helplessly as one of the white men placed a rope around one of Strong Wolf's other braves, and dragged him from his steed.

Hate swelled inside Strong Wolf's heart when the warrior was dragged behind a horse, gagging and grabbing at the rope around his throat, until he finally quit struggling and lay dead when the man finally stopped.

While the men became caught up in their fits of laughter, that gave Strong Wolf and his warriors the chance to finally defend themselves.

Strong Wolf leaned quickly over and grabbed his bow up from the ground, notched an arrow, and sent it through the heart of the man who went by the name of Frank.

Proud Heart and the others drew their rifles from their gun boots and killed two more assailants before the others got away in a frenzy on their horses.

Strong Wolf watched until the men were out of sight, then slid from his saddle.

He dropped his bow to the ground and ran to the warrior who lay in a heap, rope burns around his neck. He knelt down beside him and lay his head on his lap, tears of regret flooding his eyes.

"Son of Sky," Strong Wolf said, caressing the dead man's cheek. "You died so needlessly!"

Dazed, White Beaver moved to his feet. Proud Heart held onto him by an arm as they both went to Strong Wolf and stared down at their fallen brother.

Then Proud Heart looked at the dead white men, then into the distance, where the other white men had fled to safety.

"Strong Wolf, the white men are settlers who are not familiar with how things should be in the Kansas Territory?" he questioned, his voice hollow of feeling.

"No, that is not so," Strong Wolf said, glaring at Proud Heart.

"You know them?" Proud Heart said, kneeling beside Strong Wolf, also gently touching the face of the beloved departed.

"*We* know them," Strong Heart mumbled. "Did you not see the brand on the rumps of the horses? As they rode away, I saw the brand! It is one familiar to us!"

"I did not take time to look," Proud Heart said softly.

"I made the time," Strong Wolf said bitterly. "As they rode away, the cowards they became under the fire of our weapons, I recognized the brand that is used by a rancher that sits not all that far from Chuck Kody's ranch."

"His name is?"

"Bryant. Jeremiah Bryant," White Beaver said as he glared down at Son of Sky.

Proud Heart gasped. "I am familiar with the man," he said, looking at White Beaver and then at Strong Wolf. "I have seen him while at the trading post."

"And did he show resentment while you were near him?" Strong Wolf said, his eyes points of fire.

"Yes, I do remember feeling the coldness that came from him when we stood perhaps too close together while making trade," Proud Heart said, nodding.

"I have also felt his resentment," White Beaver added as he rubbed a contusion that was growing purple on his chest, where the rifle had struck him.

"He is our man," Strong Wolf said, looking in the direction of Jeremiah Bryant's ranch. "He is responsible for the death of our warrior."

"But, Strong Wolf, he was not among those who did this," Proud Heart said, eyes narrowing in thought.

"He whose men kill, condones the killing, not perhaps by giving the order *to* kill, but by having men under his employ who have the heart *of* killers," Strong Wolf said bitterly. "He is no less guilty than if he himself had tied the rope around Son of Sky's neck."

"And what do we do about this atrocity against our people today?" White Beaver said, knowing Strong Wolf's strong feelings for peace.

"Yes, what is your plan, Strong Wolf?" Proud Heart said, his eyes questioning Strong Wolf.

"And what would *you* do were you chief and had choices to make about such deeds done today, Proud Heart?" Strong Wolf challenged. "One day you alone, when you are chief, will have to make choices like those facing me today, for *your* people."

"I would not have to think hard and long about that," Proud Heart said, his jaw tightening. "I would say go and destroy Jeremiah Bryant's ranch, but be careful not to kill any more white men."

Proud Heart looked down at his friend who lay dead in the sun, then looked at the Potawatomis warriors who always wished to see another sunrise so that they would be there for their children. "There have been enough killings today," he mumbled.

"Your thoughts match my own," Strong Wolf said, nodding.

He lifted Son Of Sky into his arms and carried him to his horse. He nodded to a warrior who knew by the silent order to remove the deer that now lay behind Strong Wolf's saddle.

The warrior removed the deer and placed it on his own horse, while Strong Wolf tied Son of Sky on his.

"The deer," White Beaver said. "What are we to do with them?"

"Did I not give my word to Patrick that I would bring more meat for his soldiers' tables?" Strong Wolf said, mounting his horse.

White Beaver nodded as he slowly swung himself into his saddle.

"I keep my word," Strong Wolf grumbled. "We will take the meat to the fort, then go home and deliver the dead to his loved ones. *Then* we will make plans for an attack. We *will* avenge the deaths of our downed brother!"

"It could start a war," Proud Heart said, eyeing Strong Wolf carefully.

"What we do is right, and let the white soldiers come. They will soon know they should not interfere in our time of vengeance," Strong Wolf said coldly. "I tire of having to look the other way when things against our people continue to happen!"

He gazed down at the three dead white men. Then he nodded to two of his warriors who had no deer tied to their steeds. "Get the white men," he flatly ordered. "We shall deliver them as well as deliver the meat."

"One look at the dead white men will cause us to become surrounded by soldiers," White Beaver softly argued.

"You do not understand," Strong Wolf said, leaning closer to White Beaver. "First we deliver these dead white men to Jeremiah Bryant's land. We leave them to be found by them, not by soldiers. Then we deliver the deer."

They rode off. They first threw the dead white men at the far edge of Jeremiah Bryant's ranch, then went and dumped the deer just outside of the gate at the fort.

When soldiers came and gaped openly at Strong Wolf, and then at the one fallen brother tied to the horse, Strong Wolf gazed at them with a silent loathing.

"Take the meat to your colonel, and also take him the news that, while hunting for meat for your tables, white men came and killed my brave as though he were nothing less than deer meat himself!" he shouted.

He then rode away, his heart thumping wildly within his chest, his anger so deep and hard to control.

He rode without stopping until he reached his village. Long shadows rippled over the ground, and as he gazed heavenward, he spied the Milky Way.

"Oh, bridge of souls," he whispered. "Where souls pass from one life to the other. Tonight, welcome one more of my people!"

Then he delivered the dead to the door of his family.

Strong Wolf cringed and closed his eyes as the wailing began.

24

I wandered lonely as a cloud that floats on high,
O'er vales and hills.
                                    —WILLIAM WORDSWORTH

Like a firefly, the moon broke through the trees.
Strong Wolf rode through the night with his warriors.
They all wore war shirts made from a soft piece of
buckskin with buffalo hair fringe on the sleeves and
across the front. Red, blue, yellow, and white quills
were sewn on them, each color of quills radiating from
the other.

When Jeremiah Bryant's ranch came into sight,
Strong Wolf lifted his rifle into the air as a silent command for his men to stop.

Proud Heart sidled his horse closer to Strong Wolf
as he stared at the corral at the far back of the ranch
grounds. He watched several horses scamper about,
whinnying. "Are the horses that carried the men today
on their attack against us in that fence?" he
whispered.

"Of that I am sure," Strong Wolf whispered back
harshly. "I have told everyone what to do. Now, let
us see that it is done!"

He looked over his shoulder as several of his men
lit torches. He nodded at others whose duties were to
set the horses free, then he settled into his saddle and

watched it all happen with Proud Heart and White Beaver leading the silent attack.

The horses were set free and scattered in all directions. The fences were knocked down and dragged away.

And then came the most triumphant moment of all, when the white men ran out of the bunkhouse, stumbling as they jerked on their breeches, shouting and cursing.

When Strong Wolf was certain that no more men were left in the bunkhouse, he gave a nod to his warriors who waited with their torches.

They smiled and nodded back at him, then rode off in a hard gallop toward the bunkhouse, the white men scattering and falling to the ground in the flurry of hoofbeats.

"It is as I suspected," Strong Wolf whispered to himself. "In the white men's haste to leave their quarters, they brought no weapons. The surprise visit by our warriors made them careless. As planned, it won't be necessary to kill any of them. We have taken away their mode of transportation. We are now burning their lodges."

He gazed over at the ranch house, and his smile faded when he saw Jeremiah Bryant step from his house with his wife close at his side. Jeremiah wore eyeglasses, and the fire reflected in their lenses.

"And now the debt is paid," Strong Wolf said beneath his breath.

He then turned his eyes to his men and shouted for them to leave. His plans had been carried out without anyone being harmed. It was time to return home to the peaceful side of life again.

As they rode off, Strong Wolf looked one last time over his shoulder. He smiled victoriously as he watched the ranch hands scrambling around with their buckets of water, splashing them on the bunkhouse that was a blazing inferno.

Then he turned his eyes straight ahead again and rode tall and proud in his saddle. Yet he hoped that tonight would not have to be repeated. He hoped that the message would be loud and clear to those who chose to kill the Potawatomis, that the Potawatomis would not slink away and let it be done to them like cowardly puppies whose tails hang limply between their hind legs.

They headed back toward their village, then Strong Wolf saw something in the distance that made his heart skip a beat. He looked toward the heavens at the reflection of fire in the sky, making the black inky sky of night turn to crimson.

"Do you see it?" Proud Heart shouted over at Strong Wolf. "Fire! And not set by us! It is far from the one we have just left behind."

"Let us go and see what is the cause!" Strong Wolf said, making a wide turn in the road, his men following.

Strong Wolf bent low over his horse as he followed the fire tracks in the sky, then when he drew close enough to see whose cabin was on fire, his heart sank and he felt ill inside.

"Claude Odum's!" White Beaver shouted, gazing over at Strong Heart. "Someone has set Claude Odum's cabin on fire!"

Not hearing anything, only feeling remorse, Strong Wolf broke away from the others and sent his powerful steed into a much harder gallop. His eyes never left the fiery inferno, knowing that if Claude Odum was inside the cabin, surely he could no longer be alive.

There was a small hope inside Strong Wolf's heart when, as he got closer, he saw that the back side of the cabin, where the huge stone fireplace reached halfway across the wall, was not yet in flames. If Claude had crawled to that part of the room, just possibly he would be alive. And surely he would have tried to get there, for a door was there, an escape to freedom.

Strong Wolf wheeled his horse to a shimmying stop and dismounted, then ran toward the cabin.

Proud Heart ran after him, shouting. "No!" he cried. "Strong Wolf! No! Do not try it! Do not go inside that cabin!"

His ears deaf to everything, except the pounding of his heart in his eagerness to try and save Claude Odum, the gentle man that he was, Strong Wolf ran to the well behind the house.

He dropped the bucket that was attached to a rope down into the water, gathered water into the bucket, then cranked the bucket back up and grabbed it. So that his whole body would be soaked before entering the fiery inferno, he poured the water over his head.

He then grabbed a blanket from his horse and soaked it in the water, then placed it around his head and ran toward the cabin door.

Proud Heart came to him and tried to grab him by the arm, but Strong Wolf yanked it away. "Your people!" Proud Heart cried. "Think of your people! Should you die . . . !"

Strong Wolf heard those words, yet paid no heed. A friend *of* his people might be dying among flames! He had to save him!

When Strong Wolf yanked the door open, a great burst of smoke and flames reached out for him, giving him a taste of what it was like inside the cabin.

But not to be dissuaded, his heart thundering, he took a wary step inside, then stumbled over something.

The flames bright, the heat intense, Strong Wolf

looked downward. His gut twisted when he saw Claude Odum stretched out on the floor, his clothes burned off his body, his skin scorched black.

Strong Wolf felt the strong urge to retch as the stench of burned flesh wafted up into his nose. He shook from head to toe in hard shudders, then composed himself enough to reach down and place his hands on the burned flesh of Claude's arms and dragged him outside, away from the fire.

Proud Heart and White Beaver went to Strong Wolf. They gasped, paled, then turned their eyes from the sight.

"Who could have done this?" Strong Wolf said, his teeth clenched, his face still hot from the flames.

"Someone who does not want us to have such a friend in the Kansas Territory," Proud Heart said, his voice hollow.

"And he *was* such a friend," Strong Wolf said, bending to kneel beside Claude. He took the blanket from around his shoulders and lay it over Claude, then turned toward the sound of approaching horsemen.

"Someone else has seen the flames in the sky tonight," White Beaver said, his voice wary. "We should have been home safe by now, then questions would not be asked so quickly of us."

"Let them be asked," Strong Wolf said, moving to his feet. He wiped some of the soot away from his eyes, then stood with his arms folded across his chest when Colonel Deshong and several of his men came to a halt on their horses a few feet away.

Strong Wolf didn't take his eyes off the colonel as Patrick came toward him, dressed in full uniform. Patrick rested a hand on a saber at his right side, his eyes on the fire, then on Strong Wolf.

Strong Wolf watched as the soldiers surrounded the

Potawatomis warriors, who were still on their horses clustered together.

"This time I don't have any choice but to arrest you, Strong Wolf," Patrick said, going to bend to a knee to take a look at Claude. He choked back the urge to retch, then moved to his feet and stood before Strong Wolf. "Two fires were set tonight, and after you were attacked today while on the hunt? It looks too suspicious to ignore, Strong Wolf."

Patrick nodded toward one of his men. "Tie his hands behind him," he ordered. "Let the others go. We can't arrest the entire Potawatomis nation. Strong Wolf is enough. He speaks and acts for all of his people."

Strong Wolf winced as tight-binding rawhide ropes were used to tie his wrists together behind him. He said nothing, for he would not humiliate himself tonight before his warriors, or the soldiers who were hell-bent on arresting him for something.

It was hard for Strong Wolf to understand why the colonel would think that he would kill Claude. Patrick knew that he and Claude had been the best of friends, whose hearts were linked together in camaraderie!

But Strong Wolf had to think that the arrest was made to keep face for the colonel. Someone had to be incarcerated for the crimes tonight. It might as well be an Indian!

"Strong Wolf, you will face a judge tomorrow." Patrick stared at Strong Wolf. "Now go peacefully to the guardhouse. Your fate is no longer in my hands."

His chin lifted, Strong Wolf went to his horse. With his hands tied behind him, he could not get into his saddle. Proud Heart came to him and helped him.

"What are we to do?" he whispered to Strong Wolf.

"Think, then act," Strong Wolf whispered back. "But do not chance losing any of our men, or people.

There are peaceful ways to settle this. Think about it. You will know the right answers."

Proud Heart nodded, then stepped aside as the colonel came and stared up at Strong Wolf, then at Proud Heart.

"Proud Heart, take your men back to your village and heed my warning well when I say do not come to the fort with the notion of attacking," Patrick said, his voice filled with warning. "One shot fired against us will mean the death of Strong Wolf."

Proud Heart glared at the colonel for a moment, gave Strong Wolf an uneasy stare, then stamped away and swung himself into his saddle.

Patrick appointed those who would ride with Strong Wolf. Others would stay behind and gather up Claude's remains, then take him to the fort for proper burial.

He mounted his horse and rode off, soon catching up with Strong Wolf, and rode beside him.

Strong Wolf could occasionally feel the colonel's eyes on him, but he ignored him. He stared straight ahead, knowing that he had done no wrong, except to avenge that which had happened to his people.

As for Claude Odum, Strong Wolf's heart ached. Then he scowled and thought of those who could be so heartless as to kill such an innocent, warmhearted man.

He wanted to blame one man. Tiny Sharp. But he didn't think that even he was this ruthless.

No, he doubted he would ever know who killed Claude, or why. Perhaps the fire had started by accident.

He wished to believe that. It was easier to live with.

Then his thoughts shifted to Hannah. What would she say when she discovered that he had been incarcerated? What would she do?

He only hoped that she would not become too hasty in her decisions. She did have an explosive, stubborn nature.

He knew he would not be kept in the guardhouse long, not with so many people out there to speak up in his behalf. Even the colonel should give this a second thought. Patrick knew that Strong Wolf was a man of peace. How could he ever think that he would do anything to harm Claude Odum?

Patrick surely knew that he didn't, yet had to play the role of a leader by arresting someone!

And too often it made a white leader look bigger in the eyes of the community of white people if an Indian was arrested.

If Strong Wolf discovered that was Patrick's only reason for incarcerating him, Patrick would then have an enemy for life, and not only Strong Wolf, but the whole tribe of Potawatomis!

The fort came into view beneath the bright splash of moonlight. The wide gates were open. Strong Wolf was taken between them and on to the guardhouse.

When his horse was stopped before the guardhouse, a soldier came and yanked Strong Wolf from the saddle, making him stumble and fall.

Disgraced, Strong Wolf glared up at Colonel Deshong as he came and stood over him.

Gently, Patrick reached a hand to Strong Wolf's shoulder and helped him up from the ground. "Strong Wolf, I don't like this at all," he mumbled. "But my hands are tied. You know that it looked bad as hell for you to get caught beside the burning cabin while another fire was set not all that far from Claude's. Being out with your warriors, wearing war shirts, you look damn responsible. I had no choice but to arrest you."

"You forget words of camaraderie so easily?"

Strong Wolf said as he was led toward the door of the guardhouse. "Where is your trust in this Potawatomis warrior? Where is your understanding?"

Patrick stopped and turned Strong Wolf to face him. "Strong Wolf, can you stand there and honestly say that you did not set fire to Jeremiah Bryant's bunkhouse? That you did not chase his horses out of the corral?" he accused. "I heard about the men attacking you and your warriors while you were on the hunt getting more meat for my men. I know that one of your warriors was killed. Can you say you did not avenge his death tonight? Can you?"

"I have my vengeance, yes," Strong Wolf answered. "We burned the bunkhouse tonight. We set the horses free. But I did not burn Claude Odum's lodge. I did not kill him. He ... was ... my friend."

Colonel Deshong's eyes wavered into Strong Wolf's, then he nodded at the soldiers. "Take him away," he commanded.

Strong Wolf spat at Colonel Deshong's feet. "I will spit on the steaks you have made out of the deer I brought you if I get the chance!" he snarled between clenched teeth. "Your men will starve before my people hunt for them again!"

He was yanked away and shoved to a cell inside the guardhouse. His ropes were cut. Then he was left alone, where only thin streamers of moonlight came through the bars of the window on the outside wall.

Strong Wolf looked around him. He who loved the open spaces was nauseated by the foul odor of the dingy cell. He stared down at a tattered mattress that lay on the rough board floor.

His gaze shifted elsewhere, his insides tightening as he watched venturesome mice creep out upon the floor and scamper around.

Strong Wolf went to the window and gripped the

iron bars. He peered outside, his heart aching to be free again to ride with Hannah, to lead her to a secret hiding place where they could make love.

He ached to be with his people, to teach, to *help*, to *lead*.

His thoughts went to Hannah again. "Will I ever again touch her soft skin?" he cried to the heavens.

25

Be strong!
We are not here to play, to dream, to drift!
                              —MALTBIE DAVENPORT BABCOCK

Anxious to get to Strong Wolf's village, to discuss
plans of marriage with him, Hannah rushed through
her morning chores of getting Chuck ready for the
long day ahead of him.

She had just stepped into the parlor, to retrieve his
cane that he had left there the night before, when
she heard Tiny laughing about something outside, just
beneath the open window as he talked with some of
the cowhands.

When Strong Wolf's name came up in the conversation, and Tiny laughed sarcastically, Hannah inched
over to the window. She slowly drew the thin curtain
aside and listened more closely, glad that she had
opened the window earlier.

"They've got him this time," Tiny said as he untied
his horse's reins from around a hitching rail. "I hope
he rots in that damn guardhouse."

Hannah gasped and paled. She moved directly in
front of the window. "What is that you are saying
about Strong Wolf?" she asked, leaning out so that
he could see her.

Tiny turned sharp, angry eyes at Hannah. "Your
Injun friend?" he snarled. "Seems your wedding might

be called off due to his pending death!" He laughed
boisterously when he saw the look of alarm in Hannah's eyes. "Yup. He's gone and got himself in a peck
of trouble, and I had nothing to do with it, either. So's
don't go rantin' and ravin' at me, accusin' me of one
thing or another."

"He's ... in ... jail ... ?" Hannah responded, her
insides turning to cold shivers of pain. "Why? What
happened?"

"Now, just look at this," Tiny said, laughing as he
looked over his shoulder at the men who were gathering around, listening. "She's got time for Tiny *now*.
Just look at her. The mention of Strong Wolf being
behind bars has tamed our little miss just a mite,
wouldn't you all say?"

No one said anything, or laughed along with Tiny.
They looked guardedly up at Hannah.

"You little twerp," she hissed. "I should've known
better than to ask you anything."

"Honey, what's the matter?" Chuck asked as he felt
his way into the room without his cane. "What's all
the commotion about? Who are you talking to?"

Hannah turned with a start. She stepped away from
the window, the curtain fluttering down behind her.
"Chuck," she said, her heart pounding in her fear of
what might have happened to Strong Wolf. "Tiny said
that Strong Wolf has been taken to the guardhouse at
Fort Leavenworth. Do you know anything about it?
Have you heard anything at all?"

"No, nothing," Chuck answered, glad to have the
cane when she brought it to him. "I'll get Tiny in here
and get the answers out of him, since he seems to
know so much about it."

"No, I don't want to talk to that terrible man,"
Hannah rebutted, her voice trembling. "I'll go to the
fort." She shook her head as she held her temples

between her hands. "No. I'll go to the Potawatomis village. I'll find out from them what happened. Something has to be done. Perhaps it already has been. Surely Proud Heart wouldn't allow his friend to stay in jail. What could Strong Wolf have done to cause such animosity on the part of Colonel Deshong? He's Strong Wolf's friend."

She swung away from Chuck and walked determinedly toward the door.

"No, Hannah," Chuck pleaded, turning as he saw her pass him, her movements only lights and shadows to him. "Don't get involved. Stay home. I'll send someone to the fort to get answers for you."

Hannah was dressed in a riding skirt and blouse, the sleeves rolled up past her elbow. Her delicate cheekbones bloomed with color as she anxiously rolled the sleeves down and buttoned them at her wrists. "No, Chuck," she said, now nervously combing her fingers through her hair. "I've got to get the answers for myself. I've got to do something about it!"

"Hannah, for Christ's sake, you are only one woman against a whole fort of men," Chuck scolded, going to the door with her as she swung it open. He listened to the sound of her boots as she took determined steps across the porch.

"I love him, Chuck," Hannah said over her shoulder as she rushed down the steps. She eyed the horses tied to the hitching rail. Without further thought, she yanked the reins of one of the horses from the rail, then swung herself into the saddle.

"Hey!" Tiny shouted, coming from around the side of the house. "Get off my horse. Damn it, Hannah, get . . . off . . . my horse!"

"Just shut up," Hannah railed, then wheeled the horse around and rode off.

"Hannah! Don't go!" Chuck shouted after her.

"You're going to get in trouble! Come back here, Hannah." His voice weakened. "Oh, Lord, Hannah, what am I going to do with you?"

"She's got too much spunk for her own good," Tiny growled, placing his fists on his hips. "Damn her all to hell. Why'd she have to take *my* horse, anyhow?"

"Tiny, if you'd have kept your mouth shut about Strong Wolf this morning, she'd not have taken off half-cocked," Chuck grumbled. Then he took a shaky step closer to the edge of the porch. "Tiny, tell me what happened. Why is Strong Wolf incarcerated? He and Colonel Deshong are supposed to be the best of friends."

"Seems Strong Wolf went on a burnin' and killin' spree last night, Chuck," Tiny said, taking pleasure in saying it.

"God, who'd he *kill*?" Chuck stammered. "What did he *burn*?"

"First he set fire to Jeremiah Bryant's bunkhouse," Tiny replied, slipping his thin hands into the front pockets of his breeches. "Then Claude Odum's place was burned. Claude died in the flames."

"No," Chuck said, paling. "Claude Odum was one of the finest men around." He paused, then said slowly and softly. "And he was Strong Wolf's friend." He firmed his jaw. "Anyone who knows Strong Wolf at all, knows he wouldn't be responsible for Claude Odum's death. Someone else must have set the fire that killed him."

"Maybe so," Tiny admitted, shrugging. "But as for Jeremiah's place, it's out and out vengeance. Some of Jeremiah's cowhands killed one of Strong Wolf's warriors yesterday. Strong Wolf is guilty as hell of having burned the bunkhouse." He paused, then said, "And not only that. He also chased all of Jeremiah's horses from the corral."

"This doesn't sound at all like Strong Wolf," Chuck said, leaning his full weight on the cane. "He's a peace-loving man."

"And so he likes for everyone to believe," Tiny mocked.

He went up the stairs and placed a gentle hand to Chuck's arm. "Come inside, Chuck," he said, his eyes gleaming as he stared over at him. "Let's go over some of the figures in the ledger. I'm having some trouble balancing the pages."

"Yes, I wanted to talk to you about that," Chuck agreed, nodding.

Chuck followed Tiny into the house, then took one last look over his shoulder as he tried to see Hannah in the distance.

26

How you 'mid other forms I seek—
Oh, love more real than though
    such dreams *were* true.
If you but knew!
    —ANONYMOUS, 19TH CENTURY

Hannah slapped the reins and nudged the horse's
flanks with her booted heels. She just couldn't go fast
enough. She needed answers now! Surely Tiny had
made it all up. If not, surely someone would have let
her know what had happened to Strong Wolf?

Especially Proud Heart. He knew how much she
loved Strong Wolf. He knew they were making plans
of marriage! It just wasn't fair that she would have
been left out of something like this.

She reached her eyes to the blue heavens. "Oh,
Lord, please let this all be some sort of ugly joke
made up inside of Tiny's twisted brain," she whispered. "Please let me find Strong Wolf at his lodge.
Please, oh, please, let him be all right!"

When she came to a fork in the road, one that
would take her to the fort, the other that led to Strong
Wolf's village, she drew in a tight rein. "Oh, what
should I do?" she cried, looking down one avenue and
then the other.

Still feeling it was best to go to the village first,

Hannah made the turn in the road that would take her there.

Again she pushed the horse to its limits in speed. The wind blew through Hannah's hair, tangling it. The sun beat down onto her face, burning it.

She rode hard until finally she saw the village a short distance away. She sank her heels into the horse's flanks and her knees into its sides, sending it again into a hard gallop.

Breathless, Hannah entered the village. She patted the horse's neck, finding it lathered with sweat. "Sorry, boy," she whispered. "I don't make it a habit of pushing a horse so hard."

As she rode farther into the village, she became aware of people standing outside in clusters, wailing, as though they were mourning someone's death.

"No," she whispered to herself, dying inside at what it could mean. What if Strong Wolf *had* been imprisoned? What if he had not been given a trial and had been hung at sunup?

This thought made her head reel, then she caught sight of Proud Heart and several warriors getting their horses from the corral.

She smacked Tiny's horse on the rump and rode in a hard gallop to the corral.

When she got there, she drew a tight rein beside Proud Heart, who was just ready to mount his steed.

"What's happened?" she cried, near to tears from frustration.

"Have you heard about Strong Wolf?" Proud Heart asked, swinging himself into his saddle.

"I heard that he had been arrested," Hannah said, imploring him with questioning eyes. "Was he?"

"Yes, and we are making plans to release him," Proud Heart informed. "Tonight. When the moon is low in the sky. We will go and take Strong Wolf from the fort. We are leaving now to study the fort walls, to make plans on how we will enter."

Hannah's heart skipped a beat. "You are planning to go at night and get him from the fort?" she faltered, her voice hoarse in her fears.

"Yes, that is the only way," Proud Heart said, nodding.

"No!" she screamed. "That is not the answer! Strong Wolf will then be classified a 'renegade'—a fugitive. We must all come together as one heartbeat and go speak in the defense of Strong Wolf, the proud Potawatomis leader!"

She then leaned forward, her voice lower in pitch as she prodded Proud Heart for answers. "Tell me what happened," she demanded. "Everything."

Proud Heart proceeded to tell her about the fire they set, and then about finding Claude Odum dead at his house.

She lowered her eyes at the thought of how Claude had died. Feeling ill at her stomach, she swallowed hard.

Then she turned angry eyes up at Proud Heart. "How could Colonel Deshong have, for one minute, thought that Strong Wolf would kill his friend?" she remarked, her voice shaking. "It doesn't make any sense. We must do something to stop this lunacy."

She thought for a while, then leaned closer to Proud Heart. "Send for the two braves who have been recently attacked and beaten by white men," she said flatly.

"And why would I do that?" Proud Heart questioned, getting annoyed by her persistence.

"White men caused their bruises and contusions," Hannah said matter-of-factly. "They must go to the fort with us and show their wounds to the colonel."

"One of our warriors is dead because of white

men," Proud Heart retorted sarcastically. "Do we take him and show him also to the white men at the fort? You see, they *have* already seen them. It meant nothing to them."

He folded his arms angrily over his bare chest. "I do not wish to do as you asked," he said stiffly.

Hannah reached over and placed a gentle hand onto his arm. "Please," she begged. "But not for me, Proud Heart. For Strong Wolf. We must try everything to prove that what he did last night by burning the bunkhouse and letting the horses free was justified because of what was done recently to his people. He is a proud man. He could not just stand by and take it. He had to show some force, to prove that white men can't just keep on taking from Strong Wolf and his people while he stands by like a coward and allows it."

Proud Heart still said nothing.

"Proud Heart, give my idea a chance," Hannah said softly. "It's much better than going at night to try and get Strong Wolf from the guardhouse. You know that many lives might be taken on both sides. My way, a peaceful approach at trying to prove Strong Wolf's innocence, might work. Please ... give ... it a try?"

Proud Heart thought hard for a moment, then nodded. "Yes, we will give it a try, and then if it does not work, tonight we take him by force," he stated.

"Thank you," Hannah said, beaming.

She sat quiet in the saddle as the two braves were sent for. When they came to the corral, looking puzzled, she smiled down at them.

"Take off your shirts," she ordered softly. "You must show your scars, bruises, and contusions to the general at Fort Leavenworth."

The braves turned questioning eyes at Proud Heart. He nodded, giving his consent.

Once their shirts were removed and they were on a horse, Hannah thought of something else.

"Proud Heart, get the fallen warrior's bow," she commanded, flinching when he gave her an angry stare. "Proud Heart, we must take that bow to the colonel and tell him that it belongs to the dead warrior, and tell him that his bow or any other Potawatomis' bows will never be used for hunting again for the men at the fort."

Proud Heart saw the logic in the suggestion. He sent a warrior after the bow.

"Something more, Proud Heart," Hannah added quickly. "Are there any gifts that Claude Odum gave to Strong Wolf that you can show the colonel, as solid proof of Strong Wolf and the agent's undying loyalty to one another? To prove once and for all that Strong Wolf could never kill him?"

Proud Heart's eyes widened. "Yes, there are such gifts," he said revealed bitterly. "A beautiful pipe and shell beads of wampumpeag, or wampum, have been exchanged as signs of good faith and friendship between Strong Wolf and the agent."

"Please get them so that we can take them to the fort and show them to the colonel," she said, seeing him stiffening at the suggestion. "Please, Proud Heart. Do this one last thing. I won't ask anything else of you, except to go with me and stand at my side as I argue for Strong Wolf's release."

After these were secured in a buckskin bag, and the bow was there, ready to be taken to the fort, Hannah smiled a silent thank you to Proud Heart, and then to the rest of the warriors. She was in awe of how they trusted her.

Yet why would they not? she thought to herself. She had been chosen by their leader to soon join them in the capacity of 'wife'!

Sitting proudly tall in the saddle, Hannah left the Potawatomis village with a soft prayer in her heart that the colonel would listen and believe!

27

I crave the haven that in your dear heart lies
After all toil is done.

—CHARLES TOWNE

Colonel Deshong was awestruck by Hannah and how she had so suddenly assumed the role of spokesperson for the Potawatomis in Strong Wolf's absence while he was imprisoned. He sat behind his desk and looked slowly from Hannah to all of the warriors who stood crowded in his tiny office.

His eyes stopped on Proud Heart, recognizing him as Strong Wolf's best friend. He was not Potawatomis, by birth, yet was there also to defend the rights of his friend.

Her eyes filled with defiance, Hannah glared moments longer down at the colonel, then gestured with a hand toward one of the braves who wore no shirt. "Wind on Wings, please step forward," she then said, giving him a soft gaze.

Wide-eyed, his shoulders proudly squared, although he still ached from the recent beating, Wind on Wings came and stood at Hannah's right side.

She turned to Bird in Ground. "Bird in Ground, please come and also stand beside me," she murmured, smiling as he came to her left side.

"Colonel Deshong, I have proof here of the recent beatings done at the hands of whites." Hannah's eyes locked with the colonel's. "Each of the braves were accosted. One while on the hunt. The other, while innocently getting honey to take home to his family. Both braves were unmercifully beaten and left to die. But being strong-willed, and strong of heart, they survived."

She turned to Wind on Wings. She ran a hand over the scars on his chest. "He will be scarred for life," she said, her voice breaking.

Then she ran her hands over Bird in Ground's arms and chest, then turned his back toward the colonel. "He will also be scarred for life, not only physically, but mentally as well," she added solemnly. "I am certain that he is confused by having done nothing to bring on such a beating. He may never understand, except to know not to trust white people ever again, and to hate most of them with a passion."

"I see the braves, and I find it unfortunate that some misguided men sought to have some fun at their expense," Patrick replied, nervously drumming his fingers on the top of his desk. "But I see no connection in them and Strong Wolf's incarceration."

"Fun?" Hannah inquired, her voice lifting a pitch higher. "You call what those men did to these braves fun? Surely you have chosen the wrong way in which to phrase your feelings."

"All right," Colonel Deshong said, sighing heavily. "I didn't mean to say ..."

"Colonel, too often apologies come when something more must be done concerning the atrocities against the Potawatomis," Hannah stated, placing her hands on her hips. She swallowed hard. "Do you recall, sir, that only yesterday Strong Wolf brought you more meat for your dinner tables?"

"Yes, and I am grateful," he admitted awkwardly. "But still ..."

Hannah interrupted him again. "Do you recall, sir, that while Strong Wolf was on the hunt for your men, some white men came and ambushed them, killing one of his most valiant warriors?"

"Yes, I am aware, but ..." he mumbled, Hannah again interrupting.

"Sir, since nothing is ever done against those who take advantage of the Potawatomis, and Strong Wolf knew who was responsible at least for the *killing,* he took it upon himself to avenge the life of his loved one," she continued, her voice shaking with emotion. "While he raided the ranch, he killed no one. He only destroyed a bunkhouse and set some horses free. Now, I ask you, *sir,* had it been *you* who were ambushed by Indians, and your men were slaughtered by them, would *you* just go and burn a lodge and set animals free, or would *you* command your soldiers to go and kill and maim the Indians who were responsible?"

"I ..." Patrick started to say.

But Hannah still was not ready to let him say his piece. As long as he would tolerate her standing there, in defense of the Potawatomis, she would.

"Sir, did you not also accuse Strong Wolf of killing Claude Odum and setting fire to his cabin?" she inquired, her eyes narrowing when his eyes took on an uneasiness as they wavered.

"Strong Wolf had already burned one building, who was not to say whether or not he set the other fire in his frenzied anger over the killing of his warrior?" Patrick protested quickly, before she interrupted him again.

"Haven't you seen the kinship between Claude and Strong Wolf?" Hannah pleaded, her voice softening. "Didn't you know just how much they admired one another?"

"Yes, but when someone gets angry, all reason can slip from their mind," Colonel Deshong countered, placing his fingertips together before him. "Hannah, now is that all? I've things to do besides listen to your ramblings."

"Haven't I made any sense at all to you?" Hannah argued, her voice breaking when she felt that she might lose the battle for Strong Wolf's release. "You have been a friend with Strong Wolf since he arrived at the Kansas Territory. How could you not understand him better than this? You know that he is a man of peace. Last night, when he avenged the death of his warrior, he could have wreaked havoc along the countryside. Yet, he chose a more peaceful way to make his point. You should commend him for saving lives, not condemn him for the little thing that he did."

She turned to Proud Heart. "Proud Heart, please bring the bag forth," she said, reaching a hand out for the bag.

When he gave it to her, she turned toward Patrick again. She gently placed the buckskin bag on his desk in front of him. "Please look at what's inside the bag."

"Hannah, I . . ." Colonel Deshong was again interrupted by her.

"Sir, you have arrested Strong Wolf for the death of Claude Odum," Hannah blurted. "Please see what is inside the bag. After seeing the gifts of friendship from Claude to Strong Wolf, can you honestly say that Strong Wolf could have killed this man?"

Sighing, Patrick slipped a hand inside the bag. First he pulled out the pipe: a peace pipe. Then he pulled out the wampum.

He placed them before him and stared at them, tears filling his eyes as he recalled the very moments these gifts were given to Strong Wolf. He was at

Strong Wolf's village with Claude when the Indian agent had presented the gifts to Strong Wolf.

In return, Strong Wolf had given Claude a thick bearskin robe, and then had turned to Patrick with the same sort of skin, except that his was made of perfectly white rabbit pelts.

That day, everyone's friendship had been strengthened. And no, he did not see how things could have changed between Claude and Strong Wolf.

No, in truth, he could not see how Strong Wolf could have set fire to his friend's lodge.

No, he could no longer condemn Strong Wolf for having taken the law into his own hands, by burning the one outbuilding at Jeremiah Bryant's ranch or setting the horses free. The horses had been rounded up. Not one had been lost to Jeremiah except for those who had been killed during the raid on Strong Wolf and his warriors.

Yet Jeremiah would not set aside his anger for Strong Wolf having done what he did to the bunkhouse.

But that didn't mean that Patrick had to keep Strong Wolf locked up like a common, ordinary thief. Everything that Hannah had said now hit him like a cold splash of water in the face. Too many things came to mind: his times with Strong Wolf, their camaraderie, Strong Wolf's utter kindness toward mankind.

"I've been wrong," he said, placing the articles back inside the bag.

Hannah's heart skipped a beat. She was almost afraid to breathe, fearing that her next breath and heartbeat would turn the colonel back to being stubborn, whereas she *had* heard him just say that he had been wrong!

She gave Proud Heart a flickering smile, then turned eager eyes back to Patrick and waited to see what he

might say next. She crossed her fingers behind her,
hoping that he would say all of the right things.

"Yes, I've been wrong about a lot of things in my
lifetime," he acknowledged handing, the bag back
toward Hannah.

Her fingers trembled as she took it.

"And, by damn, I was wrong to arrest Strong Wolf,"
he admitted, moving quickly up from his chair. "The
good he has done outweighs the bad." He gazed at
the braves' scars and swallowed hard. "It is with much
regret that I couldn't have stopped that from happening to those braves."

He gazed over at Hannah, apology in his eyes. "But
I can't be everywhere all of the time, watching those
white men who still see Indians as savages and something to mock and sometimes ... kill ..." he stammered. He walked from behind his desk. He stood
before Hannah. "Come with me. Let us set Strong
Wolf free."

Tears of joy, of gratitude, splashed into Hannah's
eyes. She wanted to fling herself into Patrick's arms,
but refrained from doing it. She would never forget
that he had made Strong Wolf stay one whole night
behind bars. That was a sin in itself.

"Thank you," she uttered, swallowing hard.

Proud Heart came to her and hugged her, then they
followed the colonel from his cabin.

The Potawatomis warriors following behind, they all
walked across the sun-drenched courtyard until they
reached the guardhouse.

Only Hannah and Proud Heart were allowed inside
the guardhouse. And when Hannah saw Strong Wolf
behind the bars, clutching them, everything within her
felt that deep hurting pain of remorse over him having
been treated so badly.

She ran to the bars and twined her fingers through

his. "Darling," she whispered, their eyes touching, as though they were a caress. "I'm so sorry. I wish I had known last night. I . . . would . . . have come *then*."

Proud Heart stepped up to the cell. "My friend, you are to be released," he announced, reaching through the bars to grasp a friendly hand onto Strong Wolf's shoulder. "And you have Hannah to thank. Her words have set you free."

Strong Wolf gazed still into Hannah's eyes. "My woman spoke in my behalf?" he marveled.

"I said what I felt," Hannah said, tears streaming down her cheeks. "I told the *truth*. Patrick listened. But he had forgotten for a while that he was a friend."

"And so let's get it done," Patrick said as he stepped up beside Hannah with a thick ring of keys.

Hannah stepped aside and watched Patrick place the key in the lock, her pulse anxiously racing for the moment that Strong Wolf could step from behind those bars. She felt proud and relieved that she had been able to talk sense into the colonel. If she hadn't been able to, some judge could have set down a sentencing of hanging.

Now no judge would be required. Colonel Deshong had become judge and jury the moment he had placed the key into the lock that would release Strong Wolf to freedom.

The door creaked open. Strong Wolf stepped from the cell and grabbed Hannah into his arms. He held her close, his heart hammering like claps of thunder within his chest. "Thank you," he whispered as he placed his lips against Hannah's ear. "My woman, I will never forget what you did today. Never."

"Patrick could have ignored me," Hannah said, stepping softly way from him as he embraced Proud Heart long and hard.

Hannah turned smiling eyes over at Colonel De-shong. "Thank you. I'll be forever grateful."

Patrick nodded, then went to Strong Wolf and reached out a hand of friendship. "I apologize for having wrongly incarcerated you," he professed. "Can we place it behind us and move forward into a future of newfound trusts and friendships?"

Strong Wolf's spine stiffened, then he slowly reached his hand out and clasped his fingers around the colonel's hand. "Trust and friendship," he said, seeing a sudden relief rush into Patrick's eyes.

"From today forth, never again shall I be so quick to judge *any*one," Patrick declared. "I am truly sorry, Strong Wolf."

"I have one request," Strong Wolf said, easing his hand to his side.

"That is?" Patrick asked, forking an eyebrow.

"I would like to have the body of Claude Odum to bury among my people, since he has no family of his own to mourn him," Strong Wolf said solemnly.

Hannah placed a hand to her lips, touched to her very core over Strong Wolf's continued show of feelings for those he cared for. She gave Patrick an "I told you so" look, then wiped tears from her eyes as Patrick agreed to give up Claude's body to Strong Wolf.

When Strong Wolf stepped outside and saw his warriors waiting for him, he was touched deeply by their show of love. He took the time to embrace each and every one, lingering longer on the injured braves.

Then he turned and smiled at Hannah as she came and stood with him. He quickly embraced her again. "You have such a big heart," he said, reveling in the feel of her body against his. "Ah, but I chose well when I chose you to be my wife."

Through the long night, thoughts of her had made

him stay sane, as rats and mice came and went from his cell.

"I may not always be able to be as convincing as I was today." She laughed softly.

"I do not doubt anything that you set your heart to," Strong Wolf said, then eased away from her and gazed at the two braves again.

He then questioned Hannah with his eyes.

She saw the questioning, and how he had stared at the braves. "I urged them to come today, to show the colonel the viciousness of their attackers," she explained. "That caused him to rethink your being incarcerated."

"Yes, she's quite a smooth talker," Patrick said, coming to swing an arm around Strong Wolf's shoulder. "And like I said before, if she wasn't already spoken for, I might give you a run for the money."

All the while Patrick was talking to Strong Wolf, his eyes and thoughts were elsewhere. Claude Odum's body had just been brought out and placed on a flatbed wagon, then covered with a blanket. He stepped away from the colonel and stood beside the wagon. He stared down at the covered body, then gazed over at Hannah and Proud Heart.

"It is time for us to pay respects to our dearly departed," he said solemnly.

Hannah went to Strong Wolf. "I shall ride in the wagon," she murmured. She tied her pony to the back of the wagon as Strong Wolf's horse was brought to him.

Soon they were on their way back to the village in a solemn, slow procession, the presence of Claude having taken away their jubilance of Strong Wolf having been released.

When they arrived at the village, the people came in a rush toward Strong Wolf. He dismounted and received the loving arms of welcome as each of his people took time to embrace him.

And then everyone followed Strong Wolf as he carried Claude to the burial grounds of his people. "He will have a white man's burial," he said as he nodded for one of his warriors to dig the grave.

With no casket available, Claude's body was wrapped in thick layers of sheets of birch bark, then lowered into the ground.

Hannah stood over the grave and spoke verses that she had memorized from the Bible, that she had learned while attending church as a child.

Strong Wolf said his own words for his friend over the body, then stepped aside and watched as dirt was shoved into the grave.

Hannah gathered wildflowers and placed them on the mound of dirt after the grave was fully covered.

They left the grave site. Hannah went with Strong Wolf to his lodge. They embraced again.

"I must be alone with my thoughts," he then said as he stepped away from her.

"As I must return to the ranch, to reassure my brother that I did not get myself in trouble by coming to your aid today," Hannah said. She flung herself into Strong Wolf's arms again. "I'm so glad that you are no longer in that dreadful cell. Oh, how I love you."

He kissed her long and hard, then stepped away from her. "Go, my woman," he said softly. "Our time together will be sweeter another day. Much lies heavy on my heart."

"I know," Hannah murmured. He took her hand and walked her outside to her horse. It had been untied from the wagon.

She swung herself into the saddle. He reached up and took her hand and held it a moment longer, then gave it up to her. "Soon, my woman," he said. "We shall be together again soon, when these things that trouble me are finally swept away, as only bitter memories."

She nodded, slipped her hand free, and rode away. As she left the village, she was aware of the sky darkening. She gazed up and watched thick thunderheads gathering in the east. Overhead, the loud hacking call of the rain crow predicted rain.

She snapped her reins and rode harder, in a fast gallop, hoping to get home before the heavens opened up in a torrent of rain.

Strong Wolf went to a grove of silver birches just outside of his village, where he could be alone with his thoughts. As lightning zigzagged across the darkening heavens in lurid, vivid flashes, he talked to the tree spirits, the wild thunder echoing Strong Wolf's heartbeats as he sat there so filled with tumultuous emotions.

It was awhile before the rain set in, enough time, he hoped, for Hannah to get safely home.

Then when the rain began to fall, he lifted his eyes to the heavens and let himself be cleansed of remorse and hatred against the white men who had gone against him and his people.

28

I will share with thee my sorrows,
And thou thy joys with me.
—CHARLES JEFFERYS

Chilled to the bone from the rain, Hannah returned home. Soaking wet, she stood on the porch and stared up at the play of lightning in the sky. Listening to the thunder, she didn't hear Chuck come to the door, telling her to come in out of the rain.

She was filled with many emotions. She had never truly known just how deeply resentments lay against the red man, until now. It was heartbreaking to witness, especially when that red man was the man she loved with her very soul!

"Hannah!" Chuck said, grabbing her arm. "Come inside! Do you want to get a death of cold?"

Hannah came suddenly out of her reverie. She looked quickly over at Chuck.

He held her close, then went with her back inside the house. "Tell me what happened," he said as he shut the door behind them.

"He is free," Hannah said, slipping her boots off. "But Lord, although free, think of the scars left inside him over this horrible mistake!"

"He's strong," Chuck reassured. "He will come out of this, unscathed. You will see, Hannah. He's a fighter. He will never let anything take away his courage, his *fight*, his pride."

Then he reached out and touched her hair, then her clothes. "Sis, you've got to get out of those wet clothes," he said.

She nodded and fled to her bedroom.

As she stripped herself nude, she couldn't get Strong Wolf off her mind. He seemed so quick to send her away today, she thought to herself.

She could not help but wonder if his one night of confinement might have given him time to think over this notion of marrying a white woman.

Had he only pretended to be happy to see her, when deep down inside he resented her along with the rest of the white community?

She bit her lower lip, the thought of possibly losing him almost too much to bear.

29

I want you when in dreams I still remember,
The ling'ring of your kiss.
                                    —ARTHUR GILLOM

Because of the dangers that always threatened travelers these days, Strong Wolf had decided that he didn't
want Hannah to ride alone anymore. He was on his
way to her house now, to escort her back to the
village.

When a loud whistle reverberated through the air,
Strong Wolf drew a tight rein and wheeled his horse
to a quick stop. He gazed in the direction of the Kansas River, then he heard the whistle again.

The whistle continued this time, shrieking over and
over again. It sounded as though a riverboat might be
in some sort of trouble.

Then Strong Wolf remembered what Colonel Deshong had said about the riverboats not getting
through because of cholera. Did the boat's presence
in the river today mean that the fear of the disease
was now over?

He thought about Patrick and the men under his
command at Fort Leavenworth. It was best for them
that the boats were getting through again with supplies. Strong Wolf would never again send his men
out on the hunt for them. He had been humiliated for
the last time by white men.

He had decided that except for his love for Hannah and his association with her family, there would be few alliances with white people. When Claude Odum had died, Strong Wolf realized that the Potawatomis would be blamed for what, in fact, white men did to themselves.

It was going to to be a new world for the Potawatomis.

There *was* going to be one more exception. He would allow one more white person in his village besides Hannah. Word had been received that a white teacher would be arriving soon, to set up a schoolhouse in his village for the children; they would be taught the same subjects as white children.

He had requested this teacher long ago, and had only recently received a positive response.

"Perhaps she is on the boat arriving today," he whispered to himself. He was glad that the teacher was going to be a woman. It would be easier for the teacher to gain the trust of the Potawatomis children, whose trust in white men had waned since the recent experiences with them.

From the children's experience with Hannah, they had learned that white women could be trusted.

Also Strong Wolf had felt that having a white woman teacher living at his village would give Hannah someone of her own kind to befriend once she came to him as his wife. Although he wished for Hannah to learn all things Potawatomis, he knew the importance of her having someone of her own culture to talk with.

"In time, things *will* come together for me and my woman," Strong Wolf whispered to himself.

The constant, troubling whistle wafting from the river made Strong Wolf change the direction of his travel. He rode in that direction.

But when he heard the thundering of hoofbeats coming up from behind him, he turned and looked in wonder at Proud Heart as he rode toward him with several warriors.

Proud Heart reined in at Strong Wolf's side. "The constant whistling," he said, looking in the direction of the river. "It is frightening our people. What do you think is the cause?"

"Whatever it is, I do not see how it could mean anything good," Strong Wolf said, frowning over at Proud Heart. He reached a hand and placed it on his friend's shoulder. "It is good to see you care so much for my people. It will be hard to say farewell when you take over the leadership of the Chippewa in place of your chieftain father. I will miss your friendship, Proud Heart. But I will understand your absence. You and I will be following the calling of our people. I will be a Potawatomis chief. You will be Chippewa chief. It will be from the heart that we both lead our people."

"Yes, and Father has spoken recently of giving up the title of chief. I will be saying a farewell to you and your people before I wish to," Proud Heart said, then tensed and looked toward the river when the whistle started its loud blasts again.

"Let us go now to the river," Strong Wolf said. "Then I must make haste to my woman before she thinks that I have forgotten about her."

"She knows that you could never forget her," Proud Heart said, chuckling. "Your hearts are twined together as one heartbeat. It was your destiny to meet."

"Yes, our destiny," Strong Wolf said, sinking his heels into the flanks of his horse, sending it into a gallop beside Proud Heart's.

His gaze was drawn elsewhere as Hawk rode up among the other warriors and made himself known, surprising Strong Wolf since Hawk had been avoiding him.

"And so you also are curious about the noise that has startled the birds out of the trees?" Strong Wolf said, arching an eyebrow over at Hawk. "Hawk, your mother will die many deaths inside when she learns that you have aligned yourself with he whom she considers her enemy."

"I should have never listened to her," Hawk grumbled. "I was but a woman while under her guidance! She is a misguided lady. How could I have not seen that?"

"Your mother is beautiful and has persuasive ways, that is why," Strong Wolf said. "Did she not use her charm on your father to get him to marry her? I am sure that he has regretted often his weakness in the eyes of a woman."

"No, no regret is felt on his part, or he would have sent her away and married another," Hawk said. "Even with all of her faults, Father loves Mother. He has seen the goodness in her also. That is why he still loves her."

As they came closer and closer to the river, it was impossible to carry on any more conversation. The whistle became louder and louder.

When they finally reached the river, they drew tight rein and stared at the great white riverboat, its smokestack puffing out billows of black smoke into the air. Strong Wolf noticed that not all that many men were visible on the decks of the ship, which seemed strange to him. He had seen the arrival of riverboats more than once at Fort Leavenworth, and always the tiered decks were packed with throngs of people.

Today there were no people at the rails.

He made out the captain of the boat as he stood just outside the captain's cabin, his hand constantly tugging on the handle that made the whistle continue its blasts.

Then Strong Wolf gazed elsewhere. He now saw why the boat captain was trying to draw attention to the riverboat. He needed help. His great white ship was stuck. And Strong Wolf understood why. This was a particular bend in the river that he had come to know over the years. It was an oxbow that almost doubled back on itself. A sandbar crept way out into the bend before dropping away into a twenty-foot hole choked with logs, tree limbs, and other assorted brush. The river had claimed many canoes. Now it had claimed a huge riverboat.

Only moments ago, while thinking about how harshly he felt about most white people, Strong Wolf glared at the riverboat. Until the recent humiliating experiences with the white people, Strong Wolf would have helped dislodge the boat with his strong warriors.

But now? He was not sure. If he got involved with white people again, he might be asking for more trouble and humiliation.

Yet he saw this as an opportunity to once again show the goodness of the Potawatomis and cause the white people to be ashamed for their devious actions against them.

He looked over his shoulder at his warriors. "Let us go and lend our muscle to those who are in trouble!" he shouted, a quick decision having been made.

Their chins held high, their shoulders squared, they all rode off toward the riverboat.

30

We ought to be together, you and I.
                    —HENRY ALFORD

Hannah and Chuck stood at the opened door, listening to incessant whistling that came from the riverboat. "They must be in some sort of trouble," Chuck said, then stepped outside on the porch just as Tiny and several of the cowhands came toward them.

Hannah went outside on the porch with Chuck. She glared at Tiny as he gazed up at her, then focused his attention on Chuck.

"Should we go and see what's wrong?" Tiny asked. "Should we see if we can give a helping hand?"

"Yes, I think that's best," Chuck said, nodding. "It's probably that damn sandbar. If there's a captain aboard the boat that's not familiar with the river, he wouldn't know to watch out for that sandbar. It kind of sneaks up on you."

"I'm going to go with them," Hannah said, rushing down the steps. "I'm sure several people from Saint Louis could be on the boat. Maybe it's someone we know, Chuck."

"I don't think it's best, Hannah," Chuck said, reaching a hand out toward her shadow image. "Remember the cholera plague that has kept the boats upstream. There might still be a danger of it being transmitted by those who are on board the boat today."

"Surely there is no danger," Hannah said, untying her pinto's reins from the hitching rail. She went and swung herself into the saddle. "The authorities upriver wouldn't have let a boat travel downriver if there was still a danger of someone carrying cholera on board the boat."

"Hannah, don't be so bullheaded," Chuck said, feeling for the steps with his cane. "Come, now, Hannah. Stay behind. Let the men take care of things."

"Chuck, I'll not be gone for long," Hannah said, wheeling her horse around, riding away.

Tiny and his men soon caught up with her. She ignored Tiny as he sidled his horse too close to her pinto. And she knew that she had been wrong to go against her brother's wishes. But she wanted to investigate herself what was happening on the river today. Could the wires to her parents and sister have already arrived? Could they have decided to come ahead and surprise her instead of letting her know by wire?

The one thing she dreaded was the possibility of her father coming with the intent of stopping the marriage. What worried her most was that he was more stubborn than herself. He might even try to hog-tie her to stop her from getting married.

She smiled slowly at the thought, knowing that Strong Wolf, being obstinate himself, would intervene in any scheme of her father's.

Suddenly the whistle stopped. Hannah wondered if that meant no one was stopping off at Fort Leavenworth. A keen disappointment assailed her, for she still worried about her parents' reactions to the wire.

But the boat was still there. She could hardly believe her eyes as she stared at Strong Wolf and several of his warriors in the water, trying to remove the debris that the boat was stuck in.

"Seems he never learns his lesson," Tiny snarled.

"He sticks his nose into all of the white man's business."

"He's trying to *help* the white people," Hannah said, frowning at him. "Can't you ever give Strong Wolf any credit for the good that he does? For his generous nature? It's men like you who have caused the Indians so much grief. I would suggest you go back to the ranch. You don't want to dirty your hands, do you, by helping Strong Wolf and his warriors try to get the riverboat unlodged?"

Tiny said nothing back to her. Only glared. They rode onward.

Just as Hannah drew a tight rein beside the riverboat, Strong Wolf and his men came from the water, drenched with mud and debris up to their waists.

Hannah slid out of her saddle and ran to Strong Wolf. "Lord, aren't you a sight," she said, her eyes dancing into his.

Finding no humor in what she said, so disgruntled by not being able to dislodge the riverboat, Strong Wolf sighed heavily. "It is not going anywhere," he said as he glared at the boat.

Hannah half heard what he said, for she was now staring up at the decks of the riverboat, stunned to see no one but a scant crew standing there. And she knew that riverboats did not travel without passengers.

When the gangplank was lowered to the land and the captain came down from the boat, Hannah stood stiffly at Strong Wolf's side. The captain's eyes sank into his face, in dark hollows. His white uniform was stained and dirty. He appeared not to have shaved for days, gray whiskers thick on his face.

"I want to thank you for lending a hand," Captain Abbott said, lifting a trembling hand toward Strong Wolf for a handshake. "My men don't have much strength. That's why I didn't offer their help."

"What's wrong with the men?" Hannah asked, her voice wary. "And why don't I see any passengers on your ship?"

Captain Abbott gave her a wavering stare. "Miss, I hate to say that it was my impression that it was safe to travel without the fear of cholera," he said thickly. "But it took only one ill passenger to make me realize that I was wrong. I was advised against it. I paid no heed to the advice."

Hannah paled. "Are you saying that those on board your boat are ill with cholera?" she gasped, her thoughts returning to her parents and sister. Oh, surely they wouldn't be on board. She prayed there had not been enough time since she had sent the wires for them to have made plans of travel.

"Yes, seems so," Captain Abbott said, dropping his hand to his side after giving Strong Wolf a weak handshake. "Thank God, though, most of the crew isn't sick with the disease. They are just worn out from caring for those who are."

He took a quick look over his shoulder at the boat, then looked solemnly at Hannah again. "We had a doctor on board the boat, or more would have died," he said.

"A . . . doctor . . . ?" Hannah said, her heart sinking. "His name, sir? What is the doctor's name?"

"Howard Kody," the captain said, forking an eyebrow at her reaction when she grabbed for Strong Wolf, in an effort to steady herself.

"Lord, no," Hannah cried. She inhaled a quavering breath.

Then she broke away from them and ran toward the boat. Ignoring those who shouted at her to stop, Strong Wolf among them, Hannah ran on up the gangplank and shoved the crew aside, who stood gaping at

her. She ran in and out of the cabins until she found
that which housed the ill.

Her knees grew weak when she discovered her father kneeling beside a bunk, trying to force water
down the throat of a lady whose face was gaunt and
leathery, her eyes closed.

"Father," Hannah gasped. "Oh, Father!"

Howard turned around. He dropped the cup of
water and rushed to his feet. He went to Hannah,
grabbed her by a hand, and quickly led her out of
the room.

"What the hell are you doing?" he said in a half
shout. "Don't you know this is a death boat? Half of
the passengers are dead, Hannah, and you come
aboard and expose yourself to cholera? You know
better, Hannah. Lord, you know better."

Hardly recognizing him, Hannah stared at him. He
was so ashen. His hair was unkempt and hung limply
along his collar line. He looked as though he hadn't
slept in days. And he had lost considerable weight.

His clothes, which were always immaculately clean,
were soiled and wrinkled. His coat was discarded and
he was in his shirtsleeves, the sleeves half rolled up
to the elbow.

"Where's . . . Mother . . . ?" she managed to ask,
her voice thin with concern. "Father, please, *please,*
don't tell me that Clara is also on the boat."

"Both are here," Howard said, taking her into his
arms, hugging her.

Then he held her away from him and gently gripped
her shoulders as he told her a truth that would cut
clean into her very soul. "Clara . . . she . . . is quite
ill," he finally managed to say, clutching Hannah's
shoulders harder when he saw her grow limp with despair. "But Mother is well, Hannah. She's with Clara
now. She's seeing to her comfort."

"Is . . . Clara . . . dying?"

"We are doing what we can," was all that he said.

"Did you receive my wires?" Hannah asked, tears rushing from her eyes. "Am I the cause of you being on this horrid boat?"

"What wires?" her father asked, forking an eyebrow.

"Then, you are here for another purpose than my marriage to Strong Wolf?" Hannah said, searching his tired eyes for answers.

"Marriage?" her father gasped. "To an Indian?"

She meekly nodded.

"No," he said, wearily. "I did not receive such a wire as that. We . . . are here . . . for a much different purpose than that."

"Why, Father?" Hannah asked. "Why?"

"Your mother and I accompanied Clara on the journey," he said, his voice breaking. "You see, Hannah, Clara made a decision we did not approve of, yet we supported her, since she was so determined to do it."

"What . . . decision . . . ?" Hannah asked softly.

"She wants to teach Indian children," he blurted. "She was on her way to the Potawatomis village. She is going to teach *there*."

His eyes lowered. "She *was* going to," he said, swallowing hard. "Now . . . I . . . don't know. We had no idea that someone came aboard who was ill with cholera. Damn it, the disease spread through the passengers like wildfire. Clara? She helped with the ill. Now?" He hung his head in his hands. "Now, I just don't know."

Hannah was dumbstruck by the news.

Then panic filled Hannah's eyes. "Strong Wolf," she whispered. "His people." Eyes wide, she stared up at her father. "Oh, Lord, Father. I must go to Strong Wolf and tell him what's happening on this boat. I

can't chance him coming aboard. He might get cholera. The disease might even be carried back to his
people. Indians are known to have a weak resistance
against white man's diseases. Lord, Father, it could
wipe out his whole village!"

Although she was anxious to go and see her sister
and mother, Hannah's thoughts lingered on the man
she loved.

She turned and ran down the gangplank just as
Strong Wolf had begun to walk up it. She grabbed his
hand and led him quickly from the gangplank, and
then away from the boat.

She then spun around and faced him. "Strong Wolf,
please take your warriors and return home," she said
in a rush of words. "Many on board the boat are ill.
They have cholera. You can't chance getting the
dreadful disease. You can't chance carrying the germ
back to your people! Please leave! I must rush back
to my sister's side. She . . . she . . . is quite ill with the
cholera herself."

"Cholera?" Strong Wolf said, his jaws slack with
the horrid knowledge of what this meant, not only to
his people, but also to Hannah. He grabbed her shoulders. "You cannot go back on that boat! Come with
me. Protect yourself against the disease! Hannah, you
are my world!"

She placed a gentle hand on his cheek. "Darling,
don't you know?" she murmured. "I was on the ship
long enough to have already been exposed. Now I
must remain on board with the others. If I chance to
come through this all right, and the crisis is over for
everyone, only then shall I come to you with open
arms."

She wrenched herself free from his grip. "Now, go,
Strong Wolf," she said, taking slow, shaky steps away

from him. "Please. Your people's future lies in your hands."

"My future includes you at my side," Strong Wolf pleaded. "Come with me. You can live separate from my people until we see whether or not you contract the disease. But do not chance getting exposed again! Do not go aboard that boat again."

"My sister needs me," Hannah murmured. "And, Strong Wolf, don't you see? I have to be there for her, to care for her. She has come to teach your children." She paused, then gazed wistfully up at him. "Why didn't you tell me that a teacher would soon arrive to teach your children? Did you know that it was going to be my sister?"

"No, I did not know the name of the woman who was assigned to come to my village to teach," Strong Wolf said, glancing nervously up at the ship as someone screamed in despair. Surely someone's beloved had just crossed over to the other side.

Hannah's insides grew cold at the sound. She closed her eyes and said a soft prayer for her sister.

Strong Wolf gazed at Hannah again as she lifted her wavering eyes to his. "Of late, things have become too hectic to remember to tell you about the plans to have our children taught ways of counting and reading," he softly explained. "And it seems as though they just keep getting more and more complicated."

Hannah only half heard what Strong Wolf was saying. Her thoughts were on her sister. She needed to be at her sister's side. Even though she knew her father didn't want her on the boat, he would take this opportunity to show her just how skilled she could be at caring for the ill. He surely still dreamed of her going to medical school.

It was futile to try and explain to him that nothing he did or said would sway her decision from marrying

Strong Wolf. She had her own life to lead; her own desires to fulfill. And she would follow her heart into marriage with Strong Wolf.

She swallowed hard at the thought of that possibly never happening now. If she contracted cholera, everything they had dreamed could be gone, forever.

Knowing that, as far as her sister was concerned, every minute counted, Hannah gazed with a deep longing at Strong Wolf. "I love you so," she cried, then turned and fled back up the gangplank.

When she reached the deck, she turned and gazed at Strong Wolf. "Please leave!" she cried. "And please don't worry about me. I shall be all right!"

He gave her one last lingering look, then ran to his horse and swung himself into his saddle.

"Let us return to our people!" Strong Wolf said glumly. He flicked his reins and rode away in a gallop, then slowed his horse to a trot as he rode past Tiny and met him eye to eye.

Tiny sneered at him.

Strong Wolf looked arrows at him, then rode away, his heart aching to know that this might be the last time he would have been with Hannah. He knew the chances of her not surviving the dreaded disease.

But he also knew that nothing he could have said would have made her turn her back on her family. He was proud of her loyalty to her family, knowing that one day soon, if fate allowed it, her true, undying loyalty would be to him, her *husband*.

Hannah watched Strong Wolf ride away, tears streaming down her cheeks. This might be the last time she saw him. If she got cholera, and . . .

Her father came and took her by the hand, but she still did not go with him just yet. When she saw Tiny ride up closer to the boat, panic again filled her.

Chuck! Through all of this, she had forgotten about her brother!

She couldn't allow Chuck to come to the boat of death. He was frail as it was. If he contracted the disease, he would never survive!

Hannah ran back down the gangplank. She went to Tiny as he sat on his horse, staring down at her. She pleaded up at him with her eyes. "I never thought that I would ever ask a favor of you," she said, her voice breaking. "But I must. Tiny, everyone on board this boat has cholera. My parents and sister are on the boat. My sister is quite ill. Please go to Chuck. Explain things to him. Tell him that I am staying here, to help my father take care of those who are ill. Please tell my brother not to worry, and please tell him not to come here. He could get cholera. He isn't a well man. He might die! You must give me your word that you will keep my brother from coming. Please, Tiny. Please?"

Tiny paled as he stared up at the boat, then smiled crookedly down at Hannah. "Well, now, Hannah," he said, chuckling. "It seems things have changed, doesn't it? You, the high and mighty sister who came to look after her brother, is now havin' to beg the man she loathes." He scooted his hat back from his brow and leaned down into her face. "I like it. Yeah, I kind'a like it."

"You would take advantage of the situation," Hannah said, sighing heavily. "And I was stupid to ask such a thing of you. It would be to your advantage if my brother did die. You'd be able to alter all of the books in your favor before anyone who knows beans about bookkeeping could come and take a look at them."

"Are you callin' me a cheat?" Tiny growled, his eyes narrowing.

"I call them like I see them," Hannah said, placing her hands on her hips. Then her eyes softened. "Tiny, you are the only person I can depend on at this time to make sure Chuck is taken care of. If you do him wrong, I'll make sure you hang!"

"Threats?" Tiny said, forking an eyebrow. "Miss stuck-up, you pick a crazy time to hand me threats."

"I give up," Hannah said, flailing her hands in the air. She stamped away, then softened inside when Tiny spoke up behind her.

"All right, Hannah," he said in a civil tone. "I'll go and tell Chuck what's happened. And don't fret none. I'll look after him, fair and square."

Hannah turned tear-filled eyes at him. "Thank you," she murmured, then broke into a run and hurried back aboard the ship.

She embraced her mother, so grateful that she had not yet been affected by the disease.

Then when she went to the cabin in which her sister lay so ill and pale, her breathing raspy, Hannah covered her mouth with her hands and emitted a soft cry of despair.

"Clara!" she cried. "Oh, Lord, Clara!"

31

'Tis very sweet to look into the fair
And open face of heaven—to breathe a prayer
Full in the smile of the blue firmament.
                              —JOHN KEATS

Several days had passed since Hannah had immersed herself in helping those who were ill. Every day she had watched for the symptoms of cholera in her parents, as well as herself.

And thus far, they had not contracted the dreaded disease.

Although exhausted, Hannah and her parents had tended to Clara and the others without scarcely a wink of sleep.

Needing a bath, her hair full of tangles, Hannah watched her father as he came toward her, equally disheveled. He had hardly let up on her since the day they had begun caring for the ill together. He had told her time and again that she was proving just how much compassion she had for people, and how skilled she was at caring for them.

Today, when she could hardly hold her eyes open for lack of sleep, she attempted to walk away from her father.

But he was too quick.

Especially since her knees were almost too weak to hold her up.

"Take a look around you, Hannah," Howard said, gesturing with a hand toward cots of people who were recovering. "If not for your tender care, their graves would be added to those who died."

"Yes, Father," Hannah said, her voice drawn. "I know. And I'm proud."

She blinked her eyes, in an effort to stay awake.

She swayed somewhat, then grabbed for the back of a chair to steady herself.

"Then, Hannah, surely you must see how much you are needed in the medical field," Howard urged, his eyes pleading with her.

"Father, I understand how you feel," she murmured. "But please. Not today. Please don't start on me again today. I ... need ... to go and get some sleep now that the crisis has passed for everyone."

She gazed over at Clara, who was awake and taking nourishment as Hannah's mother slowly fed her sips of broth from a spoon. "And thank God Clara is going to be all right," she murmured. "Had she died, I just don't know ..."

"But she didn't die," her father said, interrupting her. "And she owes that, in part, to *you*."

"Father, I only did ..." Hannah said, but he again interrupted her.

"Hannah," he said, gently gripping her shoulders as he gazed into her weary eyes. "Admit it. Let me hear you say that you *know* you are skilled at caring for people. You have proven that you could be a doctor. You must forget that crazed idea of marrying an Indian. Go to school. Get your license. Come and join my medical practice. Let me have something to brag about, honey. Let me show you off to the world."

"Are you saying that if I don't become a doctor, you won't have anything nice to say about me?" Hannah asked, her heart aching because he had such a narrow, one-tracked mind. "That if I don't become a doctor, you would rather disown me?"

Her father paled. He dropped his hands to his sides. "No," he said shallowly. "I didn't say that at *all*."

"Well, that's how it sounded to me," Hannah said, lifting her chin stubbornly.

Again she blinked her eyes.

They were so heavy from lack of sleep.

She felt dizzy from it.

All she wanted now, since she knew that Clara was going to be all right, was to sleep for weeks!

Her father gazed down at her. He took her hand and led her outside, on top deck, where the air was sweet and fresh; the sky was clear and blue.

Hannah breathed it all in and said a soft prayer to herself that for the most part, this nightmare was over and would soon be totally behind her. She would resume her life again, a life with the man she loved. Oh, how she had missed Strong Wolf these past dreary days.

Howard drew her into his warm embrace. "Honey, don't purposely misinterpret what I am saying," he said softly. "But surely you don't want to be a mere Indian's squaw when you could go to school and be a doctor. You would be admired. You would be helpful to those who needed you."

Hannah found the strength, perhaps the last *of* her strength, to wrench herself from her father's arms. "Father, do you realize that I am old enough to know my own mind?" she said, sighing heavily. "Yet you are still trying to tell me what to do. You are still hell-bent on running my life. And please listen to me when I say that I am going to be with the man I love. *He* needs me. I need *him*."

"I ... don't ... want you to marry a damn savage," Howard blurted, his eyes dark with fury. "Your life is worth more than that, Hannah. Much more than that!"

Stunned by how he had referred to Strong Wolf as a savage, Hannah took an unsteady step away from him. "How dare you," she said, her voice trembling. "Strong Wolf is . . ."

Having pulled the last ounce from inside her to fight for her rights, Hannah felt a keen light-headedness quickly seize her.

She grabbed for the chair again, but missed it.

A black void enwrapping her, she sank to the floor in a dead faint.

"Hannah!" Howard gasped. He fell to his knees and gathered her into his arms.

Grace had come on top deck and stood in the shadows, listening to the debate between daughter and father. She went to Howard, her tired eyes glaring. "You just couldn't leave her alone, could you?" she accused. "Why can't you let it be, Howard? Hannah is no longer your little girl. She is a grown lady. And she *is* going to marry Strong Wolf."

Her hands were soft on Hannah's brow. "My sweet, precious daughter," she said, sighing with relief when Hannah's brow was cool to the touch. "Thank goodness she's not ill. She's just completely worn herself out." She glared up at Howard. "And not only from working so hard day in and out these past several days. From listening to *you*, Howard."

Howard carried Hannah to his cabin and placed her gently on his bunk.

Grace knelt down beside the bunk and kissed Hannah's brow. "Sleep, darling Hannah," she whispered. "When you awaken, you will be with the man you love."

Howard gasped. "What?" he said, his eyes locking

in silent battle with his wife as she turned glaring eyes
up at him.

"Now that the crisis is over and the danger has
passed, I am going to ask someone to take Hannah
to Strong Wolf," Grace said. "And don't try and stop
me. I imagine that man is almost out of his mind with
worry over Hannah. We've kept her from him long
enough."

She rose shakily to her feet, herself feeling faint
with exhaustion. "And we're going to take Clara to
Chuck's ranch this morning," she said. "We are no
longer needed on this boat. And the crew has managed to get it dislodged from the sandbar. It can now
be on its way downriver."

"Suddenly you are telling me and everyone else
what to do?" Howard said incredulously.

"It's about time, I'd say," Grace said stiffly, defying
him with a steady stare. "Yes, it's about time I became
my own person who speaks her own mind. Thank
God, Hannah has learned earlier than I. She'll be
much happier for it."

She looked at Hannah for a moment, then cast her
husband another tired, but determined gaze over her
shoulder. "And she'll have much more respect from
her husband," she said, her voice breaking.

32

Toiling, —rejoicing, —sorrowing,
Onward through life he goes.
—HENRY WADSWORTH LONGFELLOW

The room was deep in shadow as the sun rose and
Tiny slowly opened the door to Chuck's office. He
tensed when the door squeaked ominously in the early
morning hours; Chuck should still be asleep.

Tiny scarcely breathed as he looked over his shoulder at the closed door to Chuck's bedroom across the
hall. He listened carefully for the sound of Chuck's
cane against the wood floor.

He didn't hear it. Tiny's eyes narrowed. He went
on inside the office.

He gave the door a questioning stare. He would feel
much more secure if he could close it, yet it was too
dangerous to chance making it squeak again. Since
Chuck's eyesight had weakened, his other senses had
been strengthened: namely his hearing.

Knowing that time was of the essence, Tiny tiptoed
across the room to the desk. His fingers trembled as
he opened one ledger, and then another.

At any moment the rooster in the barnyard would
crow. The rooster was Chuck's morning alarm and had
never failed to wake him.

Tiny smiled when he found the ledger he was after.

This was the only one that had not yet been altered in his favor.

Dollar by dollar, Tiny had stolen that which he had erased from the finances shown in the journals. Soon he would disappear, and no one would be able to trace him, *or* Chuck's money.

Tiny had given up believing that he could ever own Chuck's land—the land that bordered the Potawatomis's. Now that Chuck's relatives were involved, Tiny had lost all opportunities of taking anything but cash money.

"Damn that Hannah," Tiny whispered as he sat down behind the desk and opened the journal. "If not for her, I'd be home clear. And now another sister will be here to see after Chuck's welfare. It's time for me to take what I can, and *leave*."

Smiling crookedly, Tiny dipped a pen into the inkwell. Slowly, methodically, and skillfully, he began altering the figures on the pages.

He gazed over at the safe. Thank God he knew how to open it. Today he would remove the money that he had been setting aside beneath a thick bundle of journals.

Tiny had swindled Chuck out of enough money to live the life of luxury for the rest of his life.

By tonight, he would be so far from this ranch, no one would ever be able to find him!

So absorbed in what he was doing, Tiny didn't hear Chuck entering the office. After hearing the door squeak, Chuck had purposely not used his cane to feel his way from his bedroom to the office.

Chuck stood at the opened door and sniffed. He could smell the mixture of perspiration and horseflesh and knew from that, that Tiny was in the office.

Chuck squinted through his thick eyeglasses, yet was unable to make out anything, or anyone.

But his ears picked up the sound of a pen scratching its way along paper. His keen smell picked up another familiar scent. Ink.

Tiny had come at a strange time to work on the ledgers. The reason could only be that he was doing something underhanded.

"And so you are eager to work today, are you, Tiny?" Chuck said as he felt his way across the room.

Tiny was so startled by Chuck's sudden appearance, he knocked over the inkwell, spilling ink all over the top of the desk and the journal in which he had been altering the figures.

"Damn," Tiny said, reaching quickly for an ink blotter. As he looked guardedly up at Chuck, he soaked up the spilled ink. "Chuck, you scared the livin' hell outta me."

"And why would my appearance in my own office frighten you?" Chuck said, stopping to stand over the desk.

He glanced over toward the hazy, dull light of morning that he could just barely make out at the window. "I don't believe I heard the rooster crow yet," he said. "That has to mean that you are working before breakfast." He smiled smugly down at Tiny. "Want to tell me why you have such a sudden interest in working over hours?"

"I . . . I . . . just had to take a look at the journals," Tiny stammered. "I worried about some recent entries. I . . . I think I may have made some mistakes."

"Yes, I think you have," Chuck said. He placed his hands, palm side down, on the desk and leaned closer to Tiny. "Now, would you like to explain to me about those . . . eh . . : mistakes, Tiny?"

"I . . . I . . . just rushed through making the entries, that's all," Tiny said. He slowly eased himself up from the chair. "But now they've been corrected."

"Give me a look," Chuck said, moving around the desk, to stand beside Tiny.

"What?" Tiny said, moving on out of the chair. He backed away from Chuck. "What do you mean? You can't see."

"Now, are you absolutely certain of that, Tiny?" Chuck said, chuckling low.

Suddenly Tiny pretended to fall over the chair, purposely to bump against Chuck and knock his glasses off.

The glasses fell to the floor. Tiny crunched them beneath his boot. "Oh, no," he said, pretending alarm. "Look what I did. Your glasses, Chuck. I . . . broke . . . them."

Chuck steadied himself as he held onto the edge of the desk. His jaw tight, he fumbled around until he found a key that he had hidden beneath his desk.

Then he gave it to Tiny. "Unlock the bottom drawer," he said icily.

Tiny's hands shook as he opened the drawer, his eyes never leaving Chuck.

"Now, reach inside and get me my other pair of glasses," he said, smiling devilishly down at Tiny when he heard him gasp. "And not only that, Tiny. Get me that magnifying glass. I've found it quite useful these past several days. You'd be surprised to know what I've discovered in these ledgers."

Tiny paled. Knowing that he had been caught, he backed away from Chuck, then bolted and ran from the room.

Chuck sighed and eased into his chair. "Damn, damn, damn," he said, pounding a fist against the desktop. "He's been cheating me all along! How could I have been so stupid? Just how much money *did* he swindle me out of?"

His fingers trembled as he slipped his glasses on.

Then, feeling defeated, he went to his safe and slowly turned the combination. He had made notches in the dial when he had started going blind. These notches led him to the right numbers.

The safe door swung open. Chuck fumbled around inside until he found his stack of journals and boxes of papers that he had stored there long before he had started losing his eyesight.

One by one he removed things from his safe, his fingers recognizing each box, each journal, each keepsake, each bundle of money.

Then his eyes widened when his fingers came upon something foreign after removing everything down to only a few things. It had been a long time since he had made inventory on what was inside his safe.

Now that he was finally doing it, he found a box that was unfamiliar to him.

It had been hidden beneath everything else.

His fingers trembling, Chuck took the box from the safe. He placed it on the floor before him, then slowly raised the lid. The scent of money, which he always associated and identified with dirty hands and mildew, wafted upward into his nose. He ran his fingers over the several bundles.

"Damn," he whispered, paling. "Tiny hid the money he swindled from me under my very own nose!"

A chill raced up and down his spine. "He was aiming to leave soon," he said, realizing his intent. "This would pay his way. Had I not caught him, he'd be a rich man!"

Deliberately, his jaw set, his heart beating soundly over his anger at this man who had taken advantage of his illness, Chuck scooted the desk aside.

He then felt his way along the floor beneath his desk.

Smiling, his fingers searched until they found a loose board.

Picking up the board away from the others and laying it aside, he felt down inside it until he found a safe; he had used this one before he had started going blind and before Tiny had come to work for him.

"You damn cheat," he whispered beneath his breath as he placed all of the money in this safe. "Just try and come back and take what isn't yours. Won't you get a surprise!"

He swallowed hard. "I should've listened to Hannah," he whispered, his insides aching to know if Hannah was all right.

He wondered about the welfare of his family and whether Clara had survived. He had not wanted to chance contracting cholera, so had not gone to check. His life was miserable enough being blind.

Then he felt guilty for thinking of himself, when his sisters' lives lay in balance.

His eyes widened when he heard the sound of a wagon arriving outside. "Could it be?" he whispered.

He lifted the floorboard back in place, scooted the desk back where it belonged, then felt his way out of the room.

Out in the hall he grabbed his cane, then found his way to the front door and opened it. He could hear the wagon drawing closer as he stepped out onto the porch.

"Chuck!" his father shouted. "Son! Everyone is all right, son! Clara is here! We're bringing her to recover the rest of the way at your house! Oh, son, it's so good to see you!"

Tears ran from Chuck's eyes as he felt his way down the steps.

Soon he was enveloped in the strong arms of his father, then the soft, gentle arms of his mother.

"Chuck?"

His sister Clara's sweet, gentle voice drew Chuck out of his mother's arms.

Chuck went to Clara. He climbed into the back of the wagon and drew his sister into his arms. "Sis," he whispered. He slowly rocked her back and forth as he held her.

Then he grew cold inside when he realized that Hannah wasn't with them.

He eased Clara from his arms and turned to his father.

"God, where's Hannah?" he gasped.

"Like I said, son, we're all fine," Howard said.

"Then, where is *Hannah*?" Chuck persisted.

"She's with Strong Wolf," Howard said matter-of-factly.

Chuck was taken aback by the knowing.

33

> To fondle and caress a joy,
> Yet hold it tightly;
> Lest it become necessity,
> And cling too tightly.
> —ANONYMOUS

As Hannah slowly awakened, she was aware of being held in muscled arms. Blinking her eyes, she gazed up at Strong Wolf.

"Strong Wolf?" she murmured, reaching a trembling, weak hand to his face. "You came to the boat? Oh, Lord, Strong Wolf, I asked you not to. Now you might get ill with cholera. Your people! You might even take the disease back to them!"

She tried to move from his arms, but he insistently held her there, then placed a gentle kiss to her brow.

"We are not on the boat," he said, gazing warmly into her eyes. "Look around you. You will see where you are, and where you are going to stay."

Hannah was stunned to find herself in Strong Wolf's lodge. The fireplace sent out a golden glow of light and warmth. Everything was so quiet; so peaceful.

She turned anxious eyes up at him then. "Clara!" she cried. "Did she die? Did I contract cholera? Strong Wolf, I don't remember anything!"

"Your sister is at your brother's ranch now, recuperating," Strong Wolf said thickly. "And you? No. You have not been ill. You just fainted from exhaustion."

"Mother? Father?" she murmured, stunned to know that she was so lapse in memory about everything.

"They are with your sister at your brother's ranch," Strong Wolf said, brushing her hair back from her eyes. "The boat has left. The crisis is over. We may now resume our lives. We will be married."

Hannah sucked in a quivering air of breath. "I remember it all now," she said. "It was like a nightmare, Strong Wolf." She flung herself into his arms again. "Hold me. Please just hold me."

"A beautiful maid of nineteen winters lies on my bed of sweet grass," he said in almost a whisper as he caressed her back through the thin fabric of her dress. "And I love her more than life itself."

"And I love you," Hannah said, clinging. "I missed you so while away from you." She visibly shivered. "At times, it was almost unbearable. Those who died? It was as though I lost someone of my very own kin. I tried so hard to help keep them alive."

She leaned somewhat away from him and gazed into his eyes. "Father badgered me constantly about becoming a doctor," she murmured. "Perhaps in time I would have considered it had I not met you, and had I not been introduced to the ways of doctoring while on that death boat. Now that I have seen suffering and death, firsthand, I wonder how anyone can be a doctor?"

"You are too compassionate to face death and illness each day," Strong Wolf said, smiling at her. "You see, I am certain it was like a small part of your heart was torn away each time someone died."

"That *is* how it felt," Hannah said, eyes wide.

"Then it is wise that you are leaving the doctoring to your father," Strong Wolf said, again drawing her into his embrace. "This is where you belong. Only *here*."

Hannah paled. She leaned back and looked up at Strong Wolf. "My parents," she gasped. "Surely they don't approve of my being here. How *did* I get here?"

"It seems that while you were with your parents during that ordeal on the riverboat, you managed to persuade them that your future was with me," he said softly. "When the crisis was over on the boat, and you fainted from exhaustion, your parents had you brought to me."

"So that when I awakened, I would find myself in your arms?" Hannah said, her eyebrows raising. "I had not known that I was *that* persuasive when I talked to my father about my feelings."

Strong Wolf saw no reason to allow her to know that it was only her mother whose mind had been changed toward Strong Wolf, not her father. It would only cause her pain to know that her father still had deep, negative feelings about Hannah's choice of a husband. For now, Strong Wolf would just give her information that would not cause her added grief.

"Your parents love you," he said, leaning a soft kiss to her brow. "They want you to be happy."

"I had no idea that my words were sinking at *all* into my father's consciousness," Hannah said, laughing softly. "He is such a stubborn man. And usually, he gets his way about everything."

Now completely awake and aware of things, Hannah could smell the unpleasantness of her armpits, and her hair was so dirty it felt as though tiny bugs were crawling around on her scalp.

She eased from Strong Wolf's arms, her face red with embarrassment. "How can you stand for me to be near you?" she said, inching farther away from him on the bed. "I smell horrible." She ran her fingers through her hair and cringed. "And my *hair*. It hasn't been washed in days. How horrible I must look to you!"

"You could never look anything but beautiful to this man who will soon be your husband," Strong Wolf said, then rose from the bed. He took her hands and led her up from the bed. "Are you strong enough to stand?"

"Now that I have rested, yes, my strength has somewhat returned," she murmured, testing her legs as she stood up before Strong Wolf. She laughed softly. "My knees no longer feel like rubber."

"Then, we shall go to the river and bathe," Strong Wolf said.

He left her long enough to gather up some fresh, clean clothes from the back of the lodge. He placed two pairs of breeches and two shirts over his arms. He grabbed a piece of soap from the basin.

"Come," he said, reaching his hand out for her. "We shall bathe together."

So relieved that she was no longer on the boat, and so glad to be with Strong Wolf, Hannah took Strong Wolf's hand and left the lodge with him.

When she got outside she stopped with a start, in awe of how many of Strong Wolf's people were there, their eyes seeming to brighten as they gazed at her.

Hannah sidled over closer to Strong Wolf. "Why are they here?" she asked softly.

"They know of my love for you," Strong Wolf said, smiling into the crowd. "They came to see if you were going to be all right."

A small girl came to Hannah. She held out a corn-husk doll toward her.

Hannah turned questioning eyes up at Strong Wolf.

"Talks Softly is offering you a gift," Strong Wolf said. He placed a gentle hand to the child's elbow and led her closer. "This is her way to show her happiness

over you being all right. The doll? She made it. She
has always loved it."

"If it is so special to her, does she truly wish to part
with it?" Hannah asked, hesitating.

"She offers her special doll to you to prove how
much she wishes to be your friend," Strong Wolf said.
"If you do not take it, you will humiliate her."

Hannah's lips turned into a smile as she reached
her hand out for the doll. "I would love to have your
pretty doll," she murmured, taking it. "And when I
have a pretty little girl like you, can she also play
with it?"

The girl's eyes lit up. She nodded. Then, her long
braids bouncing, she turned and ran back to her parents and stood between them, holding their hands.

More and more people, children and adults alike,
came to Hannah and placed gifts at her feet. Her jaws
began to ache from smiling so much as she thanked
them.

When everyone turned and returned to their evening chores, the sky darkening, changing to the color
of dark grape jelly, Hannah bent to her knees and
began gathering the gifts into her arms.

"There is so much," she said. "I am so very touched
by the generosity of your people."

Strong Wolf knelt beside her and helped her.

"Their acceptance of you touches my very soul,"
Strong Wolf said, walking into the lodge with Hannah.

"I hope to never disappoint them," Hannah said,
placing the items on the floor against the wall opposite
the fireplace.

"And you never shall," Strong Wolf said, emptying
his own arms.

They left the lodge for the river. The moon was
now bright and made a path of light through the thick
brush as Strong Wolf and Hannah went farther and

farther away from his village, to assure their full privacy while bathing.

When they reached a place of overhung rock, and
where a sandy shore reached down into the water,
Strong Wolf took Hannah's hand and stopped her.

Her heart pounding, Hannah gazed up at him as he
dropped the clothes and soap to the ground and
turned to her, his eyes dark with a longing that she
recognized.

She felt the same longing deep within her soul. It
had been too long since they had been alone in ways
that sent her heart into a slow, sensual melting.

And she knew that they would do more than bathe
when they got into the water. They would come together as one heartbeat, their bodies locked in passionate embraces.

"Is this truly happening?" she whispered as he drew
her dress over her head. "Are those horrible days finally behind us? Are we really together again?"

His pulse racing, the excitement building in his
heart, Strong Wolf cupped her breasts within the
palms of his hands, his thumbs rubbing sensually over
her nipples. "It is real," he said huskily. "And let us
not look back at what was. We have now. We have a
future together."

Hannah suddenly recalled something else. "Clara!"
she said, eyes wide. "She is going to teach your children. Isn't that wonderful?"

"If she is as good at heart as you are, yes, it will
be a right decision made on my part to bring her here
in the capacity of teacher," Strong Wolf said, bending
to his knees, removing her shoes.

"I remember now that my father said that Clara
would care for Chuck after school hours, while hired
help would care for him through the day," Hannah
said, closing her eyes in ecstasy as Strong Wolf ran

his hands slowly up her legs, across her belly, and then cupped her breasts again. "She will make sure that Tiny doesn't make wrong entries in the journals anymore. In fact, she might even be able to point out the discrepancies to Chuck. I'm certain they are there."

"Tiny has left your father's ranch," Strong Wolf said, stepping away from her, removing his clothes.

Hannah's eyes widened. "What?" she gasped.

"Tiny left after your brother caught him in the act of deceit," Strong Wolf said, tossing his fringed buckskin shirt aside. "As far as I know, he has left the country."

"Finally he is gone," Hannah said. She ran her fingers over Strong Wolf's muscled chest, relishing the touch of his smooth, copper skin against her fingertips. She sucked in a wild breath when she moved her fingers lower, just barely grazing the tip of Strong Wolf's manhood.

She went limp with desire when Strong Wolf swept her into his arms and carried her into the water. He held the bar of soap in one hand as with his free hand he turned her to face him, her breasts pressed against his chest as she locked her legs around his waist.

He carried her until the water was lapping at his waist, then stopped and kissed her.

They kissed for a moment, then he placed her feet to the rocky bottom of the stream.

He washed her hair with the soap, then rinsed it and lay it over her shoulders, where it lay like spirals of golden, spun silk.

Their eyes locked as Strong Wolf began rubbing the soap over her body, lathering her breasts, slowly, first one, and then the other, causing her nipples to grow hard and taut with a pleasurable ache.

Strong Wolf caressed her breasts, then moved the soap lower across the slimness of her body below her breasts, down to the supple broadening into the hips, with its golden, central muff of hair.

Hannah held her legs apart as Strong Wolf moved the bar of soap in a slow circle on her throbbing center. She closed her eyes and held her head back with a sigh as he slipped one finger inside her, and then two as he dropped the soap.

She clung to him as he continued the thrusts with his fingers, then she felt something else. Something more wonderful. Something warm and thick was sliding inside her, magnificently filling her.

She opened her eyes and smiled at Strong Wolf, then twined her fingers through his hair and drew his lips to hers. Their tongues met as their lips parted in a frenzied kiss.

The moon played on their naked bodies as Strong Wolf carried Hannah to dry land and spread her beneath him on the soft sand. He slid himself inside her again as she opened her soft, full thighs to him.

Strong Wolf's hands moved frantically over her, not able to get enough of her. His tongue left a wet path as he moved his mouth from her lips and went to her breasts. He gently squeezed a breast between his hands, leaving the nipple taut and free for the tip of his tongue.

Swirling and moist, he lapped at the nipple with his tongue, then nipped it with his teeth, causing Hannah to moan with rapture.

Strong Wolf swept his hands along her body, then reached around where her buttocks were soft and sweet as she pressed her body into his as he continued to send quick thrusts into her.

He could hardly hold his feelings at bay. Each touch, each thrust brought him closer to that point of ecstasy that he sought.

But wanting to delay it, not wanting to give her up

to the night just yet, where they would return from their paradise on wings, Strong Wolf moved slightly away from Hannah and slipped his throbbing manhood from inside her.

"Why did you stop?" Hannah asked, looking at him in a drugged fashion. "Please go on, Strong Wolf. Take me where there is nothing but you and I."

"There is more," Strong Wolf said huskily. He knelt on his knees beside her.

Bending over her, his tongue found her breasts again. He licked first one and then the other, smiling to himself when he heard her soft moan of pleasure.

He made a wet path downward, then changed his positions, so that he was kneeling between her legs as he spread them wide on both sides of him.

"There are many ways to make love," he said as he looked heavy-lashed up at her.

When she reached her hands to his cheeks and smiled, he gazed at her a moment longer, then knelt down, low over her, and ran his fingers through the cloud of shadowed hair between her legs, parting it, so that the whole of her womanhood was revealed to his feasting eyes.

The moon lay its silver light where he gazed so intensely. He flicked a finger over her swollen point of desire, then bent and swept his tongue over it, drawing a guttural, pleasurable sigh from deeply within her.

Strong Wolf loved Hannah long and leisurely in this way, his lips soft and gentle as he brought her closer and closer to the brink of total pleasure.

Then he leaned away from her and gazed at her, his own need pulsing and painful as he took one last look at her before taking from her the ultimate of ecstasy.

Her golden hair was disarrayed around her smooth and creamy shoulders.

Her hips curved up voluptuously.

Her breasts were heaving in her excitement of the moment, their nipples a dark pink, taut and erect.

Strong Wolf ran his hands over Hannah. Her skin was warm, smooth, and a little moist. He kneaded her breasts. She whimpered tiny cries when his lips sank over one of the nipples as he rose over her.

Her hand reached out and enfolded his manhood within her fingers. He gasped with pleasure and closed his eyes when she ran her fingers slowly up and down his velvety, tight heat.

His buttocks tightened and the muscles of his legs corded when she led him to the valley of her desire, then dropped her hand away from him.

In one maddening thrust he was inside her again. Over and over again he plunged into her. He kissed her as their bodies strained together hungrily.

The sensations searing, Hannah's body hardened and tightened as she absorbed the bold thrusts within her. Then she felt the bliss spreading, euphoric in its sweetness. She clung to him and moaned against his lips, throwing her head back in ecstasy as he moved his mouth to a breast and swept the nipple between his teeth, groaning out his own fulfilled pleasure against it.

Afterward they rolled away from each other and lay on the sand, their eyes watching the play of the stars in the heavens, twinkling as though they might be tiny lanterns.

"I didn't think I would ever get to be with you again in this way," Hannah said, turning on her side to face Strong Wolf. "These past few days made me aware of how quickly one's life can change. Let us take advantage of every moment, Strong Wolf, for who knows what tomorrow might bring."

"Yes, sometimes life can be cruel, even to those

who deserve the best of everything," he said. He sighed deeply when she reached a hand over and caressed his belly, just above his dark vee of hair, where lay his spent manhood.

She crept her fingers upward and ran them over the smoothness of his hairless chest. She leaned up over him and flicked her tongue over one of his nipples.

And then she ran her fingers down his body, and then her tongue. She moved to her knees and leaned over him. She kissed her way down his body, where her fingers had just traveled. She teased and stroked his tender flesh with her tongue and lips. Her hands sought and found that part of him that could give her much pleasure.

She moved her mouth over him as his manhood grew in response to her caresses. Her fingers gripped him, her tongue and breath hot on his flesh.

"Hannah," he groaned, twining his fingers through her hair, pulling her mouth closer. He closed his eyes and took from her what she gave. His head swirled with pleasure. His heart pounded.

And then she sat down over him, straddling him, as she positioned him inside her. Her hair bounced on her shoulders as he reached up inside her with his eager thrusts. He breathed hard. He gasped.

And then he spilled his seed up inside her again at the same moment she found her own release.

Laughing softly as she gazed down at Strong Wolf's flushed cheeks, Hannah fell away from him. "My, oh, my, I feel wicked tonight," she said, pulling her hair back from her eyes. She blushed as she turned on her side to face him. "I don't know what got into me," she murmured. "I am not one who even thinks of such things, much less does them."

"It is the magic of the midnight hour," Strong Wolf said. He moved on his side. He reached his arms around her and drew her against him, her breasts crushing his chest. "And the night has only just begun, my woman."

Hannah trembled sensually when he slung one of his legs over hers, revealing to her that he was again ready to take her to paradise.

"Do I have the strength?" she whispered to him, eyes wide. "I only recently . . ."

"I shall be gentle," Strong Wolf whispered back. "You need do nothing but lay there and let yourself float away as I again give you pleasure. My woman, it is the best way imaginable to relax. Just close your eyes. Just be aware of the sensations I arouse in you. Let them overwhelm you. Let them take you to paradise!"

"Yes, yes," Hannah whispered as she closed her eyes and held her head back with a sigh. "I am relaxed. I am ready. Please, oh, please love me again. I want nothing now but to be with you, to know the ecstasy of being loved by you."

His mouth covered hers with a gentle, kiss as he slowly rocked within her. He held her gently close. "Slowly," he whispered against her lips. "I will go slowly so that you will feel the euphoria of the ecstasy that will build within you. Let it come. Enjoy it. And remember, my woman, I shall be here for you for the rest of our lives. Every night I shall love you in such a way. You shall return such love. We are meant to be together. You are my world. You are my universe!"

"As . . . you . . . are mine," Hannah whispered, hardly recognizing her own voice in its huskiness.

She sighed and allowed the pleasure to fill her very being.

34

Sing, little birds, above her head,
Bloom, flowers, beneath her feet.
—ANONYMOUS

Soft church music wafted through the air. Tears sprang
to Hannah's eyes to know that her brother had cared
enough for her happiness with Strong Wolf, that he
had transported his organ to Strong Wolf's village for
the wedding ceremony. It had been placed beneath
the shade of a towering elm tree, where he had played
his beautiful music since sunup.

"I can hardly believe it is my wedding day!" Hannah said as her mother wound flowers into the one
long braid down Hannah's back. She clasped her
hands together on her lap to try and stop their
trembling. "Mother, thank you for being here. Without you and Father's approval of my marriage, I would
have never been totally happy as Strong Wolf's wife."

"But now?" Grace said, stepping back to admire
her daughter's hair. "You are certain you will be
happy?"

Hannah rose from the chair and turned to her
mother. "Mother, take a look," she said, beaming.
"Don't you see how I wear my happiness on my face?
I feel as though I am glowing from within. Surely you
can see it!"

Tears came to Grace's eyes. "My darling," she murmured. "I've never seen you as beautiful."

Hannah laughed softly with a joyous bliss, then
gazed down at the dress that Strong Wolf had asked
her to wear on their wedding day. "This dress is

Strong Wolf's mother's," she murmured. "Before he
left his home in Wisconsin, his mother gave him the
dress and told him that should he find someone to
marry before he saw her again, to please ask her to
wear her wedding dress. His mother was very much
in love with his father the day they married."

"And what about Strong Wolf's father?" Grace
asked softly.

"He died long ago, before Strong Wolf was born,"
Hannah murmured. "And Strong Wolf won't talk
about it. I imagine it is too painful to think about,
having never known one's very own father."

Hannah ran her hands down the front of the dress,
adoring the white rabbit skin from which it had been
fashioned. Around her neck she wore a necklace of
shells and feathers. She wore beautiful white leggings,
fringed and intricately beaded, the moccasins
matching.

"Isn't all of my wedding attire beautiful?" she
asked, smiling at her mother.

"Yes, quite," Grace said, yet frowned. "But I hate
to see Strong Wolf turning you into something you are
not, by asking you to dress entirely in Indian fashion."

Hannah paled and stared at her mother. "But,
Mother, I will be living among his people," she murmured. "I must not stand out like a sore thumb by
wearing clothes that differ from theirs."

Hannah ran her hand down the front of her dress
again, admiring it anew as she gazed down at it. "And
I truly feel special in this dress," she said, its softness
like a caress against her fingertips. "It is as though I
am someone else."

Hannah looked over at the bed. All across it lay an
assortment of buckskin dresses. They were gifts from
Strong Wolf's people during a celebration only yesterday. She had also received various cooking utensils,

freshly baked bread, and assortments of jewelry, some of which she wore today.

Several days passed since she had come to Strong Wolf, exhausted from her long, weary days in the riverboat.

Being among those who were dying had made each day more precious to Hannah.

Now her brother played his organ, drums beat in a steady rhythm, and people chatted and laughed outside by the large outdoor fire; everything was perfect.

"My precious, sweet darling," Grace said as she went and drew Hannah into her gentle embrace. "I am happy for you."

"But not entirely, are you?" Hannah said, giving back the hug. Then she eased from her mother's arms. "I wish you could just feel half what I am feeling, then you would know that what I am doing is right."

"Yes, I know that you feel this is right for you, or you wouldn't do it," Grace said, swallowing hard. "But life here is different than that to which you are accustomed."

Grace gestured with a hand as she looked around her, at the way Hannah would be living, in Strong Wolf's cabin. "This will be a miserable life for you, Hannah," she said solemnly. "In Saint Louis you had a luxurious bed in which to sleep. You had plush carpets in which you could sink your bare toes. You had maids and servants who looked after you. You never wanted for anything. You lived in the lap of luxury. How can you possibly expect to get accustomed to . . . to . . . *this*?"

"Mother, all that you described, and all that *you* cannot live without, has nothing at all to do with *me*," Hannah said, gently taking her mother's hands. "Yes, I loved my bedroom with its satin draperies and bedspread. It *was* wonderful to be able to curl my toes into the carpets on those long, cold days of winter. But I have never needed those things to be happy. Please remember how I sought the outdoors every chance I had. I preferred it over the richness of our house. And, Mother, you were so strict I sometimes was afraid to walk *on* that carpet, or sleep in my very own bed. If I mussed up anything, you scolded me."

"Was I that terrible of a mother?" Grace gasped, slipping her hands from Hannah's.

"Mother, I never said you were terrible," Hannah said, sighing heavily. "I said you were strict. And I understand. When you and Father were first married, you had nothing. And then when you *did,* you felt as though you had to protect it with your *life.* It was instilled in you from being poor so long."

"Thank God you understand," Grace murmured. She placed a gentle hand to Hannah's cheek. "And you understand more than I ever knew you did. I had no idea you realized the grief I experienced at the first of my marriage. At times, I wished I had ... not ... married your father. When I saw women with more than I, I so envied them!"

"Mother, I didn't know *that,*" Hannah uttered. "You never seemed the sort to be envious of anyone."

"That's only because you have known me since I have had everything a woman would ever want," Grace said. She reached for Hannah and hugged her again. "I am so glad that you did not inherit the ugly side of your mother."

Strong Wolf came into the cabin. He stood in the shadows, watching Hannah and her mother, and listened. He smiled to himself when he heard Hannah tell her mother how she felt about living among his people and in his house. More and more he saw how he had chosen the right woman. She was at home with his people, as though she had been born into their world, blood kin to them.

"My woman, it is time for us to speak our vows," he said, stepping out of the shadows.

Hannah paled. "Strong Wolf, it's bad luck for the groom to see the bride before the marriage on the wedding day," she said, yet she could not take her eyes off him and how wonderfully handsome he was today. His hair was long and flowing down his back. His face shone with a quiet pride.

He was dressed in a fringed white doeskin outfit, colorful beads in designs of forest animals on the shirt. His moccasins were fashioned out of the same doeskin material and beads.

Their eyes locked, and Hannah then realized how foolish it was to think that seeing each other was bad luck.

Today was theirs!

"Come," Strong Wolf said, reaching a hand out for Hannah. "Everyone waits to see my lovely woman." As she stepped timidly toward him, his gaze swept slowly up and down her.

"Like I am sure my mother was on her wedding day in that same dress, you are a vision," he said huskily as she went and took his hand.

He drew her into his embrace. "I never told you, did I, how beautiful my mother is?" he said, his eyes warming her insides as he smiled into them. "She is taller than most Potawatomis women. And some say her loveliness outshines the stars in the heavens." He brushed a soft kiss across her lips. "But now I would say she has keen competition in you."

"How can you say that," Hannah said, their eyes locking. "You know how I feel about myself. I have never seen myself as beautiful. I almost fear meeting your mother. If she is so pretty, I will feel even uglier."

"My woman, still you have not looked long enough in a mirror, or you would see how wrong you are to say that you are not pretty," Strong Wolf said. "You are even lovelier than my mother."

"I certainly hope not," Hannah said, laughing softly. "I would hate to think that your mother might resent me the moment she sees me."

Someone clearing their throat made Hannah suddenly remember they were not alone. Blushing, Hannah turned to her mother.

"Mother, it's time," she said, reaching a hand out for her. "I soon will become a bride! Please be happy for me! Please share my wondrous feelings!"

Grace reached for a lacy, embroidered handkerchief inside her dress pocket. She dabbed her nose and her eyes with it, then nodded. "I *am* happy for you," she murmured. "And never doubt how beautiful you are."

Hannah broke away from Strong Wolf and hugged her mother. "Thank you," she whispered. "Oh, Mother, I will miss you so when you return to Saint Louis."

"Your father and I must leave immediately after the ceremony," Grace said. "The riverboat from Saint Louis should be arriving within the hour. We are going to travel downriver for a while before returning home. Your father and I need a vacation."

"That's wonderful," Hannah said. "You do need time to yourselves."

Hannah stepped away from her mother, then went to Strong Wolf. She took his hand and smiled up at him.

They stepped aside as her mother left the cabin first, then they followed her outside.

Everyone stood with eyes wide and in awe of Han-

nah as she made her way toward the central, outdoor
fire, where a platform had been erected beside it for
her and Strong Wolf. Flowers were scattered everywhere along the ground, sending off sweet and spicy
aromas.

Earlier, several warriors had killed several ducks
and had planted sharp-pointed sticks in the ground
around the leaping flames of the huge outdoor fire.
On each stake they had fastened a duck to roast. They
had buried several under the ashes to bake.

Other meat hung from spits over the fire, dripping
their tantalizing juices into the flames. The smell of
corn, squash, beans, and many more vegetables wafted
through the air from the large pots positioned in the
coals around the edge of the fire. Coffee boiled in a
huge pot. Tea had been prepared, as well as honey
water.

While Hannah had been walking toward the platform, she had not been able to see Chuck at the organ
through the crowd, or her mother and father, who
were now standing close to the platform, waiting for
them.

Hannah was surprised when she saw a minister
standing there holding a Bible, a wide smile on his
thick-jowled face. She looked questioningly at her parents, who smiled and nodded back at her, then to
Strong Wolf, seeking answers.

"Your father asked that you not only be wed in
the Potawatomis tradition, but also the white man's,"
Strong Wolf said, smiling down at her. "I agreed. They
sent for a minister. Today there will be *two*
ceremonies."

Hannah smiled up at him. She felt doubly blessed
by her God today, and Strong Wolf's Great Spirit.

Everything became quiet as Strong Wolf and Hannah stepped up to the preacher. Out of the corner of

her eyes, Hannah saw Clara leading Chuck from the
organ. The ceremony didn't start until they were
standing there with everyone.

Then the preacher began reading scriptures from
the Bible. Hannah felt all warm and wonderful inside
as she listened. She could hardly believe that, at long
last, everything was fitting into place so wonderfully.

However, when she glanced up at Strong Wolf, she
noticed that same troubled look she had seen before
in his eyes. She wondered what bothered him? What
had he not told her about himself?

Would he *ever* open himself completely to her? She
would relax only when she understood the self-doubt
he burdened himself with.

Not wanting to allow this to spoil her special day,
Hannah wrenched her eyes away from Strong Wolf
and listened to the preacher. Her hand reached over
to hold Strong Wolf's. She glanced up at him again
quickly when she felt his hand trembling. Again she
saw that haunted look in his eyes.

Suddenly nervous herself and now not so sure about
what she was doing, Hannah looked away.

Strong Wolf half listened to the word of the white
preacher. This was his wedding day, and he *still* had
not confided in his woman his darkest secrets, which
haunted him every day of his life.

He knew he should have told her before their vows
of marriage, and that he would have to tell her
eventually.

But he had not been able to find the courage.

He doubted now that he ever would.

He could not tell her something that might make
her turn away from him with a loathing!

If he lost her, he would lose his reason for living.

When the preacher stopped and nodded at Strong

Wolf, he left his fear behind and went on with the ceremony.

He turned to face Hannah and gently took her hands. "My woman, here I am in your presence. Make it so forever that only I may occupy your heart."

Tears filled Hannah's eyes as she gazed into his. "My husband, here I am in your presence. Make it so forever that only I may occupy your heart, for mine is yours, forever and a day."

She brushed her fears aside as he then married her in his Potawatomis fashion.

They embraced and kissed and clung, Hannah's fears returning, for it seemed that Strong Wolf was holding her from sheer desperation. Her heart ached, to know that something was bothering him to this extreme on their wedding day. Surely he didn't doubt her sincere love for him! She had shown him in every way possible just how much she cared!

The celebration lasted all day, then good-byes were said to Hannah's mother and father. Chuck and Clara had also left, to see them off at the riverboat. Hannah clung to Strong Wolf as she watched them leave in a buggy, a wagon following close behind carrying the organ.

"Now we are alone," Strong Wolf said, closing the door with his foot. He held Hannah in his arms and carried her toward the bed. "My wife! Do you hear me, Hannah? I can now call you my wife!"

"I like the sound of 'my husband' better," Hannah said, giggling, feeling drunk from the whole day of magic. She had long since forgotten why she had doubted Strong Wolf during the first of the wedding ceremony. Everything had changed so quickly into jubilation; into wonderful laughter, food, and dancing. So euphoric over having finally become Strong Wolf's bride, Hannah felt as though she were floating on air.

"I promise to make you happy," Hannah whispered,
brushing her lips across his mouth.

"You vowed during the ceremony that you would,"
Strong Wolf said, placing her on the bed. "I do not
doubt you, or your word."

"My darling husband, I shall tell you time and again
my promise to make you happy, for you are now the
center of my universe," Hannah said as he disrobed
her.

Then he wasted no time at disrobing himself as
Hannah lay there silkenly nude waiting for him.

When Strong Wolf came to her on the bed, his eyes
smoke black with passion, Hannah held her arms out
for him and welcomed him. As he kissed her, hotly
and tenderly in the same breath, she marveled and
groaned when, with a silent rush of power, he drove
himself into her, swiftly, surely, deeply.

She twined her arms around his neck and clung to
him. She wrapped her legs tightly around his waist and
rode him as he came to her with his slow, deep thrusts.

"My darling," she whispered as he slid his lips
downward, to kiss the tall, sweet, soft column of her
throat.

And then he swept his tongue around one of her
breasts, licking, biting, chewing.

She cried out in soft whimpers beneath the erotic
caress of his urgent mouth and hands, his strokes in
her never losing their rhythm.

Hannah's hands moved seductively over his body,
rediscovering the bands of muscles along his shoulders
and down his back. They were so rocklike, so much
like steel to the touch.

Every nerve within her came alive with a hungry
need as she swept her one hand around and managed
to touch his manhood when he partially withdrew be-

fore plunging even more deeply inside her velvet moistness.

With quick, eager fingers, his hands were in her hair, drawing her mouth against his in a fiery, feverish kiss.

His mouth forced her lips open as his kiss grew more and more uncontrollable, more passionate.

Hannah was shot full of strange, wondrous desires that she had never known before. Each time she made love with him, he taught her more skills, the mysteries of love. She was on fire with the sensations of excitement. Her body yearned to know even more, to be what he wished her to be, to do what he wished her to do.

She moaned throatily when he brushed his lips in feathery kisses down to her breasts, then once again claimed a nipple between his teeth where he sucked until it throbbed from the pure, frantic pleasure.

Her head began to reel when she recognized those familiar feelings that came with her reaching the ultimate of pleasure. She clung to him. With her teeth, she nipped at the corded muscles of his shoulders. Her blood surged in a wild thrill.

Strong Wolf felt the pulsating of his longing in his hot loins. His lips brushed the smooth, glassy skin of Hannah's breasts, his excitement like a deep rumbling of a volcano soon to erupt. He could feel the pleasure spreading in hot splashes throughout him.

Strong Wolf swept his arms around Hannah and drew her closer, sculpting himself to her moist body, molding himself perfectly to the curved hollow of her hips.

He pressed endlessly deeper, feeling the suction of her warm and sweet place, as though warm fingers were inside her, grabbing, sucking, caressing.

Then it came to him in a sensual shock as the pleasure burst forth inside his brain, as though someone had sent sparkles of moonbeams throughout him. He felt it explode as a great shuddering in his loins matched Hannah's sensual spasms of delight.

He swept his hands down to her buttocks and dug his fingers into her flesh. He lifted her closer as she strained her hips up at him.

He could hear her breath catch and hold, then smiled as she cried out at her own total fulfillment.

Breathing hard, Hannah and Strong Wolf clung to one another when they came down from their height of pleasure. Strong Wolf rolled away from her and lay with his eyes closed as his heartbeats slowed.

Then he turned to Hannah, his hands touching her, turning her, drawing her into the warmth of his body. "I never can get enough of you," he whispered.

"Nor I you," Hannah said, closing her eyes with ecstasy as his fingers teased circles around her belly, up to her breasts, just missing the nipples each time so that they strained with added anticipation.

Then he moved away from her, silent for a moment.

He leaned up on an elbow and gazed at her. "Hannah, I've had to make a decision lately that I hope you will understand," he said.

Hannah's breath caught, praying to herself that this wasn't the time that he would reveal to her things that she knew he had kept from her. She wanted nothing to spoil this night. She only hoped that her fears were not founded—that he had kept something *terrible* from her!

"What is it?" she asked, her voice guarded.

He laughed loosely and drew her over, giving her a soft kiss on the lips. "Don't sound as though you don't trust what I am going to say," he said softly.

"Then, what *is* it?" Hannah said, her eyes searching his face and eyes for answers.

He leaned away from her again. He grabbed her by the waist and drew her close to his side.

"Hannah, seeing how quickly a disease can render a people helpless, I have decided that it is time for me to return to Wisconsin," he said. "I must now lead my people to *this* land. I know that no land is perfect, nor are the white people who will be our neighbors. But this is the best I can do for them. It is time for them to be with me, as one heartbeat."

He paused, then said, "There is one main concern of mine," he said wistfully. "My grandfather, who is now chief, is elderly. This journey might be too hard on him. I will fear for him every inch of the way. Yet he is weary of that land that has not been good to our people. He will be anxious to finally get to leave it."

"I wish to go with you," Hannah said, relieved to know that *this* might have been what had troubled him during their marriage ceremony. Surely *this,* his concern for his grandfather and people, as a whole, was what had caused him to occasionally get that haunted look in his eyes at *other* times.

Oh, if only it were so! Too often she had feared some dark secret that he was keeping from her!

Sometimes she had even thought that the haunted look was because he had doubts of marrying her!

But now?

Perhaps it had nothing at all to do with secrets, or . . . *her.*

"Hannah, the journey is long," Strong Wolf said drawing her thoughts back to the present. "I don't want to tire you. You have only recently been overwhelmed by exhaustion after caring for the ill."

"How can you even think that I would not insist on accompanying you on such a long journey?" Hannah said, her eyes wide. "I would *never* stay behind. I am your wife. I belong with you."

"But, Hannah . . ."

"Strong Wolf, if you had planned not to share everything with me, then why did you marry me?"

Hannah left the bed and stood over the fire, her pulse racing.

Strong Wolf was stunned by her outburst and knew now that he should have never kept anything from her. He now knew just how she might react when he told her the true facts about himself!

Yet now he knew to guard that secret even more than he ever had!

He could not chance losing her.

Strong Wolf left the bed and went to Hannah. He placed his hands at her waist and turned her around to face him. "Hannah, do you realize that we just had our first argument as man and wife?" he said softly, his eyes imploring her.

"I didn't mean to argue," Hannah said, her voice breaking.

She crept into his arms. "I'm sorry," she murmured. "But I just feel so strongly about things, sometimes. I don't want to be left out of any portion of your life. I want to share! Please allow it."

He unbraided her hair until it lay silken and long down her naked back. "You will go with me," he agreed. "And you must understand something about me, Hannah. I have never been married before. There will be times when . . ."

Hannah placed a gentle finger to his lips to seal his words behind them. "Shh," she murmured. "We both have some adjusting to do. Loving each other so much, that shouldn't be so hard to do."

He smiled down at her, then swept her into his arms and carried her back to the bed.

They made love again and again.

35

The air was heavy, the night was hot,
I sat by her side, and forgot—forgot!
                              —FRANK DESPREZ

Strong Wolf was now several days into his journey
home, to Wisconsin. He had left what he hoped were
enough warriors to care for the needs of his village in
the Kansas Territory.

Camp was being made for the night. Strong Wolf
had seen to it that his entourage to Wisconsin had
filled their parfleche bags with food stores for the journey. They had brought dried turnips, thistle stalks,
milkweed buds, chokeberry pemmican, and dried
deer meat.

Strong Wolf watched some prepare their bedding
while others built a large outdoor fire. The fire would
ward off the chill of the night, as well as keep away
any beasts who might come sniffing around their
camp.

Strong Wolf's eyes shifted. Proud Heart was making
a comfortable pallet for his wife, Singing Wind.

Hawk and Doe Eyes were embracing down by the
river, seemingly never to tire of one another.

No pangs of jealousy entered Strong Wolf's heart
over someone else holding Doe Eyes. Although
Strong Wolf and Doe Eyes's marriage had been
planned since the day of their birth—since they had
been born on the same day and at almost the same
hour to women who were best friends—he would

never forget the moment he realized that Doe Eyes
was someone he could never love.

He would also never forget the humiliation he had
felt when Doe Eyes had stared at him as though he
was a demon, having witnessed him become someone
she didn't know. Yes, he was afflicted by an illness
that his mother carried in her genes.

He was very grateful that it had happened only that
one time to him. He hoped that with time, everyone
who *knew* of his affliction then had forgotten.

But *he* lived with the knowledge that it *could* happen, at any given moment, at any given time. And so
did Doe Eyes!

"Darling, what are you thinking about so intensely
as you stare at Doe Eyes?" Hannah said as she came
and stood before him, blocking his view of the beautiful woman.

"What . . . ?" Strong Wolf said, his eyes wide as
he was drawn out of his dreaded reverie. "What did
you say?"

Hannah looked over her shoulder at Doe Eyes, who
was in Hawk's arms, looking adoringly up at him as
they talked.

Then Hannah gazed questionably again at Strong
Wolf. "Please tell me I don't have any reason to be
jealous of that woman," she pleaded.

When Strong Wolf swept his arms around Hannah
and drew her against his hard body, his eyes warm
and filled with love for her, she knew that question
had been foolish.

Yet there *was* something bothering him. It entered
his eyes every time he looked at Doe Eyes! Hannah
so wished that he would confide in her about this.

Yet she was never going to be a nagging wife. She
wanted to be everything sweet and good for her husband, not someone he dreaded to face every day.

"My woman, how could you ever think that I would look at Doe Eyes with a lusting, when I have *you*?" Strong Wolf said, brushing a soft kiss across her lips. "One day I shall open my heart to you and tell you why I *detest* that woman; not hunger for her."

"I didn't mean to pry," Hannah said, laying her cheek against his muscled chest, then became even more aware of his pounding heart as she felt it against her cheek. It was like distant thunder as she listened to it, a heartbeat that was only caused by torment.

It did not seem the same sort of reaction as when he held her, or made love to her.

Yes, she knew now that something terribly wrong had happened between her husband and Doe Eyes. Would she ever know *what*? Something told her she . . . wouldn't. It seemed too horrible a thing for him to confess to!

"Let us make camp down by the river away from everyone else," Strong Wolf said, picking up his buckskin bags and blankets from the ground. "We are newly married. We should have more privacy, do you not think so, my wife?"

"Yes, I think so," Hannah said, trying to feel lighthearted again, after becoming filled with such doubts.

She lifted several thick pelts from the ground, on which she and Strong Wolf would soon be making love. She hoped that she could soon forget what had only moments ago troubled her. She loved Strong Wolf too much to have such doubts about him!

"The only audience we will have tonight will be the moon and stars," Strong Wolf said, laughing as they walked away from everyone.

"It is good to hear you laughing," Hannah said, casting him a troubled glance. "Darling, tonight you seem more moody than usual."

"Yes, and I apologize," he said quietly. "But I have

concerns that I carry with me, over having left my people back at my village. Too many white people are shrewd and land hungry. While I am gone, should they ..."

"Darling," Hannah said, interrupting him. "Colonel Deshong won't allow anything to happen to your people while you are gone."

She dropped the pelts from her arms when they reached a secret place that was sheltered by thick brush and a heavy stand of birch trees. "Please don't worry about it," she further encouraged. "You are doing what you were meant to do ... go for your people in Wisconsin, to lead them to their new home in Kansas."

Strong Wolf lay the blankets and his travel bags on the ground beside the pelts. He drew Hannah into his arms. "You are so good for me," he said, his hands caressing her back. "When I feel low, you lift me up. When I worry, you give me reason to hope again. How could I have been so lucky to have found you? You are a woman of much wisdom, *and* heart."

"*I* am the true lucky one," Hannah said, framing his face between her hands, bringing his lips to hers. "Kiss me, husband. Please kiss me."

His lips came to hers gently. He cupped her buttocks through the fabric of her buckskin dress and yanked her against him, where she could feel his tight bulge as he ground it into her.

The feel of him, although only through the fabrics of their clothes, made her grow dizzy with passion.

She reached between them and stroked his manhood through his buckskin breeches, evoking a deep groan from the depths of his throat.

"We ... must ... first ... build a fire," he whispered huskily against her lips, yet leaned into her hand, so that she could grip him, then stroke him again. "My woman, you are making me mindless."

"We don't need a fire," Hannah whispered back. She reached her hand down inside his breeches and sucked in a wild breath of rapture when she felt the true flesh of his shaft, aware that some of his juices had spilled from the tip.

She rubbed the moisture into his flesh, then gripped him and slowly moved her hand on him again. She could feel his body stiffen and his breath quickening. She gazed at him, not surprised to find his eyes closed, and his head held back as he groaned again, again, and again.

Her heart pounding, afraid that she was arousing him too much, so badly wanting to join him in this ecstasy, Hannah eased her hand away and slid it from inside his breeches.

Breathing hard, Strong Wolf yanked her against him. His steel arms enfolded her as he kissed her.

She felt his hunger in the hard, seeking pressure of his lips, and she answered his kiss with a need of her own. It rose up within her, spreading and swelling. She ached almost unmercifully at the juncture of her thighs.

She gasped with pleasure when he bunched up the skirt of her dress with one hand and pushed it up past her thighs, the fingers of his other hand splaying across the heat of her passion.

His hand caressed her, then when he slipped a finger up inside her, she became light-headed with rapture.

Ecstatic waves of pleasure splashed through Hannah. She ground her mouth into his, her tongue flicking as he opened his mouth to receive it.

Their tongues danced.

His finger began thrusting, his thumb caressing the

core of her womanhood until she was almost mindless
with the pure ecstasy of it.

And then he drew away from her.

With a racing pulse and a heart beating so soundly
her knees would hardly hold her up, Hannah watched
as Strong Wolf spread blankets and pelts on the grass
beside the river.

The moon was bright, like white satin as it poured
from the sky.

The stars twinkled like jewels in the inky black
heavens.

An owl hooted from somewhere close by.

And then the air was filled with the tremolo and
yodel of a loon sounding its eerie chorus across the
water.

Overcome with a feverish heat of need for Hannah,
Strong Wolf went to her and gazed at her as he
reached for the hem of her dress and began slowly
smoothing it up over her, struck anew by her loveliness. She was, ah, so awesome in her beauty.

When her breasts were revealed to him, her nipples
taut, the ache in his loins became more pronounced.
He yanked the dress on over her head and tossed it
aside, then cupped her breasts within the palms of
his hands.

He bent low and flicked his tongue over one nipple,
and then the other, then he covered one with his
mouth, sucking, licking, nipping.

Hannah's heart was pounding even harder as she
closed her eyes and enjoyed the euphoria that filled
her entire being. Her breasts throbbed with his kisses.
Her passion was so intense, his mouth was so hot and
sweet, she was finding it hard to bring her breathing
under control.

Shaken with desire, she reached her hands inside
his shirt and swept them over his powerful, sleek

chest. And as he kissed her breasts, holding their weight in his hands, she placed her thumbs and forefingers at the waist of his breeches and slowly lowered them.

She did not have to look at him to know that he was totally aroused. As his breeches fell away from him, she reached a hand to his throbbing shaft and circled her fingers around it.

She heard his quick intake of breath, knowing now, by experience, that he became so sensitive there before making love to her. She was careful not to go too fast with her caresses, or hold him too tightly with her fingers. She wanted him all to herself; the ecstasy shared.

Strong Wolf, hardly able to bear the wild ripples of desire that were licking through him in heated flames, reached down and grabbed Hannah's hand. He took it away from his aching heat, then enfolded her within his arms and led her down onto the blanket.

He knelt down over her. He lowered his mouth to her lips as once again one of his hands found her warm and secret place and began his slow caresses.

Wanting more, hungering for the feel of him inside her, she gently shoved his hand away and placed her hands around his manhood and led it to her throbbing center.

"Love me," she whispered against his parted lips. She flicked her tongue across his lips. "Take me to paradise. Oh, my darling, how I need you. I need you *now*."

A tremor went through her body when he shoved himself into her. It felt as though he was reaching much farther than usual, touching places inside her that she didn't know existed.

As his pelvis moved rhythmically against her, his

thrusts became maddeningly fast. He sank deeper and plunged over and over within her.

Hannah threw her head back and sighed as the incredible sweetness swept through her.

Strong Wolf buried his face in the valley of her breasts, smothering his repeated groans as he felt the passion rising, spreading, turning to a liquid fire within him.

Having never felt as alive, so desired, Hannah opened herself wider to him, and her hips responded in a rhythmic movement all their own as she clung and rocked with him.

The pulsing crest of Strong Wolf's passion was near. His mouth closed hard upon hers as he kissed her, his hands stroking her softly pliant limbs, caressing her skin feverishly with his fingertips. His hands searched all of her pleasure points until she shuddered with desire.

Then he held her in a torrid embrace when he felt the storm building within.

Her hands clung to his sinewed shoulders when she felt the pleasure building, climbing, spreading.

And then that sudden onslaught of passion overwhelmed them both. Hannah clung to him as his body became rocked with spasms, and he sent his seed deeply within her.

Her own silent explosion of need sent her senses reeling. She gave herself up to the rapture as her fingers clamped onto his muscular male buttocks, feeling them tightening each time he plunged into her.

Then it was over, their ecstasy sought and found. Their bodies were pearled with sweat. Their hearts were pounding. Their breathing was raspy.

Strong Wolf leaned low over Hannah and pressed his lips to her throat. "I love you so," he whispered against her flesh.

Legs entwined, their bodies straining together as they turned on their sides to face one another, Hannah reverently breathed his name against his cheek. "Strong Wolf, my husband, my wonderful, sweet husband," she said. "Life was nothing before I met you. You have made me realize what it truly feels to be a woman. I have proven that I am more than a tomboy, haven't I?"

He leaned away from her, his eyes dancing. "Much more," he said, then kissed her softly. "You are all woman, and you are *mine.*"

"I wish to have your child," Hannah said before she even realized that she had been thinking about it. "Darling, let us have a child soon. I so badly want that."

Something she said seemed to seize hold of Strong Wolf as though a dark, dank wind had blown between them. He rose quickly to his feet, dressed, and started gathering wood for a fire, leaving Hannah on the blankets and pelts, staring disbelievingly at him.

Trembling, afraid, now suddenly aware of the chill of the night, Hannah rose slowly to her feet and grabbed a blanket around her shoulders. Staring, she watched Strong Wolf light the fire, then stand over it, his back to her, his naked body a copper sheen beneath the moonlight.

"Strong Wolf?" Hannah said cautiously.

When he didn't respond, she took a blanket and placed it around his shoulders.

The blanket warm, he gripped it around himself, but nothing would ease the torment that made him cold inside at her mention of having children. Of course, when he first thought of marrying her, his dark past came back to haunt him, to know that marriage usually brought children into the world.

But every time he had thought of them possibly

having children, he had cast it from his mind. He had wanted nothing to get in the way of their marriage!

He wanted only to have Hannah, any way he could have her.

Then everything else would come later ... the worry, the concern, the downright dread of having children!

If their children inherited the traits of his family that came from his mother's side, then that child would have to live with the same secrets he had carried with him all of his life.

It would not be fair to the child; yet besides that one fear, for him*self*, life had been *grand*!

As for now, he had a woman who met his every need, who fed his desires, who filled his arms with her sweetness.

She made him have faith in himself again.

Only she!

And now? She had seen his fear. She had felt it. He could no longer hold it within himself like a dark sin that he had no control over. He could no longer live a lie!

The blanket dropping away from him, Strong Wolf turned to Hannah and gripped her by the shoulders, causing her own blanket to flutter to the ground. He drew her into his embrace, their bare bodies pressed together as he held her.

For the moment he enjoyed the pleasant, sweet smell of her, the gentle way she clung to him, the way she pressed her cheek against his chest.

She could have plied him with questions!

For having left her so quickly, after having just made love, she could even hate him!

"I have much to tell you," he suddenly blurted, feeling her grow tense within his arms. "Hannah, I should have not waited so long to tell you. But I was afraid of losing you. I may even lose you now. If I do, I am not certain I can go on. Please listen. Please understand. Please do not go away hating or loathing me."

Hannah scarcely breathed as she heard his pleas. Her eyes were wide as she clung to him a moment longer, afraid now for him to tell her the secret that she knew he had held from her. It seemed not at all to do with his people's welfare, after all, as she had hoped. It was something else ... something frightening.

He seemed *so* afraid to tell her. What if she couldn't understand? What if what he said *did* cause her to want to leave him?

Oh, how she loved and adored him. Surely there was nothing that he could say that could change her feelings for him.

"Please tell me," Hannah said, easing from his arms. She gazed up at him and saw the silent torment; the wavering of his eyes as he stared down at her. "How could you possibly think that anything could change how much I love you?"

He reached down and grabbed a blanket. He wrapped it around her shoulders, bringing the ends around his, so that they were locked together amidst the warmth of the blanket. Gently he led her down beside the fire, then secured the blanket again around them.

"You don't have to tell me," Hannah said, gazing over at him. "If you feel so strongly against my knowing, you ... don't ... have to tell me."

"I must," Strong Wolf said, trembling inside at the very thought of what she would soon know. "I feel that you are the sort of woman who won't look at me with disgust when you know that secret part of me and my family. I *must* tell you. It has to be said. I should have told you before we exchanged vows. Then, should you have not understood and wanted to back away from me, it would have been easier. But now we *are* married. We might soon have children. You must be told my reasons for fearing fathering a child."

Hannah froze inside as she gazed into his smoke-black eyes. "I'm listening," she said. "And, darling, I will never stop loving you. No matter what you say, I will love you."

He brushed a kiss across her brow, then looked away from her. He stared into the fire as he began telling her what happened all those many years ago between himself and Doe Eyes.

"Doe Eyes and I were born on the same day, at almost the same hour, to best friends," he began. "My mother, Swallow Song, and Doe Eyes's mother, Dawnmarie, plotted on that day that their son and daughter would be the best of friends who would then grow up and marry. I went along with their schemes, not seeing harm in them, since I was so enamored with Doe Eyes, at our young age of ten . . . until Doe Eyes revealed her true self to me."

"What did she do?" Hannah asked, her eyes wide as she listened. She wasn't jealous of Strong Wolf loving someone so much at such a young age. She had gone through many puppy loves herself at that age. The only true love that she had ever felt was for Strong Wolf. She had to believe that it was the same for Strong Wolf.

"It was not so much what *she* did," Strong Wolf said, gazing down at Hannah. "It was what I did to cause her reaction *to* me, that turned her to loathing, not loving me."

Hannah's pulse raced realizing that finally she would be told what caused that haunted look in her husband's eyes; yet now she feared that knowledge.

Strong Wolf took both of Hannah's hands and held

them in a tight grip. "On that day, Hannah, my mother's fears became a reality," he said thickly. "On that day, Hannah, my body became something unfamiliar to me. It was then that I discovered that I had inherited something from my mother that was humiliating, degrading, and loathsome."

"What ... did ... you inherit?" Hannah asked, her voice barely a whisper, for now she realized how much her husband feared her knowing. And what if his fears were founded? What if she saw him as someone who made her turn her head with disgust?

"What?" she persisted. "Tell me what happened? What did you inherit?"

"I was with Doe Eyes," Strong Wolf said, releasing Hannah's hands. He lowered his eyes. He swallowed hard. "We were only ten. We shared our first kiss. Then ... then ..."

He turned his eyes away from her and moaned, as though someone had hit him.

Hannah moved to her knees. The blanket fell away from her. She knelt in front of him and placed her hands to his face. "Darling, please go on," she encouraged. "When you get this behind you and realize that I shall always love you, then don't you see? Your life will be like a newborn child's. You won't have to ever think about this again. You can begin fresh. I will be with you all of the way. I love you so!"

His eyes locked with hers. "While kissing Doe Eyes, my body began to tremble strangely," he said, his voice breaking. "I suddenly jerked away from her, not by choice, but by being forced to as my body began shaking and jerking strangely. I was thrown to the ground by the impact of the shakes. My head was thrown back. My eyes rolled back inside my head. I almost swallowed my tongue, my body uncontrollably shaking."

He paused and swallowed hard.

"At that moment I lost sense of time," he continued solemnly. "Of reality, of self. I only became aware of the horrors that happened when the shakes stopped and I found Doe Eyes staring down at me. There was a look of total disgust, of loathing on her face. She was gagging, as though she might throw up. And I knew that I was the cause of her reaction."

He took her hands in his and held them to his chest. "Hannah, when I moved to my feet and tried to reach out for her, she recoiled," he said bitterly. "She told me that I disgusted her. And then she ran away. Since that day, she has not said one word to me until she came and spoke in behalf of Hawk. I had to live with knowing that my body could betray me at any time, that I could be the target of people's loathsome stares. It has been a life of torture, Hannah, to think that I might have to relive those moments again."

Hannah stared at him for a moment, stunned by the truth. Then she felt something more. It wasn't pity. It was an intense caring, an intense wish to make things right for this man she would die for!

"Oh, my darling," she cried, flinging herself into his arms. She pressed her body against his, loving the feel of it, and hardly believing that anything as beautiful could ever be ugly. "I love you still! I understand how you must feel! Please let me help you forget! Please know that I love you no less now than before you told me. Doe Eyes was a coldhearted fool! How could she do that to you? She betrayed you, Strong Wolf! She betrayed you!"

"Her betrayal was complete when she jerked off a necklace that had been worn as true proof of our devotion to one another," he said somberly. "When we were born, we were both given the same identical necklace to wear. She stood in her disgust of me and tore her necklace away and stamped on it!"

"How horrible," Hannah gasped. "I can see how that day affected you so terribly. But this is now. Please forget what happened in the past."

"What brought it back so strongly tonight was Proud Heart's announcement that his wife was going to have a child," he said. "I began to think about us, about possibly having children, and fear filled me like bolts of lightning that our child might inherit the traits of my mother's family, as *I* inherited them."

"And that is something we shall concern ourselves with if it happens," Hannah said, brushing his brow with a kiss. "As for now, let us be happy with what we have. Our love. It is so special. It is so deep."

Strong Wolf was relieved over her reaction, yet he had to know just one more thing.

It was easy to say to him that she understood.

But what if . . . ?

"What if you should witness one of my seizures?" he uttered. "Can you honestly say that you would not be repelled and look away in disgust?"

Hannah took a deep breath. "Darling, I could never do that," she murmured. "I would be there for you. I would hold you in my arms to comfort you until the seizure is passed. I would make you see just how deep my love goes for you."

"How can you be so sure?" he asked, his eyes imploring her.

"When I was a little girl, I would say about twelve years of age, I was downtown with my father, when suddenly a woman fell down in the middle of the street and began having seizures," Hannah said softly. "My father ran to her and held her until the seizures were passed. I sat down beside her and held her hand. I felt so badly for the woman, I wanted to cry. But when she awakened and discovered what had happened, the courage she showed made me know that no pity was needed. She thanked my father for helping her, she gave me a quiet, sweet smile, then rose from the street and went on her way as though nothing had happened. Her courage, and her showing no shame made me admire her so much. As you can see, as a child I did not turn away in disgust. As an adult, I shall be even more loving and comforting."

Strong Wolf seized her into his arms. "My woman," he whispered, slowly caressing her back. "You are filled with such heart, with such caring. I will not fear any longer that which has plagued me since I was a child. You have helped me place it behind me. Thank you, Hannah. Thank you for being you."

"Shall we try once more tonight to make a baby?" she asked, snuggling against his broad, hard chest. She felt that was true proof to him that she had been sincere in what she had said to him. To have a child. *Theirs*.

He gave her a lingering, warm look, touched by her sweetness, then grabbed her up into his arms and carried her to the blankets.

When he lay over her, their bodies touching, their hands exploring, he gave her a heated kiss, one that made her head reel with the passion.

They made love with more feelings, with abandon, their hearts thudding within their chests!

Strong Wolf felt as though his demons had been finally released from inside him.

He was now free to truly live . . . and love. . . . !

36

Nothing could make the river be
So crystal pure but she.
        —ANDREW MARVELL

The Chippewa village sat on a hill overlooking a dense
forest close by. A river snaked through the forest.

Hannah had entered the village proudly at Strong
Wolf's side, her pinto keeping stride with his magnifi-
cent steed. She had taken in everything—the wigwams
made of poles that were bent and covered with the
bark of trees and cattail mats, the tethered ponies,
the toddlers playing games, and the women fleshing
yesterday's kill. Fresh meat hung from drying racks,
bloodred. White sheets of buck fat also hung from
tripods close to the wigwams.

Enjoying the merriment and celebration, Hannah
now sat in the council house, a large one-room building made of logs with clapboarding to keep the weather
out. The roof was made from wooden shingles. The
floor was the ground, with a covering of straw.

Straw was also spread on the roof. Two guards were
stationed outside to call the alarm if the straw caught
fire from the sparks flying up from the central fire pit
inside the building.

There was one door that opened into the interior.

Hannah sat beside Strong Wolf on a raised platform
that was covered with rich pelts. From the moment

she had arrived at the Chippewa village, she had been comfortable with the surroundings, and the people.

She had been introduced to everyone right away. She glanced over at White Wolf, who sat on a platform next to the one on which she and Strong Wolf sat. His wife, Dawnmarie, sat beside him. A loose robe hung in folds over White Wolf's right shoulder. Dawnmarie was dressed in a white doeskin robe.

White Wolf, of the Lac du Flambeau clan of Chippewa, was Proud Heart's father and the chief of this village. From first glance, Hannah had seen that he was a chief with much power, a man with charisma.

Hannah had been told that White Wolf's name was always spoken when old men sat around talking about proud feats of valor.

Old women praised White Wolf for his kindness toward them.

Young women held him up as an idol to their sweethearts, for although he had reached the age of sixty, he was still steel-muscled, quick of movement, and breathtakingly handsome.

His eyes proved his gentle, peace-loving nature.

As he smiled over at her now, Hannah's insides melted, so much that she sought Strong Wolf's hand quickly, to make her remember that she was married to a man who was just as handsome, whose charm matched White Wolf's.

And Hannah had been taken quickly with his wife, Dawnmarie. Not only was she sweet and friendly, a half-breed who bridged two worlds of white and red people with her Kickapoo heritage, she was beautiful, with violet eyes.

Dawnmarie's hair was gray, yet lovely in how it swirled around her delicately featured face. Only a few traces of wrinkles creased her brow, and around her eyes and mouth. Usually those wrinkles were hidden in her deep, friendly smile.

Hannah's eyes shifted, and she looked around Strong Wolf at an elderly lady who sat at Dawnmarie's right side on a platform next to the one on which Hannah and Strong Wolf sat. This elderly lady, who had reached and passed her hundredth birthday, was shriveled up and tiny, her wrinkled skin tautly drawn across her bones.

Her head bobbed uncontrollably as she sat with her hunched back, a huge knot at the base of her neck. Her old eyes seemed sightless, yet she proved even now that she was alert as she watched the dancers performing around the council house central fire.

Dressed in a loose-fitting buckskin dress, adorned with various colorful beads, her long and flowing gray hair reaching the floor behind her; the woman kept time with the music as she patted a fan of feathers against one of her knees, her legs crossed beneath her.

Hannah smiled as she thought of this woman as young and beautiful, and perhaps someone who had been quite skilled at dancing. Surely that was how she got the name Woman Dancing!

Then Hannah looked elsewhere. Her eyes stopped on Proud Heart and his wife, Singing Wind, who sat on a platform at White Wolf and Dawnmarie's right side. It was obvious that Proud Heart was happy to be home. He was all smiles as he watched the dancers, one hand linked with his wife's. They had only moments ago revealed to Proud Heart's parents that Singing Wind was going to have a child.

Hannah glanced over at Dawnmarie again and how she beamed with the news that she was going to be a grandmother.

White Wolf sat just as proudly smiling over the news.

The only drawback was that White Wolf and Dawn-marie were soon to depart from this village. Dawn-marie was going to search for her true people, the Kickapoo, in Mexico. Proud Heart would then be chief of this village. By leaving, White Wolf and Dawnmarie would not have the opportunity to watch their grandchild growing up.

But Dawnmarie explained to Hannah that she had waited a lifetime to finally search for her people. She explained that her mother, Doe Eyes, for whom Dawnmarie's own daughter had been named, had been abducted from her Kickapoo village long ago. She had been forced to marry a white trader, Dawn-marie's father. Her mother had always wished to join her true people again, but death had claimed her be-fore she had been given the opportunity. Dawnmarie had promised that she would go there herself when their son, Proud Heart, became old enough to take over her husband's chieftain duties.

Now was the time. Proud Heart would not be re-turning with Strong Wolf to the Potawatomis village in the Kansas Territory. He would stay behind, in his rightful place, with his own people.

Hannah shifted her eyes to Doe Eyes, who sat with Hawk, on a platform next to Proud Heart's. It had been evident that White Wolf and Dawnmarie had disapproved of their daughter's choice in men. Al-though White Wolf saw Hawk's father as a friend, his mother—whose Sioux brother Slow Running had been an ardent enemy of White Wolf—was anything *but* friendly. She had carried her hate for White Wolf deep inside her heart ever since her brother had died fight-ing with White Wolf and his warriors.

She had always blamed White Wolf for his death, overlooking the fact that her brother was a demon on two feet while he had lived!

Slow Running no longer posed a threat, but when White Wolf looked at Hawk, he seemed to be looking at Slow Running; Hawk had taken on his uncle's appearance, as though he was the reincarnation of Slow Running.

Doe Eyes had talked with Hannah earlier in the evening, speaking about Hawk's mother. Doe Eyes dreaded facing Star Flower with the news that Hawk had not slain Strong Wolf and Proud Heart, as ordered, and with the news that Hawk and Doe Eyes would soon be married. She expected Star Flower to go into a fit of anger! Oh, how she dreaded that moment!

Strong Wolf leaned closer to Hannah. "We will leave for my people's village tomorrow," he whispered. "But it is good to be here with such friends as White Wolf and Dawnmarie. Are you enjoying yourself? You seem so quiet. So studious."

"Yes, I'm truly enjoying myself," Hannah whispered back, giving Strong Wolf a soft smile. She reached for one of his hands and twined her fingers through his. "I guess I got caught up in thinking about White Wolf and his family. They are all so kind, aren't they?"

"As far back as I can remember, my grandfather traded and had council with White Wolf often," Strong Wolf said, glancing over at White Wolf. He was amazed at how the last thirty years had hardly aged him. And he had seen how Hannah had been taken by his noble presence.

For a moment Strong Wolf had been jealous!

"And your mother?" Hannah asked, drawing Strong Wolf's eyes back to her. "Did she come often also and visit with Dawnmarie?"

"They were, they still *are,* the best of friends," Strong Wolf said, nodding. He smiled as he again glanced over at White Wolf. "But for a while, when they were both seeking husbands, there was some competition between my mother and Dawnmarie. My mother told me that she had first loved White Wolf, then my father, Sharp Nose. She said that White Wolf saw no other woman in his eyes once he caught sight of Dawnmarie."

Strong Wolf shifted his gaze. "Violet Eyes," he murmured. "White Wolf calls Dawnmarie Violet Eyes. And I see why. Her eyes are quite intriguing, wouldn't you say?"

"Yes, they are so beautiful," Hannah said, following his gaze. "So deeply violet in color, like the violets that spread across the ground in early spring."

"But yours, the color of new *grass* in the spring, are as intriguing," Strong Wolf was quick to say as he placed a finger to her chin and drew her eyes around, to lock with his. "You are ever so beautiful tonight, my woman. When this celebration is over, we shall return to our camp down by the river. We will attempt, again, to make a baby."

Hannah laughed softly, squeezed his hand, then leaned into his embrace at his side as he placed an arm around her waist and drew her against him.

"I've never been as content," she murmured, his tightened hold on her assuring her that he had heard her.

Together they watched the dancers perform their dances. Everyone had already eaten a feast of dried venison, bear's meat, and wildfowl. They had also been served stewed pumpkin and succotash, baked bread, crisp little corn cakes, corn soup, fresh blueberries, and pine-needle tea.

Hannah didn't see how the dancers could be performing so vigorously after having eaten such a feast. The young braves and Chippewa maidens mingled as

they danced, their movements following the rhythmic
beat of drums made of hollowed logs covered tightly
with deerskins, the low tone of cane flutes, the shrill
wail of bird bone whistles, and the staccato rasps of
rattles made of polished gourds.

To the rhythmic throbbing of the drums, the young
braves leapt and rebounded with feathered headgear
waving. They gave a wild spring forward, like a panther for its prey.

The young girls' faces were glowing like bright red
autumn leaves, their glossy braids bouncing over each
of their shoulders as they followed the movements of
the braves, the fringes of their dresses swaying.

Hannah's eyes were quickly averted when a woman
entered the council house in a huff, causing the instru-
ments to become suddenly quiet and the dancers to
stand ghostly still.

Hawk standing quickly to his feet drew Hannah's
attention to him.

Then she looked in jerks again at the woman, and
followed her movements as she stamped up to Hawk
and suddenly slapped his face. The sound of her hand
against his flesh made a strange, hollow sound in the
large room.

Gasps reverberated around the room as Hawk reached
a hand to his burning face, where his mother's hand-
prints were engraved onto his flesh from her having
hit him so hard.

"Mother . . ." Hawk said, his voice almost failing
him.

"You are no longer my son!" Star Flower screamed,
livid with anger. She slapped him again. "How could
you? Word came to me that you were here! You are
in the council house of my enemy? You sit as friends
sit while a celebration is in progress?"

She turned and looked slowly around the room, her

whole body stiffening when she found Strong Wolf
slowly moving to his feet, and then Proud Heart.

Again she turned to Hawk. "They are still alive!"
she screamed, starting to hit Hawk again, but this time
stopped as Hawk reached a hand up and grabbed her
by the wrist.

"Mother, you should not be here," Hawk said
sternly, his ability to speak having finally returned.
"And, yes, Strong Wolf and Proud Heart are still
alive. I would have it no other way. And although you
wish them dead, they have become my friends again,
as they were when we were children."

Tears rolled down Star Flower's cheek. She
wrenched her wrist free and hung her hands in tight
fists at her sides. She looked slowly over at Doe Eyes,
fire entering her eyes at the sight of the woman standing beside her son.

Then she glared up at Hawk again. "And you even
take the daughter of my enemy to be your woman?"
she cried. "Hawk, you have disgraced me. You
shame me!"

"Mother, Doe Eyes and I have loved each other for
many moons," Hawk said, keenly aware that everyone
was watching and hearing. Shame filled him over a
mother who could belittle him in such a way in front
of people he now saw as his friends. "We are going
to be married."

"No!" Star Flower cried, lowering her face in her
hands. "I wish to die! I ... wish ... to die!"

Another presence in the room drew everyone's eyes
to the door. Buffalo Cloud, Star Flower's husband and
Hawk's proud Sioux father, came on into the room
and swept Star Flower up into his arms and held her
close.

His eyes wavered as he looked slowly around him,
his gaze holding on White Wolf as Star Flower

pounded on his chest, ranting and raving to be set free.

"I apologize for my wife," Buffalo Cloud said, his voice coming through loud and clear over his wife's continued tirade. "She has not yet learned how to forget a brother whose spirit even now laughs from the hereafter at her foolishness for fighting for something he gave up long ago when he died at the hands of the Chippewa."

Star Flower's screams ceased as Buffalo Cloud held her closer. She shrank into a tiny ball within his arms as she buried her face shamefully against his muscled chest.

"I will take my wife home now," Buffalo Cloud said, his voice breaking as he glanced over at his son. "And, son, please forgive your mother. At times she knows not what she does. It seems as though a demon is set loose inside her. Please see past it as I have learned to do, for when she is her normal self, no one could be as sweet and kind."

Hawk nodded, then went to his mother and placed a gentle hand on her shoulder. "Mother," he said softly. "Please turn and look at me."

Star Flower's body tightened. She clung fiercely around Buffalo Cloud's neck.

"Mother, please?" Hawk said, a little boy again who always wished to please his mother.

Star Flower sobbed, then turned her red and swollen eyes slowly around to gaze at Hawk.

"Mother, I am sorry if I have disappointed you," Hawk said, his eyes imploring her. "But I am not a murderer. I am a man who seeks peace with everyone. I was wrong to leave when you asked me to, to travel to the Kansas Territory. Even before I left I knew that I could not do as you asked. But I thought ... that ... perhaps time away from you would be best for both of us. I went to the Kansas Territory and renewed friendships. Please forget the vengeance that eats away that sweetest part of your heart. For your sake, for mine, and for Father's? Please, Mother. Try and forget the ugly past. Live for the future, for time is so fleeting. Soon you will be nothing but an old woman who still hates, who still thinks vengeance as your sole purpose for living."

"Son, I . . . am . . . sorry," Star Flower said, reaching a hand out for him. "I have been filled with hate for White Wolf *and* Strong Wolf's grandfather for so long, it will not be so easy to place it behind me."

"But you must, Mother," Hawk said, trying to keep his voice steady.

"I shall try," Star Flower said softly, lowering her eyes.

"I will take your mother home now," Buffalo Cloud said, taking a step away from Hawk. "I believe things will be all right now. Please bring Doe Eyes to our village soon. We wish to grow to know her as we would a daughter."

After Buffalo Cloud and Star Flower were gone, the celebration seemed unable to get back on a solid, merry footing. Everyone disbanded and went their separate ways.

Hannah and Strong Wolf sat down beside their campfire, which was set aside from the rest. Strong Wolf had built them a lean-to up against a stand of thick young aspens.

As Strong Wolf placed more twigs of willow on the fire just inside the lean-to, Hannah slipped off her doeskin dress and placed a soft robe around her shoulders. She kept reliving the evening, the worst part, where Star Flower had so terribly embarrassed Hawk.

She was still in awe of Hawk, and how he could forgive her so easily. If Hannah had been humiliated in such a way by her mother or father, she was not sure how she could ever forgive them.

She felt thankful that her father and mother had finally accepted her love for an Indian.

If not, she might have faced the same sort of ordeal that Hawk faced tonight.

"My woman is still in deep thought," Strong Wolf said as he sat down beside her.

"I can't quit thinking about Hawk, and what his mother did to him tonight," Hannah said. "He is so even-tempered, so compassionate." She smiled. "Just like someone else I know."

"Ah, and who might that be?" Strong Wolf said, taking her by the wrists, drawing her onto his lap. He swept the robe away from her shoulders. It fluttered on the pallet of furs beneath her.

His hands cupped her breasts, his eyes roaming over her silken nudity. "My woman, tonight is ours," he said huskily. "Let us not think or talk anymore of other people's woes. I have waited this long day through to be alone with you."

As he kissed her, Hannah's eager hands slipped his shirt off, then raised herself up from him just enough, so that she could slip his breeches down away from that part of his anatomy that always gave her such a thrill.

Understanding why she was trying so hard to maneuver his breeches away from him, Strong Wolf placed his hands at her waist and lifted her off him.

He removed his breeches, then reached for her again, placed her on his lap, and gathered her into his arms. His mouth took hers by storm, his palms moving seductively over her, his fingers teasing her sensitive places.

Hannah clung to his shoulders and sucked in wild breaths of pleasure as he began probing with his vel-

vety tight heat where she was open to him. She cried
out against his lips as he shoved himself into her rose-
red slippery heat and began his rhythmic thrusts.

She gripped his shoulders as his mouth brushed her
cheeks and ears lightly in soft kisses. He kissed her
eyelids tenderly, then again their lips met in a frenzied kiss.

As frogs croaked along the riverbank and coyotes
howled in the distance, Hannah and Strong Wolf became lost in a world that was sweet and filled with
passion.

Afterward they sat watching the river. Hannah cud-
dled close to Strong Wolf beneath a shared blanket.
She gasped when overhead the northern lights flick-
ered. It was like wind rustling the tent of the sky as
they played their magic across the sky in colors of
pale greens, blues, and pinks.

"How beautiful!" Hannah sighed.

"It is an omen," Strong Wolf said, placing a finger
to her chin and turning her eyes to him. "A *good*
omen."

Again he kissed her and lowered her to the ground,
where he again made maddening love to her.

"Surely tonight we will have made a child," Hannah
whispered, giggling as he took her to paradise with
him again. She felt as though she was a part of the
beautiful heavens.

Amidst making love, her mind momentarily strayed
to what they were going to do tomorrow. They were
going to his village. What if his mother didn't approve
of her, a white woman? She shivered at the remembrance of what happened tonight as Hawk's mother
had told him that she did not approve of his choice
of woman, and *his* choice had been someone of his
same skin color.

"My woman, your mind is not on what you are

doing," Strong Wolf said, pausing in his lovemaking. "What are you thinking about?"

A sudden strange look came into Strong Wolf's eyes, one that Hannah quickly noticed.

"You spoke of making a child tonight," Strong Wolf said, searching her face and eyes for answers. "Is that what has caused you not to enjoy our lovemaking as much? You are worried about our child possibly inheriting the dark side of my character?"

Hannah gasped and paled. "No!" she quickly answered. "I've never thought once about . . . that. Darling, I love you so much. Will you please quit worrying about that?"

"Tomorrow I face my mother with a wife," Strong Wolf said. "Is that what you were thinking about?"

"Well, yes . . ." Hannah said, not sure if she should admit to such a truth.

"Then worry no more," Strong Wolf said. "She will love you as I love you. She is nothing like Star Flower. Just like you, my mother is everything sweet in this world."

She wrapped her arms around his neck as he rolled her over onto her back and plunged inside her again. "My wife," he uttered softly.

He kissed her gently, his hands caressing her breasts as he rhythmically rocked back and forth inside her.

"My husband," Hannah whispered against his lips. "My dear, wonderful husband."

They rocked and clung and whispered and melted.

37

The red rose whispers of passion,
And the white rose breathes of love.
—JOHN O'REILLY

Strong Wolf's village was some distance downriver from the Chippewa village. He relished the feel of his mother in his arms while the Potawatomis people came from their lodges, their eyes eager and bright when they discovered Strong Wolf was there.

Hannah was standing at his side. She smiled at the people as they came and gathered around. Then she watched Strong Wolf and his mother. She remembered Strong Wolf telling her how beautiful his mother was.

And she was beautiful and looked younger than her age. She had hardly any wrinkles on her tiny, sculpted face. Her hair was still as black as charcoal. And her shape was one of a youthful woman.

Hannah was surprised that Swallow Song had not married again, yet when she thought about it, she understood possibly why. If everyone knew about her having seizures, that could cause men to look away from her.

Then a thought came to Hannah. Just perhaps Swallow Song had not married again because it was *her* choice not to. Perhaps her love for her husband had been too strong for her ever to love again.

Hannah knew that should anything happen to Strong Wolf, *she* could never love again. She would even want to die with him, for life without him would be torment!

Hannah was saddened over Strong Wolf's chieftain grandfather's passing, yet proud now that Strong Wolf was a great chief.

How proud she would be to show him off to her family as a powerful chief of his people!

"My son," Swallow Song murmured, clinging to Strong Wolf. "How good it is that you are here. I have often wished that Father had never asked you to go and find our people a new home. Time is so precious, so *fleeting*. I did not want to grow any older without you."

She swallowed hard. "And when Father died, it was hard to endure without you being here to help me," she then said.

"I shall visit his grave and say a prayer," Strong Wolf said. "Hannah, my wife, will join me at the grave. She will also say a prayer. My grandfather will hear her. He will know her."

Swallow Song reached her hands out for Hannah. "Come to me," she murmured. "Let me hug you, Hannah."

Hannah welcomed Swallow Song's arms as she hugged her.

"It is so wonderful to finally get to know you," Hannah murmured, returning the embrace. "Strong Wolf has told me so much about you. And now I know why he is so proud when he speaks of you."

Swallow Song stepped away from Hannah. "Thank you," she said in her sweet, soft voice. She smiled at Hannah. "And I wish to know your mother well."

"You will get the opportunity when you return with

Strong Wolf and me to the Kansas Territory," Hannah said. She stepped back to Strong Wolf's side.

She loved the protective way he always slipped his arm around her waist. "As soon as we return home, I will send a wire to my parents about your arrival," she said as she gave Swallow Song another smile. "They will come from Saint Louis. We can have a celebration."

"And also you will meet her sister and brother," Strong Wolf said, smiling down at Hannah as she gave him a quick, appreciative glance. "They live close to our Potawatomis village. Like Hannah, they are good people. It is refreshing to have found white eyes who can be friends. Hannah's sister, Clara, lives among our people at the village. She is teaching our children ways of white children."

His voice trailed off as his thoughts momentarily strayed to Claude Odum. *He* had been different from other whites. And he was now dead!

Strong Wolf suddenly felt an urgency to return to the Kansas Territory, not only to make sure his people were protected, but also Hannah's brother and sister. Although Hannah had not mentioned worrying about it, *he* knew that Chuck and Clara were vulnerable because of their kind nature.

No one knew where Tiny had disappeared to. He was a menace. He was capable of doing anything underhanded!

And some white people in the area resented Clara teaching the Potawatomis children. Prejudices ran strong about a white woman teaching Indian children when there were scarce teachers for the white community.

Yes, he would return to the Kansas Territory as soon as he could gather his people together here at the Wisconsin village and get them ready for the journey to their newly established home.

"Oh?" Swallow Song said softly as she gazed at Hannah. "Your sister is skilled at teaching?"

"Yes, she attended college, purposely to become a teacher," Hannah said, wondering about Strong Wolf's sudden strange silence and faraway, worried look. "I am so pleased that she chose to use her skills at the Potawatomis village."

"She is a woman of good heart," Swallow Song said, nodding. "I will enjoy meeting her. And perhaps she could teach me things I have always longed to know about your culture? Perhaps I could attend your sister's school?"

Hannah's lips parted in a soft, surprised gasp. "Why, yes, Clara would be glad to have you there," she murmured.

"I have shied away from too many things in my life," Swallow Song said, her voice thick with melancholy. Her eyes wavered as she gazed at Hannah. "My son has explained that part of our lives, his and mine, that plagues us?"

Unsure of how to answer her, yet almost certain about what she was referring to, Hannah gave Strong Wolf a quick glance.

"Yes, Mother," he said, his eyes looking at Hannah in a silent understanding. "She knows. And she accepts."

"That is good," Swallow Song said. "*That* is why I have kept so much to myself. But I have not been plagued with the terrible seizures for many moons now. I wish to open my life to new things, new adventures, new *people*. This journey to our new home will give me that opportunity."

Strong Wolf went to his mother and swept her into

his embrace. "I hope to make everything possible for you in your new world," he said.

"And how did you find White Wolf and Dawn-marie?" Swallow Song said, easing from his arms. "And Proud Heart? Has he returned to stay with his people?"

"White Wolf and Dawnmarie are well, and, yes, Proud Heart has returned to stay with his people," Strong Wolf said, already missing his friend. "Some-day soon White Wolf and Dawnmarie will be leaving to seek Dawnmarie's true people in Mexico. White Wolf will step down from being chief. Proud Heart will then be the leader of their people."

"I fear I will never see Dawnmarie again," Swallow Song said, her voice quivering with emotion.

"Yes, Mother, you will," Strong Wolf reassured. "Dawnmarie and White Wolf promised that they would come through our village on their way to Mex-ico. We shall greet them with much feasting and celebrating."

"I so look forward to that," Swallow Song said. "Dawnmarie and I have shared so much in our lives."

She smiled over her shoulder at the gathering be-hind her, then smiled up at Strong Wolf as she took one of his hands. "My son, it is time now for you to greet your people as their chief," she murmured, tears silver in her eyes. "And we will soon have our own feast and celebration, a celebration of my chieftain *son* and his wife."

Strong Wolf smiled as he looked slowly around him, seeing the eagerness of his people to greet him. He gave his mother one last assuring hug, then stepped away from her.

As the sun lowered in the sky, Strong Wolf hugged every one of his people, from the smallest child, to the most elderly.

Then after Strong Wolf and Hannah visited his grandfather's grave, and returned to the excitement that was building among Strong Wolf's people over the journey that lay before them, the celebration began.

Hannah had enjoyed the feast and celebration at the Chippewa village, but here, among Strong Wolf's people, it seemed filled with much more exuberance, much more passion!

Beside a great outdoor fire, which cast a golden glow high into the heavens, with food cooking in huge pots over burning coals, Hannah relaxed in the fun of it all, laughing, smiling, loving. It was strange how quickly she was accepted and made to feel she belonged.

Huge bouquets of wildflowers were thrust into her arms.

The children danced and sang around her.

By the time it was all over, her jaws ached from having smiled so much.

And although it was a fun evening, she was glad to finally be alone with her husband.

"This is the lodge of my childhood," Strong Wolf said, gesturing with a hand around him at the inside of the cabin. His mother was asleep in the loft overhead, worn out by the day's activities. A fire roared in the great stone fireplace. "When I dream of my childhood days, I dream of being here, sitting by the fire, popping corn with my grandfather and mother. The memories are sweet, those sort that a child enjoys carrying with him into adulthood."

"I think that's wonderful," Hannah said, sitting down on a pallet of furs before the fire with Strong Wolf. "It is good to have pleasant memories of the past."

She moved to her knees before him and twined her

arms around his neck. "I shall always remember today," she said, then giggled softly. "Darling husband, my stomach is so full of honey, bear meat, popcorn, persimmon bread, and ash-lye hominy. As my plate emptied, it was filled again."

She laughed again. "Do your people see me as frail, so in need of food, that they tried to fatten me up like a little pig in one evening?"

Strong Wolf held his head back in a fit of laughter, then placed his hands to her waist and drew her onto his lap. "They did not even notice how much food they were forcing upon you," he said, his eyes dancing into hers. "It was just their way of welcoming you, the wife of their *chief*. When much food is available, that is cause in itself to celebrate. My people are fortunate. They never lack for food, for the Potawatomis braves are skilled, valiant hunters, and the women are skilled in ways of gardening and storage of the food gathered from their gardens."

"Then, I doubt our child will ever be hungry," Hannah said, watching his expression, to see if he understood the true meaning behind what she said.

"Not as long as I have breath in my lungs will the child born of our love ever be hungry," Strong Wolf said, drawing her into his embrace, gently hugging her.

"Strong Wolf, even tonight our child was nourished by the food of your people," Hannah said, scarcely breathing as she listened for him to grasp onto the truth of what she was saying, for she was certain that she was with child! She had missed her menstrual period by a week and it was not ordinary for her to be late.

"What ... did ... you say ... ?" Strong Wolf said. He gripped her shoulders and leaned her away from him so that he could look her square in the eye.

His heart pounded with hope that he had heard her correctly.

"I truly believe that I am with child!" Hannah said, her eyes filled with the excitement of the moment. "*Our* child, Strong Wolf." She ran a forefinger slowly across his parted lips. "Yours ... and ... mine, sweet husband. Tell me that you are happy with the news. I am ever so blissfully happy myself!"

Strong Wolf was so taken off guard by the news, for a moment he was at a loss for words. Then when it truly sank into his consciousness that, yes, he was going to be a father, all doubts, all fears, were swept away in his pride and joy of the moment.

"My woman," he said, yanking her into his arms, giving her a tight, warm hug. "You have given me so much already, and now you are going to give me a child."

He placed a finger beneath her chin and lifted her eyes to his. "You have filled my life with a hope I hardly ever felt possible as a child after ... after ... that day with Doe Eyes," he said. "And now this?" He laughed softly, again pulling her into his arms, gently holding her against his chest. "And ... now ... this!"

He swept her into his arms and carried her outside beneath the moon and the stars. He carried her down to the riverbank. He nodded toward the heavens. "Legend says that the Milky Way is a place of happy and endless hunting," he said in his rich, soft voice. "Legend says that bright stars are wise old warriors. Legend says that the small, dim stars are handsome braves."

"And what do your legends say about the women?" Hannah asked, watching the play of the stars overhead, so perfectly content as she clung around Strong Wolf's neck. She had never realized that anything in this world could feel so perfectly sweet and wonderful as it felt to be married to Strong Wolf, and now to be carrying his child.

"What do they say?" Strong Wolf said, drawing her eyes to his. "They say that I am the luckiest man of them all, for I have *you*."

He kissed her with a passion all consuming.

She returned the kiss, her soul melting into his, as though they were one person, one heartbeat.

She smiled to herself, for there was another heartbeat now, one that lay amid the cocoon of her womb, and she could hardly wait until she could lie with Strong Wolf in their house in Kansas and hear the breathing of their baby as it lay in a crib beside their bed. Oh, how her world was so quickly changing; to something magical and sweet!

Yet there were fears that lay just at the surface of her happiness . . . the long journey back to the Kansas Territory. Would it be too hard on her now that she was pregnant? If anything happened to the child, she would then feel only half a woman.

She clung to Strong Wolf and brushed those worries aside as she became lost in the moment of his lingering kiss.

38

Oh, is it not enough to be
Here with this beauty over me?
My throat should ache with praise, and I
Should kneel in joy beneath the sky.
—SARA TEASDALE

The October autumn sky was sapphire-clear. Crimson
thickets lined the creeks under parasols of tall golden
cottonwoods. The angry, thin cry of a red-tailed hawk
could be heard from downriver. And flying higher
than Strong Wolf had ever seen them fly, was a flock
of circling buzzards, probably migrating.

Strong Wolf noticed the buzzards ever closer now,
drifting south. Somber creatures, they drew big circles
in the sky, sometimes going back north, but always
ending in each swing a few yards farther south.

Astride their horses and wagons laden with their
belongings tucked in deerskin pouches, Strong Wolf
and Hannah rode at the lead, Swallow Song riding her
gentle mare at Strong Wolf's left side, the Potawatomis people trudged onward, their Kansas Territory
village now in sight.

Touched by those who had braved the long journey,
no matter their age, Hannah looked over her shoulder
one last time before entering the village. One bent old
grandmother trudged along on foot, leaning heavily
against a crooked cane. Toothless warriors, like the
old women, came more slowly, though mounted on
lively ponies.

Warriors the same age as Strong Wolf sat proudly
erect on their horses. Some wore their eagle plumes

and waved their various trophies of former wars as
they saw their friends and relatives at the village catch
sight of them, now coming in a fast run toward them
on the road.

As they entered the village, Hannah saw that several large black kettles of venison were suspended
over the great outdoor fire, for Strong Wolf had sent
a party of warriors on ahead to pass along the news
to his people that he and those who followed him
from Wisconsin would soon be arriving.

The tantalizing aroma of other foods cooking in the
coals of the fire wafted through the air, causing Hannah's stomach to growl. She placed a hand on her
stomach, smiling, to know that she had made it just
fine on the journey from Wisconsin. Her child was still
safely tucked within her womb. Soon she would be
able to feel its soft kicks.

Hannah rode proudly beside her husband as his
people flocked around him and the travelers.

They reached up and touched.

They cried and shouted.

They clung and kissed.

It was a happy reunion, one that had been too long
in coming.

But there were those who saw the importance of
finishing their labors in the cornfields before the sun
set in the west. They stopped and stared, their faces
beaming with happiness, then returned to their labors
that would feed their people, as a whole, during the
cold winter.

Hannah looked in the distance and saw these men
and women resume harvesting the corn, husking it,
pulling the husks down so that the ears could be
braided together. Those wide braids of corn, along
with squash cut in circles, would be strung to dry from
the rafters of their lodges.

Beans and dried corn kernels would be placed in the elm bark containers, and the surplus vegetables would be stored in clay pots, baskets, or skin bags until needed.

As they rode farther into the village, Hannah saw large canvases spread upon the grass, where sweet corn was drying on it. Small children guarded it from birds and animals.

Hannah smiled as she watched one little girl playing with a doll made from an ear of corn. She was braiding the soft fine silk for hair, and gave it a blanket from the scraps found in her mother's workbag.

Hannah was reminded of the little girl who gave her doll to her as a token of friendship. If Hannah had a daughter, this doll would be her very first toy.

Elsewhere, Hannah saw women slicing great pumpkins into thin rings, then doubled and linked them together into long chains. They then hung them on a pole that stretched between two forked posts. The wind and sun would soon thoroughly dry the chains of pumpkins. They were to be packed away in a case of thick, stiff buckskin.

Then Hannah's gaze was taken elsewhere, when she heard some warriors talking loudly and excitedly to Strong Wolf as Strong Wolf drew tight rein before his lodge. Hannah stopped beside him, giving Swallow Song a soft smile as she also drew her mare to a gentle stop on Hannah's left side.

Hannah listened as the men spoke in part Potawatomis tongue, and then in English. She gathered from what they said, that in Strong Wolf's absence, several settlers had moved in on land that belonged to the Potawatomis.

Strong Wolf quickly dismounted. Hannah slid slowly from her saddle and went to Swallow Song and helped her down to the ground.

"And why did you do nothing to stop them?" Strong Wolf said, trying to keep his voice steady, when in truth, his insides were a burning inferno of frustration.

"We went and told them to leave," White Beaver said, clutching fast to his rifle. "They looked at us as though they did not see us and resumed building their lodges. And now they are in our fields! They are harvesting corn from the patch of land they claim now as theirs!"

"And what did you do when they looked at you as though they saw nothing?" Strong Wolf said, angrily folding his arms across his chest.

"We warned them again that they were trespassing, and that no good would come from it," White Beaver said, his eyes narrowed with hate. "But we did not actually threaten them. We did not see it as our place to start a war with whites. We did not want to feel responsible for the deaths of any of our people. We waited for you to make this decision since you are now chief and the wisest of us all."

"And did you not go to Colonel Deshong?" Strong Wolf said, glaring from warrior to warrior.

"He is no longer at Fort Leavenworth," White Beaver said. "He has been replaced by a much younger white man. This younger man listens, but does nothing about this invasion on our land. You can tell that he is a man of prejudice. He will see us all leave and be happy for it!"

"This land is ours by treaty," Strong Wolf stated. "And no one, especially not a young colonel, is going to remove us from it."

Hannah and Swallow Song's hands were clutched tightly as they stood back and listened to Strong Wolf's building rage.

"Nor will we allow trespassers on land that is ours by treaty!" Strong Wolf shouted, waving a fist in the air. "We will remove them and if the young colonel comes to us with threats, I will personally escort him from our land!"

"But this might bring us into a war that none of us wants," another warrior shouted. "And do you not see, Strong Wolf? You have only today brought our beloved relatives to their new home! Must we already be thinking about moving them to another? If we retaliate against the whites, they might, in turn, retaliate against us."

"We will fight for what is ours, and if warring is required, so be it!" Strong Wolf cried.

He looked around him, at the throng of people, old and young, weak and strong, and knew that this was the only way. He must make a stand now, or never be able to again. If he and his people were forced from this land by an act of cowardice on their parts, then they would never be a people of pride again!

"Gather up your weapons," Strong Wolf shouted. "We shall go now and send the whites from our land." He laughed sarcastically. "They think they can have a crop that was nurtured by Potawatomis hands? They are foolish to think so little about the Potawatomis's pride and strength! We will burn their homes! We will take what they have harvested!"

He laughed throatily. "We might even thank them for the effort they saved our people!"

Hannah went to Strong Wolf. "Please don't do this," she said desperately. "So much is at stake, darling." She placed her hand on her abdomen. "Our child, Strong Wolf. If anything happened to you . . ."

He placed a gentle hand across her mouth. "My woman, it is because of the child that I do what I must today to make a safe place for our child's future," he said solemnly. "Please go inside our lodge with Mother. I will return home soon. You will see then that there was no reason to doubt the abilities of your husband."

Hannah paled. "I don't doubt you," she murmured, easing his hand from her lips. "It's just that . . ."

Again he interrupted her. "I will return home soon and then we can all celebrate coming together as one with my people," he said reassuringly. "It has been a long time since my people have all been together under one umbrella of sky."

He cast a sharp glance at the darkening heavens. Then he looked around him. "Let us leave now before the inky black of night will distort what we wish to achieve," he shouted, swinging himself into his saddle.

He gave Hannah a lingering gaze, and then his mother, then he grabbed his rifle from the gun boot at the side of his horse and waved it in the air. *"Aieee,"* he cried, the war cry sending spasms of fear up and down Hannah's spine.

She watched him ride away until he was lost from sight, then she took Swallow Song's hand and led her inside their lodge. Someone had come ahead of them and had gotten a comforting fire started, that which was needed on these cool days of October.

Hannah trembled as she sat down on a pallet of furs before the fire with Swallow Song at her side, but not so much from being chilled, as it was from being afraid. "Our future was so beautifully etched out, until tonight," she murmured as she gave Swallow Song a wavering look. "Swallow Song, you haven't said anything. Please tell me how you feel about everything."

"I trust my son's judgment in all things," Swallow Song said softly. She reached a comforting hand to Hannah's arm. "Please relax and do not worry so much. You must think of the child." She smiled sweetly. "I have had only one child in my lifetime, and it has been so long since I held that child in my arms. I so look forward to holding my grandchild. It will be like heaven on earth for this woman who never married again, and whose womb has been long barren."

"It is good to have you here," Hannah said, suddenly pulling Swallow Song into her arms. "We will be such fast friends. Your grandchild will adore you."

Hannah never once mentioned her fears of her child having the dreaded seizures. And she was going to guard the secret well, so that her child would never know such seizures existed, unless the child experienced the seizures himself.

"Perhaps we should eat," Swallow Song said. "It has been awhile since we have. It is not good for the child if you do not eat at regular intervals."

"I don't think I can stomach food right now, not while I am concerned over Strong Wolf's welfare," Hannah said, settling back down on the pallet, her eyes watching the fire caressing the logs.

"I will go and get something," Swallow Song said, rising to her feet. "You *must* try to eat."

Hannah gave Swallow Song a weak nod.

When Swallow Song left, Hannah looked slowly around the cabin. Ever since she had known that she was with child, she had thought of how wonderful it would be for the child to be there, to share life with them.

Now if anything happened to Strong Wolf. . . . !

39

Though bright her eyes' bewildering gleams,
Fair tremulous lips and shining hair,
A something born of mournful dream,
Breathes round her sad enchanted air.
—PAUL HAMILTON HAYNE

As the setting sun cast an orange glow along the horizon in the west, Strong Wolf and his warriors surrounded the cornfield where several white people were plucking corn from the cornstalks.

Strong Wolf sent several other warriors to the settler's houses that had been built on Potawatomis soil. He had instructed them to hold those white people as prisoners. He would come, as chief of his people, to each cabin, and set the law down himself. He would personally see that they left, and if they dared not to, it would be up to him to decide what their fate might be.

But he had smugly known that the show of force on the part of the Potawatomis should frighten the whites into fleeing.

Strong Wolf held onto his rifle and rode up to the men and women who had been harvesting corn until they had caught sight of the Potawatomis warriors.

They now cowered together, their eyes filled with fright, as Strong Wolf drew rein before them.

"You are illegally on land of the Potawatomis," he said, his voice tight with anger. "Why do you think you have the right to harvest corn that was planted by someone besides yourselves?"

"This land belongs to whomever squats on it," a

bulbous-nosed, middle-aged man said as he stepped
forth in bib overalls, his face bronzed by the wind and
sun. "Now git!"

"You speak bravely, yet your voice reveals the fear
behind the words that you speak," Strong Wolf said,
his lips tugging into a tight smile.

Strong Wolf shifted his gaze to the two women and
the children clinging to their skirts.

Then he turned cold eyes back to the man whom
had seemingly appointed himself the spokesman.

"If you value the lives of these women and children,
you will turn your eyes and voice from me, gather
them protectively within your arms, and usher them
from land that belongs to the Potawatomis by treaty!"
Strong Wolf said with force, chuckling when the man obviously understood now that Strong Wolf meant business.

Slowly the man stepped back away from Strong Wolf,
through the rows of stalks of corn, his eyes wide.

"I am chief of my people and whatever I choose to
do with you, will be done," Strong Wolf threatened
as he edged his horse closer with each of the man's
steps backward. "Had I not been gone to guide the
rest of my people to this land that is now ours, I would
have been here to stop you from building your lodges
and taking the land as though it was yours. You would
have not cut down that first tree, and you would have
not taken our first ear of corn."

Strong Wolf continued to hound the man as he
edged his horse still closer while the man stumbled
and clawed his way back to his family. "This chief is
here to stay, and I will make sure that once you are
gone, you will not return," he growled. "Take your
families. Run. And do not look back at your lodges.
I will take care of that for you. I will burn them and
all of your possessions to the ground."

When the man paled and gasped, Strong Wolf

smiled slowly again. "Now do you see why it would have been best had you heeded the warnings of my warriors when they first came to you and told you that you were trespassing? At that time you could have saved all but your houses when you left," he said somberly. "Now you lose everything but yourselves and the steeds that carry you away."

"Please don't. . . ." the man pleaded. "It has taken a lifetime to build up our possessions into something worthwhile. Please let us get them before we leave."

"It has taken the Potawatomis a lifetime to gain respect from the whites, and still we do not have it. Why should this Potawatomis chief be generous to you who would again take from us what is ours?" Strong Wolf said, raising his rifle threateningly into the air.

"No!" Strong Wolf then shouted. "Nothing but your skin and bones and your steeds will be saved. Feel blessed for even that, for at this moment I feel vengeance inside my heart more than I have ever felt it before in my life. It sickens me to think that you, just because you are white, feel that you can take from us, whose skin is red. You have been misguided in that logic, white man. Now leave! And do not go to the fort with your complaints. I soon will be there myself to tell them what happened here today. You are thieves. Do you wish to be hanged over this land that was not yours?"

"No, I . . . we . . . don't wish anything now but to be able to go on our way, *alive*," the man stammered. He turned and ran to his children and swept one up in each of his arms. He shouted at his wife to follow him. The other man and woman and children also ran off in a panic.

Strong Wolf's heart ached to know that he had been placed in the position to treat people so unfairly, for he knew that he should have allowed them to take their possessions.

But lessons must be taught so that these white people might not try to repeat their thievery elsewhere.

He rode slowly behind the people, his warriors following him. When he reached their small plots of land, where they had built neat cabins side by side, Strong Wolf stopped and waited for them to leave.

After they were gone, he gestured toward the cabins with his rifle. "Burn them to the ground!" he shouted as he looked over his shoulder at his warriors.

He sat glumly quiet in his saddle until the cabins were only smoldering ashes, then rode on to the next squatter's land and again supervised the burning of the lodge, until all of the whites were gone, and all of their lodges were destroyed.

"It is done except for facing the colonel at Fort Leavenworth!" Strong Wolf shouted, again waving his rifle in the air. "Let us go and introduce ourselves to him in the right way!"

His warriors whooping and hollering on all sides of him, Strong Wolf rode off toward the fort.

Just before arriving, he drew his reins tight and wheeled himself around to face his men. "Place your rifles in their gun boots," he said somberly. "We must arrive at the fort with dignity. We also do not wish to enter the fort's gates with war cries on our breath! We must remember, at all costs, that the young colonel sees us as peacemakers. We must make him understand why the settlers' homes were destroyed, and why they were forced from our land!"

His men nodded. Then they rode onward.

When they reached the fort, there was a commotion of activity, for the soldiers had seen the fires in the distance and were prepared to go and see what had caused them.

Strong Wolf and his men blocked the gate so the soldiers could not leave.

The young colonel, all spruced up in full uniform, his pant legs creased neatly, rode up to Strong Wolf on a beautiful white stallion. "And what is the meaning of this?" he asked, his hand resting on his sheathed saber.

"I am Chief Strong Wolf," Strong Wolf said, his voice void of emotion. "I have recently returned from a long journey from Wisconsin. When I arrived home, I found settlers squatting on land of the Potawatomis. These people were even bold enough to harvest Potawatomis corn, to be used in the pots of the white people."

Strong Wolf nodded over his shoulder at the smoke in the distance. "Strong Wolf sent the people away, set fire to the lodges that were illegally on Potawatomis land that is ours by treaty, and have come now to set things right with you," he said in a dignified yet threatening tone. "I was told that Colonel Deshong is no longer in charge here."

"That is so," Colonel Mooney said, nodding stiffly. "And I regret having to make your acquaintance under such uncomfortable conditions." He reached a cautious handshake out for Strong Wolf. "I am Colonel Mooney."

"Is it true that you refused to send the whites from our land when my warriors came and asked your assistance in my absence?" Strong Wolf said blandly, ignoring the proffered hand.

"Yes, I was not quite sure about this land that you claim as yours," Colonel Mooney said, swallowing back a fear that was creeping up his spine, a fear he had always had of Indians. He slowly eased his hand down to his side.

"Why did it have to be proven to you in such a

harsh way?" Strong Wolf said, sidling his horse closer to the colonel's. "Surely you were instructed by Colonel Deshong about this land that is ours by treaty. Did you not listen, or did you not care to? Are you a man of prejudice?"

"Why, no, certainly not," the young colonel uttered. He looked past Strong Wolf and saw just how many Indians had accompanied him to the fort. He cursed his orders from Washington, lessening the number of soldiers at Fort Leavenworth since there was peace between the white and red man. Now he wished that he had refused this post! He was being forced to allow the Indians to have the upper hand, for their number was twice that of the fort's.

"Then I can return to my people and tell them that there will be no more intrusions on our land?" Strong Wolf said, smiling to himself when he saw the young colonel's frustration.

"Yes, I will see that nothing like this happens again," Colonel Mooney said, nervously raking a forefinger between his tight collar and scrawny neck. "No more settlers will take land that is yours. *And* there will be no retaliation over you having burned the settlers' cabins."

"You are a wise man," Strong Wolf said, then reached a hand of friendship toward the young colonel. "Come soon and make council with Strong Wolf."

The young colonel hesitated, then his hand shook as he clasped it around Strong Wolf's. "I would be delighted to have council with you," he said evenly.

Strong Wolf clasped Colonel Mooney's hand for a moment longer, then released it, wheeled his horse around and rode from the fort, his warriors following close behind. Strong Wolf sank his heels into the flanks of his horse and sent his steed into a hard gallop, anxious to resume what had been sidetracked by the news of the whites having settled on his land.

The inky black of night hung over the land like a dark shroud when he rode into his village.

Hannah heard the approach of the horses. She ran from the cabin, and tears splashed from her eyes when she saw Strong Wolf in the lead of the warriors who had come home victoriously.

Strong Wolf saw her standing there. He reined in quickly and slid from his saddle, then went to Hannah and grabbed her up into his arms and swung her around, laughing.

"We showed them!" he shouted. "There will be no more trouble from the whites! They know better than to trespass on our land again!"

Hannah held her head back and laughed, so happy, so relieved!

40

Her neck is like the swan,
Her face it is the fairest
That e'er the sun shone on.
—WILLIAM DOUGLAS

A chill wind blew across the river. The trees were bare of leaves. Autumn was gone. Winter was quickly taking a firm grip on the countryside.

A large crowd of Potawatomis were assembled, their eyes wide as they watched the final stages of the children's schoolhouse being completed.

The children were not as frisky as usual. They stood as quietly and poised as the elders. They had something now that usually only belonged to the children of white people. They were eager to learn, especially since they adored Clara, their teacher. They admired and respected her.

She was so kind and generous to them all; to them she was almost like a second mother.

Clutching a warm shawl around her shoulders, a bonnet protecting her head from the wind, Hannah stood back with her sister Clara as the last shingle was hammered into place on the roof of the new Potawatomis schoolhouse.

Hannah reached for Clara's hand and clung to it

as she so proudly watched Strong Wolf climb onto the roof.

Struggling and groaning as he lifted a bell one inch at a time up the ladder, White Beaver climbed up after Strong Wolf.

Finally there, White Beaver handed Strong Wolf the large bell.

As Strong Wolf steadied the bell against the roof, White Beaver scrambled onto the roof beside him.

Hannah held her breath as Strong Wolf and White Beaver inched their way to the small steeple that had been built on the very top center of the roof, where the bell would ring every school day morning.

"I hope they don't slip," Hannah said, giving Clara a nervous glance.

"Lord, if they do . . ." Clara gasped, eyes wide as she watched them.

Hannah's gaze held on Clara for a moment, warmed through and through to see her sister so healthy. Two years older than Hannah, tall and slim like Hannah, Clara stood with her back straight and shoulders squared. Her shawl partially hid a high-necked white blouse beneath it that was trimmed with delicate lace. Clara also wore a black velvet skirt that only barely showed her black patent-leather shoes as the brisk breeze shifted the hem from place to place.

Hannah smiled to herself as she gazed at her sister's hair. Clara wore it the same now, as she had for so long. Her brown hair was swept up in a tight bun at the back of her head.

Hannah's gaze shifted to Clara's gold-rimmed eyeglasses that were perched on a long, straight nose. Her sister's cheeks were pink with excitement, the dimples on each cheek deepening whenever her thin lips would quiver into an excited smile.

Strong Wolf's voice and the loud applause and shouts from the crowd drew Hannah's eyes back around. She gazed up at her husband, sighing when she saw that he and White Beaver had managed to get the bell hung. To her it was so beautiful. The meaning behind it was so wonderful. These lovely children would now learn ways to fight back when the whites tormented them in their future.

It was wonderful to know that the way these children would defend themselves would not have to be with weapons, but with words, and the knowledge of reading and mathematics.

Yes, the future for the children was bright, and she was proud to be a part of it all!

"Let us now hear how it sounds!" Strong Wolf shouted from the rooftop. He dropped a rope that was attached to the bell through a small hole in the roof, down to the one room of the schoolhouse.

The people became even more excited when they heard the bell begin to toll. The children began to dance and sing. The women rushed to the large outdoor fire where they had placed pots of food for a celebration. The elderly gazed in wonder at the school once again, then went back to smoking their pipes beside the fire.

"Hannah, they've done it!" Clara said, clasping Hannah's hand harder as the bell's peals resounded through the air, clear, crisp, and beautiful. "Do you hear it? Isn't it the loveliest sound?"

Hannah smiled over at Clara. "Yes, so lovely," she murmured. "And, Clara, I can never tell you enough times how happy I am that you have chosen to teach here at the Potawatomis village. You could have chosen to teach even as far away as New York state. It would be much too long between visits."

Clara, tears rushing from her eyes, turned to Han-

nah and drew her into her embrace. "I have you to
thank for so much," she murmured. "You, Father, and
Mother. If you hadn't cared for me, night and day,
during my recent illness, I wouldn't have made it. I
never want to be far from my family, and Lord knows
that Saint Louis is far enough away from Mother
and Father."

"We'll go as often as we can," Hannah said, then
stepped away from Clara and placed her hands over
the small ball of her belly that stretched the cotton
material of her dress tautly across it. "But I won't
be doing much traveling myself. Not until my child
is born."

"I can hardly wait to be an aunt," Clara sighed,
gazing down at Hannah's show of pregnancy.

"The baby kicked!" Hannah said, eyes wide.

"Let me feel it," Clara said.

Hannah inched her hands aside, to make room for
Clara's.

Clara's eyes lit up. "Oh, my Lord, Hannah," she
said. "I *do* feel it."

Then Clara let out a squeal of delight. "And I feel
something more," she cried. "The child moved, kind
of like rolling. I could swear I felt an elbow!"

"Or a knee?" Strong Wolf said as he stepped up to
them. He swept an arm around Hannah's waist. "My
little miracle worker wife. She is making a baby whose
spirit matches its mother's."

Clara laughed softly, then smiled at White Beaver
as he came to stand beside her.

"The schoolhouse is finished," White Beaver said,
his dark eyes gazing into Clara's. "I would like to go
inside with you to see it, Clara."

Hannah's eyes widened with surprise when Clara
walked away with him, toward the school.

Now having a reason to, Hannah gave White Beaver

a second, lingering stare. He was a shorter man than
Strong Wolf, yet as muscled. He stood at least one
head shorter than Clara. He was at least ten years
older than Clara, who was twenty.

Hannah had noticed before that White Beaver's facial features were not as chiseled as Strong Wolf's, yet
he was handsome in his own way. He generated much
warmth as he spoke to people, and he had replaced
Proud Wolf in Strong Wolf's life, as best friend. He
and Strong Wolf were inseparable now, their logic always matching the others. They laughed and talked
and challenged each other in games.

"There seems more to White Beaver asking my sister to see the schoolhouse with him than meets the
eye," Hannah said. "Did you see how they looked at
each other, Strong Wolf?"

"I can tell you how White Beaver feels about
Clara," Strong Wolf said as he watched Clara and
White Beaver enter the schoolhouse.

"You know something that I don't?" Hannah said,
turning to Strong Wolf.

"White Beaver is in love with Clara, and he says
that she is in love with him," Strong Wolf said matter-
of-factly. "They met down by the river one evening.
They just happened along during each other's
baths."

He chuckled. "They were alone when they met,"
he said. "They became acquainted."

Strong Wolf's eyes danced as Hannah stared incredulously up at him. "Yes, they made love, Hannah,"
he said. "And I do believe we shall soon witness a
wedding."

"Why didn't you tell me about this before now?"
Hannah asked, her words trailing off when through
the glass at the window she saw her sister and White
Beaver kissing.

"I felt it was your sister's place to confide in you about things that were so private," Strong Wolf said. He took her hands and drew her next to him. He gazed into her eyes. "My woman, is not everything good happening for us now? And soon we should be having visitors."

"You mean White Wolf and Dawnmarie?" she murmured, relishing his lips as he brushed soft kisses across her cheeks. She was happy for her sister.

"Yes, on their way to Mexico to find her true people, the Kickapoo," he murmured.

He turned with a start when he heard the sound of horses arriving at the far edge of the village. "Perhaps they are here even now. As you know, I have been watching for them every day."

Everything in the village became quietly numb as the horsemen grew close enough for everyone to see that they were pony soldiers from Fort Leavenworth, Colonel Mooney at the lead.

"No," Hannah said, sighing heavily. "What now? Can't they leave us in peace?" She gave Strong Wolf a questioning gaze. "I thought you said that things were all right between you and the young colonel."

"That is what I was led to believe," Strong Wolf grumbled, frowning as he looked at the sabers in their sheaths at the one side of the soldiers' horses, rifles sheathed at their other. "They come heavily armed today, so I would not think it is to have a peaceful council with my people."

He turned serious eyes at Hannah. "Go home," he said thickly. "Mother is not well today. Stay with her. Be there for her as well as to keep our child from any danger."

Hannah nodded and turned a pensive stare toward the school. When Clara came outside with White Beaver, Hannah ran to her and grabbed her hand. "Come with me," she said.

"Why?" Clara asked, giving White Beaver a quick glance over her shoulder as Hannah led her away from him. She watched White Beaver rush to Strong Wolf's side.

"Clara, don't ask questions," Hannah said, running past Strong Wolf on toward their house. "Just come on. It is best this way."

"But I want to stay with White Beaver," Clara cried, again giving him a frightened stare.

"As I would like to stay with Strong Wolf," Hannah said, half shoving Clara through the door of the cabin. "But I am with child. I am no longer able to behave in the manner I did when so many called me a tomboy. Now I am a woman, responsible for more than my own welfare."

Once inside, panting hard, Hannah turned questioning eyes over at Clara. "Why didn't you tell me about White Beaver?" she asked softly.

"You know, then, do you?" Clara said softly.

"Strong Wolf told me," Hannah said, nodding.

"I wanted to be absolutely sure, Hannah, that he truly loved me," Clara said softly. "Now I am sure. Isn't it wonderful?"

Hannah gave Clara a warm hug. "I'm so happy for you," she murmured.

A soft cough behind them drew them around. They walked to the fireplace. They gazed down at Swallow Song, who lay on a pallet before the fireplace, sleeping soundly.

"I'm worried about her," Hannah said. She bent to her knees and placed a hand on Swallow Song's brow. Then she gave a bright smile up at Clara. "Her fever is gone. She is going to be all right."

"Thank God," Clara said, settling down in a uphol-stered chair, sighing.

Hannah sat down opposite her. "Now, tell me about White Beaver," she said softly, trying not to awaken Swallow Song.

Hannah stiffened when she heard Colonel Mooney and Strong Wolf exchanging conversation. She willed herself not to go to the door and listen. This was be-tween her husband and the colonel.

Yes, she was learning that she had her own busi-ness to tend to ... the household duties, and soon a child. She could no longer interfere in her hus-band's business.

"Hannah, all that should matter is that I'm in love," Clara said, beaming. "And he loves me! I was going to tell you today about our plans to be married."

Hannah rushed from the chair. She went to Clara and hugged her. "And isn't it so perfect?" she mur-mured. "We will both live in the same place, and we will both raise our children together!"

"I do hope that I have a child soon," Clara said as Hannah went and sat down again.

"But this changes many things," Hannah said, thinking of Chuck, and thinking of the schoolchildren.

"Yes, I know," Clara said, staring into the fire. Then she smiled over at Hannah. "But truly not that much. I shall take my child to the school every day I teach. I shall spend evenings with Chuck, caring for his led-gers. And he has good help now, who care for his other needs. Hannah, he's going to be so surprised to hear about White Beaver!"

"Yes, he will, but oh, so happy, Clara," Hannah said, then unable to hold back any longer, went to the door and slowly opened it.

She held her breath as she listened, then paled when

she heard Colonel Mooney tell Strong Wolf that someone had stolen a good amount of their dynamite supply sometime during the night.

"Are you accusing the Potawatomis of the theft?" Strong Wolf said, his hand inching toward his sheathed knife.

Hannah died a miliion deaths inside as she awaited the colonel's reply.

41

And I am desolate and sick of an old passion,
Yea, hungry for the lips of my desire!
—ERNEST DOWSON

"And so someone stole dynamite from your fort last night," Strong Wolf persisted. "Is your presence here because you have come to accuse us of the deed?"

"No," Colonel Mooney said, shifting his weight in his saddle. "I have not come to accuse, and not so much to even question about the theft, but to warn you that the dynamite was stolen."

Strong Wolf's tensions lessened. He inhaled a slow breath, then stepped closer to the colonel's horse. "You have come to warn us?" he said, arching an eyebrow. "And why is that? Why would you think that warnings are necessary?"

"Whoever stole the box of dynamite did it for a purpose," the young colonel said, his voice drawn. "Who is to say who it will be used against? Or what? I do know that I saw in my files, when I took over the duties from Colonel Deshong, that there had been some trouble not long ago about dynamite."

"Yes, it is true that I stole dynamite," Strong Wolf said, again stiffening. "But if you delved into the full truths about why, then you would know that I used the dynamite to correct something wrong done against my people. The theft was overlooked. Colonel Deshong agreed with what I did. And you? Do you disapprove?"

"Whatever Colonel Deshong did while he was in command at Fort Leavenworth, and how he handled it, was his concern," Colonel Mooney said, resting his hand on the handle of his saber. "But now *I* am in charge. And the dynamite is what lies in question here. Dynamite is a lethal weapon in the wrong hands. In yours, it was used to destroy a dam. In someone else's, who is to say what it might be used for. Whoever stole it had a purpose. It is my job to discover *what*. It is *my* job to spread the word that the dynamite is perhaps in the hands of enemies."

"And so you came to my village to warn us that perhaps someone might be planning to use the dynamite on my people?" Strong Wolf said stiffly.

"It could possibly happen," Colonel Mooney said, nodding. "Some of my men brought me up to speed on things that have happened in the area these past months. I was told about a man under a Chuck Kody's employ." He kneaded his chin contemplatingly. He cocked an eyebrow as he tried to think of Tiny's name. "Ah, yes. His name was Tiny Sharp."

"Chuck Kody is my wife's brother, and Tiny Sharp was his foreman," Strong Wolf offered. "Tiny Sharp disappeared a few months ago. No one has seen or heard of his whereabouts. Why do you mention him now?"

"I was told that he was a troublemaker," Colonel Mooney said, clearing his throat. "I was also told that he had disappeared after having been discovered in many underhanded activities. Isn't it true that he was your ardent enemy?"

"Yes, he was my enemy," Strong Wolf said, nodding. "In truth, I expect he has no true friends. He is a man with a dark heart, a man who could never be trusted."

The young colonel rested a hand on the pommel of his saddle and rested his weight against it as he leaned down closer to Strong Wolf's face. "Do you think he is the man we might be after?" he said. "Do you think he might have stolen the dynamite? Do you know what he might have in mind for the dynamite?"

"I have not thought about him for some time now," Strong Wolf said. "I have been involved in the affairs of my people."

The young colonel sat straight in his saddle again and stared at the new schoolhouse. "That is a grand building you have there," he said, then smiled down at Strong Wolf. "It is good that your children will have the same opportunities that the white children have. Someday I would like to come in and sit through the lessons, if the teacher would not mind."

"The teacher is my wife's sister," Strong Wolf said. "I am sure she would not mind having an audience while she teaches." He smiled over at White Beaver, who seemed pleased to have his woman discussed in such a favorable way, then gazed up at the young colonel again. "The teacher is a woman. She will soon marry my friend, White Beaver."

White Beaver stepped closer to the horse when the young colonel offered a handshake.

"I would also like to attend the wedding," Colonel Mooney said, eagerly shaking White Beaver's hand. "I would enjoy becoming involved in all affairs of your village, and people. Until I met you, Strong Wolf, I greatly feared Indians. Now I wish to know more about them, to be *with* them."

"And that can easily be arranged," Strong Wolf said. "It will pleasure me to share our people's customs with you."

A great explosion in the distance, that which shook the earth beneath everyone's feet, drew the conversation to a quick halt.

Having felt the explosion—it having even awakened Swallow Song—Hannah, Clara, and Swallow Song came from the cabin in a run. Hannah and Swallow Song clutched Strong Wolf's arm as Clara went to cling to White Beaver.

Another explosion rocked the ground. A billowing of black smoke shot suddenly into the sky.

"That seems to have come from the direction of the mystery cave," Strong Wolf said, watching the smoke turning the sky to something similar to black ink.

He turned to a young brave. "Saddle my horse!" he shouted.

White Beaver ran and got his own steed. Many warriors followed.

"I wish to come with you!" Hannah cried as Strong Wolf swung himself into his saddle.

"The child, Hannah," Strong Wolf said, reaching down to place a gentle hand on her cheek.

"Then, please be careful and hurry back to me," Hannah said, trying hard to remember that she must not ride a horse now, or do anything else that might risk the child's life.

The Potawatomis and the soldiers rode off in the direction of the smoke.

Hannah sighed heavily, then gazed at length at the buggy she used while on her outings with Strong Wolf.

"No, Hannah," Clara said; she seemed to have read Hannah's mind. "We really mustn't."

"What can it hurt, Clara?" Hannah said, then gave Swallow Song a look when Swallow Song placed a gentle hand on her arm.

"Come inside, Hannah," Swallow Song said in a

motherly tone. "We will sit beside the fire while we wait for our men to return."

Hannah sighed, then nodded. "Yes, let's," she said, flanked on each side by women she loved. Clara took her right hand. Swallow Song took her left.

They went inside Hannah's cabin and sat by the fire.

To get their mind off their concerns, Clara read a novel, Hannah worked on Christmas decorations, and Swallow Song untied long tasseled strings that bound a small brown buckskin bag. She spread many colored beads on a mat beside her. On a lapboard she smoothed out a double sheet of soft white buckskin so that she could make a new pair of moccasins.

When they heard another blast, they glanced at each other, then lowered their eyes again and resumed their hobbies.

42

Life goes on forever
like the gnawing of a mouse.
—EDNA ST. VINCENT MILLAY

"Clem, hurry up and get those rocks away from the cave entrance," Tiny said, his fingers raw as he continued to throw one rock over her shoulder, and then another. "Damn dynamite. It ain't worth spit. We should've been able to get inside that cave by now."

"Just quit your jawin' and keep on workin' at it," Clem said, throwing rocks aside as others slid in the way. "We're almost there, Tiny."

"Yeah, but will it be soon enough?" Tiny growled, looking guardedly around him. "One blast of dynamite was all that was needed to draw those damn Injuns here. I'm sure they even heard the blast at Fort Leavenworth. That's all we need. To have both the soldiers and Injuns breathin' down our necks. Hell, Clem, I heard there was enough gold in here to last a lifetime."

"Who told you?" Clem asked, glad that he had run across Tiny again recently during a poker game at the back of a saloon in Saint Louis. "Was it a reliable source?"

"Sure as hell was," Tiny said, laughing boisterously. "He had just read an account of this mystery cave in some book or another. He was trying to recruit someone who knew the area. I spoke up quite quickly and told him that I knew everythin' about this damn mystery cave."

"Yeah, you knew everythin', yet you didn't know about the pirate chest of jewels?" Clem said, laughing sarcastically. "Tiny, your brains don't match your mouth. I'm probably dumb as hell comin' back in these parts with you after high-tailin' it outta here after our disagreement. I'm not eager to have a rope slipped around my neck."

"And you won't have no rope around your neck," Tiny scoffed, stopping to wipe beads of sweat from his brow. "Just let's get this damn cave open and get the jewels. We'll then go back to Saint Louis and live the good ol' life. I already know how I'm goin' to spend my money. And you? What's your plans?"

"Just stayin' alive," Clem grumbled, finally seeing some space between the rocks. "I hope there ain't no Injun hocus-pocus connected with this cave. The smoke is mysterious as hell. Where do you think it comes from?"

"You idiot," Tiny said, casting Clem an annoyed stare as he tossed another rock aside. "There are hot springs beneath the ground. The steam is what creates the smoke. Now hurry up. I've got a strange sort of crawling at the back of my neck. That usually indicates that trouble is near. If it's Indians, I want to be far away before they come and see what's happened here at the cave."

"Tiny, I never thought to ask before, but what happened to the gentleman who told you about the pirate chest hidden inside this cave?" Clem asked, pausing to brush hair back from his eyes. "You just told me that he had told you about it, as he was recrutin' men to come with him. When you told me about it, you didn't tell me anythin' about anyone else knowin' about it."

"That's because no one else does," Tiny said, laughing ruthlessly. "It's only you and me now, Clem. Only you and me."

Clem paled. "Are you sayin' what I think you're saying?" he said guardedly.

"Exactly," Tiny snarled back at him, his eyes squinting with a look of dark, deep evil.

"God, Tiny, you killed him?" Clem said, taking an awkward step away from him.

"His neck snapped as easy as a rotted twig," Tiny said, taking a step closer to Clem. He glanced at the cave, seeing the opening. His heart beat soundly at the thought of being so near to the actual pirate's treasure chest. He needed no more help. The rest was a breeze.

He yanked his knife from its sheath with the speed of a lightning's flash. In one lunge he had the knife imbedded deeply within Clem's chest.

Clutching at his chest, blood spurting between his fingers, Clem gave Tiny a look of disbelief, then he slumped forward, his last breath taken after a brief spasmodic gasp.

"*Now* I've got it all to myself," Tiny said, yanking the bloody knife from Clem's chest. He wiped the blood on Clem's breeches. He kicked Clem aside as he slipped the knife back inside his sheath.

Tiny shoved the last of the rocks aside. Reaching for a kerosene lantern that he had brought purposely to take with him inside the cave, he lit the wick. His hands trembling, his eyes wide, Tiny took slow, careful steps into the cave.

He ducked and gasped when a bat fluttered quickly past his head, and then another and another and another.

"Damn bats," he whispered, his face hot with excitement as he spied the treasure chest up ahead, only a few footsteps away.

"I can't believe my eyes," he said, too stunned by the sight to move. "An ... actual ... pirate's chest."

He cocked an eyebrow when he noticed that the lid was somewhat ajar.

Then he gasped and teetered with a sudden fear when he saw several skulls and bones lying near the chest on all sides.

"I'm ... not ... the first ..." he uttered.

Then he smiled. "But there ain't no reason why I can't be the last," he said, taking sure steps forward now. "There ain't no one here to stop me."

Tiny knelt down on his knees before the chest. He set his lantern to the side on a tall rock, so that the minute he got the chest opened, he would see the jewels shining back at him.

"There just ain't been no one as clever as me before to *come* for the stash," Tiny whispered to himself, laughing in a crazed cackle. "Come to me, Mama. Come to me and let's have some fun."

The lid now almost open, Tiny's eyes feasting on the shine of the jewels already, he could hardly contain his excitement.

Then he jumped with a start and let out a loud scream as the lid fell back, and a rattlesnake suddenly appeared and lashed out at Tiny.

The sting of the bite on Tiny's left wrist sent him sprawling to the floor of the cave. He gripped at the wrist, moaning. He yelped and hollered.

He rolled on the floor away from the snake as it uncoiled from inside the chest and came slithering toward Tiny.

"Get away from me, you damn varmint!" Tiny cried, his eyes wide.

The snake kept approaching.

Tiny grabbed his pistol from his holster. He aimed, fired, and laughed when the snake's head was severed from his body by the gun blast, and flew through the air.

Then Tiny's laughter faded. Cold sweat covered his body when he heard the first squeak and squawl of timber overhead. Dirt fell on his face. Terrified, he watched the timber creak and sway as more dirt slid from the roof overhead.

"No!" he cried, trying to scramble to his feet.

He was light-headed from the bite. His wrist throbbed. His knees wobbled. His eyesight was becoming quickly blurred.

As spurts of strength would allow, he dragged himself an inch at a time toward the cave entrance as dirt kept spilling all around him from the roof of the cave.

Then he remembered the jewels.

Damn it, he thought to himself. He ... had ... to get at least some of the jewels before the cave came tumbling down onto his head.

He turned around on the dirt floor. He crawled past the dead snake's head. He ignored the rocks that began to fall from overhead.

Finally at the chest, he heaved himself up, to rest against it, his eyes blurred, yet still able to see the shine of the jewels.

Then suddenly a large boulder fell from the ceiling and crushed the lantern beneath it, taking away Tiny's light.

He gasped and stiffened. He looked wildly above him. His scream became muffled when the rest of the roof caved in and buried him beneath it.

Strong Wolf scrambled down the path that led to the mystery cave, the soldiers as well as several of Strong Wolf's warriors following close behind him.

Strong Wolf leaned his ear toward a sound that he

thought was a man's scream, yet it had been so muffled he was not sure.

They hurried on to the cave where they found Clem lying across the ground, dead from a knife wound.

They found Clem's and Tiny's horses tethered side by side.

But they didn't find Tiny.

"Come and look at this!" White Beaver said as he lifted the empty box of dynamite.

"That's what was stolen from the fort," Colonel Mooney said, going to inspect the box. "The damn idiots used every stick."

Strong Wolf knelt beside Clem. "This is the work of Tiny Sharp," he snarled. He rose slowly to his feet and stared at the cave's entrance. He could tell that the boulders that were once there had been replaced by others. "Tiny is inside the cave. The cave has caved in and buried him alive."

"You're sure?" Colonel Mooney said, kneading his chin as he studied the cave. "You are sure he is inside?"

"Is not his horse still here?" Strong Wolf said, nodding toward Tiny's horse.

"You know for certain that is his horse?" Colonel Mooney said, staring at the horse.

"I know his horse as well as I knew the man," Strong Wolf said, going to kick away a few of the rocks. "And the dynamite? It was used on the cave. That is how Tiny is inside."

"But why?" Colonel Mooney said, scratching his brow. "Why did he go there?"

"Perhaps he discovered the mysteries of the cave and thought it worth the risk of his life to go after it," Strong Wolf said blandly.

"Do you know what is inside the cave?" Colonel

Mooney said, bending to a knee, studying the debris that had fallen when the cave had caved in.

"The man has taken the answers to his grave," Strong Wolf said, turning to walk away from the cave. He turned to the young colonel. "And I would not consider trying yourself to find what the mystery is. I would say that spirits guard the cave, or why is it that no one is ever allowed to leave once they have entered it?"

The young colonel stared at Strong Wolf, then nodded toward one of his men. "Take this dead man with you on your horse," he ordered. "We must see to his proper burial."

"Yes, sir," the man said, nodding.

Then the young colonel stopped and stared at the smoke rising from the land and water. A chill ran through him. He turned to his men. "Forget what you heard here today," he said in a solid command. "I do not want to hear that any of you have returned here. There is no need in anyone else losing their lives."

He turned and gazed over his shoulder one last time at the cave, then walked up the narrow path behind Strong Wolf.

Strong Wolf loosened his reins and swung himself into his saddle. "And now, with Tiny dead, we are certain of peace," he said as Colonel Mooney eased into his own saddle. "Come. Have council with me. Share a smoke."

Smiling, the young colonel nodded.

They rode away together as more rock tumbled in on Tiny's body.

"Winter is near," Colonel Mooney said, in light, friendly conversation.

"Yes, and should your men ever grow short of meat, just come to me and my warriors will gladly go on the hunt for you," Strong Wolf said, smiling over at the young colonel. "Your table will never be without meat, even on the coldest days of winter."

"Why, thank you," Colonel Mooney said, returning Strong Wolf's smile. "You are a most generous man for making such an offer."

"It is made by a *friend*," Strong Wolf said.

"Yes, a friend," Colonel Mooney said, nodding.

The sun was lowering in the sky. The trees overhead were silent, the birds having flown south for the winter. Acorns suddenly showered the path as the breeze picked up and became a howling wind.

"*This* friend most certainly needs the warmth of a fire before heading on to the fort," the young colonel said, drawing his jacket collar closer around his throat.

"We will be at my lodge soon," Strong Wolf said, nodding.

The colonel gave Strong Wolf another smile and rode off, Strong Wolf at his side.

Strong Wolf rode tall in the saddle, his thoughts now on Hannah. Just thinking of her made his heart soar and sing! For now, at least, everything seemed perfect for him and his wife, and his people.

But he could not help but worry about someone else. White Wolf and Dawnmarie. They should have arrived by now. If they waited too much longer, they would be threatened by the ice and snow of winter.

He gazed up at the sky. The sun was setting, painting the sky the color of chokeberries. He wondered where White Wolf and Dawnmarie were now as *they* gazed heavenward?

Hopefully near!

43

Ere the oldest star began to shine,
Or the farthest sun to burn,
The oldest of words, O heart of mine,
Yet newest, and sweet to learn.
        —HILDEGARDE HAWTHORNE

The aroma of freshly baked plum pudding and bread wafted through the air as Hannah prepared the cabin for the arrival of her parents for Christmas.

Alone in the house, Swallow Song with Strong Wolf outside enjoying a walk through the thin layer of snow that had fallen through the night, Hannah stopped and looked around at her creations. Evergreen sprigs clipped from the forest framed her fireplace mantel. Candles that Hannah had made of rolled cotton and the silky down from milkweeds flamed and danced on the mantel, shedding soft white light across the room. A tree as tall as the ceiling, displayed glass balls dangling from the limbs, as well as stoneware ornaments, crisp blue on white, that Hannah had hand painted and sponged with native designs. A Christmas angel stood at the top of the tree, glistening white. Gold-braided garland adorned the tree.

Above the door hung a handmade wreath of preserved leaves and flowers in winter white, gold, and cream, with a muslin bow a generous twenty inches wide. And beside the door stood Chuck's organ. He had sent cowhands to Hannah's house only this morning with the organ, so that everyone could sing Christmas carols.

Her mother had always had a romance with the

holidays. She had spent the full week before Christmas decorating the house and baking breads, cakes, and cookies.

Some of Hannah's fondest memories were of family holidays when she was young. She was going to carry on the tradition, anxious to be the one who had a house full of friends and relatives, laughing, and singing Christmas songs together.

The room exuded a warmth that came naturally from being loved, for Hannah did adore her home. And she couldn't be happier.

She placed her hand over the tight ball of her stomach. "Come spring, child, you will also join the fun," she whispered proudly.

The sound of sleigh bells drew her quick attention. "They're here!" she whispered, yanking her apron off.

With a pounding heart she gazed around her again. Her gaze stopped at the wrapped packages beneath the tree. She had had such fun choosing the gifts from the trading post for everyone.

"And Strong Wolf is learning how we white people celebrate Christmas," she whispered, smiling as she recalled how he questioned her about everything that she did in preparations for this special day: The tree, the ornaments, the holly and sprigs of evergreens, her insistence of baking everything that she could think of these past several days on the new wood-burning stove that Strong Wolf had surprised her with one day.

It even had a portable oven, that which made baking cookies and plum pudding great fun. There was also a sheet-iron heat stove in the corner of the room, glowing cherry red from the flaming fire inside.

"Hannah?"

Hannah's face flushed a soft pink with anxiousness

when she heard the soft voice of her mother outside the door. She grabbed a shawl from a peg on the wall.

She then flew to the door and opened it widely, not even noticing the rush of cold air on her cheeks as she ran on outside and flung herself into her mother's outstretched arms.

"Mother, it's been so long," Hannah murmured, relishing the feel of her mother in her arms. She inhaled the expensive French perfume on her mother's black velveteen cape. "I wish I could have come to Saint Louis before now, but Strong Wolf doesn't allow me to travel very far now. I've only been as far as the trading post and Fort Leavenworth."

Over her shoulder Hannah saw her father walking toward Strong Wolf who was coming back from the river with his mother. It made her heart sing and swell with joy when the two men embraced.

She then watched Strong Wolf introduce Swallow Song to her father, and smiled to herself when she saw the look of appreciation in her father's eyes as he gazed upon Swallow Song's earthy loveliness.

"Where on earth is your father?" Grace said, stepping away from Hannah. She turned and gazed around her, then smiled when she caught sight of Howard now walking with Strong Wolf and Swallow Song toward the house.

Grace turned toward Hannah. "And is that Swallow Song?" she asked, brushing flakes of snow from Hannah's hair as it began snowing again.

"Yes, that's Strong Wolf's mother," Hannah said, hugging herself with her arms.

"Why, she doesn't look a day older than thirty," Grace said, gazing at Swallow Song again.

Then she turned to Hannah, frowning. "We must get you back inside the house before you take a death of cold."

Hannah hurried back inside. "Yes, Strong Wolf's mother is quite beautiful, and she has aged gracefully," she said, slipping the shawl from around her shoulders.

She hung it on the peg again, then helped her mother with her cape. She swung it around a chair so that it could dry.

"How lovely!" Grace said, lifting the hem of her silk dress into her arms as she stepped farther into the room. "Oh, Hannah, it reminds me so much of the earlier homes that your father and I lived in, and the way I decorated them for Christmas."

She stopped and fingered the decorations on the tree, then turned and took a slow look around her. When she spied the stove in the kitchen, her eyes widened. "And you have two new stoves? One for cooking? One for the living room?" she marveled. She inhaled the aroma of the baked goods. "Do I even smell plum pudding?"

"Yes, plum pudding, apple pie, and sorghum cookies," Hannah said, hurrying into her kitchen. "Come, Mother. See how your daughter has changed from a tomboy into a cook. I am so proud of all that I prepared for today's celebration."

"Oh, I forgot to tell you, Hannah, Chuck will be along shortly," Grace said. "He is coming by way of Clara and White Beaver's house. He will bring them in his sleigh."

"Isn't it grand, Mother, that Clara found herself such a wonderful man such as I?" Hannah said, setting a teakettle of water on the stove, for tea.

"It's not something I would have expected from Clara," Grace said, laughing softly. "She always had her nose pressed in books, men seemingly the last thing on her mind."

"And now she is not only married, but with child,"

Hannah said, beaming with the news that had only been brought to her yesterday.

"With ... child ...?" Grace said, her jaw going slack with surprise.

"I shouldn't have said anything, Mother," Hannah said, reaching up inside her cupboard to take a stack of coffee cups from the shelf. "I should've waited and let Clara tell you the news." She placed the cups on the table, and then reached for the saucers and placed them on the table beside the cups.

She went to her mother and took her hands. "But, Mother, I am so excited about Clara's news, I can hardly contain myself," she said. "I will be an aunt." She laughed softly. "Aunt Hannah. How do you like the sound of that, Mother?"

"I shall be a grandmother twice in so short a time," Grace said, sighing. "I wonder if it will make me feel so much older? Always in my mind's eye, when I hear a reference to a grandmother, I see someone much older."

Hannah stepped back from her mother and looked her slowly up and down. Her pale blue silk dress, with its embroidered decorations of iris on the skirt, nipped in delicately at her tiny waist, and her face had only a trace of wrinkles. "Mother, you do not look your age at all," she said. "Why, you look hardly older than twenty."

Grace laughed softly. "Now, that is stretching it just a mite, wouldn't you say, Hannah?" she said, then turned as everyone started coming into the cabin.

Strong Wolf stepped aside as his mother entered, and then Hannah's father.

And while Hannah and Grace had been talking, they had not heard the arrival of two other horse-drawn sleighs.

Chuck came into the room, his cane out before him

searching each step. Clara was at his right side, gingerly holding his arm, and White Beaver was at his left, also helping him along.

But who came in after them made Hannah almost faint with surprise. "White Wolf!" she cried, "Dawnmarie?"

"Finally we made it from Wisconsin on our way to Mexico," Dawnmarie said, her laughter ringing in the air with its soft sweetness. "My heart is strong, my face is calm, my eyes are eager for new land—the land of my true people, the Kickapoo."

Hannah hurried to everyone and gave each of them hugs, then when she came to White Wolf, she hesitated long enough to gaze up at him, still in awe of his noble presence and utter handsomeness at his age of sixty.

"It is good to see you again, Hannah," White Wolf said, himself doing the honors of taking her into his arms. He gave her a hearty hug, then stepped away from her as Strong Wolf came to Hannah and took her by the hand.

"It is good that you are here," Strong Wolf said, reaching his free hand to White Wolf's shoulder. "We had thought you had changed your mind about traveling to Mexico. When winter set in, we gave up looking for you."

"We had missed our son Proud Heart for so long, we decided to stay awhile to enjoy being with him since we will not see him again for many moons," White Wolf said, helping Dawnmarie with her white rabbit fur cape.

Hannah quickly took the cape and laid it across another chair for drying, then took White Wolf's white doeskin jacket and laid it beside his wife's cape.

"Did you run into much bad weather on your journey?" Strong Wolf said, stepping between White Wolf and Dawnmarie. He placed gentle hands to their elbows and led them to the fire.

"We are foolish, *ay-uh,* for taking out in such weather, but we are prepared well enough for even the deepest snows with the sleigh," White Wolf said. "When we reach the warmer climates down south, we shall then travel by horse. My wife is a skilled horsewoman."

"You traveled without escorts," Strong Wolf said, easing an arm around Hannah's waist. White Wolf and Dawnmarie eased down into upholstered chairs.

"I am capable enough to care for my wife on the lengthy journey," White Wolf said, smiling warmly over at Dawnmarie, who was dressed in a brilliant-white doeskin dress resplendent in beads. Her hair was long and loose over her shoulders, almost as white now as the dress. "And traveling with many would draw too much attention. We wish to arrive at Mexico without any interferences."

"And how is Proud Heart and his wife?" Hannah asked, remembering that his wife should be quite heavy with child by now.

"They are faring well," White Wolf said, nodding. "My son carries the title of chief well on his broad shoulders."

"Yes, I am sure that he does," Strong Wolf said, filled with melancholia over missing his friend so much.

Soft Christmas music began wafting across the room as Chuck sat playing the organ. Everyone went and stood around the organ. Hannah and her parents began singing the carols as the others, who were not familiar with the songs, listened.

"The spirit of Christmas lives in the soul of the people," Strong Wolf had told her when they had discussed Christmas.

Hannah smiled over at him now, feeling so lucky to be with the man she loved on their first shared Christmas. They were learning each other's customs well.

She was glad that Strong Wolf had entered into this holiday with such zest and understanding. And it thrilled her to know that next Christmas they would have one more person with whom to share the holiday. Beneath their tree would lie presents for their child!

She lifted her voice above the others in song, never having felt so at peace with herself and the world. She laughed softly as Clara gave her a soft nudge in her side.

"Hannah, you are drowning out even the organ music," Clara teased.

"Yes, I guess I am," Hannah said, reaching for her sister's hand, gently squeezing. "But don't you see? We have so much to be happy for. I want to sing and sing and sing!"

Clara gave Hannah a hug, then began singing just as loud, feeling the happiness and gaiety of it all.

Hannah's eyes widened when she heard someone else enter the singing. Strong Wolf had listened close enough to learn the words as the most special Christmas carols had been repeated.

Hannah twined an arm around his waist and leaned against him. She joined him in song and joy.

44

He holds thy hands,
He claspeth mine,
And keeps us near.
—JULIA BAKER

Sparkling moon, The month of March. . . .

As Hannah walked to the far edge of the village beside Strong Wolf, she noticed the leaves on the oak
trees were now the size of a squirrel's ear, a sign that
it was time for the Potawatomis people to plant
their crops.

She looked at the fields spread before them, punctu-
ated by blackened spars. Those trees, girdled by the
men the past spring, had been scorched when the
brush had been fired in the fall, the ashes providing
nutrients for the soil. When fertility waned after many
seasons, other fields would be cleared, farther and farther away.

She looked with pride at the rows of hills in the
cornfields, each twice the length of a man's foot and
as high as a man's calf, three feet apart. Those hills
remained year after year, the cornstalks buried back
into them at the end of each harvest. That organic
matter improved the tilth of the soil, allowing air and
water to move through it more easily.

Soon she would be among the women who would
be placing seeds together carefully in the top of each
hill. They would plant two rows in one field, then
move on to plant two rows in another field. The work
would go quickly as the women would talk and joke

among themselves. Only when each field had some
rows planted would they return to the first field. Thus
no one would feel that her field had been favored.

"You are so quiet," Strong Wolf said, snuggling her
closer to his side. "What are you in such serious
thought about? Our children? We checked on them
before we went for our walk. Their stomachs content
with their mother's milk, they went fast asleep."

"No, I'm not thinking about our children," Hannah
murmured. "I look forward to being a part of the
planting season this year. That was what I was thinking about."

"I have other things on my mind," Strong Wolf said
huskily, giving her a playful nudge closer.

"Then, let us return to our cabin and pursue those
thoughts," Hannah teased back as she smiled seductively up at him. "Show me, darling, what's on your
mind, don't just tell me."

Laughing softly, they ran through the village, almost
breathless when they reached their cabin and hurried
inside, closing the door behind them.

Spring was in the air, soft and warm. The night
scents abounded in fragrances of wild roses and lilacs.
The moon was wafting its silver light through the window and across the bed when Hannah and Strong
Wolf stretched across it, their hands gently touching
and caressing each other's bodies.

"Your stomach is flat and smooth again," Strong
Wolf said, running his fingers over its flatness. He
straddled her and bent low, to flick his tongue in and
out of her navel. "But it tastes the same, like honey."

"That tickles," Hannah giggled, the flesh of her
stomach rippling beneath his teasing tongue. The ache
of need blossomed between her thighs when his
tongue dipped lower and he found her sweet place
nestled between her thighs. She closed her eyes and

slowly tossed her head back and forth, the ecstasy building within her.

"Does that tickle, or does it do something more for you?" Strong Wolf asked, his eyes dark pits of passion as he gazed up at her.

Hannah twined her fingers through his glossy black hair and smiled down at him. "You know how it feels," she murmured. "Wonderful."

"Then shall I continue, or would you rather I . . . ?"

He didn't get the chance to finish. She had her hands gently at his neck, urging him fully over her.

"I'd rather," she murmured, her fingers in his hair again as she urged his lips to hers. She melted inside as he kissed her and plunged his thick shaft inside her, half lifting her off the bed with the thrust of entering her.

His lips drugging her, Hannah's body hardened and tightened. When he cupped her breasts, she groaned with pleasure against his lips. She arched her hips and pressed her pelvis against him. He showered her face, ears, throat, and breasts with loving kisses.

Hannah was swirling in a storm of passion that shook her innermost senses. For too long they couldn't share these special moments. She had made love with him only in her warm pink dreams.

But now, as the babies lay in matching cribs not that far from Hannah and Strong Wolf's bed, she was able to be everything to Strong Wolf again, and he to her.

Their bodies strained together hungrily.

They could not hold back the ecstasy any longer.

Their kisses became frenzied.

Their moans of pleasure mingled.

Their bodies shook and quaked.

When they came down from the clouds, panting and satisfied, Hannah leaned up on an elbow and gazed at the cribs. "Mother never told me that there were twins in our family," she whispered. "Can you imagine, Strong Wolf? We have a daughter *and* a son. I think it's a miracle."

She sucked in a wild breath of rapture as Strong Wolf came up behind her and pulled her back against his hard body. She reached behind him and stroked his muscled buttocks.

"You are the true miracle," Strong Wolf whispered in her ear. "That you came to me and filled my life with so much more meaning, and that you have given me a son and daughter. How could a man ask for more?"

Hannah sighed as he leaned over, lifted her hair, and brushed a soft kiss across her neck. She laughed softly, when through the silence she could hear her children breathing, so sweet, so soft, so precious.

Hannah sat suddenly up and wrapped her arms around her knees. "Listen, Strong Wolf," she said, scarcely breathing herself so that she could enjoy listening to her children breathing. "Hear them? Hear them breathing? Sweet Snow Princess, Sweet Wolf Fire, our precious children."

He scooted himself into a sitting position beside her. "Yes, is it not a sound to be treasured?" he said, drawing Hannah next to him.

"Darling, when I was with child, and was not aware that I was carrying two children in my womb, I had so looked forward to the time when we would be listening to our child breathing in the same room with us at night," she murmured. "I never in all of my wildest dreams thought that I would be listening to two sets of breaths. I still can't get over knowing that we have two children in our lives so quickly!"

He placed his hands at her waist and gently urged her onto her back. He knelt over her, a knee parting er thighs. "Let us make a third child," Strong Wolf whispered huskily.

Her eyes dancing, her heart pounding, Hannah nodded. She twined her arms around his neck and drew his mouth to hers.

As they kissed, rocked, and swayed, Hannah could not help but think about the way it *could* have been, had they not fought and won the many battles they had been faced with since the day they had met.

She knew that they would be faced with many more challenges during their lifetime together. But for now, he would just be grateful for what they had.

Hannah's heart beat like wild thunder as the warmth of pleasure spread through her. "My wonderful Potawatomis chief, I . . . love . . . you . . . so," she whispered against his lips.

"My woman . . ." he whispered back to her. "My one and only; my desire."

Dear Reader,

I hope you enjoyed *Savage Rage*. Those of you who are collecting my Indian romance novels, and want to hear more about them and my entire backlist of books, can send for my latest newsletter, autographed bookmark, and fan club information, by writing to:

Cassie Edwards
6709 North Country Club Road
Mattoon, IL 61938

For an assured response, please include a stamped, self-addressed, legal-sized envelope with your letter. And you can visit my Web site at www.cassieedwards.com.

Thank you for supporting my Indian series. I love researching and writing about our beloved Native Americans, our country's true first people.

Always,

Cassie Edwards